AF373903

The MoonDawn Games

By A. J. Frost

For the daydreamers.
Welcome to mine.

Tampte Mountains
Northern Reach
Crelde
Pothah Flatlands
Crystal Forest
Salt Lake
Pothalyr
Darboth Bog
Blackfall
The Dredge
Inur Forest
Ferreway
Synsee
Pyrtar Cliffs
Switch Lake
Aizmen Bay
Heartwood Forest
The Fallen Waters
Seawall
Stonecrest
New Grosham
The Twin Islands
Qintra
Quantis
Venom Isles
Map of Syrelle

1 - Mysarin

Elegant and shining under the soft morning sun, she wore blood like gloves.

Mysarin waded into the cool stream of the river as she inspected her hands. Grime and filth dripped into the water, blots of red spreading like ink before her. She worried that it would never wash off—that the blood had become an extension of her rather than something she could discard once she was done getting dirty.

Like a scar or a stain.

A rising gag clogged her throat at the thought. She dunked her hands into the water, but the familiar stream offered no reprieve. Instead, her skin burned with the same crimson coloring as she rubbed, scraped, scratched. Desperate. A fleeting thought crossed her mind—it will remain. Like a scarlet tell written in her flesh for everyone she would meet to know. A brand to tell them about the monster that she was.

She paused her purification and shut out the Heartwood forest. She counted to five, breathing deep with each passing number. Her breath shook like a beaten dog, and even when she was done counting, she remained still. She remained scared.

When she finally found enough courage to peek through one eye, she saw that the gloves were off. The blood was gone. Mysarin looked up through the foliage at the quiet brightening of the sky, casting its bidding pale-blue hues. She should be in the pleasure house now, preparing for the day, not alone and naked in the forest.

The soil pressed into the soles of her feet, cool and grounding, as she inched her way between the overgrown trunks of the Heartwood trees. The warming summer breeze caressed her body as she followed a path only known to her. She crept along it until she reached a heap of broken wood beams crowded with wild plant growth.

She grabbed a white chemise and a heavy cloak from the creaking, rotting, floor.

It went the same way every time; she awoke smothered in innards and carrion, vulnerable, heart wrought and aching. She cleansed away her shame in the stream and found her clothing in the shack. It had been many years since her first forgotten night that by now she had come to accept it as a fact of her life:

Mysarin would always be a beast.

Her shaking body slipped into the familiar clothing. She whispered a story to herself as she walked barefooted back into the city of Stonecrest. It was a child's tale about a girl named Lyonisa. She was a courtesan, just like Mysarin. Her beauty had been her savior and her undoing, just like Mysarin.

As the story goes, Lyonisa had been cursed—her name had meant beautiful, and it had meant ugly, and she spent her life being one, or the other, or both, or none—just like Mysarin.

Cursed is what Mysarin's name had meant after all.

Nobody now took the meaning of names as seriously as they once did, yet, it was a concept that entranced her since she was a young girl hearing the story for the first time. Perhaps it was because namely-blessings were no longer given from the deities. Nothing was. The deities had all but completely forgotten about their own children: the humans, the elves, the crossbreeds, and the monstrosities.

It's as if they had all gone to sleep, or some godly war had been raging above. But they had all disappeared. All of her prayers had remained unanswered. She wondered if her namely-blessing was the last to be given, as some sort of sick joke.

Even still, feeling her voice dance over the story in the dewy mornings was all that could keep her calm. She finished her whispers as the city began to wake; folk opened their windows, Ladies set out on morning strolls, mothers entered bakeries to gather what little food they could for their rising children, and Mysarin stepped over the threshold between them all. She kept her face low beneath her hood and hoped none would notice the last remnants of what she had done trailing on the stone walkways behind her. She imagined she looked similar to a wraith in the moment, making their silent crossing back into the Lands of Wind after a night spent free in the material plane; her muddy footsteps being the only proof that she was ever here at all.

Except, she wasn't a wraith. She was a serial killer who had conveniently forgotten the whys, the hows, and the whats behind her kills. The only thing that had greeted her in the mornings was the who, if she was lucky enough to not have disfigured their face.

All she could tell about the person whose life she had taken last night was that he was male with graying hair.

She stopped when she reached the pleasure house—on the outskirts of the slums—and pushed her palm against the ajar door.

She creeped through the foyer and into her room, stopping before her vanity. Her eyes stung with a dull ache when they snagged on a glimpse of herself in the mirror. The cruel reflection of the person she might never fully know looked back at her. Dark hair, silver eyes, tawny-brown olive skin. Everything was in its usual place, except, it didn't feel like her at all. She couldn't remember the last time it did.

The expression on the woman in the mirror turned sour. She felt the angry heat fill her veins at what she had become as her feet marched her body forward. Using the remaining scraps of her own free will, she pushed over the mirror and let it shatter it on the ground. A quiet roar rumbled out of her lips at the broken pieces before her. The different versions of her splintered at her feet.

Then anger showed its true face: sorrow. It took all of her might to not drop to her feet and wallow in it. To mourn for whoever it was she was supposed to be instead of *this*. But then she looked around at her room, her bed, her business. It needed to be ready to receive patrons and earn enough coin to pay back her debt. So, as a cool tear crawled down her cheek, she simply began to clean up the mess. She went to properly bathe and dress, and used her glamor magics to cover up the remaining darkness beneath her eyes. She threw away the memory of waking beside the man with graying hair turned red, and opened herself for business.

She had to move forward. Pretend her life was simply ordinary.

As far as she could tell, she had a month before the next time she awoke next to a corpse.

The day went on as usual: men, women, wine, coin, repeat. Not necessarily in that order for the wine. That came in intervals frequent and plenty; it stopped her from thinking too much about, well, everything. It allowed her the confidence needed to banter, seduce, and gain the next step in buying a way out from under her Lady Madame, Grenlide. The sniveling she-wolf herself stopped in Mysarin's room after she had finished off the first bottle of the day.

"Mysarin, you have a guest." Her light brown hair, now graying in sparse areas, was strung up and placed around her thin face like a true Lady's. Tanned russet skin was beginning to wrinkle in places that showed she was often dissatisfied with her girls' income. Calculating green eyes told her to make things quick, as it was not to be a paying customer.

The elven man walked in, with his high cheekbones and round eyes. Mysarin smiled.

"Don't take too long, you're lucky enough I allow such visits," Grenlide said just before she closed the door.

"Deime," Mysarin breathed his name like a prayer.

He was handsome in his own way; he always had a clean shave and short cut hair the color of wheat fields, kind honey colored eyes, and a smile that made a girl feel welcomed.

"To what do I owe this delicious pleasure?"

"I missed you last night," he replied.

"And I adore being missed," she said as she rose. A pink flowing fabric hardly covered her body in the place of a respectable dress. Deime's hands grazed her exposed skin when she moved into his arms.

Mysarin knew that Deime was the best thing she could've hoped for. He was tender, gentle, he made her feel safe. Which was hard to find in the common folk of Stonecrest. Most people who dwell in the city only look out for themselves; they stole, lied, fought, all to get their hands on what they needed. Deime was only looking for someone to spend his days beside, and that's what made her so fond of him.

And he never dared to peer to close at her shadows.

It also helped that he didn't take issue with her current line of work. He was a baker's son, not a man of any noble standing, but she supposed it was noble of him to let himself fall in love with a courtesan. In a city obsessed with titles, it was a brave thing to do. And she loved him back for it. Perhaps she would only drag him down with her, and she already had in the eyes of his father, but she had never cared. Deime had never cared.

Maybe that made her more like Grenlide than she thought. A wolf. A predator. And Deime was her sweet, juicy, doe.

She pulled back and lightly pinched the tips of his rosey-gold pointed ears.

"When are you going to let me adorn these wonderful things?" she asked playfully.

He tensed. "I already told you, I do not plan on exaggerating the features that humans like to hate me for, it feels like asking for trouble," he replied.

"All elves do it," she laughed, "if anything, not adorning them will make them pick on you more." She was prepared to let her teasing go on until she saw his mouth set into a tight line.

"It's hard enough as it is, being an elf who isn't royalty," he softened his voice and laid his hand upon her matching and bejeweled pointed tips. "You know this more than most."

Mysarin resisted flinching at Deime's words. She closed her eyes and shut out the memories of her work. The memories of the human men and their cruelty, and the memories of their ruined bodies laying at her feet. Another thing she had to bury at the bottom of her consciousness.

She took a deep breath and smiled up at Deime. "Do I smell strawberry cakes?"

He laughed even though the smile didn't quite reach his eyes. "I knew not to come here without your favorite treats, you would've already kicked me to the curb if I hadn't." He lifted his cloth tote to her eye line.

She snatched it out of his hands and sat at the small table in the corner of her room. When he sat down on the old wooden chair across from hers, she had already started on her second strawberry cake.

"You know, I came over today not just to bring you lunch like the good lad that I am, but to tell you something important," Deime started to cut a freshly baked loaf into slices while he talked.

A nervous tick of his—he was always doing something with his hands when he was feeling unsure.

He cleared his throat, "I know that you've been struggling here."

Mysarin stopped chewing and raised a brow.

"And, I know you don't like to talk about business with anyone else, you're stubborn like that." Deime smiled bashfully.

'*Business*,' she repeated in her mind as she struggled to not roll her eyes. No matter how accepting he may be, he always had a hard time saying the real words. *I am a whore, I sell my body, I let men pay to fuck me*, she thought.

"But you know I worry about you, it's just what I do. I'm hopeless and I spend my days baking and thinking. Thinking mostly about you."

Oh Great Twelve, where was this going?

"And I think to myself 'Mysarin has already worked so hard to be where she is, has gone through enough. What can I do to ease her and her mind?' And well I started to brainstorm—"

"Deime, please stop rambling and say it." She began to sweat.

He huffed a laugh. "I'm sorry, you-you know how I am when I'm nervous."

Deime's round eyes darted around the room, looking for a comforting place to land on. He must've decided his hands were the best.

"Deime." She felt her entire body tense.

"Well I was thinking we should get married," he rushed the words out of his mouth, as if he said them any slower, they would not make their way out.

"You could come live with me and my father, and when he finally decides he's too old to work, Sea Salt Bakery becomes mine and there's already a loyal clientele and we don't do to bad for ourselves and then you never have to lift a beautiful finger again, except to maybe bake some bread every now and then and..."

The doe was running. Deime's words started to fade out of her head as the room began to sway. Mysarin should've known this was coming. They've only been seeing each other as more than friends for a few months now, but the two had been close ever since she worked her first royal party as a courtesan. Deime was there with his father as they worked handing out those same little cakes that sat before her now. She remembered feeling so thankful that there were other elves there who were not a part of a royal house, and that Deime had snuck her a strawberry cake underneath the table where she sat.

That's when she built up the nerve to ask the handsome elf his name. '*Deime, that means* dependable *doesn't it? Or* fickle *but I don't really take you for that sort.*' It was the first time in so long she had felt like a normal girl again.

And ever since that party, through the years that passed, Deime had always been there. *Dependable*.

Mysarin realized that Deime had stopped talking and was now just staring.

She smiled, real and true. This was all she ever wanted.

"Yes, I will marry you."

His face lit up in surprise. "Truly?"

She laughed. "Yes, Deime. Of course I will."

She extended her hand to him with a limp wrist, and watched as he gleefully fumbled around in his pocket. Then he slid a ring onto her finger. The band was woven gold with a thin deep-yellow stone in the middle, her favorite color. It was nowhere near a lavish and expensive ring, but Mysarin's breath caught at the sight of it. She knew at that moment the sacrifices he had to have made; the months of silent saving, the anticipation, the dreams he had been slowly building upon. As if he knew he would one day be asking for her hand in marriage, even before they decided to be more than just friends.

The weight of all that he was—his unwavering devotion—landed and pressed down onto her chest.

She needed a solution to her lost nights. She needed to find a way to stop the killings, unless she wished to kiss this man and all of her hopes and dreams goodbye. She needed to convince Grenlide to let her go from under her service. She needed to sober up.

"I... Let me talk to Grenlide today. I must convince her to let me leave, I—I still owe her a debt."

Her head swam. Was this a dream come true or a new nightmare? How would he react to her leaving in the middle of the night once a month? Coming home in the mornings with soil and sanguine covering her?

Would he end up as one of the bodies at her feet?

"Of course, I should be going anyway." He stood, leaving behind the lunch he made for her. "Mysarin... You've just made me a very, very, happy man."

She struggled to hold her grin up. Her brows creased, her gut churned, as Deime left Mysarin sitting there with the ring sitting happily on her finger, just above a crimson silk glove.

She blinked until it went away.

First things first, she needed to convince Grenlide into letting her out of service. If she could do that, then she no longer had to work for coin. If she no longer needed to spend her time with hungry men, then she could devote it to finding a way to stop her amnesia. If she could stop forgetting what exactly she had done, then she could finally stop killing.

Except, it wouldn't be the first time Mysarin had wanted to leave, and getting Grenlide to agree would be no easy feat. She knew she still owed a debt that Grenlide was unlikely to forgive without anything in return except for the loss of one of her best girls. Still, Mysarin stood on wobbly legs, and made her way through the halls.

Moans filled her ears. The smell of sweat and incense hung heavily in the air. The carpets were dirty and fading, and the lights held dim at all hours of the day. There were no windows in Siren's Labyrinth, no way to tell how long a Lord or Lady had spent with the love of the day. Mysarin held her arms over her chest. A rabid beat sang behind her ribs. When she reached Grenlide's office, she hesitated.

How in the world was she going to do this? She hadn't much but a small secret treasure of coin to barter. No reasoning other than '*a man is stupid enough to want to marry a courtesan.*' Not to mention that they were only a few weeks away from the busiest time of the year—the time when nobles from all over Syrelle visit for the annual MoonDawn games.

She turned around.

Perhaps she would just run instead. Leave in the night and hope Grenlide's paid swords weren't smart enough to find her. And when things quieted down, she would return to Deime.

The door opened behind her.

"Ah, Mysarin. Ready to get back to work?" Grenlide's voice was deceivingly warm, like a mother's coo. It's how she convinced Mysarin into joining her brothel when she was fourteen and fleeing from Synsee, her hometown. That warmth convinced her even now to turn back around and face her.

"I—How much is my debt?" she asked.

Grenlide crossed her arms. "Why must you ask?"

"Just tell me how much is left."

Her greedy green eyes dropped down to Mysarin's hand, to the ring Deime had placed onto her finger.

"He asked you to marry him?" she laughed. "That poor idiot."

"He's not an idiot," she said, feeling intensely defensive despite the fact that she had just thought a very similar string of words. "He loves me. He wishes to help me be free of this place, be free of you."

"Well, well. He certainly won't be able to pay the debt for you, if that's what you're thinking. He's a merchant, correct?" Grenlide smiled, her overly red lips parting to show more of that bright color on her front teeth. "He might have been able to pay, but he bought you that instead. I'm guessing he hadn't even thought that there would be a price to pay for you."

Mysarin felt her face twitch. She wanted to punch Grenlide right in her rouge slathered teeth.

"Just tell me what the debt is, and I'll pay it. Please, Grenlide, I've paid my dues. I've brought in plenty of coin for you already. Let me leave. Let me be free."

"No." The warmth in her voice turned to ash. "You are my prize mule. My star. I wouldn't let you leave for any price. It would never outweigh the amount you bring in, my darling beauty."

She grabbed onto Mysarin's arm, long nails digging into her skin.

Anger was a familiar feeling for Mysarin—a caress from a selfish lover. But in this moment, when she felt as if all of her problems were clasping around her throat and all she needed was for *one* of them to let go, she felt that caress turn into a fire.

"Fuck. You," said Mysarin, as she tore Grenlide's hand off, leaving scratches on her skin. Grenlide made for another grab, and Mysarin pushed her back.

Grenlide flew to the floor, her head banging against the doorframe behind her. Mysarin was shocked. She hadn't meant to shove her so hard.

"I'll have you whipped, girl!" Grenlide made to stand, to call for her swords.

But Mysarin was choking, aflame. The anger for the woman before her overshadowed everything. Red lines fed into her vision, feathering the world around her. Her heart rate was the only thing she could hear.

She was going to kill her.

No.

Not like this.

She stumbled back, resisting the urge to tear Grenlide's skin from her bones. But the rage pushed her. Grenlide's blood begged to be spilled over the fading rugs.

"Ixmon!" Grenlide screamed for her toughest guard.

The call shattered her frenzy. The red began to recede, and as Mysarin regained a sliver of her control, she ran. She shoved passed other courtesans out in the foyer and burst through the doors of the pleasure house.

2 – Estair

Estair did not fear much. She did not fear the giant water dragons called sea-strikers and their acid breath. She did not fear a battle with another pirate, or soldier, or any man, as she knew she would always best them. She did not fear crowds, or public speaking, or heights, or spiders. Yet as the wooden plank creaked beneath her feet and she heard the frenzied shouts of her crew behind her, she realized what she did fear—death.

A hand reached over the gunnel and pressed into her back, pushing her further out into the open ocean. Her feet shuffled forwards under the force, and she swallowed a scream.

"Walk the plank!" A voice sounded out.

"A life for a life!" said another.

This was her own crew cheering for her death. It was a standard punishment that no one within the Karnoch pirates was above. Not even if you were Boonefaentelle Karnoch himself. She slid her feet further out onto the wooden board with her hands tied behind her back. She then peered down into the Fallen Waters below, her dark hair falling into her eyes. It was storming, like usual, and the water slammed into itself violently. There was no way Estair would be able to swim in that. Not with her hands bound.

"Someone push her off! The lazy cunt." Cheers in agreement rang out behind her.

She felt another presence step onto the board, and felt her fear begin to claw its way up her chest. The rope restraints dug into her skin as she tested their strength. They were expertly tied. She slowly turned around to see one of her crew members creep their way out to her. It was Shwen, one of her most loyal members. The man who had promised to always look out for her.

His brown eyes glowed with anticipation as his bulky body shuffled towards her own. He would most likely take her place and become First Mate once she was gone, the bastard. The thought of him leading her ship, *The Dragon's Mane*, had anger bubbling in her veins. She then thought of stinging cold water filling her lungs until the world faded into black.

She had to do something. Estair was not ready to die.

"I request Trial," she stated loud and clear for all of the sweaty, stinking men to hear.

A loud collective sigh was their response. They wanted blood, but they were bound by the markings on their wrists. Oisoen's Promise is demanded each time a new member was to join the Karnoch, sealing their word into a wheat marking on their arm like a birthmark. No one here worshipped Oisoen, Grandfather of Trust, Deity of Harvest, Trade, and Community, but the ritual was the only way to ensure that the thieves, mercenaries, and slavers would stick to their word. Estair's own wheat symbol sat just above her actual birthmark—an ink spill that vaguely resembled a dragonfly.

There were two things that they must always abide by: a life for a life, and Trial. Most men would rather see their soul float into the Land of Wind and meet Siefris, Saintess of Stars, than go to Trial. They would rather drown than have Boonefaentelle Karnoch, a deeply unpredictable man, dole out a punishment. Some men have been dangled by their wrists over the walls of his palace in Qintra to be cooked under the harsh sun. Some set free into the wilds of the Venom Isles with nothing but the clothing on their backs. One man had spent the rest of his life as a living personal footstool for the Pirate Prince.

It was a risk—a punishment that could be worse than death. She looked down into the gray waves below one last time before hopping back onto the deck. Hopefully Boone was feeling merciful when they arrived at shore.

The markets were packed, stalls stacked atop one another as Estair's crew brought her through the sandy streets of Qintra. Women with beautiful long hair like her own stared at her as she passed. Their eyes asked if she was alright walking amongst the brute men. They asked if she was safe. She nodded her head to them. It was part of the culture of the Twin Islands for the women to protect their own, especially when it came to saving them from the hands of pirates. But what the other women did not know is that Estair could save her own skin. That she already had and would again and again.

The heat was dry and the sun beat down onto her deep copper-brown skin, coating it in sweat. Her leathers clung to all the wrong places as they made their way to Boonefaentelle Karnoch's Scorpion Palace in the heart of the city. It was crafted from light yellow sandstone and dark wood, and held the remnants of an old warship within its structure. Its highest peak held a balcony made from the helm of a ship, with the likeness of a female Suijin, Prior of the Depths, Deity of the Four Seas, Lakes, and Rivers Between, as the figurehead. Estair kept her sights on that beacon, stark against the clear blue sky, until they entered the doors to the Grand Room. A breeze from the servants' large fans dusted her sticky face.

Then her knees were aching with dull pain as they hit the wooden flooring. Two hands grasped her shoulders, shoving her down before Boonefaentelle, who was sitting on a throne made of melted down stolen gold in the center of the room. She looked up at him through her long hair and held his green-eyed stare. Estair had seen, spoken, and pillaged with Boone before, but in this moment, he looked more like the Pirate Prince than he ever had. Beside his throne stood more of the First Mates, clad in filthy leather clothing. They made his silk green and black tunic look more expensive in contrast, and his short black hair and mustache seem clean and kingly.

He smiled down on her, showing off his two golden front teeth. She grinded down on her teeth, thinking about how she should be up there, with him.

"Estair, would you like to tell me why your men have demanded your head?" His voice was like gravel, rough and thick from smoking prunn and tobacco from his pipe for too many years.

"I have killed one of my men," she said. Her voice was steady, confident, and lacking remorse.

There would be no hiding here. Not with her entire crew, who had witnessed the aftermath of her crimes, standing behind her to call out a lie before the King of the Free Cities. Boone controlled the Twin Islands, Qintra and Quantis, and the primitive Venom Isles south of it all. Stonecrest Royalty controlled the rest of Syrelle.

"Who?" he asked as he snapped his fingers.

A short and scrawny man with grayed hair ran before Boone, dropping to his knees and hands. Boone stretched his muddy shoes onto the man's back.

"I do not know his name. We had bought him from the Seawall Prison the day before. He was to start working as a steward," she said.

"Great. You killed a Karnoch member and you wasted my money. My two favorite things."

"He was going to…" she stopped herself, unsure she could finish.

He began to speak in Syrellen instead of Diarmar, the native language of the Twin Islands, as an insult to her intelligence.

"No, please, tell me. What garnered this response from you? My First Mate? A captain of his own ship? And the only one who is a woman nonetheless. I risked a lot letting you take your position, you know. And now you embarrass me."

"He was going to rape me," she finally said, continuing in Diarmar and ignoring his belittlement. "We all promise a life for a life, and yet, if he would've taken me the way he had wanted, you all would not sing for his death, would you?"

She looked around at all of the men in the room. The ones who she had witnessed doing the same with other women of the islands. Her crew who she had forbidden from pillaging bodies as well as riches.

"It is the same. He would not have taken my life but he would have killed my soul." She heard her heart thrumming in her ears. Felt the rage burn her skin.

"So I spilled his blood for it."

Boone leaned forward in this throne at that, kicking his human footstool out of the way. Estair resisted a flinch when the old man sprawled on the floor. He crawled out of the way, Boone lifted a palm out to the man to his left, Carni. The tall man with golden eyes, like hers, set the jasper pipe into Boone's open hand. He lit the pipe with a flame that spurt from his golden-brown fingers, and deeply inhaled. A bead of sweat fell from her nose onto the floor as she waited. She looked at the gray-haired man in the corner and swallowed. He was getting quite old… She silently prayed that she would not turn into the next piece of breathing furniture.

Boone exhaled the black smoke in little floating circles. He returned his speech to Diarmar when he finally spoke again.

"As you know, we are trying to build some relations with the Syrellen Nobles. Buying prisoners from Seawall, trading with New Grosham. But the Loraenars in Stonecrest want our loyalty."

He took in another puff of his pipe, and then blew it out of his nostrils. He tapped his idle fingers against the arm of his throne.

"They want allies. Ones who can defend the waters. And they promise more gold than the other cities."

"What does that have to do with me?" she asked. She was feeling impatient. Boone was toying with her.

He wheezed a laugh. "I'll sell you to them."

"What?"

"Yeah, I'll sell you to them with our other slaves. They want more men for their army as well as allies. You should do well there."

"No, I don't want to leave Qintra. This is my home."

"Oh! How could I have forgotten that! So I assume you'd rather be my footstool then when this one croaks? It should be soon," he leaned back into the chair and smiled, "I keep kicking him in his organs."

"Boone, please," Estair said softly.

"It's done then. We'll ship you out on the morrow. Take her away."

The two hands that were pressed into her shoulders scooped up her arms and dragged her out of the Grand Room of the palace. They led her down a flight of stairs and into a dungeon cage. Before they left, they grabbed a sword and cut off her long hair so it would sit above her brow. Another embarrassment to her as a woman of the Twin Islands. Then they chained her hands and feet, and left her to the silence of the cage. She sat upon a pile of hay and pressed her forehead into the wall.

Estair knew nothing of Stonecrest, knew nothing of their culture. Knew nothing of their royalty and politics other than the ruling families names. She held a rising sob deep within her as she sat alone in the dungeon. Boone wanted to sell her on purpose. It brought her the same loss of autonomy she would have felt if the prisoner had gotten his way. The same feeling of helplessness that she had felt when her parents had first sold her to the Karnoch Pirates as a child. The same deities-forsaken feeling she had when she first learned the meaning of her own name: *expensive*. Her teeth ground together thinking of the high price Boone was to set for her, and how easily it would be paid.

3 - Mysarin

The summer heat doused her skin, and even the flowing fabric of her loose dress was not enough to stave it away. But it didn't matter. Nothing else mattered except for what she was about to do. Mysarin stormed through the streets of Stonecrest, looking over her shoulder for any of Grenlide's men that would be on her tail. She ran through the slums, through the piles of the sick and the poor, while prunn smoke wafted into her face. She started to feel a little high as well as drunk when the blue slate roofs around her became more vibrant. The rose bushes and ivy vibrated as they climbed their ways up the exteriors, stretching to meet the sun in the sky.

But she didn't stop, she ran all the way through gray stone alleys and cracking paths until she could immerse herself in the dense crowd of the shopping district. Here, bodies would be her camouflage. They would give her the time and the cover to do what she needed to do. Because here, she would find a sword for hire of her own.

One to kill Grenlide.

She scanned the crowd for a mercenary; someone who looked tough, someone dirty, someone in armor with a sword at their side. Anyone other than herself.

She couldn't be the one to do it. She was too messy—all of her kills had ended gorged and splayed, like an art piece. Like a sacrificial lamb. No, she needed to hire someone to do it clean. To do it in a way that couldn't be traced back to her, lest she wanted to give herself away as the beast who killed all those corpses left behind in the Heartwoods.

She checked the alleyway she had just come from one last time. No signs of Ixmon.

The smell of sea salt and vinegary musk from the unwashed persons around her smacked into her senses. Shoulders brushed past her own as she squeezed herself between bodies. She scanned the booths and fronts of shops surrounding the once beautiful water fountain, now crumbling in places and spouting murky water. Her eyes landed upon a small booth underneath an arch of marigold, the orange flower of Ikaamte, The Healing Hand, who was the Deity of Cures and Medicine. Then she noticed the man standing beneath it.

He was in a simple tunic and pants the color of the sea, standing tall and proud. His hair was chest-length and shone a dark reddish-brown in the sun, half of it pulled back into a lazy pile. He had the cunning smile of a fox spread wide across his face.

That was her sword. He was dressed like a merchant, and running a booth, but with the way his eyes observed the small details of everything around him, his posture and large build, he had to be a soldier or mercenary. Or perhaps a spy, since he was posed as a disciple of Ikaamte, but she knew a soldier when she saw one. He was capable. He seemed hungry for coin.

He was the one.

She moved close enough to overhear him selling some sort of elixir to an older, human man.

"This will fix your cough right up, I swear it on Ikaamte himself," the man said assuredly.

He had a voice that was butter smooth, and pulled the ear toward the sound the way the ivy vines were pulled to the skies.

"And I'll tell you what, just for you, if you find yourself within the next week with the same cough, then you can march right here and take back your coin. That's how sure I am that my elixir will work."

The old human man who reeked of prunn passed over his coin and grabbed the bottle from the merchant, and then chugged the elixir right there. He then began to cough uncontrollably, and Mysarin thought perhaps the elixir would cure through death. He hunched over, bracing his hands onto his knees as he attempted to catch his breath. Once it returned to him, he picked up his head and glared at the merchant.

"Well it takes more than a few seconds to kick in," he chuckled. "Like I said my good sir, give it a try everyday for a week and if Del's cure doesn't soften your lungs and fix your ailments, then I will give you back every coin."

The old man then simply nodded his head, traded an egregious amount of coin for 6 more elixirs, and then slowly made his way into the direction of the slums.

Mysarin was about to turn around and look for someone else. This man was clearly just a charlatan and not someone who would kill for her; if that man was smoking prunn, his lungs would never be saved. It was something she had seen with other courtesans—the ones who had turned to the addictive hallucinogen instead of wine like her. But the charlatan locked eyes with her then.

"My Lady, I have what you need right over here!" the voice like a soft wave said. "Please, come forth."

She felt drawn in, all urgency leaving her body only to be replaced with the need to follow his words.

"What are you struggling with my dear? Del's cure can fix all." Every word the man spoke floated like poetry.

"I..." She stopped herself. The prunn she breathed in made his eyes swirl around, but his voice made her want to tell him everything.

"Go on. Nothing to be ashamed of here."

"Can it cure amnesia? I awake in the morning with no memory of what I've done the night before," she heard herself say.

"Amnesia? I believe it can help with that. Tell me more."

She opened her mouth to continue before she stopped herself. This wasn't right. Why in the world would she tell a stranger this?

Then it hit her—he was *charming* her.

She stepped back, away from his touch. Her head cleared and she remembered why she was here. He flashed that intoxicatingly vicious smile. She wanted to slap it off of him, but she practiced her restraint. Instead, a new, better, idea formed.

"Your charms won't work on me, scoundrel," she said.

The smile dropped. His smooth, sand colored skin went from the beach beneath high-noon to the paleness of bleached stones. "Fine. Be on your way then."

Mysarin laughed. "Oh, not so fast. You're going to teach me that spell, or..."

She leaned in close.

"Or I'll stand here all day and tell every single customer that approaches what you're up to. You'll make no money, and instead this crowd will eat you alive for tricking them. And if they don't, I'll come back every day and continue on and on and on. Until my voice gives out, or until you give up and leave."

He stood there with his muscular body tensed, and Mysarin thought that maybe this was not the type of man to play these sort of games with. Some men reacted in drastic ways, unafraid of any consequences or law. Maybe she would get to slap him afterall.

But then, he started to laugh. A real, loud, belly laugh of pure entertainment.

"Well met, my friend!" She felt her body relax as he continued to cackle, "I haven't had a shake down like this in ages!"

Sounds of a struggle broke through the crowd. Mysarin and the man turned to see a woman with dark curly hair be taken away by a group of royal Taurean Castle guards. The woman had olive skin, and was wearing a dress in the same shade of pink as Mysarin's. She swallowed. She needed to hurry, needed to learn this spell before they came to get her next. It was likely that Grenlide would get the royal guard involved, to threaten Mysarin into never pulling a stunt like this again. To reprimand with the firmest hand.

Unless... They are looking for me because of what I've done. Have they found the bodies I'd left behind? Did someone see me? Her head swam. Mysarin had what felt like the entirety of Stonecrest out to get her.

But she had just gotten lucky. She could learn this charm, and then use it on Grenlide to let her go. She wouldn't have to kill her, and she would be able to keep her secret stash of coin for herself. She kept her head down, not ready to give up just yet. A perfect plan that had fallen into her lap.

"I'll tell you what, I made enough money for the day here, and after that rather tense event," he looked around and into the uneasy eyes of the marketplace that watched guards drag the woman away, "I don't think I'll be making anymore from these poor souls. Give me a moment to pack up some of my things, and let's head somewhere else. I'll teach you what I know."

"Wonderful," Mysarin replied. "How about Bull's Eye Tavern?" She needed a drink.

He nodded his head and began to break down his booth into a small trunk. She stood close by, eyes peeled on the crowd, looking for any signs of danger. The woman's screams faded back into the blur of the city, and Mysarin spied no other royal guards. And still no signs of Ixmon. She looked back down at the ring on her finger, the amber jewel shining back at her, and she felt the upturn of her lips.

It was all falling into place.

"Alright, let's go," the man said. His voice was different without the magics coating it, his tone deep and airy. "Mind telling me your name?"

They moved through the crowd together.

"Mysarin, and you?"

"Delvuvius Crune," he said.

"Wow. That's awful."

He laughed, "Yeah, well my friends call me Del."

"Did you know Delvuvius means *lucky*? Or *hapless* and that's why you're here preying upon the sick," she said.

"Hey now, I said I'd help you, did I not? Doesn't that warrant at least a little bit of manners? You'll hurt my feelings otherwise."

She looked at him to see a lopsided grin. He was quite handsome, with green eyes unlike Grenlide's. They were softer, gentler, and had amber mixed in.

"Really? A charlatan asking for manners? Complaining about hurt feelings?"

He shrugged. "I guess I need something to keep me from being completely barbaric."

She squinted her eyes at him. He was teasing her. The fox toys with the wolf.

"Buzzard."

He snickered and looked at the dress she wore, the exposed skin in so many places.

"Are you a courtesan?"

Her body stiffened.

"No judgement." He raised his hands. "Makes sense is all."

"What's that supposed to mean?"

"You didn't say you had a surname. And you're… uhm… very striking."

She rolled her eyes. "I'm their resident glamor mage. I help the girls make more money," she lied. She wasn't sure why she did, it didn't matter what he had thought of her anyway.

They arrived at the tavern and immediately moved to a table that was in the darkest corner of the room. She recognized many previous patrons here, and she prayed to no one and nothing that none of them would come to speak with her. Once a bar maiden came by with wine and mead, Delvuvius noticed the ring on her finger.

"Are you a married woman? Inviting a man out while your husband is away," he clicked tongue, "I ought to find the man and tell him of what you've done, after the way you agitated me earlier. Though, I will say, I am flattered." He looked up at her and winked.

"Not married," she quickly replied, "yet, anyway. He proposed this morning." Her cheeks warmed.

"Oh, no. Don't tell me you plan on breaking this poor man's heart!" He clutched his chest in exaggeration as he tipped back his head. "Please Mysarin, fair lady, give me your hand eternally and I shall never leave you lonely!"

He smiled and looked out of the corner of his eye at her, amused by himself. Mysarin thought how exponentially entertained this man must always be.

"I do not plan to break his heart, I simply must find a way to—" she stopped herself, flustered. "Let's just get on with it. Teach me the spell."

"Sorry, touchy subject I see, I never quite knew how to navigate those," he cleared his throat and went on. "For the spell, well, you said you were a glamor mage, correct?"

"Yes, yes. I know my way around magics."

"Good. So, for this spell, it goes like any other," he flitted his hand about, "you recite the lines a few times and get used to the feeling of the magics. If you are aiming to perform this spell like how I did today, you need to practice. You see, I didn't have to recite the prayer at the market as it would ruin the whole point of using it on another person. They would know they're being charmed and then they'd come back for their coin immediately after it wore off. So that's what we will do. We will practice. Let's start with actually learning the words."

"Wait. That's not what I've done before."

"What do you mean?"

"Saying the words. When I do glamor, I just… do it."

He raised an eyebrow at this, his face turning curious.

"You don't pray for it?" he asked.

"No. Never."

"Hm. You must've had a Chosen in your lineage, then. Lucky you." He said the last words with resentment laced over them.

Chosen, she thought, *in my own lineage. Does that have something to do with my lost nights?* The Chosen were the mortals who were blessed by a deity, typically only during wartime, allowing unrelenting access to their magical domains. She didn't think either of her parents had been Chosen, but, maybe they had hid it from her?

"Chosen lineage or not though, glamor magics is Paramos' domain, and persuasion is Umakes. So, you'll need to pray."

She sighed. "Fine, tell me the words."

"*Lolorasrojumpur Umakes, etineriam persuacionic pryse.* Now repeat that."

She repeated the words as best she could. Delvuvius continued with his instruction only after she had perfected the old languages' strange inflections.

"Now, you're going to say the words again, and this time I want you to think of trust and what that means to you as you do it."

She recited the words and thought of the color blue, she thought of every time Deime had placed a soft touch on her skin and a kiss on her lips, she thought of how still the other courtesans would sit as she pulled and arranged their hair into place, she thought of her parents.

"Do you feel it?" he asked.

She felt a swell in her throat and then a warm tingle along her tongue, "I do."

Her voice sounded like hers, only not. Smoother, lighter, full of air and promises. "So what do I do?"

"You can do anything," he said. "Demand something, ask something. You'll get the results you want. If you're in public though, it's best that you're not obvious about it. Others will catch on fast."

She nodded and smiled as she remembered how she hadn't gotten to smack that look off his face earlier. "Why don't you give a beautiful woman a laugh, and slap yourself?"

Mysarin saw the slight resistance as his hand raised and swiftly landed upon his own face, and then he started in surprise, mouth agape.

"You," he paused, and then he laughed. "You vile woman!"

She responded with her own unrestrained laugher, and she noticed how even that sounded more alluring. "I'm sorry! I just wanted to see it in action, that's what practicing is all about isn't it?"

"I cannot disagree with that, as distressing your methods may be." He shook his head, smiling. "Now the most important part is that you remember the feeling that the magics gave you. That tingle in your mouth and the swelling warmth in your throat? That's the persuasion coating your voice. You can use the spell until you know the feeling well, and then you can summon that persuasion magics in your mind without the words once you become more acquainted."

"Right, okay. Let me try again, I promise there will be no more slapping." She giggled to herself and once more recited the words. She thought of the color blue until she felt the magics again.

She took a moment to force herself into memorizing the feeling of summoning it, and the sunshine it wrapped around her vocal chords.

"Tell me something about you, Delvuvius Crune, I know you are a charlatan and a cheat, but what else is there?"

"Well, for starters, I do not enjoy preying upon the sick... I simply do what I must to survive."

"Please. You're magically adept, you're well built, why haven't you become a soldier?"

"I sure tried. I made it through all of the schooling, the training, but when it came to the Breaking..." He paused, the charm wearing off, and his eyes darkened.

Her throat felt dry as the persuasion magics slipped away. She took a long swig of wine.

"You did the Breaking?" she asked about the common ritual used to grant soldiers more magics.

"Body and soul," he replied. "It just didn't quite take with me. I was lucky enough to have survived. Heh, guess the meaning of my Deities awful name rang true after all."

A beat passed. She wasn't sure what to say, so instead she changed the subject.

"Why hadn't your charm worked on me earlier?"

He half-smiled again. It seemed he wore that flirty look like a mask. "Every spell has its loopholes. Just like how every name has more than one meaning. Magics are from the gods and the gods are always fickle."

"You've got that right."

"So cynical," he sneered.

"Like I have a reason to be anything but," she grumbled, pouring another glass of wine.

"You mean the whole '*I awake in the morning with no memory of what I've done the night before*' thing?" His voice went up a few octaves as he tried to mimic her.

She glared at him. "That's not fair, you charmed that out of me."

"And you charmed information out of me that I didn't want to share, either. It seems we are even." He paused, looking at her goblet. "Either you were drunk, or something else was taking up space in your mind when I charmed you. That's why it didn't work."

"Ah, so my vice is also my saviour. Better than nothing, I suppose."

"Well, you better offer me some if we are to continue practicing. I clearly need some protection from you."

The tavern turned deathly quiet as the doors swung open in the front. She turned around to look, only to find more of the royal guards walking in.

The Taurean Castle armor, crafted of silver and gold with winged embellishments, created a stark contrast against the dull-colored and dirty clothing of the townspeople sitting around them. The eyes of the golden bull's head symbol of the city met with the wishful stares and awe-gazed faces that were glued onto the noble finery. Mysarin's stomach growled in its vacancy.

Suddenly she began to feel very hot, and she began to scan the walls for another exit. Every bone in her body screamed they were here for her.

"Are you alright?" Delvuvius asked.

"I need to go." She stood, and spied a door near the bar.

"What? Mysarin!" he called after her, but she was already slipping through to the side of the tavern. The summer sun hit her skin as she walked out to find a man in leather armor standing before her. Her fear dropped down onto her chest and weakened her legs.

He had silver hair, and deathly pale skin. A lunar-elf. And the only one that she had seen in Stonecrest was Ixmon. He turned around, eyes landing on her as she sprinted in the other direction. She moved like the wind around the side of the tavern, and into another alleyway. His footsteps echoed hers, faster than wind, until he was close enough to grab onto her arm and yank her back.

She fell to the ground. The air she breathed evaded her lungs, and she struggled to cling onto it. She had taken too long with Delvuvius, letting him distract her. *Stupid*, her inner monologue scorned her. As her chest stayed hollow and her shoulder pulsed, Ixmon pulled her up to standing. His face was blank, like always, as his deep plum eyes looked her over. She gave up on fighting him. She could usually defend herself decently enough against Ixmon if she really wanted to, but he had knocked all of the fight out of her.

Yet, perhaps it would still work out. She would get a beating from him, and then the next time she saw Grenlide she would use her new spell to charm her when she least expected it. And then she would be free.

She went compliantly as his icy fingertips chilled the skin of her wrists. He said nothing as he led her back to where she had come from.

"What's happening?!" Delvuvius stood at the door she had tried to escape from.

She said nothing in reply as Ixmon guided her through the streets of Stonecrest.

4 – Estair

Estair cried as she sailed over the Fallen Waters from her home in Qintra. She envisioned the soft white trees that would remain on the First Twin of the Twin Islands as the tears came rolling down her cheeks.

The first time she was sold she was only nine; her parents had given her the name Estair when she was born in hopes that she would grow strong enough to fetch a fair price from the Karnoch pirates. Now, she was at the age of eighteen, falling from the grace of being the only woman who was a First Mate. She was back to being treated like goods arriving at the port, ready to be devoured by the peoples of the city. She tugged at her chains in frustration.

Estair was trained from the moment she was bought to become a First Mate, due to her rather large build and seemingly natural reflexes. She trained on the seas, terrified of the creatures lurking below the deep blue waters until she screamed in fear no more. They taught her to fight with a sword, to use the magics she had in battle, until she was good enough to captain her own ship. Yet, some part of her had always known that one day one of the men would come for her and her womanly body. So, she continued to train far into the night when the other drunken pirates would pass out for the few hours they had, vowing to surpass them all.

Estair practiced and honed her magics, becoming one of the best fighters in the Karnoch. She did so every night she could until the time finally came. She would never forget the way the bulky elven man spoke in her ear after sneaking up on her while she trained in the night on the deck of *The Dragon's Mane*.

"I've never had a lady as big as you," he had whispered as he roughly grabbed her waist and pulled her towards his body. She could still smell the vinegar of the bitter seawater wine on his breath. She could still feel his oily face pressing into her neck while he tried to take whatever he wanted, unafraid of the tall and muscular body that held onto a sword. An oaf of a man to think that just because she was a woman, she could do no harm to him.

He had no idea who she was and whose ship he stood upon. He had only arrived earlier that day, the persecution of his crimes following him out into the open sea after ten years behind bars. Estair hadn't cared to meet him when he first got on, as she was too busy in her quarters sorting through *Jiafornia*, a flower of the Venom Isles, and deciding what was good enough to process into prunn.

It hadn't mattered whose ship it was. It hadn't mattered that she had earned the respect of her crew and that they had viewed her as their equal. He gripped onto her and none of her crewmates would've tried to stop him, not after she had banned them from doing the same to the women of the Twin Islands. So, she had taken her practicing sword, and even though it was dull and bent, she swung it around as she used her might to rip her way out of the elf's grip. It struck right into the crook of his neck, on the opposite side of where he was kissing hers.

Estair wiped her tears onto her shoulder as she turned away from the shores of Qintra, and straightened her back as she looked off into the distance where she could almost see the towering height of Taurean Castle.

She learned earlier in the day that the tensions between the royal houses had been rising within the past few months, as Princess Syndra Loraenar had not yet made a great display of her magics. If the Princess could not prove her might, Seawall or even the Northern Reach might get the idea to make a move on the throne. It's what made Boone jump at the chance to trade with them. The Loraenars knew that the Karnochs ruled the Fallen Waters that lay between Stonecrest and Seawall, and to have the pirates on their side was to have the waters expertly defended, should the armies of Seawall dare to cross. And now Boone would have plenty more gold to add to his throne.

Estair, chained by her wrists and ankles to a Syrellen handler, followed the line of unbound soon-to-be soldiers and servants of Taurean into the cramped cabins beneath. She silently sent out a prayer to Suijin, Prior of the Depths, that their ship would sail smoothly.

Estair was shaken awake in the night by her handler, a man with a long black beard and oily skin. His large and clammy hands gripped her shoulders as he yelled for her to get up.

"ALL HANDS ON DECK!" Spittle flew from his mouth onto her face as she blinked away the deep sleep.

"SEA-STRIKER ATTACK!"

Estair jumped from her cot, hands and ankles still connected together, as the man continued to go bed to bed waking the rest of the men.

"GRAB ANY WEAPON YOU CAN AND REPORT TO THE UPPER DECK."

She watched him as her heartbeat began to drum in her chest. "I am still chained. How could I do anything?" she asked in Syrellen.

She lifted her arms, halting at her chest, to show him.

He looked at her for a brief moment, contemplating.

"Grab a weapon and swing, you can do that chained. Just don't let it spray you."

He then grabbed a curved sword from a table and tossed it at her feet. "And use your magics."

He then continued through the cabin shaking the unbound prisoners awake and yelling.

Estair picked up the sword with both hands and rolled her eyes. Her chains pinched at her flesh, twinging, as she tested the slack of the binding around her hands and feet. It would have to do.

Men pushed past her as they scrambled up the wooden stairway to the upper deck, threatening to knock her off balance. Her chains continued to pull at her skin each time she took a strained step up the stairs, digging their way deeper into her ankles. She grit her teeth. It was utterly ridiculous that they continued to keep her restrained when the rest of the men were free to roam. All because she defended herself and was now deemed 'unstable' by the Syrellen crew.

When she had finally reached the upper deck, each man had stationed themselves before the gunnels and either manned a cannon or prepared their magics. The wind blew fiercely and the waves crashed as rain poured from the skies. It was chaos, and it was art. The cruel beauty of the sea caught in a storm was something Estair would never get used to. She awkwardly ran to the front of the bow and peered out into the unending gray of the Fallen Waters. Squinting her eyes through the weather, she tried to pin down the sea-striker. Men hollered and gripped the cannons as a large wave came crashing into *The Warbeast*, sending it tipping to the left. She bent her legs to balance as she continued to watch the waters rage.

When a massive bright green fin peaked above the surface a few miles out, she smiled. She had no fear; she had fought this beast many times before, and hadn't failed yet.

She gripped her sword tight when she heard the cannons fire into the sea. She winced as a roar rumbled in her ears; one of the desperate shots had made a direct hit. Estair whipped around in time to witness the sea-striker's head emerging from the gray mass. Its pewter and green scales dripped salt water. Its red, glowing, eyes locked onto a large black haired crew member standing beside a cannon. He raised his club in the air, igniting it in fire magics and hurdled it towards the striker, aiming at its whiskered nose.

Estair quickly shot a gust of wind towards the club to steer it up into the nostril of the beast. It was the only way to harm the creature as the fire would do nothing against its thick armor-like scales. The fire went straight up into the cavernous hole in a perfect motion, and it was just the right size to squeeze into the weak spot. The beast roared again, rearing its head. Estair almost lost footing. She stabilized herself as it dunked its head back below the surface.

For a moment, there was a stillness in the air—an eerie lapse of time. The storm paused in anticipation and the men began to look overboard for any signs of the striker. A tangy sulfuric smell swept through the air, and Estair knew what was coming. She quickly summoned a deflecting water shield around her body as the beast burst through another towering wave and began to spray yellow, powdery, breath along the surface of the ship. Two Syrellen men who had not been fast enough melted. *The Warbeast* was made of enchanted wood and stood firm against the acidic mist's properties, but the men had dissolved into a puddle along the deck.

That's when another cannon was shot, this one engulfed in blue flames, and it exploded upon impact onto the sea-striker's red eye. Black blood sprayed the deck as the beast screamed. It was a deafening wail, dragging claws through Estair's brain. Her vision turned red. The rest of the men were able to cover their ears, but her hands were still bound as she was forced to hear its last retort.

With the vile scream still ringing, her eyes rolled into the back of her head and she collapsed. Then the beast retreated back into the depths of the Fallen Waters.

5 - Mysarin

Grenlide hadn't ever held back with punishing Mysarin. Not like she had with the other girls, who would get a simple slap on the wrist for misbehavior. But perhaps that was because the other girls weren't as deviant as Mysarin. They didn't have her natural talent for defiance.

When Yrana—the girl who lived a few rooms down—came to visit Mysarin, she gasped. Mysarin's face was swollen, her arms bruised and her back burning and tender from the lashes of a whip. Mysarin had begun to work on her glamor to cover it all at her desk. The frame of the mirror she had broken sitting hollow atop it. Yrana closed the door and rushed to her side.

"What did you do, Mysarin?" she asked.

Mysarin faced away from her, but recognized her by the sound of her honeyed voice and the cracking of her ankle each time she had taken a step. Yrana had been here for almost as long as Mysarin had, showing up here when her father had broken her ankle in an attempt to stop her from running from him. And that's all Yrana would ever say about that. Anytime anyone had asked her *why* she had run from her father—why she would have preferred being *here* than with him—she grew mean and spiteful. And then she would pick up her pipe.

Yrana bent down at the side of the chair Mysarin sat in. Her full, tightly wound, bronze curls framed her deep saffron-brown skin. Her two front teeth, with a small needle of a gap, sat just below her plump upper lip held open by a slackened jaw. Her almost black eyes roamed over Mysarin.

"I need you to tell me where it all is. So I can cover it," Mysarin's voice cracked. "And pour me some wine."

Yrana rose to fetch the wine decanter on the opposite side of the room. "Are you going to tell me what happened to your mirror, at least?"

"I broke it."

"Twelve curse you, Mysarin. Paramos will make sure to give you seven years of bad luck for that."

"Paramos can bugger off."

Yrana flinched when she brought over the glass. "You're going to get me cursed, too. Stop it, will you?"

Mysarin laughed a humorless breath. "Fine. Just help me with covering this."

Yrana then began to gently place her fingers over the spots of bruising as Mysarin wove her magics over them. Her skin tingled and warped in on itself, the smell of roses wafting in the air. Mysarin felt more stiff when it was done; glamor magics had always felt uncomfortable, like a thick layer of mud caked onto the skin.

Yrana let her know when she looked normal again, and Mysarin finished her decanter. The pain eased, as did her mind.

"Can you do me one more favor, sweet Yrana?"

"Of course."

"Go tell Deime that I must see him." After what Ixmon had done to her, she yearned for the comfort of his presence. She wanted his gentle touch and his promise of a normal life.

"Oh, Deime, huh? I'd go see that handsome man any day," Yrana purred.

Mysarin smiled. She remembered how once Yrana had told her that if Mysarin decided she no longer wanted the elf, the human woman would be ready to take up her place. What a sight it would be, to see Yrana with her impulsive decisions beside Deime's compulsive habits.

"Just tell him to come tomorrow morning, or late tonight. Tell him I'm close to getting out of here."

"You're going to leave?" Yrana's playful face dropped.

"One way or another," Mysarin said. The next time she saw Grenlide, she would persuade her and dangerously let herself hope that it would take hold for long enough to get out.

Mysarin spent the rest of the day working in pain and practicing summoning her persuasion in the downtime. She considered herself lucky that business was abhorrently slow due to the calm before the storm of the MoonDawn tourney. She resisted a flinch each time a patron went to caress her back, and each time they went to grab onto her arms. The pain had caused her to keep filling her stomach with wine, and eventually she had drank so much that the room had begun to spin and shake and quiver.

Suddenly, she was no longer on top of a man, but on the floor puking.

She decided to deny any more requests for the day after that. Yrana had brought her bread and tea to hopefully settle her stomach and drive the effects of alcohol away, and soon after she had left, Grenlide finally showed her face.

Grenlide usually liked to avoid Mysarin after beatings, shying away from her own wickedness. But now, Mysarin had her chance.

She just wished she wasn't so drunk.

"Aw, did Ixmon hurt you too much?" The warmth in her voice was enough to ignite a wet log.

Mysarin said nothing, trying to focus her sights, and to stop the ground from moving.

Grenlide squatted down before her.

"You're drunk during business hours?"

Mysarin ignored her, trying to remember what Delvuvius had taught her. Trying to remember the feeling of summoning that sort of magics. *It was… a warm throat, like drinking tea. And… What did Delvuvius say? Thrust—No.* She giggled. *Trust. I trust*

Deime… and I trust Yrana. She brought me tea. I'll drink it to make my throat warm.

She took a long, slow sip, as she tried her hardest to focus her mind on the only two people she could give her trust to.

She, miraculously, felt the magics swell and coat her voice. Her heartbeat picked up. Mysarin's hands were shaking, and the room finally, *finally*, stilled. This was her moment.

Grenlide grabbed onto Mysarin's chin, forcing their faces close together. She was likely about to say something awful and soul crushing. So, Mysarin spoke instead.

"You're going to let me leave. For freeee. I've worked here long ggeeenough you bitch."

It sounded very convincing.

Grenlide let go of Mysarin's face, her fingers gracefully returning to her lap.

"I'm going to pack my stuff, and then I'll neverrrrss see you again."

It was working, it had to be.

Grenlide laughed.

"You can take the night off, but you know that just raises the debt you owe. And all of the wine that you drank? That costs you, too." Then she stood, and left the room without another word.

Shit.

Grenlide had left that night, still nowhere to be seen the next morning when Mysarin woke with her head throbbing. At least her wounds felt slightly better. She rose on still shaking feet and began to reapply her glamor to the places where Yrana had placed gentle fingers. A knock rapped on her door, sounding like the loudest thing in the world. But, she knew it was likely Deime on the other side.

"Come in," she said.

"Hello, uhm, are you Mysarin?" a woman's voice said.

Mysarin turned to find a tall, auburn-haired, elven woman with tanned rosy skin standing where Deime should've been. Mysarin hadn't finished with her glamor and watched as the woman's eyes grew wide at the sight of the bruising on her arms. She quickly finished the job as she prepared herself to work. Requests this early in the day were unusual, but it was better not to question it.

"I am. Here, love, come make yourself comfortable."

She rose and sat upon her bed, tapping on the space next to her.

The woman continued to stand there, looking unsure.

"I… I can sit over here, if that's alright," she said, and gestured to the table in the corner of the room.

"Oh, you want to watch? Mmm, I do love to put on a good show," Mysarin drawled.

She began to undress herself.

"Wait, what? Oh! Stop. Please. Del told me you were a glamor mage—I might have the wrong room but the woman out front said I could find you here…"

Mysarin immediately put her breasts away.

"Oh."

"I'm so sorry, do you know where I could find the glamor mage?"

"No, no, that-uh, that's me. Apologies." Her cheeks burned. "What's your name?" she said, trying to quickly move on from her embarrassment.

"I'm Telme. I… I was hoping to get your help with getting a woman to notice me," she said.

She sat herself down at the table, just as ready to move on from Mysarin's uncomfortable display as she was.

"She's the handmaiden to Rionaes Theinguard and she hardly notices me and I'm Syndra's handmaiden myself so a lot of planning must be made between us, yet, every time I ask her to take a walk in the gardens with me, she doesn't seem like she wants to but then I catch her staring at me sometimes and you know the Oswesians, they're all so aloof, and at this point I'm desperate because Lila is simply the most stunning woman I've ever laid eyes on. I was thinking you could help me, make me prettier, teach me to glamor myself up or something. Please, help me."

Holy word vomit.

Mysarin blinked.

"Sorry. I had that speech planned out a bit more eloquently but then…" Telme dropped her eyes to Mysarin's chest.

"You're handmaiden to Syndra Loraenar?" was all Mysarin could think to say.

"Yes, and she's trying to court Prince Rionaes as I'm sure you've heard and I thought it might be so lovely if Lila and I were to…"

More words at incredible speeds and yet Mysarin's thoughts faded elsewhere.

Handmaiden to Syndra Loraenar. I wonder how much of an influence this woman could have on the Heir. She might provide a motherly perspective to her, if the meaning of 'Telme' holds true... And Syndra, the kind of money the royals have... The library in Taurean Castle. *This could be everything that I need. They could buy me out of here, and I could look through their library for anything on amnesia and bloodthirst.*

Screw charming Grenlide! This was infinitely better than all of her other ideas.

Mysarin stood up and examined Telme. She had deep blue eyes, like the ocean at dusk, and a crooked nose. High cheekbones and an oval shaped face. She looked very charming, and Mysarin thought of how she would dress her if she were a courtesan.

"You don't need my glamor magics, you just need to part your hair like this."

She rearranged Telme's short auburn locks to flow from the middle, and tucked them gently behind her pointed ears.

"And wear some orange-red rouge, perhaps. And then, the next time you see—Lila, right?"

Telme nodded.

"The next time you see Lila you're going to touch her. Any chance you have. If you're laughing, you're laying your fingers on her shoulder. If you're asking her a question, hold onto her hand. You seduce her. It seems she is allured by you already, but you have to be the one to make a move. Be bold."

Telme had said she was Oswesian. The continent to the east had held a population of lunar-elves, like Ixmon, who all worshipped Siefris, Saintess of Stars, Deity of Past and Future, and the Lands of Wind. A skittish, reserved, group of people.

Telme smiled. "You really think that will work?"

"My dear, look at where I live. I *know* it will work."

"Then I will try it. Thank you, I—how much do I owe you?" She began to rummage in the coin purse at her hip.

Mysarin held out a hand. "Oh, don't bother. I hardly did anything."

Then a wild demand within her had her locking eyes with Telme instead, light gray entwining with deep blue. Her breathing felt unsteady with hesitance as she bent over and laid a hand upon Telme's calloused fingers.

It had to work this time. It *had to.* She focused everything she had on it, her mind finally clear without consuming any wine today. Her heartbeat bubbled as she summoned the warmth of persuasion magics to her throat, letting it silken her vocal chords.

"I just ask that you help me out in return. A favor." Mysarin prayed to any deity who might still be listening that this persuasion would last the long walk back to the castle.

"Convince Syndra Loraenar to seek my services, so she can form a true bond between her and Rionaes Theinguard. Tell her I have more up my sleeve than just glamor magics. I know love and illusion spells. I can do elemental magics. Anything that will convince her."

She gave a confident squeeze to Telme's hand to disguise the trembling of her own. She then backed away as she waited for Telme's response.

"What a fantastic idea," Telme smiled and stood. "I know she's also been struggling to connect with Rionaes," she huffed a laugh, "Oswesians, right? I shall tell her as soon as I return."

Mysarin let loose a breath she did not realize she was holding.

"Wonderful, then I hope to see you again, and soon." She dipped her head in goodbyes, and then watched as the woman made her way out of her room.

There was no way that Grenlide would be able to resist giving Mysarin to the Loraenars. *Everyone* wanted to be on their good side, and Grenlide had been trying to earn their favor for years. There were two things that she had valued most: coin, and relations with nobles. There would be no way to resist a Loraenar's offer, and then Mysarin could simultaneously figure herself out.

Then once it was done she could be normal. She could marry Deime.

Perhaps they'd live in that old shack in the woods that Mysarin always traveled to when she awoke in the forest. The shack where she'd always leave her clothes. They would rebuild it, make new memories. His presence could wash away her years of horror.

Mysarin felt giddy thinking about the daydream.

All she had to do now was wait for Syndra Loreanar to summon her to the castle, and once she did, convince her that she needed Mysarin.

It shouldn't be too hard.

6 – Estair

Estair remembered a cold cloth pressed against her head. And darkness. She remembered a bowl of gruel. She remembered beads of sweat rolling down her back, and then more darkness. She spent the rest of her trip in and out of consciousness, burning and delirious from the scream-fever. The sea-striker's last resort before it must retreat from battle, or be defeated, is the blood-curdling scream. Estair had battled many strikers and had always known to block out the noise, known the warning signs.

This was her first time continuing a battle while the enemy was out of sight.

Her handler woke her again, this time with a cold bucket of water to the face, telling her they had arrived. She had been out for two days.

"Faster," his voice brusque and impatient. He pushed at her shoulder as she was ushered off of *The Warbeast* and onto the docks. Outside was wholly white. She blinked her eyes repeatedly, slowly, trying to stave away both the sun and the darkness still beckoning her. Men were lifting nets of fish and sacks of trade and rushing along the wooden boards all around her, voices overlapping in the distance. She hardly noticed.

"I've never had a lady as big as you," a voice whispered into her ear.

Lazily, she turned her head to find no one there, then stretched her face. Not real. A drop of sweat encroached on her eye and she nuzzled her face into her shoulder, trying to wipe it away. While she was distracted, her foot caught on a lifted plank of wood and soon her face met the dock.

"Great Twelve, get up." Real.

Her handler gripped the back of her cotton shift and yanked her back to her feet. His knuckles felt cool on her neck and she almost sighed in relief. He gripped her chin and forced her to look him in the face.

"Gods, you're sicker than a MoonDawn beast. You need to control yourself."

He had eyes as blue as the open sky. She wondered where in Syrelle he hailed from; most people in the Twin Islands were born with brown or golden eyes like hers.

His mouth was still moving, "Are you hearing me?" He shook her.

Estair nodded, her mouth was too dry to speak.

"And shall you find the Lands of Wind, shall you meet the dust of realms, I shall hope to find you there. I shall, I shall, I shall..." Her mothers voice. Not real.

Her handler slapped her face, driving the song away. The world grew a fraction clearer and the sun became less blinding.

"Thank you," she made out, voice hoarse.

He sighed. "Someone bring her some water or Twelve curse you."

Estair followed the other men through the halls of the castle, led by Taurean guards, gaining more lucidity by the second. The walls were opulent with golden and silver markings painted along them. The moldings were intricately carved, and matched the fine details that bore into the guards armor. The furniture and base colors of the walls and ceilings were shades of vermillion, gray and onyx black. Yet, even with all of the sophisticated details of the castle, the halls felt like they'd been crafted from cold bones. The thousand year history of the place radiated throughout; death clinging to life and sinking into the dust.

She couldn't remember the last time she had bathed, and felt her cheeks burn as castle-goers passed by the flock with their elbows over their noses and their eyes snagging onto her shortened hair. Their clothing was even finer than that of the guards; silken and embroidered fabrics in colorful fashions. Ladies wore tight bodices over wide, ruffling skirts. Lords looked silly in puffy sleeves and tight trousers. All while Estair was in rags; dirty, sick and chaffing where her chains were clamped onto her body.

The assembly of ex-pirates had all stopped once they reached the courtyard. They stood lined up in front of an elven man, who was tall and mighty and dressed in the same gilded Taurean armor. His chin-length, golden blonde hair shined in the morning sunlight as he surveyed the cluster he had bought from the Karnoch. He walked silently down the line, coppery-beige skin held tight and straight. Then he stopped in front of Estair.

"What is a woman doing standing among my new soldiers?" he demanded.

Estair tried to stand confidently, rolling back her shoulders as she replied in Syrellen, an uncomfortable language on her tongue, "I w-was a First Mate wwwith the Karnoch. I can fight."

Her voice was still full of dry heat. Her accent made her trip up on the words. She knew as soon as she said it, sick as she was, it wasn't convincing.

The elven man studied her for a moment. He was even taller than she was, and yet they seemed to carry the same weight. It was hard to tell his age—as elves were known to have much longer life-spans than humans did—but the delicate folds around the corners of his round eyes told her that he would be in his late thirties in a human sense. As for his real age, he could've been anywhere from fifty to a hundred and twenty years old. His irises were a golden shade, matching hers, as they roamed over her.

He took in her dewy and flushed face, drinking up her high cheekbones, chiseled jawline, and wide mouth. He smirked as his attention drew to her breasts, peeking through her worn shift dress.

After likely imagining what she looked like without her too-thin clothing, he snapped his head back up at her and grunted, "A woman has no place among my ranks, take her to the kitchens."

He then proceeded to walk down his line of inspections.

"No, allow me to showw you," she challenged.

She needed to convince him, whatever it took, for it was all that she knew. If she was forced to live in a new land, forced into new servitude, she wanted the comforting weight of a sword in her hand again. The cool feeling of leather against her skin. If she could not smell the salt of the seas any longer, she wanted to fight. Even with the scream-fever still ravaging her, she believed she could persuade this man. Perhaps it was the delirium of it all.

The elven man stopped in his tracks with his back turned to her. He then swiveled around towards her with his hand extended, the back of his armored knuckles landing upon Estair's cheek. She fell backwards, her body meeting the ground for the second time that day.

"Huh," he said. "You look better like this. More female."

He then continued to walk away as two guards came up to remove Estair from the cluster of men, and drag her to the kitchens.

She blinked rapidly this time, still trying to keep her chin high as they forced her all the way back into the castle, struggling against the weight of her. She closed her eyes as she thought of the white trees in Qintra, how soft their fluffy leaves felt brushing against her skin.

"I shall, I shall, I shall…" The echoes of her life past continued to haunt her. She opened her eyes.

The kitchens were a blur as she struggled with reality, and the warmth from the ovens threatened to suffocate her. The guards finally removed the chains she had worn for so many days when the smell of the bread baking in the ovens washed over her, waking her. Her stomach yearned for any food she could acquire.

Once the guards had left her, she searched for any scraps that she could quickly eat. She spotted an apple on one of the stone counters and made a grab for it as an old woman walked into the kitchens.

The woman jumped in surprise at Estair's massive height. "Oh! My, you startled me. What are you doing here?"

Her stomach growled in complaint as she drew her hand back to her side.

"I'm here to cook, I suppose."

Estair looked around at the dishes and ingredients that were scattered about the kitchen, trying to blink the blood that was trickling into her eye away.

"Well, you can't cook looking like that. Or *smelling* like that, no offense, dear."

The old woman grabbed a damp cloth from a nearby counter and slowly limped over to Estair. She paused with her head at Estair's waist, looking up at the wound on her head.

"I'm going to need you to take a seat."

"Oh."

Estair looked down for a moment before she found and sat down on a small stool that she was standing next to. She leaned into the relief as the elderly woman began to clean the blood from her face, numb to the pain.

"You're burning up, poor thing." The old woman frowned. "What is your name?"

When Estair didn't respond, still lost in the respite from her fever, the woman said, "My name is Bea, I'm a servant, too. I usually cook here with a few others. I've been wondering when we would get some new help."

She smiled at Estair, highlighting the wrinkles around her silver eyes. They were surprisingly warm, like the comfort of a hug. She wondered if this was real.

"My name is Estair," she finally responded.

She then gently grabbed the older woman's wrist and pulled it away from her face.

"Is there anyw-w—place I can properly bathe? I also… do not know how to cook. I'm a fighter."

"Well, there are no swords in here, so you can be our dishwasher for the time being. As for a bath, I get one started for you in the servants quarters. And perhaps you need a rest, too. Come, follow me."

Bea motioned with her hand for Estair to rise, and she clicked her tongue at the thin shift she was brought here in.

"I'll see about getting you some real clothing as well, I can't have you walking around in *that*." The woman turned and began to make her way through the castle.

Estair felt the tears well up in her eyes again, except this time, it was not from the pain on her face. She tried to will them to retreat, yet they fell down her face fast as the violent waves in the Fallen Waters. She followed Bea as she silently cried, and thought to herself how Bea's white hair had looked so similar to the trees back home. Why was she getting so emotional?

"I shall, I shall, I shall..."

She fought to keep balance as they walked through the dark halls of the Taurean castle.

Bea spoke quietly to Estair, "Word of the wise, try not to end up worse than you are now. Though, that may be easier said than done."

She looked at the cuts on Estair's face from the man's armored backhand, and then down at her raw and red ankles.

"Just don't question those who rank higher than you, and *listen*. And don't trust anyone too easily, you never know if there are rats lurking about..."

Bea's voice was slowly draining into the background, her mothers taking the forefront of Estair's mind.

"And when you call for me, I shall hear it. When you reach for me, I shall be there. When you're all alone, you should know..."

Estair tried to listen closely to the wisdom of Bea's words, yet her body did not feel like her own. Instead, she focused on the physicality of the woman. How was she this old and frail and still up on her feet like she was now? Walking and speaking with such vigor. *She must have bones of steel. The same sort of bones this place was built with,* she thought.

Bea and Estair finally reached the small servant's quarters; cramped rooms filled with many beds, furniture on the brink of falling apart, and drawers that were mostly empty. They moved into a room off to the side and Bea began to fill a large tub with the buckets of water that were lying nearby.

"The water's going to be cold, prepare yourself. It'll be better than nothing, though," Bea said. "It will help cool your fever, at least. I'll go and find clothes for you, you just focus on getting yourself cleaned up." She finished filling the tub to half of its capacity, and then left the room.

Estair undressed, and slipped into the cold water. Relief. She sat for a moment, still as the stars, before she wiped away the dirt, blood, and memories of her life before today. She wouldn't need them any longer.

She woke the next day to Bea bringing her breakfast. The woman was kind enough to excuse her from any kitchen duties the day before, allowing her to fully heal from the scream-fever. Bea had set up a small wooden table next to Estair's cot in the servants quarters that she set a bowl of soup down on, a vial of strange liquid, and a new container of salve for her wrists and ankles.

"It's to help ease the heat," Bea said when Estair grabbed the vial to inspect it. "Now drink up. Today, I'll give you a run down on what you'll be doing here, if your daydreaming has finally subsided."

She put a hand onto Estair's forehead.

"You don't seem as warm today. Did you sleep well?"

Estair uncorked the vial and drank.

"I think so." She rubbed her eyes. The vial left a strange taste in her mouth, like minty wine. "What was in that?" At least her accent had a better time working around the Syrellen words after her slumber.

"Herbs, most likely." Bea then turned to walk out of the room. "Eat your food and come to me in the kitchens."

Estair chuckled. She was beginning to really enjoy the old bat. Slowly, she ate the soup; it was hot and comforting and the best thing she had eaten since she left Qintra, and she wanted to fully appreciate it. Once she was done she stood, stretching her long limbs, and shaking out the hallucinations that were plaguing her all yesterday. A slow chill went up her spine as she remembered the voice of her mother singing her a lullaby. Part of her wondered if it was somehow real.

But Estair knew that it wasn't. Her mother had sung to her when she was a child, yes, but it was about the only kind thing her mother had done for her. The rest of the time she spent in her mother's presence was all about training. Her mother would bark orders at her in the yard of the house, forcing Estair to work her muscles until she collapsed day in and day out. She had needed to grow strong if the Karnoch were going to pay for her. Now, Estair would sometimes wonder if her mother just enjoyed the control.

The haziness of the scream-fever was still in the back of her mind, slowly receding like a morning fog. She rubbed her eyes again and then sighed as salve soothed her chafing. Today would be long.

In the kitchen, Bea was already washing up the dishes when Estair walked in.

"Ah, took you long enough." Bea rested the wet cloth down on the rim of a bucket sitting atop the stone counter. "Are you sure you're feeling well? I can excuse you for another day if you need it, dearie." She placed her hands on her hips in fists. Estair felt the corner of her mouth tug upwards.

"No, I am alright." Estair widened her arms and spun in a circle to show Bea.

"Good. Then let's start with a tour then, shall we?" Bea walked out of the kitchens and into the halls of Taurean Castle. Estair stood for a moment, watching, and then realized she was to follow. She weaved through the maze of Lords, Ladies, guards, and women wearing strange masks covering their entire faces. Some people laughed, some spoke in hushed tones, all of them wore bright colors and shiny fabrics. And they all smelled nice. Estair was used to pirates who would wash once a week in pure seawater, who wore the same dirty rags each morning.

These people *bathed regularly*. Suddenly, Estair imagined it would not be so bad here. Though she still wished she had a sword in hand.

Bea brought her to the Taurean Royal Healer's Hall connected to the servants quarters and told her that this was where the healer's workrooms would be, should she get sick again. They were only permitted to heal the royals and other nobles though, so Bea told her to get on their good side so they would sneak her medicine. Estair peeked into one of the rooms with an open door and saw a man with long thick locs and a deep sapphire-brown complexion reading a book. He looked up to her and waved, and so she waved back.

She promised herself to get on his good side.

Next, Bea brought Estair into the main area of the castle, where the ballrooms, the receiving room, and the entrance out into the courtyard were.

"Remember all of this, you hear me?"

Bea's feet took many lopsided steps as Estair would take one, she noticed, and so she slowed her pace while she nodded her head to the old woman.

"What are you doing? Keep up!"

Estair chuckled to herself again and resumed her regular speed.

The two walked up a few flights of stairs to a floor filled with rooms for guests. Bea pointed out two in particular.

"We have Rionaes Theinguard staying in this one. He's the Princes to Oswes, so make sure that this room is checked on often and kept tidy. Stay out of the way and out of sight though. That is the protocol here for servants. If he is currently occupying the room, then you turn around and you come back later."

"But what if it is dirty?" Estair asked, confused as to why she had to sneak around.

"I'm starting to think he actually likes it that way," Bea muttered.

She continued down the hall at her fast tempo before abruptly stopping before another room.

"I've been told we will have a guest here soon. You'll have to be the one to bring them food and clear away the plates. I'm too busy with everyone else."

She waved her hand about and continued her walk.

"Same rules apply though, don't interact, don't be seen. It is the way."

Estair nodded her head again, trying to remember how they even got up to this room from the kitchens in the first place. The inside of the castle was the largest building she had ever seen, and she still had not seen most of it. She remembered being told that it was the largest castle in the world by one of the men on the way there, before she caught the fever. She now knew it was the truth.

Bea then led her into the courtyard. It was a large open space within the castle gates that held three important areas, Bea had said.

"The garden, the arena, and the soldiers' training grounds."

Bea had counted each place on her fingers.

"You probably won't be doing much at the gardens or the training grounds, but we are going to host a tourney here soon, and that is going to be all hands on deck for three weeks."

"Everything is in threes," Estair said to herself.

"Huh. I guess the Loraenars like it like that. It is the way." Bea nodded her head in affirmation.

"What is that?" Estair bunched her brows together.

"What is what?" Bea stopped.

"'It is the way,'" Estair lowered her pitch and mimicked in the same authoritarian tone Bea used.

"Oh, just something from a past time. That reminds me, we have one more stop to make." Bea resumed her hurried gait.

They stopped at a small, strange, building on the edge of the courtyard that was fully made from the light-gray stone that was the exterior of the castle and the city. Inside, everything seemed to be once elaborately carved and cared for, with details now fading away from time. There was dust and stone debris laying about, casting shadows through the air and the light shining in from the large open windows. Estair watched as a ray of sunlight highlighted specs of dust dancing through the golden colors. They played a game with each other. One group would swirl and twirl forwards as one would retreat, spinning in the silence. If the rest of the castle was made from bones, the memory of death, then this place was made from the very essence of life.

She tore her attention away to see Bea's white hair placed before a stone column.

There were many stone columns around the room, placed in a semi-circle. But, it was uneven: in the corner of the room where another column should be, there was only open space and old broken stone. She turned her head back towards Bea and noticed the column next to the one she was in front of did not have a statue like the others did.

"What is this room?" she asked.

Bea continued to stand still as night before the statue shaped like a malomar—a female creature one part elf and one part snake with fins along its tail and backside.

She then replied, "A prayer room. Don't you recognize the Great Twelve?" It was a statue of Pymith, The Huntress, Deity of the Wild, Nature, and Creatures Big and Small.

Estair looked around at the figures again, focusing on their cracked and smoothed shapes. It was as if they've had fingers run along them so many times that over the years the edges began to fade. She made out the male Suijin—which was strange to see as in the Twin Islands she was always depicted as female—on the other side of Bea, and Talisi, Harbinger of Light, Deity of Justice, Scales, and Holy Fire, in the middle. One on the other side of the room was clearly Thir and Yekse, The Insatiable Heads of Pilferage, Deity of Greed and Thievery, since Estair could make out two heads on one body. The rest seemed to blend in together. Estair tried to remember who she was forgetting.

"Like I said, past times. You lot don't respect the Deities like you used to." Bea sighed and looked back to her statue beside the empty column. "If you feel like coming here and praying though, you do so at night, after all your duties are done for the day. It is the way."

"It is the way," Estair repeated softly.

7 - Mysarin

Mysarin attempted persuading Grenlide again for good measure. After her success with Telme, she knew what to do. And she was sober this time. But, she only found Grenlide growing angry with her incessant begging to be freed. Ixmon had to come into the office and drag her back into her own room.

Grenlide didn't drink. Grenlide didn't smoke prunn. It made no sense why it wouldn't work on her. Her mind was impenetrable.

Mysarin had even prayed before walking into her office, under her breath so Grenlide wouldn't hear, instead of relying solely on summoning a god's magics that hadn't given her any favor. And still, Grenlide remained the bane of Mysarin's existence and the barrier between her and everything she ever wanted.

It had been two days since Mysarin had persuaded Telme. *Two days*, and still no summons to Taurean Castle. No messenger bringing her a letter that contained the key to her cage. She was starting to panic. She felt like she was running out of time as a slave to the moon's 28 day cycle. Every day counted more than the last. Every single day Mysarin got closer and closer to killing. Again.

In the darkest parts of Mysarin's mind, she heard a whisper saying that Grenlide would be the next body at her feet. The waning moon promised that when it was filled, she would get out one way or the other.

But Mysarin didn't want to be a killer. She didn't want that stain on her soul. It's why she opted for this whole persuasion idea instead—it was the only thing saving her from killing more than she already did.

Twelve, she just wished she could *stop killing*. Stop forgetting. Stop giving her body away. Stop. Stop. Stop.

Be normal.

She was still in the throes of rage when a hooded figure opened her door.

The woman and blonde elven man in leather armor watched as she threw a goblet at her wall. Her chest was heaving, her room destroyed.

"She was right. She's the spitting image of you," the blonde elven man said. His eyes were painfully golden, his hair and skin the same shade. Mysarin thought she recognized him, but she couldn't quite place how…

And that's when the woman removed her hood to reveal that it was Syndra Loraenar herself.

Mysarin almost sank to her knees.

She stood tall and proud, and the world seemed to pause in her presence. The king and queen had named their sole heir Syndra, meaning *power*, and Mysarin knew in the moment she must've been divinely blessed; waves of undiluted influence leaked into the air around her. She was like a dark storm cloud, demanding that its presence be known by the thunderous ruptures it sends through the skies. It is said that each time a new ruler is destined for the throne, they are gifted with limitless magics by the Great Twelve along with their namely-blessing.

Mysarin had completely believed that they had abandoned this world until now. Now, she was here, looking at the evidence of their existence and realizing they had only abandoned her.

Syndra scanned the remnants of a room; the bedding covering the floors, the turned over chairs, the broken mirror still sitting on her vanity. All before her eyes landed on Mysarin.

"I heard you're a glamor mage, correct?" Her voice was young, and she looked to be about seventeen years old in both a human and elven way. Even with her age, she still reeked of authority. Mysarin was stuck staring at the heir to Stonecrest and all of Syrelle, unable to speak. She swallowed, trying to find her words. Yet, they would not make their way out of her mouth.

All Mysarin felt was fear: for the plan she executed on a whim, for the fact that it worked, for what was to come and for the woman standing before her. She felt sweat start to pool on her brow.

Syndra looked *eerily* like Mysarin.

They both had the same raven dark hair, steel gray eyes and olive toned skin, albeit Syndra's was much paler than her own. They even adorned their elven ears in the same placements. Mysarin was lost in the similarities. So she started to count what differences there were instead.

"Uhm, hello, Your Highness." Mysarin bowed, finally breaking the silence, as she thought that while Syndra's face was round, hers was more of a heart-shape.

"Are you the woman I am looking for?" Syndra asked impatiently.

"Yes, that's me. Pardon the uh… the state of the room, I didn't know you were coming," she said while noticing that Syndra's hair was straight and silken, and hers was wavy, wild and full of volume. "My name is Mysarin."

"Show me what you can do then, Mysarin." Syndra crossed her arms expectantly.

When she spied no freckles upon Syndra's nose bridge, where Mysarin's was dusted with them, she nodded her head. Mysarin then summoned a simple flame to her hand—a small elemental spell that anyone with magics could perform.

"Is that all? I thought you were supposed to be a master at glamor." Syndra raised her eyebrow.

She was dressed in all black, wearing nothing that could mark her as royalty. No corset, no farthingale under her skirt, no jewels, no crown.

Mysarin started to question if this really was the Princess.

"Fine. I'd rather not be lurking around in a pleasure house anyway," she said. She turned to leave.

"Wait," Mysarin called after her.

This had to be her. The man behind her—who she now recognized as the Golden Elf, Zendar Paelos, the Commander of the Royal Army—wouldn't be here otherwise. It was also in the way she held herself, and the matching look to the rumors of what the Princess looked like. '*She shines like a torch through the shadows,*' Mysarin had once heard.

Syndra turned around, impatience spreading over her face.

Mysarin let her own glamor drop, the heavy weight of the mud sliding off, revealing the bruising and marks that had lain below. She unveiled the darkness beneath her eyes, and the pallid tone of her skin.

Syndra smiled, unrattled by the true, gory, abominable, look of Mysarin before her.

"Good. That is satisfactory." Mysarin thought she could see a hint of something else within the heir's eyes. Something she couldn't yet place, but they blazed with an intensity that could burn right through walls.

Mysarin's stomach went into a full whirlpool within her, and she fought to keep standing.

"How can I be of service to you, Princess?" *Please, please, please. Please, work.*

"I have some events coming up, the MoonDawn games, the ball, the courting of a foreign Prince, and... other things. I need to ensure that I look my best for these events. They need to go smoothly for the great of Syrelle."

Syndra looked as if she fought to keep her shoulders back and her chin high as she spoke. Mysarin thought that perhaps all of the pressure that was placed on this young girl was weighing her down.

Heavy may be the crown, she thought.

"Of course, Your Highness, whatever you need."

"And I require you to live within Taurean during this time as well," Syndra said. *Yes, yes, oh Great Twelve,* yes.

"I can do that," Mysarin replied almost immediately.

The games were a three-week long event, with the last day being the next full moon. It was risky timing, but if she could pull it off, she would have all the time in the world to devote to finding a cure to her lost nights. If she didn't find anything within the Taurean library, that is. Which, why shouldn't she? It was a resource even the most astute scholars would kill for beside the one in Synsee. She would do her work and leave after the last tournament, making it out before her sleeping feet took her into the forest.

"Wonderful," Syndra relaxed her jaw, and breathed in deeply. "And you will be paid handsomely for doing so."

"Wait. You'll have to pay for me. Give the money to my Lady Madame, Grenlide."

"I thought you were a resident mage, not a whore."

"Either way, the money goes to Grenlide. I owe her a debt."

"Very well then, show me to her, and we will discuss your price."

"Thank you for the opportunity, Princess. You will not be disappointed." Mysarin curtsied again.

She led the two through the quiet pleasure house, the other girls asleep and resting before another day of work in the morning. Mysarin went to knock on Grenlide's door, but Syndra moved in front of her and opened it herself.

"What is this?" Grenlide said from behind her desk.

Zendar followed in after the Princess, and closed the door behind him, leaving Mysarin out in the hall.

She waited patiently, pressing her ear against the door to listen in on what they said:

"What do you people think you are doing?" Grenlide's toasty timbre.

"The Crown would like to buy one of your girls from you." Syndra.

The room was silent for a moment. Grenlide was likely realizing who, exactly, she was speaking too.

"Really?" Grenlide drawled. "Mysarin has quite the debt, and is my best girl. I won't let her go for less than what she's worth to me."

"Yes, well," Zendar speaking, "the Crown is prepared to pay any cost. Name your price."

Mysarin's heart became all she could hear after that. That dangerous feeling of hope coming back to her, consuming her. She was getting out. Her plans had finally come together. She was finally taking a step closer to a simple existence.

The two came out of Grenlide's office. Mysarin caught a glimpse of her Lady Madame, smiling from ear to ear.

"I expect you to be fully moved in by midday tomorrow. I'll have someone meet you at the gates at dawn to show you to your room and assist with moving anything in. I hope for your sake this works out favorably, I do not take disappointment lightly," Syndra said to her. Mysarin nodded and curtsied again, and resisted the urge to thank the Princess over and over.

She wanted to cry with gratitude as she watched the two leave.

The first thing that she wanted to do with her freedom was to find Deime. She ran out into the night air, immediately getting soaked by the summer rain. But Mysarin didn't care. Her life had just changed.

"It's so refreshing! It's like giving yourself a new start, letting the rain wash away any and all worries," Deime's voice sang through her mind.

Yes, yes it was. Mysarin almost tripped on the stone paths as she ran towards Sea Salt Bakery, giggling to herself. Once she reached his door, she began pounding on it.

"Deime!" she yelled out. "Deime get out here right now!"

Eventually a window above her opened, and he peeked his head through.

"Mysarin? What in the Great Twelve are you doing out there?!"

"Get down here!"

"It's pouring rain!"

"I don't care! Get down here this instant!"

He laughed, and closed the window.

Mysarin breathed deeply, shaking with anxious energy, as she waited in the dark.

He came out of the shop door with a lantern in his hand, wearing nothing but his trousers.

"My father is going to be so pissed if you wake him," he said.

"Screw your father." She grabbed onto his free hand and tugged him out into the downpour.

"I'm free!" she yelled.

"What?!"

"*I'm free*, Deime. The Loraenars bought me out from Grenlide, I don't have to sell myself anymore. I just need to move into Taurean Castle for the tourney, and then I'm *done*."

He grinned, the moonlight shined down onto his yellow hair, turning it silver. Droplets fell from his strong nose. He set down the lantern, and swooped her up into his arms, spinning her around.

"That's-that's amazing Mysarin! How did you do that?"

She laughed into his ear as the rain came down harder.

"I persuaded a handmaiden. I had her recommend me. *Twelve*, I didn't even think it would work, but Syndra Loraenar herself just came to Siren's Labyrinth to buy me out!"

He stopped in his tracks, setting her back down onto the pavement.

"You persuaded a handmaiden?" he said, smile faltering.

"I—" she hadn't meant to say that.

"You *charmed* someone?"

"No, I—"

"That's what you said."

"Deime, it was the only way."

"No. There could've been other ways."

"Why are you being like this?"

"You know why."

His mother. She was once charmed by a thief in the streets. He had made her hand everything she had over, including the money the Thunshire's had desperately needed. When she had realized it, she had told Arias, Deime's father. Then things had gone horribly wrong. She had to flee from Arias' anger, leading her out into the streets at night.

And then she was never seen again.

Deime stepped back, his body going stiff.

"Deime, I'm sorry. I, I had no other way."

"I can't believe you. It's *wrong*, Mysarin. You messed with someone's mind!"

Her skin heated.

"You know what's wrong? Manipulating a fourteen year old girl into working at a brothel when she had nowhere else to go. Making her sell her body. Endure beating after beating. Refusing to let her leave once she was old enough to look after herself."

"And that handmaiden had nothing to do with that." Deime crossed his arms.

"She had *everything* to do with it. She was the only way for me to get myself out of there. You weren't going to pay for me were you? You couldn't have!"

"I could have. I could've saved up. You should've told me."

"No! You couldn't. Just because you were stupid enough to want to marry a whore doesn't mean that she would let me go. Twelve, Deime. Did you think I worked there because I *wanted* to? No, she wouldn't let me leave even if you did pay my debt. I needed something bigger, something better. And I did it. Why can't you be happy for me?"

Deime said nothing. His big, brown eyes were locked in a wide stare. The doe was bleeding before her. Another body injured, and her teeth dripping with crimson.

"I'm sorry. I'm sorry, Deime. I-I don't know why I said that, I don't think you're stupid."

"No. You just think I'm naive."

"That's—"

"No, I get it. Maybe I am. It was naive of me to let myself fall in love with you."

"Please, Deime."

The guilt came quickly, replacing her anger. Instead of her skin heating, it was now shaded with shame. She grabbed onto his hand. She wanted to cling to him like a sinner clinging to prayer, begging for redemption.

"Just… I should go back inside," he said.

"I'm so sorry."

He was fighting some internal war with himself, she could see it on his face.

After what felt like years of silence, he took a deep breath and finally said, "Do you need help moving into the castle?"

"I… I don't think so. I don't have a lot."

"Well, I'll come by tomorrow morning, okay? I'll help you anyway. I'll see you then."

He then pressed a kiss onto her forehead, grabbed his lantern, and went back into the bakery without another word.

Mysarin arrived at the front gates of Taurean Castle, Deime in tow, just as the sun started to rise above the horizon. The air was cool, and the skies were still stained a hazy dark blue with strokes of orange painted lazily across it all.

"Are you sure about this? I don't think it's too late to back out," Deime said quietly, as if not to disturb all of those who were still asleep. He set down a few bags of Mysarin's things as he stared up at the towering presence of the Taurean walls.

Beyond the white iron gate, the largest castle in all of Tris was made from light gray stone—like the rest of the buildings in the city—yet under the dawn the stones looked a periwinkle shade. Its colossus arches between towers served as bridges where guards were posted all day and night, ready for any threats that might come their way. The light blue rounded domes atop the towers were said to have elaborate and ancient paintings left from previous rulers on the inside. Mysarin wondered if she would get to see those paintings herself.

"It's definitely too late now, I don't want those guards coming to find me if I don't show," she replied.

She looked over to Deime, breaking the intense grip that Taurean Castle had on her sights. He seemed somber still. She was afraid that his wounds hadn't stabilized yet.

"Can I tell you how sorry I am for last night?"

"Mysa, it's fine. I just… I want you to be safe in there. What if I never get to see you again?" He looked at her with a searing magnitude, as if he was searching within her eyes for the future.

"It's not like they won't let me leave, I'm not their prisoner," she laughed, trying to lighten his mood.

"You know that's not what I mean… I hear it can be brutal in there. No mistakes are allowed to the servants. When I had worked for them it was the second most stressed I had ever seen my father."

"That is why I simply will not make any," she winked at him.

When he still did not smile back at her, she continued on, "Seriously, I will be okay. They'll let me come and go as they do all their servants, and I will come see you tomorrow morning. We'll continue on as normal. It's just a job. And when it's over, we will throw a lovely and beautiful wedding."

"It will be lovely and beautiful, because *you* will be there." He moved close to her and planted a firm kiss onto her lips, and then he held on to her tightly. Mysarin could feel his heart beating wildly through his chest and into hers, and her own beats turned in time with his.

"Mysarin!" Telme yelled from just the other side of the gate, startling the two lovers and breaking their embrace.

She smiled at the two as she placed her hand upon her heart.

"Aren't you two cute?" Telme motioned to the guards to open up the gates, and Mysarin's hands began to shake.

"Goodmorning, Telme, thank you so much for doing this for me," Mysarin responded carefully knowing that the handmaiden was still unaware that she was charmed.

"Of course, honey, now you two wrap it up and let me show you to your room." Telme crossed her arms and waited for their goodbyes.

"I'll come by when I'm free, and you can show me how to bake those new fruit tarts that you've been working on." Mysarin held Deime again in an embrace, this time taking note of the way he felt pressed against her. Strong, sturdy, dependable. He was the column that held up her ceiling. She looked into his face and wondered if she saw those paintings inside of Taurean, if their beauty could even compare.

"Okay, just don't keep me waiting too long, you are my life, Mysa." He kissed her again, and she savored the way her lips felt against his.

He stepped back, and handed his bags off to Telme through the now open gate. Mysarin nodded her head in goodbye with a smile of courage. *I will be just fine,* she tried to tell him with her eyes.

She picked up the other bags she had been carrying herself and began to follow Telme up the path into the castle grounds. She didn't dare to look back, afraid she would drop her things and run back to the elf. She knew without looking, though, that Deime was still standing in the morning light, watching her make the climb that could change her life.

Mysarin finished unpacking her things only two hours later. She was unsure of what to do with herself during the rest of the time she had before she'd begin her work with Syndra Loraenar. The Princess must've assumed Mysarin had much more to unpack than she did, unaware of how large the gap of wealth between them truly was.

Her room in the castle was bigger than three rooms in the pleasure house combined. Mysarin assumed she would've been living like a servant in this castle, and was surprised when Telme had brought her here instead.

Everything was ornate and intricately carved or decorated, from the red and black floor tiles that resembled a moonlit meadow, to the ceiling that *did* have an elaborate painting of some past Danai King. Even the candle sconces along the walls had silver and gold tendrils that flowed away from the functional parts—purely there for pleasure.

Mysarin was filled with glee at the sight of the room. It had rows and rows of arched black bookshelves along the walls, with areas for sitting and dining. They sat next to an enormous fireplace that was sure to keep the entire room warm, even during the winter nights. Off to the northern corner was a paper and wood partition that was painted with black and silver and hints of an amethyst purple.

Behind the partition was her bed, resting upon a giant frame with rich fabrics swooping down from it. It looked soft and beckoning despite the cold decor, and it rested below a window that viewed the city. After unpacking, she stared out the window, trying to find Sea Salt Bakery among the mass of gray stone walls and blue slate roofs. She couldn't make out which of the buildings Deime was residing in.

Mysarin walked out from behind the floor to ceiling partition to find Delvuvius sitting in the chairs made from a deep maroon velvet and a dark cherry stained wood. He set down a book he must've picked up from the hundreds that lined the book shelves and turned to her with a look of discontent.

"You *charmed* Telme?" Each word he spoke was hushed and rigid.

Oh Twelve, here we go again.

"Was I not supposed to persuade anyone? You must've known when teaching me that I was going to use it." She walked closer to the crook, dressed in a basic black tunic. Mysarin furrowed her brow in confusion.

"Not. On. Telme. Never again, do you understand?" He stood from his seat, and began to pace around the open front of the room.

When Mysarin continued to stand there, perplexed as to how Delvuvius was even here in the first place, he continued, "You could've gotten her *killed*. That woman raised me and you could've landed her in the *dungeons*. And for what? So you could land a big job?" He stopped moving as he stood and stared at Mysarin, waiting for a reply.

"Wait, what? I—I did not know who she was to you or how clearly dangerous this could've been."

"It is still dangerous! For you and for her. If you do not perform well, *Telme* is to blame. You forced her to recommend you!" He walked up close to her as he said the last words, getting within inches of her face. She flinched.

He paused, closed his eyes and breathed in deep. One breath, two breaths. Then as his eyes bore into her own, she could swear that what she saw was fear, not anger, on his face.

"I do not mean to scare you," he said calmly, "but tell me you will never again persuade the servants of this castle. You do not understand the consequences of your actions."

"What are you even doing here?" she asked.

"Promise me."

"Fine, yes I promise."

And with that, Delvuvius turned on his heel and walked out of her room.

8 - Delvuvius

Delvuvius Crune was hot with rage; he felt the tips of his round ears burning red. He walked out of Mysarin's new room and stormed through the halls. *Great Twelve, the oaf of a woman, what does she think this place is?* he thought to himself. *She had no right. No right whatsoever. And now here she is thinking she's been rewarded for her actions. Big new fancy room, new fancy job. She's just like the royals, thinking she can do as she pleases with the servants of this castle and screw the consequences. What else should I expect from an elf?*

As he stomped through the long and winding halls of the castle that he knew like the back of his hand he thought of that misguided day that inadvertently brought Mysarin here:

Delvuvius had begun to make his way to the castle from the shopping district after he realized it was going to continue to rain all day. There were no sales to be made on a day like that. As he walked the same path he always took, he stopped by the prunn den to check on the old man he made a sale to the day before. Though he learned quickly after asking around and giving his description to other patrons that the sick man had passed away in the night.

Delvuvius had known there was no saving the man's lungs. He tried to stifle the guilt that soon rose within his body and reminded himself that he did what he had to do. At least the elixirs he sold weren't a total lie. They were common pain relievers that he was able to take now and then from Ostrac, a Taurean Royal Healer. He told himself that he had given some comfort to the man as he passed, and comfort to those who likely had looted the rest of the week's supply.

He pulled one of the orange marigolds from his trunk of supplies and placed it upon the threshold of the prunn den.

"Talisi, Harbinger of Light," he whispered softly as he kneeled.

"I ask that you help these persons overcome their addictions, and that you give safe passage to those who do not. In the name of Justice and Sacred Fire, do right by these souls."

He paused and stood as he stared at the marigold laying in front of the doorway, becoming smothered by the rain. He then added, even quieter than before, "If you're still listening."

Yes, he was a crook and a liar. No, he was not a disciple of Ikaamte, the Deity of Cures and Medicine. He was a soldier who prayed to the deity of noble warriors, even though Zendar Paelos decided he could not do it for him. That is how he was raised; within the castle walls after he was dropped off as a babe. All he *had with him was a blanket and a note that said:* Make him strong. Give his life meaning. *And so he was raised by the servants and soldiers, handling a sword and honing his magics as he grew.*

As Delvuvius continued in the rain on the path to the castle, he was consumed by the thought of never having to return. The servants had still welcomed him with open arms, sneaking him food when they could, but the soldiers... They had all shunned him after the Breaking, when it yielded no other depth to his powers. Exiled him like the previous Royals, the Danai family—who were slaughtered and usurped by their cousins, the Loraenars—after their sickness was revealed. As if his lack of superior magics was akin to the MoonDawn disease.

Telme, Ostrac, and his Deity, Talisi, were about the only friends he had now; he was used to sending his prayers out as he had since he was a young boy with the other soldiers, that the deity quickly became his silent confidant when he needed to speak of the things that would only break Telme's heart and Ostrac's moral compass. Yet, over the years, Talisi's reassurances came far and few between, leading to the complete silence that he experienced over the past few years. He had then wondered if the other soldiers still received a reply.

Delvuvius' stomach growled as he looked down to the rather empty case he was carrying. He made a plan to get more tinctures, and to possibly swipe a loaf of bread or two from the kitchens.

He'd arrived at the servants entrance just outside of the castle, soaked from the summer shower, when he spotted Bea.

"Del! How nice to see you. Telme is with the healers on the lower floor," the castle cook called out to Delvuvius.

"Bea, nice to see you as well. What brings you out into this piss-poor weather?" He looked up into the gray sky.

"I was heading to the garden to pick a few herbs. The Queen requested fresh mint tea." Bea plastered a false and tight smile onto her face.

Delvuvius rolled his eyes at the thought of sending the frail and often sickly woman out into the downpour. Perhaps she still faced retribution for working beneath the Danai reign.

"Well, don't take too long or you'll need some of 'Del's Elixirs' again, free of charge of course." He gave a lopsided half-smile to the old woman.

Bea giggled as she patted his muscular shoulder and passed him out into the rain. He watched for a moment, taking in the woman's slight limp and wetted white hair, and took a mental note to try and squirrel away that elixir for her. Just in case.

Delvuvius had entered the castle and almost sighed in relief at the smell of the servants' halls—they smelled of home. His wet shoes squeaked against the marble flooring as he made his way to the healer's workrooms. The chirps echoed off the quiet halls until he found Telme chatting with Ostrac.

"I just want something that will make me look pretty, and you have all these herbs here, can't you throw something together for me?" Telme asked the human, trying to convince him into

helping her court the handmaiden to the castle's guest that she's been talking about since their arrival.

"I guess I could make you a rouge or something for your lips… I might have some berries here but that's all I can really do. I'm trained to heal, Telme, not to help you court." Ostrac replied in annoyance.

"You see how stern these healers are?" Telme turned to Delvuvius as she shoved her chin length auburn hair out of her face.

"I need some serious help here! Have you seen the beauty that is Lila?"

"Yes," Delvuvius replied, chuckling. "I have seen the Prince's handmaiden, and though she is a sight to behold, she has nothing on you Telme."

"Oh, you only say that because you have to." Though the middle aged elf meant what she said, she still put her tanned hand upon her chest as if truly flattered at the compliment.

"Ostrac, is there nothing else you can do for this wonderful woman?" Del said as he leaned against the doorframe to the small study.

Ostrac sighed. "Like I said, I'm trained to heal royalty, not to help woo foreign court persons." He turned back around to continue muddling his herbs with his mortar and pestle, done with the conversation. The smell of the damp plants being crushed filled the small space.

Delvuvius turned back to the woman who raised him, who was leaning on the poor healer's shoddy work table. He often felt sorry for anyone who stood in Telme's way of getting what she wanted.

"I'll tell you what Telme, I have some extra coin I can give you. Take it into town to this glamor mage that I met, working in the pleasure house, and she'll give you what you need."

The words that had caused everything to go so horribly wrong. What an idiot he had been, for sending Telme to her. After Mysarin was taken away by that lunar-elf, he'd been embarrassingly waiting for a chance to check if she was okay.

Not anymore.

"Oh Del, what a sweet boy you are. Always caring for the needs of others," she held out her hand to receive the coin. "You know you've always been that way, I think you're better off not fighting with those brutes in the army."

Delvuvius resisted the urge to flinch at the words. He knew they were well-intended, but the sting of his shortcomings always pricked at his wounds.

"Just don't tell anyone, I have a reputation to uphold here." He reached into his too-light coin purse and dropped about half of what he had into the palm of the handmaiden. "This should be enough, and tell her Delvuvius sent you, maybe Mysarin will be kind enough to give you a discount."

"Ahem," Ostrac turned around and glared at the two of them still in his work room. "Can you let me work in peace?" His twilight hands made to shoo Telme's behind off of his work desk.

"Oh, don't be so surly Ostrac, we'll go," Telme leaned down to place a kiss on the top of Ostrac's thick locs, and then hopped off of the desk to link her arm with Del's.

"Before we go," Delvuvius paused and turned to Ostrac, *"I need another few tinctures, possibly one for Bea. Our* delightful Queen sent her out into the rain and you know how quick to ailments she is.*"*

The man sighed again. "Sure, come by tomorrow morning and I'll have a few for you. But this time I need juniper berries, mugwort, and I want more of that sweet mead."

"Sure thing."

Delvuvius turned to fake a whisper and raise his eyebrows at Telme. "He is rather grumpy today, I'd say."

Delvuvius and Telme giggled together as they walked out of the healer's work rooms. Delvuvius's smile grew as he heard a muffled chuckle from Ostrac when the two passed over the threshold.

He finally made it out into the gardens, the sun almost reaching midday in the sky, and marched until he found what he was searching for. The golden poppy flowers and ragged robins seemed to welcome him with a beckoning breeze. The flowers that were associated with Talisi were always a source of comfort. As if they brought Delvuvius a fraction closer to his deity. But now, their fragrant scent floating in the air seemed to mock him and his inner turmoil. He sat down on a bench next to them as he tried to collect his thoughts.

How did she even pull that charm off anyway? For it to have lasted the entire walk up into the castle from the slums... She's clearly talented... She would've made a good soldier. He clenched his fists around the edge of the bench, feeling the rough stone press into his palms. Then, he rested his elbows against his knees as he brought his palms together and bowed his head.

"Talisi, Harbinger of Light," his voice barely audible over the wind brushing through the leaves.

"Protect Telme, bestow upon her your blessing and keep her from harm's way, for she acted not within her own will. I ask that you also... teach Mysarin the true nature of this castle." His fingers interlaced in a tight weave, turning his knuckles white.

"Be kind, be gentle, but bring the balance you promise to this castle. To this city."

He stood, and picked a flower from the garden. He then waited to see if the clear skies would cloud. A test. To see if the Great Twelve had all truly all gone away. He remembered the stories told of picking ragged robins, how taking just one of Talisi's flowers would bring lightning down upon those who did.

He anxiously stood there, staring up into the endless blue skies for what felt like hours. Waiting. He gave up when the sun hit its peak in the sky, not a single cloud in sight.

Hours later, Delvuvius knocked on the door to the small study where Ostrac worked, two bottles of mead in tow.

"Come in," the smooth and steady voice called out.

The smell of ground herbs and wet soil hit Delvuvius as he entered the space, settling the anger that still simmered beneath his skin. He swung the two bottles over the healer's head and waved them in front of his face as he sat at his desk in the cramped room.

"I need a drinking buddy, care to join?" he asked.

It had become a ritual of their own—to seek out the other with a bottle of something strong in hand whenever emotions or boredom grew too large. Usually it was Delvuvius who would initiate, and Ostrac who would begrudgingly partake.

Ostrac turned to look over his shoulder and up at the face of mischief Delvuvius had on. He raised an eyebrow.

"I hope you have a third bottle lying around if you're really looking to get pissed with me." The smile that slid onto the healer's face reflected Delvuvius' own.

"Well, why don't we go looking in the kitchens then?"

The two skittered off in search of more spirits in the kitchens, and were opening up cabinets when Ostrac noticed Del's still clenched jaw.

"What made you want to drink tonight?" he asked.

"What? A lad can't take full advantage of what squatting in a castle has to offer?" Del opened up another cabinet: nothing of use.

"I mean, you know I certainly do," Ostrac huffed a laugh. "But I meant, what are you so tense for? You're doing that thing with your neck again. It's all bulgy and gross to look at."

Delvuvius opened a door that contained a rack filled with plenty of bottles of wine.

"Ah, here we are."

He walked in and grabbed one from the bottom, one that no one would miss. He found Ostrac sitting on top of the counter in the center of the kitchen, one of the bottles already opened.

"Well, I think I have girl troubles."

Ostrac just raised his brows as he took a swig from the bottle in his hands as if to say *go on*.

Delvuvius hopped up onto the counter next to him and opened a bottle of his own. He took a long drink before he continued.

"There's this woman, an elf, and well I thought we had a strange connection when we met the other day. Like, birds of a feather." He took another drink. "And then today, I find out she's in the castle and I go and find her room and I just freaked out on her."

"Why?" That familiar crease between Ostrac's brows emerged.

"Well I taught her how to use a certain form of magics…" Delvuvius omitted the full truth, knowing Ostrac would reprimand him for using persuasion magics. Again.

"And I found out that she used them on Telme, after I had sent her to the elf. This morning all I heard about at the crack of dawn was Telme going on and on about how great her services were and how she recommended them to the *Princess*. Which is very unlike her. You know Telme only does things for herself."

"Twelve, Del, out with it. What did you say?" Ostrac wore a goading smile, already knowing full well the mess Del had made. He offered to clink his own bottle against the one in Del's hands.

"I wasn't mean, swear it on my sword. I just told her how dangerous it was, and to never do it again. And even when I was furious at her, all I could do was think about how *beautiful* this woman was. And then how *stupid* she was to use the magics I taught her on the first person she saw. And maybe a little guilty for teaching it to her in the first place… I'm fucked aren't I?" Del snorted to himself in his misery.

"Well," Ostrac took another sip, "at least you still have time to make amends, if it's what you want to do." He looked down at his hands, his eyes turning distant.

"Oh, not this again." Del nudged his arm.

Ostrac snapped his head back up and smiled bashfully. "I'm fine."

"Well, I shared." Del put his hand on his chest, and bowed his head. "Now it's your turn."

"I…" Ostrac trailed off, taking another drink. "Just make amends before you no longer can."

Del patted him on the shoulder, knowing exactly what had haunted Ostrac in the moment. "I'll try my best."

9 - Mysarin

Mysarin was in a dark room, feeling hands pulling and tugging on her body. They grabbed a hold of her and she was thrown to the floor. Her heart began to race and she stifled a scream of fear as a human man leaned over her. He began to berate her, yet she couldn't understand what he was saying; the sounds were all muffled like she was underwater. *I must've hit my head.*

She reached up and touched the wet she noticed trickling down her face right before the man came down to her level and straddled her. His face was red and puffy with rage as he pinned her arms under his knees. His voice was finally clear as he leaned in.

"Spoiled elven bitch. Where are all your guards now, huh? Where's all your riches and luxuries?" His face then morphed into Grenlide's, and then into Ixmon's.

When he lifted his hand to strike her again, she noticed that his skin was losing color. She looked down at his stomach to find her hand between a large red wound, his intestines wrapped around her fingers. She screamed.

Mysarin opened her eyes and quickly lit the candle that rested upon her bedside table. She sat up in bed, still sweating and panting from her dream, as she slowly recalled where she was. She was in the castle in her room, swaddled up in the black feather-soft blankets. She sighed. She hadn't had a nightmare like that one in months. *It must be the castle.*

Her heart was still racing from her dream, and the breeze that blew in from her open window sent an eerie rush down her spine. She stood up from bed, knowing she wasn't going to get any more sleep. On quiet and slow steps, as if she did not want to be noticed awake at this hour, Mysarin grabbed her candle and walked to the sitting area. She looked down at the book Delvuvius had left on the table earlier. '*Sacred Flames and Dwindling Lights*', a book written about Talisi, as well as common incantations used by those who worship the deity.

She rolled her eyes at the thought of their argument earlier.

Mysarin sat and began to mindlessly flip through the pages as she recounted her first day working with Syndra Loraenar. Three hours after Delvuvius had left, Telme finally arrived to bring Mysarin to the Heir's rooms. It was a strange day. Syndra the entire time had made Mysarin show her "options" as she tried to stifle her guilt for persuading Telme. Mysarin spent hours and hours changing the color of Syndra's raven locks to every variation of hair color she could think of. Changing the color of her eyes and timing how long the magics would last for. Even silly things just to further amuse the Princess like summoning fire, water, wind.

When she had finally left Syndra's rooms for the day, her very bones were shaking. She was surprised she did not faint on the way back to her own. With sweat dripping from her skin and her breathing growing more labored by the moment, she was ready to collapse when she finally made the trek back. That was before she smelled the food that was laid out for her on the table. An enormous plate full of exquisitely seasoned meats, rice, and vegetables, with sides of soft bread rolls and sweet treats.

Mysarin hadn't had a decent meal in... well, in a long while.

So, only after the table was cleared did she fall asleep, right before servants came in to collect her mess of dishes. Thinking of the food now made her stomach growl, craving more only a few hours later. And since she wasn't going back to sleep anytime soon—her dream and the eerie feeling of the castle keeping her up and antsy—she stood and decided to try and find the kitchens.

She opened her door to the halls only to find a man with short, white, curly hair standing before her, his own candle light flickering against his pale skin. His shock likely reflected her own as she stood staring up at him for a moment in silence. He looked about the same age as her, early twenties, and was one of the most beautiful men she had ever seen. His eyes were wide, yet soft with his lilac irises and long white lashes. His nose was a delicate slope, leading into his soft and plump lips. The white-haired man must've been a lunar-elf, Mysarin noticed, with small opal stones adorning his pale white ears.

She wondered what he was doing so far from home.

He looked as if he had been crying, with a tinge of red around his lids, and it seemed like wandering around in the night was something he did often by the darkness beneath his eyes.

"I am so sorry," he whispered, a flush of pink rising in his cheeks.

"What are you doing? Who are you?" Mysarin whispered back.

"I… I was up walking around and I heard you screaming." He paused for a moment and then quietly added, "I was not sure if it was real."

He then looked down at her, and took a full inspection of her wellbeing. "Are you well?"

"I didn't realize I was screaming," she looked down and away from his intense eyes. It was her turn to feel embarrassed. "I was dreaming."

"Oh."

She looked back up to see him… Contemplating on what to say next, perhaps? His eyes shifted around as his head tilted side to side.

"I get them too. Nightmares."

She did not expect to walk into the halls and have a heart to heart with a random elven man, no matter how pretty he was. She debated on just closing her door and flopping back down onto her bed once more, but she couldn't shake the feeling that there were eyes embedded into the castle walls, watching her. She didn't want to be alone. And then her stomach growled. "Do you know how to find the kitchens?"

"I do. Follow me." He turned on his feet and started walking down the halls.

"You didn't tell me your name," she whispered behind him, afraid to wake anyone else who might be occupying the other guest rooms.

"It is not as important as you believe," he whispered back to her as he kept on leading her in the darkness.

"What's that supposed to mean?" Her heartbeat started to pick up; whether it was in fear of the cold atmosphere, or still from exhaustion after expending so much of her magics, she wasn't sure. She looked around at every shadow his candle light created, convinced she was seeing ghosts in her peripheral.

"What was your dream about?" he asked, changing the subject. She noticed he had an accent, but she couldn't place where it hailed from.

"What are *your* dreams about?" she challenged. No way was Mysarin going to delve into the inner workings of her mind with this strange man.

"Fair point," he chuckled softly.

Mysarin and the white-haired elf continued to walk through the darkness of the castle in silence. The sounds of their footsteps being the only thing Mysarin could hear, yet she kept noticing him perk up and look around at phantoms. She started wringing her fingers together, thinking that he was searching for eyes in the walls too, when she started to hear a familiar laughter in the distance.

She saw the glowing light ahead as the elf said, "I believe it is just around this corner."

"Oh! You did *not* say that to him!" the familiar voice rang out in laughter.

"No truly," another man's voice called back, "I did!" The two erupted into laughter, both trying to keep the sounds as quiet as they could.

When Mysarin and the elf walked into the kitchen, she stopped in her tracks at seeing Delvuvius, and an umber skinned human man wearing the purple and gray clothing of a Royal Healer, both sitting on the counter tops and guzzling bottles of wine.

"Oh good Great Twelve, what are *you* doing here?" Delvuvius asked when he saw the two walk into the room.

Mysarin and the elf both stood silently, staring with wide eyes.

Delvuvius smirked at the two after a moment.

"You don't have to both look like you've been caught doing something scandalous," he paused and cocked his head to the side, "unless you have? Mysarin, don't tell me that one night away from your betrothed and you're already getting into trouble with a foreign man?" He laughed as he tipped back his head, the other man giggling as well.

"You know that is not truth, uh, Delvisivis?" The elf replied.

"Dellllvuuuuviiiuuuus," Delvuvius, drunkenly, slowed out his name. "Man, you've heard my name like three times already."

He took another drink from the bottle of wine and passed it to his friend. "Ostrac, here."

"Well, in his defence, it might have one too many syllables," Mysarin muttered.

Delvuvius opened his mouth to retort, and then closed it. He squinted at her.

"What? Nothing to say now? That's certainly not how you felt earlier." Her body felt like it was on high alert, her nervous system fraying from the day. She didn't necessarily want to argue with him, but picking at their fight relieved an inner tension she had been holding onto.

His cheeks turned red. "Only because you seemed to have lost all sense. Where is the wit you had when we met? Did it all go out the door when you saw how much coin could be made?"

Mysarin let out a sardonic laugh. "Isn't that what you do every day when you sell your *elixirs* to the poor? Not to mention that the spell hardly ever works."

"I'd be a much fatter and richer man if it did."

Delvuvius stared at her, she stared back. He had intimidated her earlier, had made her feel small, just like everything else in her life had. She was sick of it. For once, she wanted to have the upper hand, no matter how small it may have been.

The elf cleared his throat, shattering the tense silence. "Could I have some?" He motioned to the wine that was in Ostrac's hands.

Ostrac passed the wine.

"You're a hypocrite," Mysarin said, and then turned to leave, forgetting about her childish fears from earlier and letting her childish need to get in the last word lead.

"And you're an idiot."

"Del," Ostrac said.

She swallowed her anger at the comment, pushing herself further away from him. Then she heard a sigh and shoes hit the ground. The steps made their way to her, catching up with her pace. A hand placed itself on her shoulder, stopping her in her tracks.

"Wait, Mysarin."

She turned over her shoulder and she saw his anger fade as fast as it came. She raised a brow. "What?"

He removed his hand, and said nothing. His face turned unreadable.

"That's what I thought. Coward." She continued to walk back to her room, stomach growling, a triumphant smile on her face.

"Did a cat claim your mouth?" The elf butchered the saying to Delvuvius behind her.

10 - Delvuvius

He needed to get out of Stonecrest. He wanted to gather up as much coin as he could and hit the road to settle down far, far away from here. And far away from *her*. So the next morning, he wandered the castle until he saw what he was looking for: a Lady. Not one that is known for her beauty, but one that is known for her finely made dresses and large coin purses dangling from her hip.

She looked to be waiting for something or someone, her small eyes unsure and frantic as she surveyed the faces of people passing by. Delvuvius had told her to meet him in this hallway, near the cliffside and beneath the third archway that bestowed a gorgeous view of the sea in the anonymous letter he drunkenly wrote her last night.

A letter claiming that he was a Lord from Blackfall that had been secretly admiring her from afar for weeks now. It was an idea that had been forming in the back of his head to earn a lot of coin, but he was never set on acting on it—not until last night that is.

He stood in the arcade hallway on the cliffside dressed in his finest blue tunic with his hair pinned to cover his round ears until he spotted her. He shook out his hands as he made his way towards her. The sun was just above the horizon, casting a golden glow over Lady Stromwen while she fiddled with her sapphire necklace. Her hair was mousy brown and she truly was not an unsightly woman by any means, yet Del had heard rumors from the servants that she had been struggling to find a suitor. He smiled when she laid eyes upon him.

"Lady Stromwen, I am very happy to see that you came." Del took her hand as he bowed before her, and laid a tender kiss on the back of it. He noticed her skin smelled strange. Ignoring it, he stood back up to face her.

"I am Lord Fisgon of Blackfall. It is a pleasure to finally make your acquaintance."

"Are you the one who wrote me that letter?" She smiled, showing crooked teeth that matched the color of her butter yellow silk dress. "You are so very handsome."

Her white freckled cheeks turned rosy.

"And you are as radiant as ever." He grabbed her hand, and let the persuasion magics coat his voice.

"Please, take a walk along the cliffside with me." The two stepped out onto the grass as Mysarin's words echoed in his mind, *'you're a hypocrite.'*

The two strolled along the secluded pathway under the morning sky, speaking in polite tongues.

"What made you decide to write me that letter?" Lady Stromwen asked after a few hollow niceties.

"I…" Del paused. He let the persuasion slip away from his voice. If he was to execute his plan, he wanted to ensure she gave him consent for at least some part of it. It would be wrong otherwise. He gathered himself again, preparing for what he was about to do. A deep steadying breath filled his lungs, and he locked his eyes onto hers.

"I haven't been able to get you out of my head." He stopped and gently grabbed her arm. Suddenly the world grew brighter as a cloud released the sun, bathing the two in light.

"I must know you. I must have you, for you are the fairest maiden I have ever laid eyes upon and now looking at you under the morning light I…" His voice grew quiet, like he was embarrassed to admit it.

"I must taste you, if you would allow me."

He wasn't sure if his words sounded sincere, if they sounded too planned out. And yet perhaps that was what he needed—to sound as if he had been preparing for this very moment with a woman who haunted his mind.

Lady Stromwen was shocked, her deep blue eyes growing wide and pupils dilating. Her breathing turned hurried. Del held her stare and smiled his signature lopsided grin as he reached his hand up to stroke the side of her neck. She let out a shaking breath in response to his touch, leaning into his body and closing her eyes. He smelled that strange smell again on her skin, and resisted the urge to drop his look of longing and want.

"I would allow it," she opened her eyes and whispered.

He then let his hands roam over her figure; from her neck, to her back, to her waist. He leaned into that same spot on her neck just above her collarbones and hesitated as Lady Stromwen placed her own hands on his backside. She smelled *sour*, like vinegar, mixed with florals he could not place. She gripped his glutes and wholly pressed her body into his as he hovered over her bare skin. He then leaned back and used his left hand to lift her chin, exposing her neck further, and turning her face away.

Then he used his right to untie her coin purse.

"You are so very lovely, Lady Stromwen, like a bloom on a summer's night," he whispered into her ear.

She giggled as her coin purse fell free into his hand. Delvuvius slipped it into his pocket and then pulled away, standing straight and tense.

She furrowed her bushy brows at him. "Did I do something wrong?"

He shook his head and waved his hands, keeping her attention away from the new weight in his pants pocket.

"No, no. I have. I apologize my Lady, this is not right. I have embarrassed myself, and have almost made a fool of you because I cannot control my desire. Please forgive me, I must go."

Del bowed quickly and left the way they had come, leaving Lady Stromwen confused.

Just when he crossed back under the open arch and into the hallway of the castle, he saw a masked woman dressed in black turn the corner. A Faceless—one of the queen's personal spies that would roam the castle for intel—using shadow magics to come and go unnoticed.

Oh Talisi, please tell me they were not watching me.

He continued to walk down the halls after the spy, feeling his body begin to shake. The Faceless turned back to look at him as he rounded the same corner, and he stopped a few feet away. Del stared at the black mesh mask covering the woman's entire face and knew in the moment she had seen it all. Every thought had left his mind as the two stood in that silent hall. He heard the distant waves crash out below the cliffs. His feet felt bound to the red and black tiles beneath him.

The Faceless slowly inclined her head in greeting, and then disappeared into the shadows.

It only took an hour. Del had rushed to change into another outfit, stash Lady Stromwen's coin purse in his room, and fix his hair in hopes that no one would recognize him. He thought he was safe when he began to make his way out of the castle only to be stopped by two guards.

"Queen Yegaran has requested your company," the one on the right said. Del recognized him from when he was training to become a soldier. Hans Lopond was his name. They had never talked much but were about the same age.

Del swallowed.

"Apologies, I'm actually on my way out right now. Perhaps another time?" He tried to squeeze between them. Hans put his hand on his shoulder.

"Delvuvius, you know that's not up for debate." He looked disappointed in Del. Disappointed in what he had become. Del's shoulders sank a bit, and he knew he was in for it.

"Alright." He tried racking his brain for ways to explain what he had been doing with Lady Stromwen. "Take me to her."

The three began to walk the long and dark halls of Taurean. Del played out every situation in his mind. He could blame it on Lady Stromwen, but after playing with her feelings the way he had, he couldn't bring himself to put her into further trouble. Or, he could perhaps say her coin purse slipped and he was going to bring it back to her later… Except, that was widely unbelievable. He was screwed.

They arrived in a small dining room when Del had realized there was no way to get out of this. He was going to be jailed, or executed, or exiled, or tortured. He couldn't decide what punishment would be the worst for him. Exile would clearly be best, he could go live in the southern continent away from here at least. Tortured? Eh, been there, done that. It was between jailed and executed, most certainly.

Queen Yegaran sat in the center of the long dining table with Princess Syndra to her right and the Faceless that spotted him to her left. The guards pulled out a chair and pushed down on his shoulders, forcing him to sit before them. He looked around the room for any potential exits.

"Delvuvius Crune, is it?" The queen spoke with a soft voice and a small smile of satisfaction on her lips. She must've been pleased that her Faceless had caught something so scandalous. Her dark brown hair was long and wavy, with a silver crown made of amethyst stars, and gold and diamond horns atop her head.

"Yes, Your Majesty." Del inclined his head to the queen, and then to Syndra. His mouth felt dry, and he wrung his hands together under the table.

"I have been very gracious to let you stay in the castle since you were left here as a babe, and even after we could not make use of you as a soldier. You had even taken time away from many servants and their duties, as they took on the burden of raising you. Telme, for instance," she motioned to the angered handmaiden in the corner, "even gave you the surname that she had forfeited. We all have been very, very gracious. Wouldn't you agree?"

She snapped her fingers as she spoke, causing Telme to bring over a pitcher of wine. He felt his cheeks burn while Telme filled Queen Yegaran and Princess Syndra's glasses, and then paused before his own. She gave him a look of motherly disappointment, and filled his only halfway.

"Yes, Your Majesty." Del reached for his glass with a hand he willed into staying still. He chugged the entire thing.

"And now, I have to hear that you are fraternizing with a Lady of the court, and robbing her in broad daylight."

Syndra made a *tsk tsk* noise, and Del shot her a glance. Syndra only smiled in return.

"Is this true?" The Queen raised an eyebrow and held a look that said there was no lying here. Only the truth would give him a chance.

His eyes wandered over to Telme standing back in the corner of the room, her arms crossed. He knew his ears were likely to bleed later on from the scolding she was to give him. His breath grew quick as he looked back at his queen, and yet he kept his face like stone.

"Yes, Your Majesty." His words came out quieter than he would've liked. He felt his cheeks grow even warmer. *Twelve, I feel like a child.*

"I thought so," said the Queen.

She waited for a moment, Del holding his breath.

"I must say I have a sort of soft spot for you. You were left here as a child around the same time I lost one of my own." Her brown eyes looked into his with the weight of old grief.

"A mother without a babe, and a babe without a mother. I thought it perhaps a gift from the Great Twelve rather than a coincidence." Her voice remained soft. Del released his inhale. He began to think he really *was* lucky for a moment.

"So Syndra and I have thought of a proposal for you, for I still see that lost child within you."

Syndra rolled her eyes. Del refused to let a smile climb onto his lips. Telme relaxed.

"You have a choice," the Queen continued. "You can be jailed and branded as a thief, or you can put your personal knowledge to use, and train someone in magics."

This time, Del couldn't resist the grin that split fully across his face. It was a reward to him. To be able to use his training again, to get a purpose again, to fight again. He felt hope for the first time in ages. This was miles better than leaving, even if he had to pass Mysarin in the halls every now and then. He would have never even thought of going elsewhere if he knew that *this* was an option. He tried to keep his smile small as he nodded his head.

"Yes." He continued to nod, not thinking twice about what he was getting himself into.

"Yes, you will train?" the Queen asked.

"Yes, Your Majesty. When do I start?" He felt a jolt of new energy coursing through his veins. He felt he could do anything.

"Tomorrow," Syndra said, eyes pinned onto him like a bird of prey, and immediately Del felt that feeling of hope drain from his body.

11 - Mysarin

Mysarin's head was pounding when she awoke at dawn to the smell of freshly cooked eggs, bacon, and bread. A servant was leaving the rooms as Mysarin peered around the partition, seeing the platter splayed out on the table.

"Thank you!" she quickly called as the door shut, wincing at the sound of her own voice. She sat down and began to eat, her hands shaking as she poured a glass of wine, when she noticed a note was left for her on the table as well. She shoved a bite of eggs into her mouth as she reached for the note with her other hand. *Meet me in the gardens at midday. - Syndra.*

Mysarin sighed, regretting skipping another dinner last night. She felt hungover from how exhausted she was, from using so much of her magics. With that and drinking less wine than she was used to since now she had to truly focus, she felt nauseous and drained.

But this was already miles better than the pleasure house. Better than anything she could've dreamed of. She no longer had to wake up and pretend to be so interested and aroused by Lords and Ladies. She no longer had to worry about a debt hanging over her head. All that was left was figuring out how to stop her amnesia.

But first, she wanted to enjoy her freedom.

Hardly tasting anything, she quickly gobbled down her food and stood to get dressed. The morning sun beamed through the window and down onto her skin as she threw on a simple pink cotton gown. She turned to the window and peered through it to find Deime's bakery again.

Looking out into the city from her room in the castle created a mirage over Stonecrest; the blue roofs and the gray stone came together to create a mirror image of the sea beyond. A vision flashed into her mind, when she and Deime had spent a day down by the waters on a small beach near the ports. It had been years ago, when they were only seventeen.

She smiled at the thought, and left the castle for the summer morning streets.

The bell by the door assaulted her ears as she walked into Sea Salt Bakery. Rising yeast, sugar and cream wafted into her senses as she locked eyes with Deime's father. He was blonde, and elven, like his son, yet that's where the similarities had stopped. His skin was copper brown like baked clay, and his eyes were the same shade of blue as everything else in Stonecrest. Deime had taken after his mother in terms of eyes, skin, and personality.

"Ah, Mysarin. We were just talking about you," he said, only giving her his attention for a moment before returning to the dough behind the counter. He shook his head to himself.

"Hello, Arias. Nothing bad I hope," she said as she watched his hands roll the dough into a ball only to flatten it back out in a hypnotic rhythm.

"How are you?" she asked.

He continued to knead. She bit her cheek as she awaited an answer.

"Deime!" His eyes remained on the project before him, voice impatient. "You have a visitor!"

Well, so much for pleasantries. Arias had never been completely sold on his only son dating a woman who had spent her life working. Not to mention a woman who had worked as a courtesan. She stopped fiddling with her hair once Deime had emerged from the back rooms.

"Mysa." The word came out of his lips like the lyrics of a song, no matter how much she hated the pet name. A smile replaced his look of irritation in the blink of an eye.

"Let's go enjoy the sunshine, shall we?" He grabbed onto her hand as he brought her out the door.

"What happened to showing me how you make your fruit tarts? I had breakfast, but I could eat more. The Princess worked me like a mule yesterday," she said. The bell harassed her sensitive hearing yet again.

Once the door had closed to the shop, Deime spoke.

"Father is in a mood today, and I'd rather we enjoy the nice weather anyway." Golden light caressed his short hair, highlighting strands of what looked like pure magics. His cheeks flushed in the morning warmth, and she thought again of that day they had spent at the shores. He looked so similar now to how he did then, as if time had left him untouched.

"Then let's go to the shore, where we went on that day you had made me get in." She poked at his sides.

"That," he grabbed her waist in turn, "is an excellent idea."

The heat of the day had already begun to kick in as they walked the long path down to the small beach. Stonecrest wasn't nearly as warm as it was in the Twin Islands or further south, was what port men had told Mysarin during her years at the pleasure house, but during the summer the weather could grow quite erratic. It seemed today would be one of those days where the temperature would spike. Her muscles ached as sweat began to wet her neck, and yet she still kept her palm embraced in Deime's.

At the beach, the smoothened stones were baking beneath her feet as she creeped closer to the Fallen Waters' shoreline. Deime trailed close behind her, stepping on the same stones to create a secret trail only those two would know.

"Arias said you had been talking about me, when I got there," she said.

"Y-yeah." He cleared his throat. "I told him of our engagement."

She stopped. He ran into her back, almost knocking her over the invisible boundary between their path and the sea. He caught her shoulder as she felt a splash of resentment at her feet. She took in those honey-brown eyes.

"He doesn't approve?"

"You know how he is." A gull cawed in the sky above them as if to say '*traditional*' in Deime's stead. Arias had never held back his opinions, and Deime had never failed to hear them. "My mother never worked, she only stayed home to take care of me. He knows what you do to earn coin—or what you used to do. I-it's just how he thinks. Maybe it was different growing up in Seawall."

"Small-minded men think like that everywhere," she said before she could stop herself.

"Mysarin—"

"You're defending him?"

"He's my father. He's all I have now." He looked out into the ocean.

She breathed in the salty air. She didn't want to fight with him again.

"It was the first time we had kissed."

"What?" There was that look of the doe. Wide-eyed, unsure, pure.

"After you had dared me to get into the *freezing* water. You wrapped your arms around me to warm me up."

"I did not *dare* you. You dared yourself."

"No, no. That's not how I remember it."

He laughed. "That is how it was! You said 'oh it can't really be that cold' only days after the spring equinox, I disagreed, and you just *had* to prove me wrong."

"A disagreement may very well be the same as a dare. You should've known better." She grabbed his arms, and pulled him with her across their invisible line.

She squealed once the water hit her ankles. "How is it still cold?! It's late summer!"

He picked her up and threw her over his shoulder, and her second scream scared away the seagull who had interrupted them earlier. He ran out of the water and the bouncing motion made her stomach twirl.

"Oh no put me down!"

He breathed heavily with a boyish grin as her wet feet met with the stones yet again. "Are you ill?"

"No," she said as she placed a hand on her stomach. "Just queasy after using up so much of my magics yesterday."

He smiled, placing his hand onto her stomach. "You're not pregnant, are you?"

She smacked it away. "No, you dolt. I can't until the yearly contraceptive wears off."

He got down onto his knees, giggling. He pressed his hands around her lower back and pressed his ear to her stomach. She held very still.

"Then in a year, I expect that I'll be hearing a heartbeat in here." He squinted his eyes. "I feel like if I try hard enough, I almost can."

He looked up at her, his eyes filled with that familiar molten-honeyed heat. She felt her cheeks and her neck flush. Then his hands moved from her back to her thighs, and dropped down to the hem of her skirt.

"Deime…" she whispered. His fingers trailed up the lines of her calves. She shivered from his touch.

She looked around, checking to see if they were alone on the beach, and then up at the sun in the sky. It was getting close to midday. She sighed.

"Deime, I should get going."

"Of course," he said, removing his hands and standing. He tried to hide away his disappointment as he leaned in and placed a kiss on her lips, on her cheek, and then on her neck, a remnant of that heat in his eyes still lingering. "Don't work yourself too hard."

Back at the castle, when she opened up her dresser to change, she found a surprise that the servant must've left when she was gone. It was a beautiful, proper gown, made of fine silk. Mysarin's eyes scanned over the pewter gray material, stopping at the aubergine embroideries in the shapes of tiny stars. When she looked closer, she noticed that there were white and icy blue glass beads sewn onto the purple stars that created an iridescent sparkle in the light.

She contemplated how she would get into the gown when she heard her door open. Telme entered the room and smiled at Mysarin.

"Looks like someone has taken a liking to you. I was sent to help you get ready."

"It's so pretty," were the only words Mysarin could find to say.

Telme walked over to the gown and took it off of its hanger, turning to look at Mysarin.

"Oh, I should probably undress, shouldn't I?"

"That would be the only way to put this on," Telme gestured impatiently. "Nothing I haven't already seen, right?"

Mysarin snorted. "Right. Sorry about that."

After dressing her, Telme began to comb and arrange Mysarin's hair into an elaborate updo, and placed a necklace of citrine jewels set in gold around her neck. She then caked her skin in a white powder, and placed red rouge onto her lips.

Once it was all done, Mysarin looked into the mirror and was stunned. Her jaw dropped at her own reflection.

She looked royal, divine, beautiful, *ripe*. Her skin shone like a glimmering star, her hair the night that encompassed it.

She wished for no one else to look at her this way, as none could ever deserve such a sight. Others would only see this portrait and begin to barter. They would push, and shove, and fight, and bleed for the chance to have her. Grenlide's mouth would water. Men would bawl and beg at her feet, stretching desperately to bite into her. Her reflection began to make her stomach turn, and the longer she gazed at herself the more cloying it became.

She resisted the urge to vomit.

She wanted to tear it all off. It felt wrong. She was a monster, a killer, a drunk and a whore. She was not the monarch that she currently played the part of.

Her freckles were almost invisible, the darkness under her eyes covered, her medium-brown skin painted white. Her curly hair was braided out of her face, and smoothed into a tight knot at the nape of her neck. This was more than she had ever done to herself with her own glamor.

"My dear, are you alright?" Telme asked, hand gently rubbing her back where the dress left exposed skin.

"Why did you do this? I'm horrendous."

"Well," she replied with offense, "I thought you looked quite lovely."

"I… This isn't me."

Telme put her hands on her hips in the background of Mysarin's reflection. "Today it is. Just try and enjoy it."

Mysarin took one last look at herself, trying not to wince, and stood. Telme began to lead her to the hall, but her hands started to shake again. She quickly gulped down a glass of wine.

"C'mon, now. We don't want to be late." Telme linked her arm into the crook of Mysarin's own and began to show her the way through the winding halls. She tried to control her breathing.

"How are you liking it so far?"

"It's… different than I thought it would be," she replied.

Telme softly laughed. "How so?"

"Well I thought I'd be staying with the other servants here, not in a room so… large. It's bigger than any I've ever had." She looked down at her dress, at the stars twinkling under the daylight lazing through the open arcade.

"Those may be the perks of being on my goodside." Telme nudged an elbow into her ribs. "I admit, I have a rather persuasive manner when it comes to the Princess. She listens to me."

Mysarin tensed at the mention of persuasion. She wondered if Telme had put the pieces together, or perhaps Delvuvius had told her the truth in his anger.

"You picked the right person to ask a favor from," Telme said.

Mysarin forced a smile at the handmaiden. If Telme did know, she didn't seem all that bothered about it.

"And should you need another, don't hesitate to ask, okay?" Telme continued on as they passed a cluster of guards, visible on a lower pathway of the castle, in their full suits of armor.

They were escorting a woman with black hair, and olive skin… like the one they had arrested in the shopping district. Her face was terror stricken. Mysarin tried to get a better look at her—

"Us servants look out for one another here, plus, Delvuvius sure seemed smitten over you. If you can make my boy happy, well then, I'd do anything to see that continue."

She whipped her head back to Telme. "Oh… no. You've got that wrong. I don't think he'd mind never seeing my face again. And I'm betrothed to another."

"Oh, the boy at the gate? Guess I was mistaken."

"Did Delvuvius say something about me?"

Telme patted her hand. "No. Just call it instinct." She winked. "But, tell me more about him. Who is he?"

The woman with the guards fainted, falling onto the red marble. From a glance, it looked like she was bleeding out. One guard grabbed onto her chained wrists, and hauled her over his shoulder. "His name is Deime, his father owns Sea Salt Bakery—is she okay?"

Telme finally seemed to notice what was happening outside of the arcade. She peered over the edge. "Oh, I'm sure she's fine. I think they caught her stealing from a Lady of the court earlier today."

Telme pulled Mysarin in the opposite direction, away from the view of the guards and their prisoner, and guided her until they reached the entrance to the gardens. Mysarin pushed the worry from her mind; she had more important things to focus on.

The gardens were a beacon of colors and fragrant smells, all guiding Mysarin deeper into their labyrinth until she forgot about the prisoner. The air was thick with the scent of roses and jasmine, and the sun created a puzzle through the leaves, casting shadows and creating light to fill in the spaces on the cobblestone paths. She followed the vibrant array of flowers and tightly trimmed bushes, eyeing the Lords and Ladies of the court who were enjoying a midday stroll.

One Lady in a yellow dress seemed to be crying. Mysarin offered a kind smile as they locked eyes, and continued on the path, leaving her to her sorrow.

Telme led her down a walkway surrounded by carefully sculpted hedges all bearing a resemblance to past rulers. Jurseca Danai, the First King, had the second most detailed hedge just behind the one for the current King, Fisrolf Loraenar. The one for the previous King, Fonmere Danai, though, was simply shaped into a head on a pike. Telme left her at the entrance to a large iron arbor covered in climbing ivy and rose bushes as she gazed at the hedge for Fonmere. A swooping feeling of sorrow grasped at her as she took his hedge in.

In the center of the arbor sat a tall fountain peeking out from the open roof of the arch. The rhythmic splashing of the fountain's cascades filled her ears as Mysarin eyed the stone in the middle of that crystal clear water.

It resembled the deity Talisi. She stood confidently with arms spread wide, a scale held in one hand and a sword in the other. Beneath her sat Syndra, and a Taurean Castle guard. They were playing a game of chess as the rest of the nine guards stood stiff in a wide circle around the walls of the arbor, with two servants waving large fans behind Syndra. The guard sat with his helmet at his side, face drawn and bored. He moved his thick bronze fingers towards his horse piece, and took out one of Syndra's pawns. She grumbled in annoyance.

"You're supposed to let me win," she said as she moved another pawn forward to be sacrificed.

"Then how will you ever learn, Your Highness?" His black straight hair was pulled into a low plait behind his head, and his almond shaped eyes searched for his next move with ease.

"I don't want to learn these stupid rules. I want to win. Why is the Queen the most powerful, and yet the King is what calls the game anyway? It's all foolish." She smacked her hand across the board, spilling the black and red pieces onto the ground. Mysarin cleared her throat.

"Hello, your Highness." She curtsied low.

Syndra turned her head and scanned the woman before her. "You're all dismissed," she said over her shoulder to the guards. "What a wonderful dress you have on," Syndra said by greeting, scanning over the intricate details of the stars.

"Why thank you, Your Highness, you got my measurements perfectly." She smiled at the Heir.

"Me? Oh, no. I didn't have that made for you." Syndra laughed at the thought. The men shuffled out from under the arbor to linger nearby as she squinted her eyes, contemplating. "But that works out very well for me."

"If you didn't, then who did?" Mysarin asked.

"It's not important right now," Syndra said. She leaned forward greedily, her eyes lighting up for the first time since Mysarin arrived. Two black crows landed on Talisi's outstretched arm, their dark feathers shining like Syndra's hair. "Can you… make yourself look like me? More than you already do?"

"Uhm, how do you mean?" Mysarin asked.

Syndra flitted her hand about in front of her. "With your magics, of course."

She thought for a moment. Overall, it might not seem like it would take a lot of effort, especially now that she was painted up as she was, but this was dangerous territory. There would be so many tiny details to perfect and— "Isn't that illegal?"

"Sort of, but I'm the soon to be Queen, so I say that right now, it's perfectly legal." Syndra rose and stepped forward.

Mysarin stepped back. "I guess I could try and transform, it would most likely use up all of my magics for the day, though." Her stomach lurched at the idea beneath the suffocating fabric of the dress. She looked around, to see if anyone was watching the two of them. Surely, she wouldn't be jailed for this if Syndra herself was requesting it, right?

"That's fine, I just want to see if it's possible, and take advantage of your fine dress. It's something I'd wear. Perhaps you could work as my double for when the tailor comes by." She smiled.

Mysarin hesitated. Another crow landed on the lip of the fountain. They all started cawing at her.

Syndra's smile dropped, her face hardening in demand as if to convey that refusing to shapeshift was not an option. "I guess I could bring my guards back over for more games. But they wouldn't be happy seeing me so disappointed…"

Mysarin swallowed. She knew it had to be done whether she liked it or not. So, she tried to center herself. She focused on even breaths, trying to ignore the sounds of the crows and focus on the rustling of the leaves. She thought of the color yellow. It took only a moment before Mysarin had summoned the glamor magics. Her face began to tingle, as well as her scalp, her eyes, her mouth, every part of her body. She stood there focusing on creating the changes needed to become the Princess.

When she finally opened her eyes after what felt like a few minutes, she immediately felt drained, and slathered in that strange mud feeling. Her hair felt heavier than usual, and her body lighter.

Syndra's eyes lit up, a slow smile creeping onto her face.

"Close enough," she said, "now, go walk around, talk to people, be *me*."

"But my voice is still the same, I don't know how to change that. I really only know the cosmetics," Mysarin replied, inspecting her hands. They were smaller and more elegant than her own. She wished she could look into a mirror.

"Look into my eyes when you speak to me," Syndra demanded.

Mysarin snapped her head up. She guessed she *was* looking into a mirror.

Syndra let the irritation trickle away, her shoulders loosening. "Go walk around then, wave, but do not speak. Then come back to me when you're done."

Mysarin, looking like what she assumed was a copy of the Princess, curtsied, and then turned to begin her walk. Her back felt weak, and suddenly she felt thankful for the tightly laced corset and the stability it was offering her. Although it did nothing for her stomach—it spun around from nerves and heat and wine and her magical hangover. Mysarin did not make it far through the maze of the gardens before she had to run off to a nearby shaded alcove. She began to hurl.

She disposed of all the contents of her stomach as quietly as she could, in fear of Syndra hearing. She realized it was not quiet enough when she heard light footsteps approaching her.

"Syndra? Are you well?"

Oh no. It was the elf from last night with a small and pale woman, studying roses as white as their hair at the opposite end of the walkway. A guard wearing white platinum armor stood in the distance as well, with a long pole attached to a curved blade behind his back: a scythe. The lunar-elf hesitantly stood a few feet away from Mysarin as she continued to gag over the grass and roots.

"Why are you wearing…" He drifted mid sentence.

Mysarin collected herself enough to look up at the elf, who seemed to be staring off into the distance behind her head. Quickly, he snapped his focus back to the imposter.

"Not Syndra."

Her eyes went wide, afraid he would leave to tell his guard of an impersonator lurking in the gardens, pretending to be the heir to the throne. She opened her mouth to speak, feeling her heartbeat, and possibly more bile, rising in her throat. A murder of crows flew overhead, their caws clawing at her.

"Did you do that all yourself?" He smiled at her, his face serene like a silent winter forest. "Do not worry, I will not tattle."

She stifled another gag as her false hand rose to meet her mouth. She felt her smaller lips, more of a rounder shape than her own, and moved her hand down in her own inspection of her chin. Softer, more curved. Syndra's features were a skewed reflection of her own, like the shattered mirror on the floor of her room in the pleasure house.

"How?" was all Mysarin managed to say.

"Well, you did very good work, if it was you who did the magics, but it is not quite right." He leaned in closer, his lilac eyes drinking in her every detail.

"I can see a few freckles. And your eyes… They still convey every emotion." His voice turned into an almost whisper. "And I have never seen Syndra show much at all."

"She made me do it." Mysarin found herself spewing out words instead of her insides.

"I had a feeling," he looked past her head and into the distance once more. She followed only to see more bushes.

"Do you like the dress?" She turned to see him smiling that calm omniscient smile as he returned to the present.

"It was you who gave it to me?" Mysarin asked, perplexed as she had only met the elf the night before. "How?" she repeated.

"I, uh, I saw it in a… a dream, a few months ago."

His face turned to look at the ground, and it was strange to see him look unsure. He lifted his gaze to look up at her distorted features once again.

"I thought it was intended for Syndra, once I learned I was to be sent here to meet with her. I had it made before I left Oswes." He lifted a hand to scratch the side of his neck, and Mysarin noticed strange tattooed symbols peeking out above his collar.

"Yet, when you told me about your dreams, I realized it was for you. And looking at you, wearing it now, it all comes together."

"I don't understand." Mysarin shifted nervously where she stood, feeling her legs begin to shake from exhaustion.

"When I was growing up, before I understood my dreams, I just thought them as horrid nightmares. And when I would wake up in the night and I felt restless and scared, I would look out into the stars." He lifted his head to the blues skies as if he could see those same stars now. "So when you told me that you had a nightmare, I thought it must be for you.

"So that when you awake in the night, you can look at the stars too…" His stare was intense as his voice trailed off. His cheeks grew pink, as if he realized he was saying too much. "Sorry, heh, I am an oracle. A gift from Siefris." The last words came out laced with a tinge of hostility.

Before Mysarin could respond, the pale elf and Mysarin whipped their heads towards the castle as they heard a scream ringing through the estate.

12 - Estair

Estair dropped to her knees, her scream echoing off the stone courtyard and filling the air of the Taurean Castle grounds.

Moments earlier she was still washing the breakfast dishes in the kitchens when a group of guards burst through the doors demanding the whereabouts of Bea. The old woman, who Estair was beginning to really open up to, was ill all morning. Estair had taken every opportunity to assist Bea, trying to repay an unspoken debt that she felt for her.

The old woman with the heart of a warship had told Estair that she often falls quickly to ailments, yet they do not last for long; she simply wakes in the mornings with a soreness to her body, her mind overcome with a restless unease, and a fever. It was usually gone by the next day, and Bea had claimed it was merely from her old age. So Estair, not wanting to question her, had drawn the woman a warm bath, and left to take on as much work in the kitchens during breakfast as she could.

It wasn't much that Estair could offer, but she wanted to try for Bea, eternally grateful for her existence despite the short time they'd known each other. It was as if Bea could be the mother that Estair never truly had. So, when the guards had arrived, Estair had rushed to bring them to the servants' rooms where she had last seen Bea. With her heart racing and her mind wandering into unknown depths, Estair thought of a million different reasons as to why the guards had demanded for the sick woman. Her mind boomed with one in particular: Bea was dying from her illness, and the guards were sent to save her.

Yet, when Estair and the group of five guards burst through the doors, Bea was upright and sitting on the bed seemingly normal. At that moment, Estair remembered that the Royal Healers would not have helped Bea while the guards were around. Confused, she finally took in the full sight of the guards as they continued to rush towards the bed. They were fully dressed in royal armor, not the armor they usually wore about the castle which was much lighter. No, they were dressed head to toe in metal plates shining with their Stonecrest bull's head seal.

"What is the meaning of this?" Estair had yelled as the guards swarmed around Bea, snatching her up by her arms. They began to drag the woman towards the door where Estair was still standing. She rolled back her shoulders and kept her hands loose at her sides as a sense of that strange and familiar calm had washed over her. She stood her ground in the doorway and repeated herself. "What are you doing?"

The guard leading the group had gruffly replied, "This is official business for King Fisrolf and Queen Yegaran Loraenar of Stonecrest. Now out of our way or you shall be sentenced as well."

"Sentenced? For what?" Estair had yelled at the guards as she felt the calm disappear from the air around her, and greeted the stifling choke of fear.

"Step aside!" The guard ordered as he swung out his arm and pushed Estair to the ground, away from the threshold.

The group of heavily armored men led Bea by her arms out of the servants rooms as Estair watched in horror from the floor. She would've immediately risen to defend the elderly woman had she not finally noticed that Bea was going willingly. Her legs followed the men as she turned back and shook her head at Estair as if saying not to interfere. Estair gathered her breaths for a moment as Bea started to disappear down into the dark corridors of the castle.

Her head continued to race as she tried to collect herself and willed her heart to slow, hand pressing upon her raging chest. She then shot up, and followed the echo of armor *clank clanking* against the black and red tile floors. Estair's thin and poorly made clothing served to an advantage, she realized, as they allowed her to swiftly follow the sounds of guards. She moved silently, her breathing uneven. She couldn't afford to be seen—the guards wouldn't just shove her aside this time.

They'd kill her for getting in the way, yet again.

Sentenced, she had thought to herself. *Sentenced to what? For what?* She had a feeling this wasn't going to end well.

She finally heard the sounds of a small crowd gathering to wherever the guards were taking Bea.

"Monster!" one shouted.

"Kill the beast!" yelled the hoarse voice of another.

Estair ran towards the commotion. It was then she again stopped in her tracks, stumbling as she entered the unfamiliar courtyard. There was a large wooden platform sitting in the middle of the gray stone area, looming over the screaming crowd. The guards brought Bea up to the middle of the platform and greeted the golden haired elven man who had backhanded Estair on her first day in the castle.

"No." The word forced its way out of Estair's throat when the golden elf raised a sword, Bea pushed onto her knees in front of him.

"A loyal servant to the Danai family," the elf had roared to the crowd and to the helpless woman before him, "is a traitor to the Loraenars. This *beast* is to be put down, to further protect the citizens of Stonecrest from the MoonDawn disease and its effects." Estair's head had swam and her body had swayed as he spoke. She looked around at all of the angry faces in the crowd before her. Then she heard a low rumbling, like howling wind.

She looked back at the platform, and watched as Bea grew larger. The guards struggled to hold her down, Zendar laughed, watching, as Bea slowly grew long teeth and her jaw opened wide. Far beyond what was normal. Estair watched in horror.

But it was over in an instant as Zendar brought his sword down onto the back of her neck.

Estair was still screaming, blinking rapidly, when she watched Bea's head roll along the wooden platform. The crowd cheered in celebration. Bea's head was back to normal, and Estair thought she imagined it all. She paused there, the trail of her scream leaving her with the rage and confusion of watching Bea die threatening to consume her.

She'd seen many die before; had caused their death with her own hands. Never before though, had she witnessed someone so undeserving to be slaughtered like cattle. Her terror caught in her throat and Estair finally rose from her knees. The deadly calm came back to her, and her shaking eased. She took one last look at Bea's head, knowing that what she saw was not real, knowing that Bea was kind, and undeserving. She strode up to the group of guards splattered with blood. Luckily for Estair, the men were too preoccupied with wiping the dead woman off of them with trembling hands.

"You idiots, why were you standing so close?" The elven man had said to the guards, though Estair hadn't really heard. "You lot better pray to the Great Twelve that you didn't get any in your eyes or mouth, or you'll end up like her. Stupid oafs, you…"

The roaring in Estair's ears drowned out what the man was saying entirely as she climbed onto the raised surface. The guards and the man would not have even noticed her arrival had it not been for the lingering crowd gasping at her audacity.

Estair felt a cool breeze wash over her face as she felt the silent, lethal, rage take over her autonomy. A guard finally turned around to face her as she shoved a hand into his chest, and reached for his sword with the other. The sharp *zing* of the steel sword rang through the air as Estair swung with deadly precision. The blade connected with the guard's neck, just below his helmet, and just above his metal armor. The head flew through the sky forcing the crowd to take off running and screaming in alarm.

They scattered like rats.

Estair was on the move to the next guard before the head hit the ground, joining another one with dark black hair, and joining Bea's. He took out his sword and prepared to defend himself as Estair dropped into a slide on her knees. She skidded to a halt just before the man and thrusted her weapon up between his legs while his sword sang through the wind above her head. She felt the resistance in her hand as the sharp tip of the sword made its way through the man's torso, a bone-chilling whine pouring out of his mouth and blood leaking from his nethers and onto her grip. She retracted her weapon with a swift pull, and he fell to the ground.

Fast as a sea-striker, Estair rolled from where she was back up onto her feet. She heard that same *clank clanking* of armor rushing to her backside before she whipped her body and arms around, using her momentum and all of her might to connect her sword with the man's metal plates. It crashed against him, making a dent in the metal, and he fell to the side.

She lifted up her leg, kicked the guard in the middle of his chest, and made to advance, yet she suddenly felt a burning sensation along her arms and legs. She growled as the burn forced her to the ground, hands and feet bound within golden shining ropes. Her sword was ripped away. The elven man walked over to her, appearing above her yet again. He smirked down at her as his hands glowed with that same golden aura.

"Well, you really can fight," he grunted. "You just killed two of my men. A woman." He laughed, his head tilting up into the clear skies.

She snarled at him.

"I should kill you, you worthless servant." He paused, sweat dripping off his forehead onto Estair's cheek as she thrashed against her restraints.

He glowered at her in silence as he thought.

"But you can fight."

Estair held his intense stare, feeling that creep of death slither around her skin. That same fear filled her, fear for what came once she no longer drew breath. It was not the first time she had killed while knowing that it would likely result in the end of her own life.

Except this time she didn't have another way out.

"Just do it already," she said, voice hoarse from her scream. She wanted it over with, as fast as possible. The faster it happened, the less afraid she could become. She closed her eyes.

"Well my issue here is, you just killed one of the men that was set to fight in the tourney."

He released her from her magical restraints as the remaining two guards snatched her arms, forcing her to stand. She opened her eyes.

"And the King and Queen will *not* be happy with me if I tell them I'm missing a fighter so close to the games. So, you can die in the arena instead." He smiled, satisfied at his solution.

Games? If it was a game of sword and steel, Estair could take down any opponents.

"And if I win?" Estair raised her chin, gathering all of the confidence she could muster. "What will you do with me then?"

He laughed that bubbling laugh yet again, tilting his head back. He took a moment to gather himself, still giggling, and looked back at her.

"You won't." He waited for a moment before he added, "Shit, I'll let you free if you do. But trust me—"

He leaned in closer, breath hot on Estair's face.

"—you won't." He smiled again, bearing his razor sharp teeth with a wicked gleam in his eyes.

13 – Mysarin

Mysarin let go of her glamor magics, a bright light emitting from her body as she returned to looking like herself.

The small handmaiden and foreign guard rushed over to where Mysarin and the elf were standing. He turned to his handmaiden, as she said, "We need to get inside. Now."

"Come with me, quickly." His pale hand went to grab Mysarin's, now returned to its normal proportions.

Taurean guards swarmed through the gardens around them and Mysarin froze. So, the elf squeezed his soft hand over hers as he led Mysarin back through the maze. She watched in a daze as other people hurriedly made their way back to the safety of the inner castle walls.

"Mysarin. Rionaes." Syndra's voice came from behind the two.

They both stopped and turned around to find Syndra surrounded by her personal guards. Her arms were crossed along her chest as she looked upon their joined hands. Mysarin felt her skin turn cold as she immediately pulled away. The elven man was Rionaes Theingaurd, *the Prince to the Oswesian Throne*. The woman was his handmaiden, Lila, the one Telme had wanted to court. The guard with the scythe on their back was a royal Oswesian Knight.

And they had all witnessed her puking.

Rionaes had witnessed her arguing with Delvuvius, and *screaming* in her rooms. Her cheeks burned bright red.

"Everyone must go to their own rooms and stay there until this is sorted out." Her gaze felt as if it was going to cut into Mysarin's skin. Syndra then looked up at the foreign Prince, jaw clenched. "And no one is to leave the Taurean grounds for the time being."

Oh Great Twelve, Syndra saw me holding hands *with her soon-to-be betrothed.*

"Yes, Your Highness," Mysarin said quietly as she curtsied, once to Syndra, and then again to Rionaes before turning to leave. She started to feel suffocated by more than just the tight corset around her waist.

"And Mysarin," each of Syndra's words were clipped as she spoke them and her face turned entirely devoid of emotion, "you have retch on your dress. What a shame."

She then walked in between the two as she made her way into the castle, several guards following after her.

Mysarin wished for any deity at all to strike her down where she stood. She gave half a smile to Rionaes, avoiding his gaze, and then hurried off to her room without another word.

Every step Mysarin had taken felt more laborious than the previous one, her feet feeling heavier and heavier every second. The moment she arrived, she undressed immediately. It was like a puzzle to figure out on her own, but she got it done, not having the energy to wait for Telme or another servant to show up for help. She took down her hair and wiped all of the white powder off of her skin.

Then she collapsed onto the bed without another thought, slipping away into a deep sleep.

She awoke just before the sun started to set on the horizon, her room engulfed in colors of orange and red. Her stomach and her head ached as she arose and dressed herself in her simple pink gown. *I've had enough luxuries for one day*, she thought to herself as she put on the loose material. Shaking the grogginess of the nap away, she made to leave, but a new book and another note sitting on her table caught her eye, along with yet another spread of divine food.

She opened and read the note, from Syndra again by the way the words were carefully written onto the paper, saying: *Study this. Learn as much as you can before we meet again. Find a man named Delvuvius near the servants quarters, he will help you.*

Delvuvius? She wondered just what his position in the castle was, why he was here at all. Maybe he really was a spy.

Mysarin picked up the book "*Elements and The Arcane.*" It was a spell book. Mysarin scrunched her face and rolled her eyes in annoyance at the heavy workload the Princess was placing upon her, and having to see Delvuvius again. She took in a deep breath as she looked down at the ring on her finger. *Remember what it's all for. Anything is better than the pleasure house.* When she smelled the spices wafting from the extravagant meal placed before her, her stomach's cavity became unignorable. It was a roasted chicken, placed on a bed of rice and vegetables. Sitting next to it was a dense soup, full of small round dumplings.

She was going to go back to Deime's bakery. After today, she needed to be next to the elf, needed to breathe in his scent of almonds and flour, needed to feel his soft skin against hers, needed his voice to tell her that everything was okay. She longed for the comfort only Deime could bring to her after the chaos from earlier, but as she looked at the meal before her, she thought of what a waste it would be to let it all spoil. So, she decided she would eat first.

A cold draft flew through the room around Mysarin, and she was deep in thought as she ate. She thought back to when Delvuvius was arguing with her, yelling that Telme could've been killed for her actions.

At the time, Mysarin had passed the comments off as Delvuvius being dramatic, since the man seemed to often have an inclination to be. But the look on his face… She hurriedly finished her meal, grabbing the book and the note from the table, and headed out into the halls of the castle. After today, she needed to get more information on just how precarious this place really was.

14 - Delvuvius & Mysarin

Delvuvius sat in the kitchen alone, drinking spirits straight from the bottle. The kitchen felt empty and quiet, not solely because he was the only person in the room, but because of Bea. She was gone. She was one of the many servants who had helped raise him, and now she was gone. He felt still.

He raised the bottle to take another sip, and then slammed it back onto the table. It wasn't fair. She was a frail, sickly woman who couldn't defend herself, and that bastard had ordered her dead. Zendar Paelos, The Golden Elf, the Commander of the Royal Army, and the man who had cast Delvuvius aside after breaking every bone in his body. The man who wanted nothing to do with Del after the Breaking had revealed nothing more to his magics than he already had. He put his head into his hands.

Del understood the paranoia of the castle; after the Danai family was usurped, the people within these walls started to constantly look over their shoulders, fearing the MoonDawn curse. The Loraenars would never forget what had plagued their cousins, nor would they let anyone else. Perhaps it was a power tactic, but more likely, it was pure hysteria. If any of the Loraenars were cursed like the Danai family, they would all end up in the ground, just like the Danais. The Chaehora family over in Seawall would make a move on Stonecrest in an instant if they heard.

But beheading any of those that could be assumed ill with MoonDawn was madness. Del knew Bea couldn't have been a shapeshifter anyway. Sure, she was working at the castle during the reign of the Danai, but she was just simply feeble. To imagine her as that vicious creature… He took another drink.

The door creaked open from behind him.

"I thought I'd find you here." It was Mysarin, breaking the silence of the room.

"What do you want?" He looked down into his spirits.

"Are you… okay?" She sounded hesitant, like she cared to know but wasn't confident she should ask.

"Did you hear what they did today?" His voice was hoarse. He continued staring at his bottle as he spoke, unable to face her. He was still pissed at her, and for this exact reason.

"I heard the scream, but, no one has told me anything. I came to ask you." Mysarin's voice wavered, and she sounded scared. Del finally turned to face her. Her face was flushed and matching her pink dress, her silver eyes were filled with concern.

"They beheaded a servant." His breath threatened to catch in his throat. "Her name was Bea."

"I'm sorry. Did you know her well?" Mysarin's well-groomed brows pinched together further.

"I did," was all he could manage. He offered her his bottle and when she declined, he took another long swig.

They stood in a stretched silence for a moment, before Mysarin came to sit next to him on the countertop. She looked at him, eyes darting back and forth between his own. Maybe it was the drinking, but seeing her this close, it was like seeing her for the first time. The way her dark hair fell effortlessly around her face, the pink in her cheeks meeting with the constellation of freckles upon the bridge of her nose. It had his heart racing.

Drunk and desperate to feel anything else, he slowly began to lean in, wanting to know what the skin above her collarbones had smelt like.

"Do you remember when you had yelled at me for persuading Telme?"

He stopped in his tracks, eyes going flat.

He sighed. "Of course I do, why?"

"You said that she could've died because of it, and then today happened… Why would it have happened?" She wrung her hands together in her lap.

"So you've finally realized this place is not paradise after all." He chuckled bitterly and resisted the urge to roll his eyes at her lack of awareness. "It's a deathtrap."

"But I don't understand why, are the Loraenars truly so evil? Didn't they free Stonecrest from the Danais' dangerous rule?"

His brow furrowed. "Well, of course. But there's more to it than that now. Do you know what happened?"

Mysarin shook her head, her hands wringing in her lap. So he put aside their now seemingly petty fight and began to tell her.

"You know how there are annual games every year right?"

She nodded.

"Well, they only started about twenty years ago, when Fisrolf Loraenar led the charge to kill all of the Danai family. It's to celebrate their victory. The Danais had become cursed. Either they were poisoned or maybe the family had the sickness all along, who knows, but they had become dangerous nonetheless.

"The MoonDawn curse, disease, ailment, whatever you call it, caused the Danais to shapeshift. People blamed the deity Gron, some thought it was sourced from something else—eh, not the point. No, the point is, is that they would uncontrollably turn into these giant, bloodthirsty beasts that tore apart the people of Stonecrest. They even took down hundreds of minotaurs in the Heartwood Forest. Almost brought those fuckers to extinction."

She stared down at her hands as he spoke.

He paused and took another swig of the spirits, trying to recall all of the things Telme had told him about Taurean's history.

"Fonmere Danai tried to hide the curse for as long as he could, blaming the killings on the minotaurs, saying they were waging some internal war and killing peoples in the wake. Then came Fisrolf. Somehow he found out, and he led the siege. He poisoned Fonmere Danai, killed the rest, and then sat himself upon the throne."

"So, they're killing people who think they might also be, what, *infected*?" Her voice shook.

"Clever girl." Delvuvius nodded his head. "It's why they killed Bea today. There's been talk of dead bodies being found in the forest and she was often ill, but, Great Twelve, *she* wasn't the monster. It's ridiculous. I've already heard people making up stories about how she started to shift in front of the crowd that was there."

"Bodies have been found?" she asked.

He looked at her then, and saw the fear in her eyes. He looked at her hands, watched her continue to wring them back and forth. "Yeah. They've been showing up, apparently in the same pattern as before. But it wasn't Bea, I can feel it in my gut. Whoever or whatever it was, it's still out there, MoonDawn beast or not."

He put his hand on hers to stop her from wringing them.

"Look, you don't need to worry so much about that. It's just that if anyone in Taurean so much as breathes wrong, it causes mass hysteria. The King and Queen demand their heads, no further questions asked. All in the name of *safety*. And then they celebrate their victory every year for three weeks as if they've done no wrong. So be careful, is all that I ask. It could be Telme next, or you, even."

"What about you?" she asked.

He laughed. "I can take care of myself."

"But are you... what do you do here?"

"Can't you tell?" he asked, half-smiling at her. "I'm the court huntsman."

She jerked her hands away. "What?"

He frowned. "I'm kidding, obviously."

"Oh," she forced a smile. "Sorry, you've spooked me with your stories."

Hm. He tried to find the lie. His vision was fuzzy, the alcohol in his stomach warm, but he squinted his eyes and for the first time began to wonder what it was that she could be hiding.

"And so what about Syndra?" Mysarin spoke softly. "Is she just as dangerous?"

"I honestly don't know." He hesitated, unsure if he should be telling this to Mysarin, but he wanted to keep her talking. Wanted to study her. "Syndra seems to me a spoiled and snotty nuisance. But she's young, and she's under a lot of pressure to prove that she can continue the Loraenar reign and marry a good suitor. The King and Queen only have her to carry on the name, no other children, let alone any sons. Everyone doubts her for being a woman."

He tilted his head back and forth, weighing his opinion on Syndra. "I have yet to hear of her ordering someone's death, but I don't know if I would put it past her."

Mysarin moved to pull a book out of the bag she had with her, and slowly revealed it to him. "Do you have any idea as to why Syndra would leave this for me to learn? Why she told me to come find you?" Her voice was hushed as she spoke.

Del read the title of the book: *"Elements and the Arcane,"* and he frowned. *She* was who he agreed to train.

"This is what beginner soldiers study, what they're required to memorize front and back before they undergo the Breaking." He set aside his bottle, deciding he'd definitely had enough; she clearly wasn't hiding anything, she was just overwhelmed here and wanting to know more about her new trainer.

He wanted to kick himself. She wasn't a riddle for him to solve. He didn't need to investigate her, because he wasn't a soldier anymore.

"Have you ever even used battle magics?" he asked.

"No, just glamor spells, minor element conjurations and what you taught me. I don't know much." She shrugged, uncertainty in her voice.

"Have you ever had to fight someone? To the death?"

There were no women in the Royal Army, yet it was all he could think of as to why Syndra would want Mysarin training on this type of magics. Maybe they wanted her to be their champion for the MoonDawn Games?

"What? No. Why would you ask me that?"

He bit down on the inside of his cheek, taking another long glance at her. "Maybe she wants you in the army for some reason, I don't understand why though. Or why she wants me to train you." He hiccuped.

"But—" Mysarin stopped herself, and looked down at the book in her hands.

"If it's any consolation," she lifted her gaze back to him, "I don't even think I'm right. For once." He gave her his best crooked smile, trying to ease her mind. "But I'll look into it for you. I know most of the servants here, and I can see if they've observed or overheard anything. Someone must know something."

Something in his gut told him to stay close to her. To keep offering to help. Offering to do more. He rolled his eyes at himself when Mysarin looked away.

"I need your help with one other thing, too," Mysarin added hesitantly.

Delvuvius looked at her with a scowl. "How else can I be of service, M'Lady?"

"Before I came here, I tried to leave to see my betrothed, Deime. But the guards wouldn't let me leave the castle… they said no one was to for the time being, with what happened today." Mysarin shoved the fear that she was next as far down as it would go.

You got someone else killed for your crimes, her mind reprimanded.

"They aren't letting anyone leave? How am I supposed to sell my elixirs?" he asked with that vulpine grin plastered onto his lips.

Perhaps I should run while I still can.

"Seriously," she huffed, "do you know an *alternate* way out of here?"

"I do," he said. "But I think now is not the time to use it. Not until we know what Syndra is up to. It could be too dangerous for you."

The fear in the back of her mind pushed forward at his words. The guilt of Bea's death weighing on her. Her chest felt tight, and she mindlessly began to rub at it, as if to ease the ache.

"I can get a letter out for you though. Just write it and tell me where to go."

Better than nothing. She could at least speak to Deime one last time before they took her head.

"Are you sure you would do this for me? If it's too dangerous for me to leave I'd assume it would be for you as well." She searched his face for his motives.

That smile again was what she saw instead as he said, "No, *I* am a lowly castle rat, not the person Syndra has placed her focus on. I'll be fine. Plus, I at least know how to use a sword if I am to be caught."

"Okay," she breathed, "Thank you, Delvuvius, for doing this."

"Mysarin, please for the love of Talle, call me Del. There's too many syllables in the full thing," he said.

"Thank you, Del." She smiled awkwardly. At least he was willing to help her. She felt a small amount of the weight lift from her chest, and the tightness eased. "Do you have paper?"

"Oh, you want to write it now?" He raised his eyebrows. "Sure, sure, give me a moment." He hopped onto his feet and swayed. She didn't realize how empty his bottle was until now.

"Don't deliver it until tomorrow, though. Not until you're more… sober," she said, thinking he'd get himself killed if he was sneaking about drunkenly. She did not want more blood on her hands, indirect or not.

"Good idea." He hiccuped. "I'll go get paper." He then walked out of the room, bumping into a small stool that was laying in his path. Mysarin held in a laugh.

"Just don't read it, please," Mysarin said as she handed over her letter to Del.

"What, there's not any smut in here is there?" He grabbed and inspected the paper, holding it up to the light as if he could read the words through its envelope. He hiccuped again.

She snatched the paper back out of his hands. "Seriously, I mean it. It's… private."

Her cheeks turned pink again, and Del couldn't help but notice how pretty it made her look. He averted his gaze. *What is wrong with me?*

"I won't read it. I swear." He looked back up to her as she gave up the letter. Their hands grazed each other while Del grabbed it, and he felt his heart pause. *Stupid drunkard,* he thought to himself, *she is spoken for.*

And she's hiding something.

"Thanks, again, for your help. I-I needed it." Mysarin was a stubborn woman, Del could tell from the moment he met her, and hearing her admit this had him struggling not to smile.

"Don't look so happy about that." She crossed her arms.

"Sorry," he laughed, "I'll meet with you tomorrow for training, 'round midday, your room?"

"Alright, I'll see you then." She smiled as she turned to leave, her hair bouncing down her back as she moved.

Del stood for a moment and watched her walk away before he turned and moved quickly to his room—a glorified broom closet, but the best he could hope for while living in the castle for free. It was something Bea had put together for him once he was kicked from the barracks, knowing he had nowhere else to go. His heart began to ache with that dull pain again, and the stillness threatened to sink back in.

He sat down on his bed, trying to shove his feelings for Bea's death away. He reached into his pocket and pulled out Mysarin's letter to Deime. He flipped the paper over and over in his hands, wrestling with his grief, wrestling with the idea of doing Mysarin's bidding, and what it was that had him questioning her.

He thought back to when they met, to when she had said something about having amnesia. It was strange, but could he really be suspicious of that? It didn't mean anything.

And yet, she had seemed so worried when he talked about Bea, the Danais, and the bodies that had been found. She had seemed guilty.

He opened the letter after the seventh flip.

Day 1 of the waning crescent, The Moon of The Red Hound,
Year 1014 of the Elven Era
    Dear Deime,
I miss you already. I write to warn you that I will not be coming
around as often for the time being. A woman was executed at the
castle today, and the guards are saying we aren't to leave. Now I
know that reading that will only make you worry, so stop. Take a
deep breath. I am fine, and I will be fine. It had something to do
with a disease, but I believe it has been handled. I will write to you
as often as I can, and don't mind the man who is delivering these
for me. He's incredibly frustrating at times, but has become a sort
of friend, and one we can trust...

Del set the letter down, stopping himself from reading anymore. Guilt sat deep in his chest after reading that she trusted him. Del longed to be the type of person worthy of someone's trust, like he had once been. There was a time where he had been epitome of dependability; a top soldier in the army, destined to become a second-ranking Commander, set to even possibly take over for The Golden Elf one day. He was the one all of the other soldiers had aspired to be and the one they all requested to spar with. He had spent his early days studying and even tutoring his fellow men on the very same book that Mysarin had.

But then he thought about the month he had spent being tortured by Zendar, and the lowest moment of his twenty years of life. Every bone he had was broken, only to be mended by a healer's magics, and on and on it would go. Zendar relished every moment of Del's torture, betting that he would give up before his moment. It only made Delvuvius hold on for longer, waiting for the Breaking—the limitless power.

But Zendar had been waiting to see Del fail, and then he did.

Other soldiers only took a week or two to Break, but he took much longer. Perhaps it was because he had grown up sort of broken already. During those long days, Delvuvius spent the entire time in anticipation, thinking about how powerful he would become, thinking he'd end up better than he ever could've dreamed of. It was foolish and childish because on that final day, when he felt the floor of his magics burst open, there was no flood of power to follow. Only stillness.

The stillness was worse than the torture. It was a void, a black hole residing where his power should've been. It served as a constant reminder of his failures, clawing their way into his mind at every opportune moment. He had lost everything: his will, his place in the world, his *purpose*. And now, here he was, on the precipice of finding that yet again. As he sat in his poor excuse for a room, clutching Mysarin's letter, he vowed under the eyes of his unheeding deity to become the man he was meant to be.

The very next day, Delvuvius decided he did not like Deime. He was too *blonde*. And smug. He knew he was picking at straws but something about Deime irked him. Del had overheard him and a man who must be his father talking about Mysarin when he had walked in with her letter, and from the sound of it, it was not the first time they had spoken on that topic. His father, sporting the same shade of sunshine hair, had been going on about how a woman should be this and should be that. And Deime had little words to say in rebuttal.

Suffice to say, Del was thoroughly irked.

"Ahem," he said dryly as he stood in Sea Salt Bakery's doorway. The two left their conversation as Deime nervously wiped the flour from his hands onto his apron.

"I have a letter for Deime."

"And who are you?" Those beady blue eyes of the older man locked onto Del, taking in every inch of his appearance.

"The name's Delvuvius Crune, Mysarin sent me." He felt the wood of the doorway press along his spine.

"You see the company she keeps? That's the sort of woman you plan to marry?" Del decided he hated Deime's father even more.

Deime's face flushed in his silence. He took off his apron and began to walk over to Del.

"The way you speak about your personal issues out in the open is an interesting way to run a business," said Del.

Deime grabbed his arm and pulled him into the street as he continued, "I'm surprised you're able to keep it all running. What if a customer were to walk in? Great Twelve forbid it be a woman!”

He yelled the last bit as the door shut in his face.

“That’s enough,” Deime said.

“Oh, so he does speak.”

Deime rolled his eyes as he let go of Del’s arm. “Look, that was none of your business, okay?” He extended his hand, open palm facing the sky. The sun beat down on the two, summer cicadas buzzed in Delvuvius’ ears.

“Sure.” He grabbed the letter from his pocket, holding it between two fingers. Then he pulled it back as Deime made a grab for it.

“Just surprising, is all. She didn’t tell me that your father was such a dick.”

“I’m sorry—how do you know Mysarin?” His brown eyes held a heavy look of suspicion.

Del guessed he could understand what Mysarin saw in the elf before him; he was a safe choice. Not a passionate love that would be written about in poetry books for decades to come, but one that wouldn’t be too hard to hold onto. He felt slightly disappointed. She seemed like the type of woman who enjoyed a fight.

“I am her dutiful trainer while she stays in the castle walls,” he said. “And now her messenger,” he added, mostly to himself.

Deime’s white and golden brows smushed together.

"Trainer? For what? And why does she need *you* to be her messenger?"

"It's all in the letter, puppy-dog." He finally relaxed his hand, letting Deime grab onto the paper.

"Puppy-dog? Seriously?"

Del shrugged. He looked like a golden retriever to him.

"Better than a vagrant," Deime said quietly. He turned around to go back into the bakery.

"Ah-ah," Del said before Deime could go back to that tired conversation. "I'm not making two trips. Read it, write a reply, and then I shall be on my way."

Deime stared for a moment. He let loose a big breath. "Fine. I'll be back."

"And don't take too long, puppy-dog, this vagrant has illegal things to do," he said in a sing-song voice.

The door's bell chimed a few minutes later as Del watched two parents swing their child between them, hands all connected. The small boy screamed in excitement.

"Here." Dieme held the new letter in front of his vision.

"Awww, you put a flower on it and everything."

"Just get out of here already. My father said you're repelling customers standing at the door like that."

"Because I'm *so* menacing and scary," Del groaned. He turned around and began to make the rocky walk back to the castle as the sun reached its peak in the sky.

"No, just a simple human," Deime grumbled behind him.

Del lifted his hand up over his shoulder and stuck out his pinky and thumb, wiggling his smaller finger back and forth in a crude gesture.

"See you next time!" He allowed a small smile to appear on his lips as he made the motion that had been cast in his own direction many times before.

'No, just a simple human,' he silently mocked the elf in his mind.

Was Mysarin aware of how uncreative the man she was engaged to was? Deime, at the very least, could have come up with something better than the typical stereotype elves threw towards humans. Pegging him as simple just for having round ears and a shorter lifespan. He could've laughed out-loud at how idiotic it was. He guessed the ignorance didn't fall far from the small-minded tree.

He wondered if perhaps this was some secret view she had also held against him. Then hoped his eyes would not roll their way out of his head. *Fucking elves.*

But, it couldn't have been true. Mysarin had never made any sort of comment that tied in with the strange war between the Deity's children. But perhaps she kept those thoughts to herself and Deime. He looked at the letter in his hands and the pathetic stem of lavender that was melted into the wax seal. He finally realized that *this* was the worst punishment Queen Yegaran could've given him.

"Talisi, help me," he said to himself.

15 – Mysarin & Delvuvius

Mysarin headed to the library the next night, ready to search for answers and unable to sleep. The first day of training with Del had been… awkward. He had been so helpful the night before, and yet after he arrived with Deime's letter, he just seemed as if he couldn't stand to be around her. Just when Mysarin thought perhaps they were on the way to making amends.

Screw him, she thought as she walked through the drifty halls of Taurean Castle with her candle light. She was grateful he was willing to help her, grateful that he had brought their letters back and forth—though she still had not read Deime's reply—and yet, he was infuriating to be around.

His sarcastic remarks, his idiotic bits, that ridiculous smirk he always wore like armor. It all stayed on repeat in her mind even hours after he left, causing her to toss and turn in her covers. She needed a distraction.

A guard on patrol was stationed at the end of the hallway that led to her room.

"Excuse me, could you tell me how to find the library?" she asked him.

"Huh, popular tonight. Just down that way and to the left," he replied, pointing to a large set of wooden doors.

Mysarin curtsied in her thanks, and continued in the dim candle-light. The castle was too quiet, her footsteps bounced off the marble floors onto the walls and back into her ears as she made her way. She saw Deime's soft tawny eyes on the day he had asked her to marry him in her mind. She looked down to the yellow stone in her engagement ring; under the flame's flicker the stone shone a fierce shade of amber. Like the color in Del's eyes.

She dropped her hand.

The library doors were heavy as Mysarin pushed against them. They creaked and shuddered against her touch. Mysarin stopped in the open doorway when she was finally able to take in the view of the library; it was a large circular space, with balconies hanging over the first and second floor. Pillars held up the mezzanines, with stairs connecting each to the floor below. The center of the space was kept entirely open, with a glass ceiling letting the moonlight shine all the way through. She stared at the crescent above her, and heard the sounds of a ticking clock.

She swallowed down her residual guilt over Bea's death. There was nothing she could do about it now.

Light-blue flames floated through the air, lighting the way along each aisle and row of books. There were fireplaces alight, and cozy seating areas all around. The bones of the room would have invited everyone and anyone into the depths. A striking difference to the dim and drafty halls she was just moving through, and she still shivered anyway.

The room resembled Synsee, the city she had loved so dearly, the city she secretly missed. She felt her knees wobble a bit as she took her first step into the room. She took in a deep breath, and it smelled like cinnamon and apples. She spotted a nice looking loveseat by the fireplace when she heard quiet chatter coming from somewhere—a singular voice. It sounded like someone was whispering to themselves. She began to slowly move towards the noise instead of the loveseat, curiosity driving her. Perhaps they spoke of Syndra, and her plots. Perhaps they spoke more about this MoonDawn curse. Perhaps Mysarin just got lucky.

She heard books moving in and out of their spots on the shelves, and scrolls being unrolled, and then rolled back up as she ascended a staircase near the back. The open center of the room acted as a horn, boosting the sounds made around the library, like an echo chamber.

"Eeskeva oon ta t'ulu ve." The voice spoke in a language Mysarin had not heard before.

It waited in silence.

"Ipvar tehahn oon eekare ve."

Silence again. Like it was waiting for a reply.

This was not the ancient tongue of magics as far as Mysarin could tell, and was not the native language of the Twin Islands that she heard… Somewhere, before. *Where have I heard it before? How can I not remember? Is it from a night I've forgotten?* She moved closer as she arrived on the second floor. *Not important right now. Focus.* She scanned the mezzanine, looking for the source of the voice when her eyes caught on a head of white hair. It was Rionaes Theinguard.

"Reroneghe ta uvsh potar."

The language must've been Oswesian. Silence again. He reached up to a large book on the shelf and pulled it off, setting it down onto the table where a stack was beginning to form. He sighed to himself as he sat before the stack and pulled a small box from his pocket. It looked like he was drawing cards.

Mysarin, knowing she wouldn't gain any intel on her situation and not wanting to be caught eavesdropping on the foreign Prince, cleared her throat. His head whipped around in surprise as she rounded the balcony to greet him.

"Mysarin." He stood and pulled out a seat. "Please, join me." His face was unreadable.

"Oh, Your Highness, I wouldn't want to intrude," she said as his body tensed up. He clearly did not want to be seen here.

"No, no, I insist. Your company is always welcome." He gestured his hand towards a chair. His sleeves were rolled up and Mysarin caught a glimpse of more of those strange looking tattoos before he sat back down.

"And please, refer to me as Rionaes. 'Your Highness' is not so necessary when it is just us two."

Mysarin made a quick nod and curtsey before joining him, her eyes turning to the table. The box had been full of cards, but they were not regular playing cards like she had thought. She studied the intricate drawings on each, all depicting different people, different scenes. Some had cups, some had swords. She wanted to ask about them, but she wasn't sure what to say or do. Wasn't sure how to behave around Oswesian royalty.

"They are called *H'ro Bet'te*, or 'divination cards' in your tongue," he answered her silent question. "I use them sometimes, when I feel I need guidance," he said softly, still lost in his world.

His eyes scanned the tiny paintings, trying to draw meaning from them, and he blinked slowly. He then stood up and walked over to another shelf, mumbling something in Oswesian again.

Mysarin wasn't sure what to make of this. Rionaes was acting like a lunatic, and yet, possibly, this would be deemed as normal in Oswes. Perhaps that's why the pale, white-haired, elves of the continent were deemed as 'lunar-elves' in the first place; the word lunatic stemmed from scholars who once claimed that the full moon caused madness. She looked back up at the shining beacon in the sky, thinking about her lost nights. They might've been right.

She examined the man before her, and thought he looked less of a Prince and more of a regular elf in this moment; he wore a simple white linen tunic with frilling trailing around the collar, which was unlaced to show his marked chest; his hair was disheveled more than usual; his body language had now relaxed back into an ease. So she found the courage to speak to him like he was one.

"What do they say?"

"Nothing good." He grabbed an old scroll and unrolled, eyes scanning frantically. He smiled. "But maybe, I figured it out."

"And what are you trying to figure out here?" She began to scan the texts of the books stacked onto the table. They all were about the history of Taurean Castle. She wanted to read one as well, as they might contain some more information about the MoonDawn curse—they might tell her if that's what was plaguing her all this time.

She had thought about asking Delvuvius for more information, but she still wasn't sure what his place in the castle really was. He called himself a castle rat, and yet, he was assigned to train her for whatever it was Syndra had planned. She decided it was best to go about it alone, for now.

Rionaes brought the scroll over and sat down beside her again. Reshuffling the cards and laying them out into a circular shape. He inspected them, his finger tapping against his bottom lip as he seemed to be deep in thought. Mysarin waited patiently for him to gather whatever it was. He looked back up to her and smiled shyly.

"Sorry, I am acting strange," he said.

"No more than usual," she teased.

He huffed a laugh. "I fear I might be cracking under the pressure." His eyes dropped any amusement as he looked into hers. "I…" His attention was drawn away by the space behind her head again.

She held her breath, watching him.

He looked back at her. "They say it is okay to tell you."

"Who's 'they'?" She felt a chill crawl up her spine. *Okay, so he is insane.*

"Wind. Or, spirits are what you call them. They speak to me, guide me, help me achieve whatever prophecy they have in store. All a part of being an Oracle. Anyway, I am torn. Between duty and *life*. It may seem easy to know all of the possibilities of your actions before you make them, but for once… I would like to jump into the unknown."

He shook his head as he glanced back at the *H'ro Bet'te*.

"Either way something is lost," he added.

It didn't make much sense to her. Rionaes spoke solely in riddles. She risked laying a hand on his shoulder, offering the only comfort she could provide in the face of a world she could never understand. The corner of his mouth tilted up. It was at least something.

"Thank you," he said. "And what brought you here?"

"I couldn't sleep, and I needed to get my mind off of… everything." She shrugged.

"A feeling I know well." He grabbed a book from the stack and opened it before him. "You are welcome to stay."

So she grabbed one too, and began her research.

The next day had passed, two since Bea was executed, and Mysarin spent every spare moment immersed in the book Syndra had left her. That, and training with Del for a few hours, and then spending her nights researching in the library with Rionaes. A strange friendship was beginning to emerge between her and the foreign Prince; they didn't talk much about anything, but the company was comforting. She spent most of her time with him secretly trying to find any information about her homicidal tendencies anyway.

She hadn't found anything yet, and started to believe that her monthly episodes had nothing to do with the previous ruling family.

Now, she sat in the open seating area by the fireplace in her room, staring at Deime's letter on the table. She hadn't found the time to open it and write a new one, and now that she finally had a moment to breathe before Del arrived for training, she couldn't bring herself to read the thing. She had not seen the elf in what felt like ages, and a little worm in the back of her mind was convinced he would be angry with her. That perhaps Arias had convinced him that she was no good.

Mysarin wondered what the interaction between Del and Deime was like; if Deime knew what Delvuvius really did to make money, he would most definitely be disappointed with her. Deime had a strong moral compass, a seed that started to grow after he lost his mother. Mysarin knew if Deime got any hint of the man's job, and the type of magics he used, he'd only assume the worst of him.

So she sat, paralyzed, staring at the unopened letter from Deime with guilt swimming laps in her gut. She heard the familiar knock on her door, snapping her back to reality.

"Come in," she called out.

"You *still* have not opened his letter?" Del asked as he entered the room, taking in the way she had sat with the sealed envelope on the table before her, shoulders tense.

"I don't know why, but the thought of what it might say makes me nervous. What if he's moved on with some other girl after I've been away?" She continued staring at the letter.

"It hasn't even been a week, Mysarin, I highly doubt that he has confessed his adulterations already. It's more likely that he will in at least another week." He tried and failed at holding a straight face as he spoke.

"Not funny," she sighed.

He sat down at the table across from her. "Sorry," he chuckled. "Would you like me to read it for you?"

"Great Twelve, no. That's even worse. Let's just get back to learning these ridiculous spells. I'll build up the courage to read it eventually."

She slid the letter off to the side and then reached for the same book they had been reading for the past few days, opening it to where they left off.

"Okay, this next spell here has been underlined by Syndra, so I really need to get this one down," she said while running her fingers over the text.

"Which one is it?" Del leaned forward trying to peer at the page.

"It's called *Flame-Shot*, so… it's throwing a ball of flame, up to *sixty feet away*?!" she exclaimed.

"Good ol' Flame-Shot," Del reclined in his chair, bringing his feet up onto the table. "You do *not* want to be on the receiving end of that one. It singed off almost all of my hair once in training."

"How am I supposed to practice this without burning down the castle?" she asked.

Delvuvius stood up, inspecting her room, her stomach twisted into knots. He walked over to the other side of the room and turned to her, a delinquent look on his face.

"Your room is about the right size, good for practicing, so I'll stand here and you throw the Flame-Shot at me. I'll create a water shield to catch it. Just make sure your aim is right." His face turned serious. "Please do not singe off my hair, it took too long to grow it back out last time."

"No. No, no, no. I will kill you." Mysarin began to sweat as if the fire was already summoned to her hands.

"No, you won't. I've done this enough times in training, and I still have enough magics to keep up. It will be fine, trust me." His eyes sparkled in the same way they did each time they practiced something new.

"Okay," she sighed, "it's your funeral." She slowly rose from the table, book in hand. "*Leloronijormiensan lewenonjh Talisi eontoneme sohna,"* Mysarin read the ancient tongue out loud as she thought of flames in her mind.

She envisioned the invoked deity, Talisi, and sent a silent prayer to The Harbinger of Light that she would not burn anything down. Memories of Synsee's blaze, the fires that had incinerated her parents home, came to mind. A ball like a small sun summoned into her hands from thin air, growing into the size of her own head.

She eyed down where Del was standing, a concave circle of water floating in front of him at the ready. She breathed in deep and threw the ball of flame, aiming for the center of the shield.

It drifted to the side of his body as it soared through the air at an incredible speed, and it looked like it would miss. Yet, his instincts were fast. She closed her eyes and squealed as the blazing ball met with Del's water shield, filling the room with a *hiss* and clouds of steam.

"Good!" Delvuvius shouted. "Again, this time just focus more on your aim even after you throw it. It's magics, not an actual object, so the normal physics don't apply here."

"How can I do that?" Mysarin asked, hand still warm from the elemental magics.

"Well for starters, don't close your eyes and squeal like a pig."

She huffed.

"And fix your eyesight onto me, onto the shield. Feel for the connection in your mind to the magics, so you can guide it should it move astray. You have to concentrate the whole time for spells like this, not just while you summon."

"Okay. Let's try again." She rolled back her shoulders and fixed her gaze upon the small whirlpool Delvuvius brought back in front of him.

She read out the words in the book, thinking of her triggers for flame. She forced herself to pay attention to the warmth that started in the center of her palm and crawled its way to the tips of her fingers as she summoned the ball a second time. With eyes locked onto the center of the swirling water, she threw it.

As it soared through the air, Mysarin searched for the thread in her mind that was connected to the miniature sun. She grabbed a hold of it, and compelled it to stay the course of a straight path, striking onto Del's shield where it stood. It didn't hit the middle, more like the upper third of the circle, but it hit it nonetheless.

The hot steam filled the room again as Delvuvius yelled, "Yes! Great work!"

He beamed with pride over at Mysarin through the mist filling the room. She couldn't help but notice the way his face had entirely brightened up compared to his usual annoyance at her presence.

"You really love doing this stuff, don't you?" she asked, studying this new side of the man.

"Yeah, I do," his eyes instantly dropped their light, returning to normal. "It's nice to do it again, I haven't really since my Break."

Maybe it was the steam in the room, but Mysarin could've sworn she saw his gaze go somewhere far away, trapped in a memory.

She continued, not wanting to disturb the delicate peace between them.

"I want to try it without words, I've been getting better at recognizing the feel of new magics and being able to summon them on their own."

"Yes, of course," he snapped back to the present and summoned another shield.

Mysarin recalled the feeling of the elemental magics, creeping and crawling its way along her skin and warming wherever it touched. Her hand held a cupping gesture as she summoned the magics, slowly extending her fingers and forcing the warmth to spread along them. The ball grew from seemingly nothing, back into the size of her head. She locked her eyes onto Del, and she noticed the way he was watching her.

He was looking at her like she was not so much a wretched thing, but rather an altar that he would get onto his knees and pray before. A symbol of something much cleaner than she was.

Mysarin diverted her eyes, staring into the center of the water's vortex instead, and gathered all of her concentration to create the path for her fireball to follow. She highlighted an imaginary tunnel in her mind, creating walls the sphere could not pass, and threw the fireball down it. She watched as it struck the center. Steam filled the room again, making Delvuvius disappear.

"Good Great Twelve!" he called out, and she heard his footsteps moving through the room. She tried to wave her arms through the air to clear the steam but to no avail.

"Are you alright?" she asked, arms still flailing around.

He offered no reply as his footsteps continued to echo through the room.

"Del?"

"I'm fine." Del appeared in front of her, his calloused fingertips gently grazing over the soft skin of her wrists and stopping her wild movements.

He lowered her arms as he looked into her eyes. In this light, the spectacular flecks of amber in his eyes wholly took over the base of green.

"You, on the other hand, are truly gifted." His voice was barely a whisper as he said the last few words.

"Thank you," she said softly, feeling the shaking of her muscles begin.

"I've never seen someone such a quick study. Have you trained in magics before?"

"N-no. I—" Her breaths slowly began to become more labored as they were locked in a stare. The water in the air was thick enough to drink.

"—I think we need to open a window," she said.

Del gasped for fresh air as Mysarin flung open her window, and he opened the door to her rooms. They both focused on breathing for a moment before saying anything to each other, and Del could feel his heart rate more intensely with every second that passed in silence.

She was *everything*; her control, her speed, her natural instincts. And he couldn't help but notice how her hair grew surrounded by the steam they created, curling in around her cheekbones. He wanted to run his fingers through it. Del prayed that she wasn't able to see the want in his eyes through all of the mist when he had touched her skin.

Stop, he thought to himself. Mysarin was engaged to the baker's son. He was their messenger and her trainer and that was all it would ever be. He looked at the letter still sitting on the table as he tried to shove all of his confusing feelings down as far as they could go.

He tried to remember how infuriating she could be.

He tried to remember that she wasn't all that she seemed. That she was hiding something.

He decided that he needed to find it out.

"How are you feeling, are you tired yet?" he asked, still feeling the tension in the air clinging to him like the steam. His eyes grazed over her olive skin.

She plopped into the velvet chair and breathed heavily.

"Yes, extremely. It's strange, I can normally go for longer."

"Well, that spell is a big one, it consumes a lot of your energy," he sat down across from her, not wanting to be too close.

"I'm honestly shocked you were able to get out three in a row without collapsing. You're strong, Mysarin."

Her eyes widened at the words and he wondered if she'd ever been told something like that before.

"You know, you never told me why you're always here. At the castle, I mean," she said. "Are you a spy?" she asked playfully.

He watched her fingers mindlessly trace an image into the velvet fabric of the chair.

He laughed. "No, I just… sort of live here."

She looked over to him again with those silver eyes.

"I was dropped off at the gates when I was a babe, and then I never really left." He added after a moment, "I want to, though."

"How come?" There was no judgement in her voice, only genuine curiosity.

He studied her with something between a glare and a gaze. A beat passed. He shouldn't trust her. He shouldn't tell her. But what was the harm in it? If he opened up, then maybe she would, too.

"Well, my whole life I was raised to be a soldier. The servants had to stick me somewhere, and when that didn't quite work out… the other soldiers, the ones I thought were my friends, they all began to act like I no longer existed. So I gave up, and looked for a way to get out. To be free."

"And that's why you started selling your 'elixirs.' For freedom." Her face scrunched. It wasn't the answer she was looking for, it seemed.

"Precisely. It was either that or become a mercenary with the Karnoch, but even then I'd still need that deeper well of magics that the Breaking didn't bring me."

His jaw ached from clenching it so tightly. He forced himself to relax, to swallow his resentment, after noticing the way Mysarin was inspecting his face.

"You're more than that, though."

He jerked his head up. "What?"

"You're more than just what you can do. Power isn't—it isn't everything. Sometimes, you're better without it." Her hands began to tremble again, as he watched them trace the same lines over and over.

"Sounds like you know a lot about it," he said. "Anything to do with that amnesia of yours?"

She froze. Then a smirk lifted her lips, her eyes dark, and Del realized that he should be afraid of her.

"I wouldn't know. I forget, remember?" She turned to face him.

"All of it?" he asked.

"All of it. Maybe it's just from all the wine I drink," she said. Then she winked, and moved to the table where her glass sat.

He watched her intently. She drank the glass, poured herself more, and then stared at him over the rim.

She looked him up and down, sizing him up, or enjoying the view. He wasn't sure which.

"I do hope you don't plan on leaving anytime soon," she said after she had gathered whatever it was from him. "As selfish as that may sound."

He smiled his signature fox-like grin, "Are you saying you *enjoy* my presence, Mysarin?"

She shrugged. "I'm just saying you're not… a bad friend to have around."

She was playing with him. Trying to distract him.

It might've been working.

He smiled, raising his eyebrows at her. "Now, did that pain you so to say?"

"Oh, extremely." She pretended to wince, and they both laughed even though they both knew it was for show. It felt like they had both seen a peek behind the other's mask, and even though the facade was gone, they continued to keep up with the ruse. Pointless, really.

What game was she playing? Was he simply overthinking everything, or was she catching onto his suspicion? She turned, looking out of the window as she sipped from her glass.

"Any news on Syndra?" she asked.

He rose to shut her room door. "Telme told me that she's been stressed about the games. That she has to perform."

"Perform what?"

"I guess this year the King wants her to make a show of her strength before the tournaments. Apparently Seawall has been secretly growing its army and they're worried that the Chaehora's are going to make a move. So a war is resting on her shoulders." He almost felt bad for the Princess.

"That still doesn't make any sense though, why would she want *me* to be trained like this?" Mysarin scrunched her brows together again.

"Incase she fails, maybe?" Delvuvius shrugged his shoulders. Truth is, he's been non-stop racking his brain for the answers, never finding any that he understood. That went for most things in his life as of late.

"I think I should ask Prince Rionaes."

Del drew back at her words. "Why would he know anything? He's courting her and asking him so casually may be ill-conceived. I don't think that will be safe."

"He said he's an oracle, maybe he can see what she's going to do."

"The Prince told you that? Are you well acquainted? People are fickle here, Mysarin. I say we can't trust him."

I don't even know if I can trust you, he wanted to say.

"I think I can, when I was in the gardens with him, he spoke about her with this sort of wariness in his voice. Like he thought she couldn't be trusted herself. And he's… confided in me. He's casual, like there are no titles between us."

Her face was set, eyes piercing, and Del wasn't sure he would be able to talk her out of this plan.

He sighed, "Don't."

She raised her brows at him. "Why?"

"Just," he paused, stopping himself from arguing, and pinched the bridge of his nose to drive the growing headache away.

"If you're going to, at least bring me with you. Just in case."

This he would not compromise on.

16 - Mysarin

The next morning, Mysarin decided to seek out Rionaes alone. Del wanted to accompany her, but she knew his presence would only make Rionaes more guarded. She told Del that they should wait and see if any other servants had more information before approaching the foreign Prince, but she needed answers now. Her nightmares had returned, more vivid than ever, with a dark figure resembling Syndra lurking in the corner of a few.

She left her rooms and headed for the gardens, the last place she'd seen him. She imagined he often strolled through the mesmerizing labyrinth, as she would have if Syndra's demands hadn't consumed so much of her time and energy. She paused only moments into her route. A woman with a mask covering her face caught Mysarin's eye in the halls. It obscured her identity entirely, with black lace mesh hardened and curving over the planes of her head.

She wondered what it would be like to walk around anonymously as the woman did. A life spent not having to worry about a past following your every movement, and the titles that attached themselves to it all. Mysarin realized then how she had gained a new title herself; she was used to being a courtesan, a runaway, a monster, an elf. Now she had to add court mage to the growing list. She found herself wishing she had a mask of her own as the woman slowly faded into the shadows. To be anonymous felt much more free than she was now.

If she hadn't had the people in her life to see her, to judge her, she wondered what path she would take. If Deime hadn't existed, would she be so concerned with her killing?

She worried that without him, she might enjoy her mornings waking up in blood.

Before reaching the doors to the garden, three guards appeared before her, blocking her path.

"We have orders to bring you with us," one of them said.

Oh no. Her blood chilled. *They've caught me.*

"Where are we going?" she asked, struggling to hold her voice steady.

"The Princess's rooms," he said, and then the other two guards joined her at her sides, the man speaking taking the lead. They were leading her to her execution. They had figured out that the bodies in the Heartwoods came from her, not Bea. Delvuvius must've put it all together after she had slipped up in front of him so many times. As they spiraled through the winding stairs and winded halls, following the maze of the castle all the way into the eastern wing, she planned her escape.

She would have to… to…

She swallowed. She couldn't do anything.

She had no idea how she had killed so swiftly. Efficiently. Mysarin knew the capability was inside of her—she's left countless corpses behind, ever since she was fourteen—but how to access that lethal skill, she had no idea.

They shoved her into a royal suite.

"Hello, Mysarin. Thank you for coming." Syndra was sitting on a dark teal chaise, surrounded by large windows overlooking the city, and out into the sea. The rooms were enormous, at least four dedicated solely to Syndra, all twice the size of Mysarin's. The guard called this one the "drawing" room, but instead of canvas and paints like Mysarin expected, it was filled with chairs, ornate side tables, and beautifully tended potted plants.

The drawing room was awash in shades of vibrant teal and gold with dark, richly tinted, mahogany wood accents. The floor to ceiling windows were part stained glass with romantic and floral themes, and the ceiling *was* painted with similar subject matter. Mysarin wondered if Syndra was the one who cared for the plants, or if it was Telme.

"Thank you for having me, Your Highness." Mysarin slowly moved into a deep curtsy, bowing her head. "May I ask what we are doing today?" She looked around nervously as the three guards placed themselves around the room, more following in.

"I want to test what you've learned, and how strong you've become." Her face was devoid of any emotion, looking bored and vaguely unsatisfied.

A wave washed away her fear. There would be no execution today.

"As you wish. What shall I demonstrate?" Mysarin felt relief even as her body coated itself in sweat.

"Glamor yourself, into me."

Mysarin looked around at the guards in the room, counting at least ten. They surrounded her on all sides, with Syndra eyeing her down in the front and center. She swallowed a lump of nerves. Mysarin closed her eyes and shifted into the image of the Princess.

When she opened her eyes, she found that she, surprisingly, was not immediately exhausted. All of the training with Del she had been doing was paying off.

"Now cast Flame-Shot, send it to one of the guards, any of your choosing." Her small smile was dripping in contrivance.

Syndra was a crow making an aerial display, showing off its skill high in the sky above Mysarin's wary head.

"Won't it… hurt them?" Mysarin looked around again at the men encircling her, lining the walls of the room.

"They can handle themselves, they're trained in this. Now do it."

With trembling hands, Mysarin summoned the small star into her palm. She set her sights on a guard who was bigger than the others, more muscular. He had tanned skin and short dark hair.

She supposed he might have the best chance of not getting hurt, if this was to go wrong. She focused on the connection to the ball in her mind, then threw it at the guard, aiming for his center.

It felt as if time slowed down for Mysarin as she watched her Flame-Shot fly through the air, threatening a random man's life.

He reached his hands out as if to catch the fire, and encased it between them in a swift movement. The fire snuffed out, leaving a trail of smoke feathering up into the air.

Mysarin turned back towards Syndra and watched her smile grow.

"Again." Syndra commanded, voice cold as steel.

Mysarin felt her energy begin to wane, so she ensured her feet were firmly planted, and her back was straight as she summoned another Flame-Shot. She threw it to the guard standing next to the first one. He pulled out a shield of water as Del had when they were practicing. Steam filled the air around him.

"Again."

She threw another ball of flame to the next guard, he snuffed out the fire between his hands as the first one did, strangling the fire with wind magics.

"Again."

Her legs began to wobble as she breathed in deeply, and threw another.

"Again."

And on and on it went, until Mysarin had almost thrown the ball around the entire circle of guards. When she reached the seventh one, she stumbled. She was panting, sweat soaking through her olive green cotton dress, as she lost her balance and reached out to a nearby chair back to retrieve it. She looked up at Syndra through the thickened air, whose face was only reveling in satisfaction. She opened her mouth to tell her she could do no more, when the glamor spell gave out on its own, illuminating the room full of smoke and mist.

"Keep practicing this. I need you to do ten, and then to put them out on your own, as me." Syndra crossed her arms. "You have until the day of the first tournament."

"But, why?" Mysarin was so exhausted she couldn't stop herself from asking.

"Do not question me." All ten guards bristled at the demand, hands laying upon their swords.

The air was thin. She pulled and pulled at the oxygen around her, trying to force it down into her lungs. "But—"

"Because I am soon to be the ruler over all Syrelle. Because my word is law. Because I am the closest thing a mortal can get to divinity and I shall not be disobeyed."

Syndra stood to her full height and walked forward, meeting Mysarin eye to eye. She stared into her with the eyes of a predator. Mysarin felt like the wolf no more, but now a bug writhing between the crow's beak.

"You're excused."

Mysarin tried to blink away her confusion as she used the last of her energy to curtsy, and then turned to leave the room. She walked through the halls, with her hand gliding on the black and gray wall, supporting her weight. The world was spinning around her, and she felt she could not take a deep enough breath. *Only a few more steps,* she told herself. A high pitched ring like the bells of Deime's shop scratched at her ears. *Almost there.*

As she trudged up a flight of stairs, the reds, blacks, and grays of the halls began to bleed together into an abstract oil painting. *Why is Syndra doing this?* Mysarin's mind racing like a stallion, she struggled to arrange the murky figures into a canvas she could understand. Syndra had to have a motive for this. For forcing her to perform such exhausting feats, for pushing her beyond her limits and stretching her will. There had to be a reason.

Her legs felt like heavy sacks of grain, scraping and dragging along the floor. She stumbled at the top of the stairs, catching herself against that cloudy wall. She was so close to her room, yet the web of corridors seemed endless and eternal. She had to speak with Rionaes, maybe he knew something from those nightmares of his. Perhaps when he was asleep he also saw the dark figure in the shape of Syndra in the corners, and he knew why she was there.

A wave of dizziness spread through her body and she tripped again, hand slipping from the wooden carvings and bleeding colors.

Then she saw her hand spurt forth long, sharp, claws.

She tried to scream, yet all of the air had fled.

Mysarin pressed her back into the wall to slowly glide her way to the floor as she now stared at her hand. That oxygen she was fighting for never heard her pleas. She blinked rapidly, convinced she was imagining the claws. A muffled voice called out her name.

Mysarin's vision began to fade as blood trickled down her fingers and her mind slipped into another nightmare.

A dark woman surrounded by hate stood above her as Mysarin shredded through a doe's midsection, spilling its organs out onto the red marble flooring. She used elongated, serrated, claws.

When Mysarin opened her eyes, she was in a room she did not recognize.

She noticed she was laying in a large bed atop soft blue linens as she came to. A human man with an angular and disciplined face sat next to her on a chair, studying her. It was Ostrac, the healer who was in the kitchen with Delvuvius that night she had run into the foreign Prince in the halls. She looked at him with confusion as he relaxed his authoritative demeanor into a small and warm smile.

"She's awake," he called out in a sing-song manner.

She looked at her hand. No claws. No blood.

Footsteps rushed from the far side of the room. Mysarin looked to their origins as she took in the full scope of the space she was in. It was the embodiment of magics. Gold and washes of blues adorned every corner, dancing together. There were floating crystals of every color twinkling playfully in the light; rainbows cast along every inch of the room, stretching outwards in greeting.

Piles and piles of books were stacked wherever they could fit, most of them bookmarked halfway through.

Synsee.

"Are you alright, Mysarin?"

It was Rionaes, dressed in a white and lilac tunic that was unbuttoned enough to show his chest. It was covered in those strange symbol tattoos that Mysarin couldn't understand, twirling lightly in some areas and jutting raggedly in others. It was like a circular map made out of a language lost to time. She realized it was probably in Oswesian.

"I—" Mysarin's throat scraped and cracked as she spoke, Ostrac quickly handed her a glass of water from which she drank deeply.

"Where am I?"

"You are in my room." Rionaes came closer and carefully sat on the edge of the bed.

"I watched you faint in the halls earlier. I carried you here while Lila retrieved Ostrac." He gestured to the man still studying his patient. "What happened?"

Mysarin looked to Ostrac with cautious eyes, unsure if she could speak so freely in front of a Royal Healer.

"I overworked myself."

She turned her gaze back to Rionaes, who was watching the shadows on the walls. She wondered if he had seen her claws, too. Perhaps she only imagined it.

After a moment of silence between the three, Rionaes came back into the world and turned back to Mysarin.

"It is okay, he came to heal you, no? Nothing leaves my walls. Tell us what happened, please." He placed a reassuring hand on her own.

She sucked in a breath. There was no way he could've seen it. It was just in her head.

"Syndra made me shapeshift into her again and throw flame at guards until I nearly collapsed in front of them all," she said quietly. "She's trying to train me for something." She took another gulp of water, her head pounded. "I was going to talk to you today, before it all happened, I need to know why she's doing this."

"I…" Rionaes' eyes widened and began to dart between Ostrac and her. He retrieved his hand, and bit his lip.

Ostrac stayed still as a statue, waiting to see what would happen.

"Please, Rionaes. I don't know what else to do. Do you know anything?"

Rionaes calmly put hands over his ears and closed his eyes. He took a breath in and slowly let a breath out. Thinking, without the 'wind' weighing in this time, she assumed.

He opened his eyes, and sighed heavily. "I was afraid this would happen. After I saw you in the gardens glamored as her I… I began to understand."

His face hardened, and she noticed that the purple underneath his eyes had only gotten deeper. His shoulders slumped.

"I have been having dreams, like the ones I often get, the first one was years ago, but they became more frequent when I arrived in Syrelle." Rionaes' lilac eyes grew distant as he recalled his visions. He filled up his lungs a second time before he began:

"There is a woman with silver eyes who craves the world. She takes bites out of those she deems more powerful than her in hopes that it will make her stronger. She spends her days wandering the realm, looking for foes to eat."

He spoke slowly and intently as he told the story, his voice smooth like the keys of a pianoforte and his melodic accent growing thicker.

"One day she stumbles across a giant silver-eyed wolf, and she becomes obsessed with the power. She is convinced it belongs to her, for they have the same eyes. She spends her days following the wolf—tracking it, taking fur and braiding it into her own hair, mixing the golden reds with her darkness. Eventually, she builds a trap for the creature. An iron crate. It waltzes inside, starving for the fresh hare lain within, and the woman slams the door shut. Locking it inside.

"She continues to take and take pieces of the wolf, grafting its ears onto her own, creating jewelry from its sharp teeth and claws, slowly becoming one. All to satiate her desire for more power. But she gives to the wolf too—she cuts off locks of her raven hair and stuffs it into the wounds she left behind, matting it with the blood that pours out. After months of torture, a man with eyes cold and dark as the night sky, her father, finds what she has done to the poor creature. He kills it out of pity and mercy after shoving her inside so she can contemplate on her behavior. Like she is a child in time-out.

"The silver eyed woman, though, has truly become one with the wolf, and she dies alongside it. The two lay side by side in the iron crate, surrounded by a pool of crimson blood swirling together. The man then locks the door on them both, ashamed of the horrors that lay within and afraid of—of the blood."

Rionaes rubbed at his face, trying to wash away the dreams that have plagued his nights for years.

"I believe the woman is Syndra," he finally added after a moment of pause.

"And what? I'm the… the wolf?" Mysarin looked to Ostrac, who looked lost. She now wondered if Rionaes could tell her more about the blood on her hands. And if he already knew every filthy detail… She swallowed, hoping he could not see through her mask.

"It is possible." Rionaes stretched his lithe body across the foot of the bed, staring up into the ceiling painted like the stars.

"I still don't understand. You think she wants to become one with me?" Mysarin began to feel her heart pound in her chest.

"Well, it is not so literal. The way I interpret it is…" He turned his head to the two. "And I could be jailed for this, so as I said, no words shall leave my walls. But I think Syndra may be trying to gather power."

"She's the heir to the throne. Born with limitless amounts. Why would she need more power?" Ostrac asked, brows still knotted.

"I do not know," Rionaes hesitated, thinking carefully about what he was going to say next. "What if she was born with none? It is not uncommon."

"Not to the heir to Stonecrest. There has never been a ruler without magics." Ostrac looked to Mysarin for her agreement. "Her name literally *means* power."

"But, she hasn't made a great display of her magics," she said. She grabbed Rionaes' and Ostrac's arms. "Has anyone seen her *actually* use magics?"

"I guess not but…" Ostrac was still in denial.

But, that was it, it had to be.

Rionaes shook his head solemnly. "I could be wrong," he paused before he added, "I have been before. My dreams…they are hard to decipher."

"If you're right though, I think… she wants me to pose as her during the performance before the MoonDawn games." Mysarin tried to steady her breath. "Del told me that the King is going to make her, so she can deter other nobles from starting another war for the throne."

Her head began to pound even harder. She needed a real drink.

"I think we need more evidence to prove this theory other than senseless dreams. No offense, Your Highness." Ostrac, the voice of reason. "Not to mention that these claims could end with us beheaded if the wrong person were to hear."

Rionaes had gone back to his other dimension, utterly distracted again by those stars looming above them.

When Mysarin finally felt well enough to return to her room, she took a detour into the library to find a book of names. She brought it back to her room and flipped through its pages at a brisk speed. She scanned each of the names, meanings, and origins seeking one in particular. She whispered a prayer to Umakes, He Who Knows, Deity of The Mind, The Voice, and The Hands, that the information she looked for would be within these pages. Yet, she didn't accept that he had heard her call, even when she found it.

Syndra - Female Name
Meanings: Power, Almighty, Endless, Void, Blank
Origins: When the Dawn of Magics arrived to the world of Tris during the Great War, it was widely believed that the Deities had blessed their children. Though some had thought it was to create more soldiers to aid   , in his cause. It was said that the Deity of   had opened up a hole from the sky that allowed all living beings to peer into the vastness of their lands above; the Lands of Stars and Darkness. It was infinite, all encompassing, and yet cold and empty. The people had named the magical gift bearing rift 'Syndra'. Syndra had bestowed

a magical blessing upon all of those who had peered into the fissure for long enough while unknowingly stealing pieces of their soul. In modern times, the name has shifted in its meaning in order to reflect the original gift of Syndra.

Mysarin stared at the page for a moment, wondering why there were two big blank spots. She racked her brain, thinking of who this deity was, and coming up with nothing. *It has to be a Deity, but... why was it never written?*

She marked the page before she set down the text, and as soon as she did, the thoughts of the missing deity seemed to drain out of her like sand slipping through an hourglass.

As if it was like her lost nights, Mysarin completely forgot everything about it.

She sat in her chair, face unmoving, for endless moments before she found air again. Her mind had only set onto one thing; Rionaes' theory, the origins of Syndra's name, and the Princesses actions all finally slotted together perfectly and completed the puzzle.

Rionaes was right.

With shaking hands Mysarin stood from her seating area and walked to her bed. She reached under her onyx pillow to retrieve Deime's letter and began to read it. Her eyes roamed over the scrawled handwriting to find those familiar words of comfort.

Day 2 of the waning crescent during The Moon of The Red Hound Year 1014 EE

Mysa,

I miss you so much it hurts. And I'm worried for you. My father is well, but he has been asking about you. Wondering why you haven't been around. I don't have the heart to tell him that you're working at Taurean Castle now. You know how he is. It would only cause another argument. But Mysarin, I need to see you, I need to know you are okay. I can't stand not seeing you everyday, not breathing in your air. Life is simply more gray without you in it. And I know you said not to mind him, but that man delivering our letters seems shifty. I don't know what it is about him but I don't think you can put all your trust into him. Either way, I know you will make the right choices for yourself.
Stay safe, my love.

Deime.

P.S. I also want to tell you that I had a dream the other night that the two of us moved into a small cottage of our own, and we had a beautiful baby girl. I hope to see that come to life one day.

After reading the same letter three times, she pulled out a pen and paper and began to write one back. She needed to see Deime, as soon as she could. Mysarin felt as if the walls around her were shrinking, and that her air was growing thinner by the minute. She thought that perhaps if she could just feel the warmth of his chest against her cheek again, if she could breathe in his smell of almonds and flour, if she could listen to his voice caress her ears and soul, then perhaps she would be okay.

She thought about one of the first lost nights of hers, and the day after. It hadn't been too long after she'd first met Deime. He came by the pleasure house, buying some of her time and taking her out into the city.

The whole time she'd thought he was going to begin groping her at any moment. It was what he'd paid for after all. But instead, he asked her questions about herself. He got to know her for who she was. He found out that she loved to read, that she came from Synsee, that her father worked at the Institute of Magics as a librarian.

She had been so terrified then, about what she'd done, and who she was—a girl trapped in a brothel with no other means to escape her fate, nothing more but a lifetime of whoring ahead of her—and Deime had shown her that there were other possibilities.

He had shown her that she could be cared about, even with all of her darkness. With him, she was able to just be the good side of herself.

She needed that now, and so she wrote to him a place and time to meet her, in the silent hours of the night, and dared to hope that Del could easily sneak her out of the castle grounds.

Then she walked into her washroom, and stared at herself in the mirror. No one had caught her yet, but the reality of today, the fact that it could happen at any point, had settled into her blood.

"What did you do?" she asked herself. She looked down at her hand, picturing them covered in blood, with those same claws.

A flicker of something flashed in her mind. A piercing weight settled behind her eye.

The full moon lingered over the night, Mysarin below it as she undressed in the shack.

She heard a creak in the floorboards, and turned around. A woman stood there. Her eyes were wide, a hunting dagger in her hand.

"You... I saw you... My husband, he—" the woman took a step closer to Mysarin, the knife pointed towards her heart.

"Go away, unless you want to end up like him," Mysarin said with a smile.

"You slept with him! Harlot!"

The woman lunged.

Mysarin gasped. She looked back at herself in the mirror, hands at her throat. "What did you do?" she asked again, her voice cracking.

She felt like she didn't know how to breathe, because blood was running down her throat. She could taste the sweet iron of the woman. She could feel the hunger inside of her grow.

17 - Delvuvius

Del arrived at Mysarin's door the next morning, fidgeting with a loose thread hanging from his tunic. He had delivered Mysarin's letter to Deime the night before, after arguing with the stubborn woman about taking her to meet up with the baker's son. He had tried and tried to convince her about the dangers were they to be caught, yet found himself saying yes after truly seeing the panic in her eyes as her whispers raised in anger.

He had walked down the lower tunnels thinking about how screwed he would be if he couldn't figure out a way to say no to Mysarin. He then realized that the danger he felt radiating from her wasn't because she had some scandalous secret, but because he did. He wasn't usually a man of many morals, no matter how much he wanted to be, and he worried that they slipped further and further away the longer he spent with her.

And he liked it.

He now steadied himself as he knocked.

"Come in."

He opened the door to find Mysarin with a book opened in front of her, but it was not the one they had been learning from. She motioned for him to shut the door, then led him to the far wall by her bed. As they sat, she handed the text over into his hands and pointed at the words on the page.

"We need proof," she said.

Delvuvius read the meanings and origins of the name Syndra, recalling what Mysarin had told him as they argued last night. *Rionaes saw it in his dream. She's going to kill me for her power or use me until there is nothing left. I need to see him, please, Del.* He looked up, meeting her wide and dilated steel-gray eyes.

"Is this not proof enough?" he asked quietly. A whisper in the back of his mind questioned why the deity's name had been blanked out of the text.

But it left as soon as it came.

"Not enough to save me. We need to destabilize her claim to the throne and bring it to King Fisrolf. In Rionaes' dream, the King was my savior."

"It's going to take a lot to convince him that his own blood is not fit to rule. I don't know if anything could." He closed and set the book behind him, wishing the thing would combust. Making any sort of claim was dangerous territory; they could lose their lives for treason—heresy. "What if he already knows? The Queen herself had asked me to train you. They all must know," he added.

"Then he wouldn't be having her perform for the MoonDawn tourney, right? I don't know how, but they must've hidden it from him." Mysarin placed a hand across her stomach, clutching at her pink cotton dress.

Del wanted to reach out and shake her, tell her that this plan was insane. Tell her to just run instead, save her own skin. But he couldn't. He knew what it might mean for Telme. And he knew Mysarin would never go for it; she wouldn't leave Deime behind or force him to leave his life here.

Del didn't want to see her go, either. "We have to tread very carefully here," was what he decided to say instead. "I will sneak you out to see Deime tonight, but other than that, I will not endanger you further… *I'll* snoop around for more evidence. Possibly, there is something in her rooms."

"I can't let you do that alone."

"You have to, because the only time I can is going to be during the tourney. When you're performing as her." He held his breath, trying to stop himself from offering her any more help.

He saw the hair stand up on her arms as she struggled to take even, rhythmic breaths.

"Great," was all that made its way from her full lips.

He looked at her, deeply, waiting for her to agree to the stupid, reckless, idiotic plan of his.

"Are you sure you can do this? Are you *willing* to do this? What if you get caught?" she asked.

"I won't," was all he said. He nodded his head in promise, and then rose. He extended his hand to her. She took it and followed him out into the seating area to continue practicing her magics.

He was trying to teach her how to make a small static charge between her hands. It wasn't any of the spells underlined in the book that Syndra had left, but she seemed like she needed a distraction from the conspiracy.

She made a small spark, but it snuffed out almost immediately.

She sighed. "This one is hard."

He moved closer, grabbing her hands in his. "You're positioning your fingers all wrong, that's why." He adjusted them for her.

Then he stopped short, staring at her middle fingertip.

"Is… is that blood?" he asked. There was a small smudge of deep red just around her nailbed. He had the strangest idea looking at it; he pictured himself pressing her fingers into his mouth to taste them.

She drew them back, taking a large step away. "What? No. It—it can't be." Her brows pinched together as she stared at her shaking hands, inspecting every inch.

"Let me see," he said, making another grab for her wrist.

She evaded him, her back hitting the wall, and she shoved at his chest. He pushed forward, seized her wrist, and pinned her other to the wall behind her.

"Del, stop," she squirmed beneath him.

He held her hand up to the light. She kicked at his shin.

There it was, clear as day.

"It must be wax," she said, her voice shaking. "From sealing my letter."

He didn't believe her. Here was the proof that she was hiding something from him. "That would be convenient, wouldn't it?"

"Let me go! It's wax, you lunatic!"

He pressed her wrist to the wall, above her head to join her other hand, and stared down into her eyes. "Now, Mysarin. Tell me the truth. I'm not letting go until you do."

"Twelve, Del! It's fucking wax. I don't know how to prove it to you."

He looked at the red on her finger once more. His mouth watered. Then he lowered it down, pressing his body against hers as he did so she couldn't escape, and licked the crimson stain.

She took in a sharp breath as his tongue slid over her finger. She didn't move.

He dropped her hand and stepped back.

It was wax.

They stood in silence for a long stretch of time, as he felt heat rising in his face.

"I don't know why I did that. I'm sorry. I—I have to go."

Late in the night, Del found himself at Mysarin's door again, dressed in his blackest and lightest clothing with an old and mostly dull longsword at his side. Just in case. He messed with the hilt of his sword the whole way there. He knocked once, and waited. She appeared silently, wearing a dark cloak that reflected his own attire.

"I wasn't sure you were coming," she said.

"I made a promise, didn't I?"

Her eyes dropped to his mouth. He desperately wished he would miraculously sink into the floor. Instead, he smirked with that lopsided smile. "We reek of mischief," he whispered.

She rolled her eyes. "You always smell that way."

"Is that bad?"

She shrugged at him, and then tried to hide her face while a playful smile spread across her mouth. He stifled a laugh as he turned and began to carefully lead her down the halls. A golden illuminated string of his own making flitted about in the space ahead of them, lighting the way.

Delvuvius knew the Stonecrest guards' shifts, and chose this exact time to leave because of it. The main guard on duty, Vixcor, was a drunken buffoon who'd only gotten this job because he was Zendar's nephew.

Yet, the plain-looking human man was notoriously late to his post when the shift switched over to his, and Delvuvius had made sure that Vixcor found a rather strong bottle of wine in his room earlier in the night. The two of them rushed through the main halls on quiet feet until they reached a secluded and mostly abandoned hall off the side of the south wing. Cobwebs clung to the corners on the ceilings, the painted dark stone and marble radiated a chill that was untouched by any hearth. Quietly, they moved to a large tapestry depicting an image of a gnarled Heartwood tree with a minotaur bowing its horns before it. The hanging, inconspicuous, weave brushed against his skin.

This was the entrance to the lower tunnels.

No one other than that drunkard was ever posted guard down here unless there was war raging. Changing that was going to be one of the first courses of action Del would've taken when he was on the path to becoming Commander. It was foolish and arrogant to leave the tunnels practically undefended, yet, for the first time he thanked his lucky stars that the Breaking had yielded nothing more for him.

He tested the handle on the door that was hidden in an alcove behind the tapestry. Locked, of course.

Luckily, the castle rat and lying merchant also happened to be adept at picking locks.

He pulled out a thin, hooked, rod and carefully slid it into the keyhole. He placed his ear against the wood and listened as he scraped around with the metal. After one click, he pulled out another and carefully fiddled with the two of them. He grinned once he felt a subtle release beneath his fingers and gently twisted the two rods.

He opened the door as it croaked beneath his touch. They then trekked through the frigid and damp corridors in silence, led by Delvuvius' golden string. The sounds of their soft footsteps and small splashes echoed off of the stone walls, and Del's heartbeat thrummed in his chest. He looked back to ensure Mysarin was still there, and saw the collected calm that had washed over her face.

And that's when he heard a third pair of boots splashing in the distance.

Quickly, he let go of the spell that created his guiding string of light and rushed to Mysarin. He grabbed her shoulders and pushed her against the wall around a dark corner that was nearby.

"WHA—" He clamped a hand over her mouth and put his other one on the wall by her head.

"Follow my lead," he whispered as quietly as he could, lips brushing against her pointed ear. She looked at him with a searing anger on her face until she heard the boots too, turning her eyes wide with panic. Del wondered how she hadn't heard them first with her superior elven hearing.

"Da na da na da daaaaaa." A sloppy tune rang out. It was Vixcor.

He must've brought the wine with him. Del clenched his free hand into a fist—he should've known.

"Stay still," he whispered.

His whole body pressed into hers, trying to make the two of them as small as possible, to blend in with the wall in the shadows. It was too late for them to move anywhere else—Vixcor would hear it. Del squeezed his eyes shut in frustration as he noticed every one of Mysarin's curves pressing into him. He tried to ignore the softness of her body as he tilted his chin up and silently prayed that Vixcor would be too drunk to notice them.

His steps grew louder. Closer.

Del noticed that Mysarin smelled sweet like warm sugar. He looked back down to find her staring straight into his soul. Vixcor was moments away when Del suddenly heard a *clank*.

"Whoops!" Vixcor laughed to himself as he splashed around in the shallow water for a moment. He must've dropped his bottle. *Ugh, hurry up, hurry up.* Del held his breath after Vixcor finally picked it up and continued to move closer to them.

But Mysarin was breathing too heavy, and *way* too loudly.

He was going to catch them and then they would be jailed for sneaking her out. And she would be punished much worse than he.

Quick, quick, think of something quick.

"What the…" As Vixcor slowed his pace and moved even closer to the two, creeping over to them, Del did the only thing he could think of.

He removed his hand and placed his lips on Mysarin's.

The two of them kept their eyes open the entire time. Del trying to say *sorry sorry sorry* as Mysarin's screamed *I will kill you.* But still, she followed along.

Her soft lips roamed across his own, feeling petal-smooth. His leg slid into the space between her own, bringing their bodies closer together and the softest moan escaped her. Her fingers laced themselves into his hair. His hands explored the curves of her body, causing his own to react and harden.

He almost forgot about what had brought them here.

He opened his mouth and brushed his tongue across hers—

"Hey!" Vixcor yelled.

Del pulled away and locked eyes with the guard, while Mysarin turned her head, acting ashamed.

"Oh, Vixcor, hello." Del straightened his clothing and cleared his throat.

"Delvuvius?" Vixcor rubbed at his eyes. "You know you can't be down here."

Del moved closer to the guard and lowered his voice. "Listen, I know. I just needed to see my lover, but with the whole castle being closed… we had to, uh, get creative." He smiled sheepishly and summoned persuasion magics to his throat. "Do you think you could put it past you, for an old friend?"

Vixcor looked over Del's shoulder to get a look at Mysarin, still standing back a few feet with her head turned the other way like an embarrassed maiden. He then looked back to Del, and stood completely still.

"Let me have a go at her, and I'll forget it."

"What?" Mysarin broke her silence, outraged.

In the same moment, Del pulled him to the ground and held his head beneath the shallow water.

His knee dug into Vixcor's back as both hands gripped his blonde hair. He counted to ten before bringing him back up for air. "How about you let this go and I let you leave with your life? You see, I'm not really the one to be scared of, but this maiden here? She will *destroy* you if you even get close."

He chuckled as he moved closer to Vixcor's ear.

"Really, I'm actually saving you."

"Alright, alright, I'm sorry! Let me go!" Del still gripped onto him, debating if he even should. He turned to Mysarin. She nodded slowly, and he released the man. Del stood before him as he drunkenly scrambled up to his feet, and ran to the castle entrance. Del tried to gather his own breathing.

"Sorry. It was the only thing I could think of. Are you okay?" He kept his back turned, unable to face her yet.

"Let's just hurry up," was all she said.

Del and Mysarin continued through in silence, avoiding looking at one another. They emerged from the tunnels, and they walked out onto the cliff overlooking the Fallen Waters just north of the Stonecrest Port. Behind them, the blue and white stone castle still towered above, perched atop the highest point in the city. They were surrounded by the same ancient trees that crowded the Heartwood forest, shielding them and the tunnel entry from view. The scent of the sea hit Del as if the treacherous waters had splashed him from below.

Mysarin ran ahead, sprinting for the figure lingering against one of those leafy trees.

They embraced as Del stood back and watched, only hearing the sounds of the waves crashing against the rocks ten miles down. He averted his gaze to the horizon, the roaring waters meeting the starry night sky, in order to give them some semblance of privacy. He watched the way the crescent moon had reflected against the ocean, only breaking where the First Twin of the Twin Islands distantly came into view.

He looked at the two again when he heard the conspiratorial whispers, and saw Mysarin beckon him to join. He sucked in a deep breath and made his way over.

"You truly think that the Princess is powerless?" Deime asked the two of them, eyebrows raised. Del let his breath go. She didn't tell Deime what had happened on the way here.

"We do, her name means *blank*," Mysarin spoke with conviction, "and she's been forcing me to practice magics while looking like her. It has to be why."

"We just need confirmation on it," Del added in.

"Mysa… How can I help? What can I do?" Deime pulled *Mysa* into another hug, stroking her curly hair.

"Nothing you really can do, puppy-dog," Del answered for Mysarin. They both looked at him: Mysarin questioning the nick-name, Deime annoyed.

"There has to be something, I'll do whatever I can." Deime spoke earnestly as he gazed back into Mysarin's eyes.

As if he'd even be capable, Del thought to himself.

"He's right, Deime. I believe it will be up to Del and I. I'll have to perform, while he'll look for proof." She lifted her chin to look up at the elf as she spoke, and then stepped out of his arms. Del resisted the urge to smirk.

"I don't want you getting hurt, Mysarin, I-I can't believe that this is what it's come to. I knew I never should've let you walk through that gate." Deime's hands clenched into fists.

"You couldn't have stopped me if you had tried," Mysarin replied, a soft smile on her face, and love in her eyes for the man standing before her. She reached out and stroked his pointed ears as Del turned his attention to the waves again.

"Can you promise me that you'll be safe?" Deime whispered to her.

"I promise. As long as I do what she says, she won't hurt me. She needs me right now." Delvuvius heard the smile grow in her voice as she continued on. "Plus, I've got some intimidating new magics under my belt now. Thanks to Del."

He looked back at the two and forced a painful grin. "We need to get back soon, Mysarin."

Vixcor might very well be telling a superior what he saw in the tunnels right about now. He looked at the baker's son.

"Sorry," was all he could offer.

Deime sighed and grabbed her by the waist, pulling her to his chest. He closed his eyes and leaned in to kiss Mysarin goodbye. As they did, Mysarin had her eyes open, looking at Del with a searing glare. She deepened her kiss with Deime, and then finally let Del out from under her gaze. It was brief, but it told Del all he needed to know.

One: he meant nothing to her.

And two: she was much better at only showing people what she wanted them to see than he originally thought.

It'd be best if he never underestimated her again.

He held back an eye roll. He hadn't told Mysarin about what his encounter with Deime had been like, and it seemed like the elf hadn't said a word about it either. And it only pissed Del off even more. Part of him wished he could push Deime off of the cliff, and yet part of him still wanted to beg for the elf's forgiveness for kissing his betrothed. He needed to sort himself out, and quickly.

"I will see you again," Mysarin said softly to Deime, "I don't know when, but as soon as I can."

"I'll be counting down the minutes," he replied.

Del cleared his throat.

Mysarin turned to him as the two began to make their way back into the tunnel entrance, her cheeks flush. She took the lead as Del's focus remained on Deime.

"She's strong, you know. She'll be okay," he reassured the elf, for it was the least he could do.

"Are you even listening to me?" Mysarin was staring right at him, arms crossed.

They had been learning how to let go of magics, how to stop a spell after it had been cast. It was what he had done when Vixcor was approaching them, and the first thing Mysarin wanted to know about when he arrived for training that afternoon.

"Yes, yes, of course. Just thinking." He rubbed at his chin, still lost in thought.

Truth was, he was thinking about the night before. About their kiss. It wasn't a real kiss by any means, and something he wished had gone differently, but it was all he had thought of since. He had even dreamt of it that night as he laid his head down for sleep and watched as it blurred the lines on reality.

In his dream they truly were lovers, running into the tunnels for privacy, and she had grabbed onto him. She had told him how it was hurting her very soul, being so far away from him. Their lips had collided again, their hands pulling each other in deeper and deeper.

"Are you serious right now?" She walked over to him with heavy steps.

"What?" He felt his cheeks burn and his eyes grow wide.

"You're staring off into the distance and still not answering what I had asked! This is supposed to be time for *training*, not for daydreams." She was directly in front of him now, hands on her hips.

He realized he quite liked the way she looked when she was annoyed.

"What was it again that you had asked?" He tried to hold a straight face.

"Oh the nerve! I had *asked* why the persuasion hadn't worked in the tunnels last night."

He continued to stare and said nothing, holding in his laughter. He furrowed his brows.

"So you've gone insane," she said, throwing her hands in the air as she paced about her room. "What am I to do now? How will I learn anything if my trainer has seemed to lose all wits, no matter how few he had to start with."

He howled when he couldn't hold it in any longer.

"Oh, so this is funny to you? Are you drunk?" She stopped in her tracks. He shrugged. She fought a smile as she closed her eyes and breathed deeply. She won the fight as her face remained set in irritation.

Then, she spoke very carefully, "Will you quit playing and answer my question?"

"*Vixcor* was drunk. The wine had already clouded his mind, and there was no room for persuasion to take hold. There are limits and loopholes to everything when it comes to magics. Especially with charms."

"That's right… So, he really did want to 'have a go' with me," she said mostly to herself. Her face grew dark.

"You thought it a side effect of magics?" He wanted to reach out to her, to comfort her, but clasped his hands together instead.

"I don't know. Sometimes it catches me off guard, how cruel men can be."

"I'm sorry. It must've been hard to be in that moment… especially after I had—"

"Don't." The darkness had evaded, her eyes turning scornful.

He lowered his gaze, bringing up his palms in resignation.

She sighed and suddenly his clothes felt too tight on his body. They rubbed roughly against his skin as he felt his heart rising up.

He cleared his throat.

"Then shall we continue?" He gestured to the table where a glass full of magical water that Mysarin created was sitting.

She said nothing, she just reached her arm outwards, and began to manipulate the water she had created, making an arrow. She aimed it at the wall and sent it flying. It stopped moments before it had hit the crack in the stone from previous attempts. Her arm shook slightly.

"Good. Now fully release it," he said.

"How?" Her arm was still raised, holding the arrow in place, her brows brought closer together in concentration.

"Find the tether that had created the arrow, created the water, and follow that up to the beginning." She closed her eyes.

Nothing happened.

"Imagine it like the roots of a tree," he continued. "The trunk, or the seed of it all, is the base of the magics. Everything else is a root, stemming from the same intention. Let go of the seed, let it fade, and the rest will follow."

The arrow and the water disappeared into the air. He looked at the glass. It still was a quarter way full.

"You missed some."

"I meant to." She reached for the glass and brought it to her lips.

"I wouldn't do that if I were you," he warned.

She had already downed it all. Then frowned. "Gross!" She coughed.

He laughed. "I told you!" He reached for her lambskin flask and handed it to her.

She took a swig and swished it around her mouth before spitting it back out into the empty glass. "Great Twelve, why did it taste like… I don't even know. Yellow?" She shivered.

"Yellow?" He asked incredulously.

"Yeah, but not the good kind of yellow. More like sulphuric yellow. And also dirt." She took another drink.

"I'm sorry, what is the 'good kind of yellow,' exactly?"

"Like amber, deep and warm like the skyline at night. Like my engagement ring. Like the color of your—" she stopped herself.

"My what?"

"Nothing."

He raised a brow.

"Just tell me why that tasted so horrendous, Mister 'all-knowing.'"

He smirked. "It's because it's not *real* water. It's magics. What you just consumed was raw element." He picked up her spit glass and brought it over to her window by the bed. He was still giggling to himself when he dumped it out.

"Is that okay to do? Should I make myself sick?"

"Yes! Hurry and get it all out before it poisons you!" He said with lips set into a goading smile.

She took him seriously and rushed to her privy chamber. He grabbed her arm as she passed him.

"I'm messing with you, you're fine."

She slapped his arm. "You're *so* hilarious."

They looked into each other's eyes for a moment and nothing was spoken. Instead, time paused. The air dissipated. The world receded.

He let go of his grip and looked towards the wall.

"Are you sure it's fine? I feel sort of queasy." She said, moving to the sofa before the fireplace.

"You will survive. People do it all the time for Crunlining, remember?" He sat down next to her, keeping his body tight to make sure there was no contact between them; he wasn't sure if he could handle any more.

"*Please* don't bring up those sick freaks in New Grosham or I *will* puke." Mysarin rested her head against her hand.

"Aw c'mon they're not eating *real* animal shit. Just *magical* shit. They feed them magical hay." She made a gagging noise as he went on. "Praise Gron, The Carnal Rot, Deity of Disease, in all his glory!" he shouted.

Her door was opened by two guards.

"The Princess requests your time," the one on the left with short curly hair said.

Mysarin and Del both stood as Syndra shoved her way past them. He felt the air in the room change. Mysarin stood still as death.

"I was coming to check in on your training and improvements. Not sure why I heard laughter out in the hallway though." She looked at Mysarin.

"Only taking a brief rest, your Highness," Del said.

Syndra turned her head in his direction. "I wasn't speaking to you, *dog*."

"Oh, how your words wound me, your Most Beloved Majesty." The guards stiffened at his tone. The one who had spoken laid a deeply tanned hand on the hilt of his sword. His green eyes struck Del where he stood.

"Del," Mysarin placed a hand on his shoulder, "I think we've trained enough for the day. You can go."

He turned and nodded to her, trying to ignore the warmth of her hand upon his shoulder, and made his leave. He tried to make the most sarcastic looking bow he could before the Princess; his hand raising with posh positioning and his leg crossing before the other. He then turned to Mysarin one last time. Her face was full of worry. He winked at her and then cleared his throat before the guards.

The blonde one grunted as he made room for Del, the other with his hand still on his sword. Delvuvius held back an eye roll. He could take them both down if he wanted to. Instead, he firmly nodded his head at them and began towards Prince

Theingaurd's room. He needed to pick the lunar-elf's brain about something.

"Show me what you've done today," he heard Syndra saying as he made his way down the hall.

A few steps and a left turn and he was there. A man in white platinum armor donning a scythe at his side stood before the door. An Oswesian Knight. Del's eyes snagged on the moonstone engraving of a tree, and the full moon watching it from above, on the front of the knight's chest plate.

"I'm here for a visit with the Prince, if permitted," he said to the knight.

The silent man just turned and knocked twice, and Rionaes' handmaiden Lila opened the door as he went for the third.

She swung it open wide before saying, "I shall go find Telme."

Del's heart warmed at the thought of Telme winning over the handmaiden she had been pining over for weeks now.

The knight closed the door behind him, remaining stationed in the hallway. He entered the room to find Rionaes laying down on the ground, shirtless, with deep blue stones laying in a strange pattern across a tattoo. He cleared his throat as he stood above him.

Rionaes held up a finger and kept his eyes closed. He mumbled something in Oswesian under his breath as Del stood there with his arms crossed. He began to tap his foot after a minute or so, and let his mind drift back to his kiss with Mysarin.

"Why did you come?" Rionaes shattered his reverie.

"Hello, your Highness. Sorry, uhm… shouldn't you already know?" he asked. He studied the intricate and swirling runes across his pale chest.

"Not always, and *please* just refer to me as Rionaes," he huffed. He seemed agitated.

"Yes, your— uh, Rionaes. You know, I could come back later, if you're too busy doing… what are you doing?"

"*Iveskene*." Rionaes said as he plucked the stones off his body and sat up. He slid them into a purple velvet drawstring bag. Del just stood there waiting for him to elaborate.

Rionaes did not.

"Sorry, and what is *Iveskene*?" he finally asked.

"It is how I get my markings. It connects me to the Lands of Wind, and Siefris herself. A ritual." He stood, and grabbed a thin white undershirt and threw it over his head. He looked like a ghost of himself.

Del decided to stop asking about whatever Rionaes was doing as it only brought him more questions.

"Right. Well, I've come to ask about your prophecy." He fiddled with a book on the table next to him, ran his fingers across the ridge of the cover.

"So, Mysarin has shared with you. She must place a big deal of trust in you."

"Well, I am her trainer after all. Teaching someone magics that could seriously injure one or the other is bound to create a bond." He read the title of the book his fingers glided over: "*The Movements of Water; An Invention between Sewage and Magics.*"

"Hm. It is not a prophecy. Only what could be." He moved closer to Del and placed a hand upon his own, stopping him from messing with his clutter. His touch was ice cold. "What would you like to know?"

"Mysarin thinks we need to tell the King what his kin is up to. I disagree. I'm wondering if *you* know if *he* knows." Del put his hands into his pockets to not disturb anything else. He observed the room that was in complete disarray.

Rionaes released an exasperated sigh. "I am not a mind reader."

"But you know something."

"I know that Syndra's father sees what she has done and forsakes both her and Mysarin. In my dream it was death. In life it could be anything. Exile. Imprisonment. Servitude. Death of life as they know it. But perhaps it was not because he finds out what Syndra has been doing, but because he does not like the results. Perhaps it is not her father at all but someone who is a father figure. I do not know."

"Whatever it is, I can't let it happen to her. She doesn't deserve it," he said, looking back to Rionaes.

"Though I do not have the answers you seek, I agree." Rionaes nodded. "May I ask you something now?"

"Oh, uh, yeah of course."

"How do you…" The Prince paused, seeking the right words. He oscillated his head. "How do you spend so much time with her, while you can not stand to be in her eye?"

"I—well, I wouldn't say that."

Rionaes mirrored Del's face of confusion. "You two were fighting, last time I saw."

"Well, yes. But, uh, we figured it out." He thought for a moment. "For now at least."

"I see. Tumultuous. For me, there is no good." Rionaes then turned around and sat down next to the window.

He made a grab for a book under two others and began to read from the middle. Del took that as his sign to leave.

18 - Estair

Estair pulled a sweet and slightly sticky tart from her bosom when she was alone in the kitchen and set it atop a plate. Bea never left her mind as she moved through the now increased load of work to be done. The unexpected care that the woman had shown her had softened Estair's heart in a strange way; she found herself grieving at night for the woman she watched die, after spending all her free time preparing her body for the games. She grabbed a spoonful of honey and attempted to artfully drape it over the tart to distract from its deformed state.

Today would unfold differently. The guest rooms were adequately prepared for the nobles from all over Syrelle to arrive, and Estair finally had her chance.

Bea's advice was what Estair thought of now—to make nice with a healer, just in case. It must've been how Bea had been able to treat Estair's fever and chafing skin, and now that the games were only two days away, it needed to be done. Today. So when it was time to send afternoon sweets up to the Queen, Estair had grabbed one and stuffed it between her breasts. At least the beige cotton gown she had to wear had one perk to it.

She placed an extra strawberry on top of the tart, and then quietly made her way to the workrooms Bea had shown her. She stopped at the one she thought was right and knocked.

The door opened.

"Yes?" It was the right room. The man with kind eyes and soft looking hands that she saw on her first day was standing there.

"I brought this for you." She gestured with the plate.

"Oh," he said, taking the plate. "Thank you."

The door moved closer to her face.

Her foot compressed between the door and the framing, with a bruise likely beginning to form. "What was your name?"

He pulled the door back after he heard the *thud*, then set the plate down on his work desk. "Ostrac, and you?"

"I am Estair. I saw you on my first day here." *Smile at him, be friendly.*

"Well, pleasure to meet you, Estair, but I'm afraid I am very busy." He looked down at the source of the *thud* still in the entryway.

"May I help you? I have nothing else to do today." Her eyes flicked across the room, landing on the various vials, herbs and books.

One book was open next to his tart with illustrations of plants.

"I can help you find those."

"You know about herbs?"

"No. But I will learn." She needed him to give her a chance. Needed his help if she were to win her freedom in the games.

He surveyed her. She pulled her legs together, straightened her spine, and lifted her chin.

"Actually," he said, "can you climb?"

"A cliff?"

He chuckled. "No, a tree. Less intimidating."

"I can do that." *Smile.*

"Alright then, follow me." Ostrac grabbed a small dagger and an empty basket, and made his way through the halls.

The castle was finally open again to let their new arrivals come and go, and Ostrac had brought Estair out through the city. It felt like her first time walking through Stonecrest without the fever clouding her senses. The heat of summer here was nothing like the Twin Islands' dry temperature, but the sounds of the city were the same; beggars shouting, merchants lying, men whistling and elves snarking all blended together as Estair passed by. She quietly observed her new world until they made it all the way to the edge of the Heartwood Forest.

Ostrac prodded about, taking the dagger out of his basket and poking at tree bark. The air out here felt cleaner than near the castle, and the sounds of birds chirping gave her a sense of calm. A tree joined the song of the birds, groaning from his blade, and red liquid spilled out from the wound.

"Do they bleed?" Estair asked. She had never seen trees like this. They were tall and mighty, with thick trunks that were her full body length in width. Their branches went up into the skies to caress the clouds. She was used to the smaller white leaves like the ones in Qintra, but the leaves on these were yellow, red, and green.

He smiled. "No, it's their sap. But they are called Heartwoods because of this." He looked up into the branches. "Are you ready to start climbing?"

"Are you not coming with me? It is easy," she said, already trying to find the right grip.

"Uh, no. I'm… I'll stay down here." He took a step back.

"Okay." The bark was rough against her palm, and sticky on her fingertips. Her foot pressed into the trunk and she lifted, swinging to a low hanging branch. "What am I looking for?" She glanced down to find Ostrac staring back at the city.

"It's a sapberry. Should be small, round, and orange. It will also have red leaves growing near it, and they should feel scratchy against your skin."

Power sprung from her feet, launching her to another branch. Leaves brushed against her cheeks as she caught another glimpse of Ostrac, who was staring at the roots jutting up from the soil. "Are you okay?"

"I'm fine," he said, "just keep going."

She found another divet in between branches and latched on, flexing her muscles as she pulled herself up. Estair had gotten about ten feet up the Heartwood when she saw a cluster of red leaves on another branch. She shimmied her way over, hugging the trunk and gripping the lumpy bark as she moved. She then made a small leap to the branch and heard Ostrac gasp. She looked down again to see his hand over his mouth.

"Are you afraid? I will not fall." She rubbed a red leaf between her fingers. It was smooth.

"Uhm. Actually yes, I'm terribly afraid of heights. I thought this would be better, but watching you do it is almost worse. Great Twelve, I feel dizzy." His legs broke beneath him planting his behind into the wet soil.

"Put the basket out and I'll drop the berries into it. You don't have to watch, I will be fine."

Ostrac said nothing more.

Be friendly.

"I used to climb trees all the time. Back in Qintra." She went up further, made her voice louder. "Everyday I would leave my home and I would climb. Everyday I would climb something taller."

More red leaves on the branch above her. Her feet were firmly stationed on a thick one now, and she stood to her full height to see if the one above was within reach. The bark scraped her palms and the inside of her wrist. *Close enough.* She jumped from the branch and wrapped her arms around the one above.

Ostrac yelped.

She pulled her chest to the branch, and swung a leg up and over.

"Then, I was with the Karnoch. Sailing the seas each day, learning how to balance." She looked down again to see he had moved the basket, and was frozen in horror as he watched her movements. "So I will not fall."

The red leaves from the cluster had a subtle grit mimicking the calluses she bore on her hands. She lifted them up and saw small brown stems growing what looked to be orange peas.

"I found the berries," she yelled.

Ostrac stood, and wavered a bit, looking up at her. At least he was standing now. "Okay you can drop them down, aim for the basket."

She plucked a handful and dropped them down fifteen feet. One made it into the basket, yet it bounced upon the impact landing it in the dirt.

"This won't work. Throw me the basket."

"How are you going to get back down if you have it?" He grabbed onto one of his long locks of hair and began to stroke it.

"Don't worry about it." She decided he worried too much.

He let go of his hair and walked as if he had just made it to land after a week at sea. Green colored wind moved from his hands to lift the basket, floating it up to Estair. The berries felt delicate between her hardened fingers, like a babe in a warrior's arms. The thin skin glistened in the sunlight that beamed through the empty spaces of the leaves, highlighting the orange liquid encased inside. She took a moment to roll a berry between her fingers, wondering how much pressure it would take to pop it.

"I only need a few sapberries. You can leave the rest to the birds," Ostrac said.

"Are they safe to eat?" She imagined the sensation of liquid bursting out onto her tongue.

"No, not in their current form, they need to be distilled and—can you please come down now?" His hands grabbed back onto his hair.

She laughed and put a handful into the basket.

"First tell me what makes you so afraid."

Making herself comfortable, she sat down on the branch, letting her legs hang free into the air.

"I—I already told you it's the height that you are at."

"Yes, but why?"

His arms folded across his chest. She swung her feet back and forth. The birds' song sounded clearer. He sighed.

"Come down and I will tell you, I can't even look at you up there anymore."

She placed the basket's handle between her teeth, feeling the twisting ridges at the corners of her mouth and began to make her descent. Going down was much easier than climbing up; it only required a few rightly aimed leaps, some careful maneuvers, and a bit of dangling from her hands. She made one last jump, her knees bending to absorb impact and her foot aching from the swelling. She removed the basket from her teeth and smiled at Ostrac, who had watched her movements in horror.

She thrusted the basket towards him. "Tell me your story."

Soft fingers grazed against her rough ones, and she tried to imagine him with a sword. He sucked in a large breath, and looked at her with those kind brown eyes again, which seemed to somehow soften further.

"A girl that I loved fell from a great height. It was when we were both young, only sixteen, and she wanted to grab eggs from a bird's nest. It was up on top of a bell tower and we were both hungry enough to risk it. She had me keep watch, as it could be considered poaching by the King. The stones crumbled and she fell. I watched as she bled out onto the streets of Stonecrest." His voice was flat as he spoke, like he was too busy holding back a wave of emotion to focus on the words.

"You could not heal her?" They passed through the thin veil of trees. The sun fully warmed Estair's skin as they walked along a path through an open field.

Taurean Castle loomed over the city in the distance, and her eyes snagged on the massive sight of it all.

"I didn't know how. It all happened so fast that there wasn't time to beg a Royal Healer to do it either… It's why I decided to become one myself." And one that offered their services outside of nobility. It made sense to her.

"I am sorry. It is hard to watch a cruel death, and harder when it happens to someone you care for." The image of Bea's head soaring through the air at that same castle flashed through her mind.

Such a radical difference there was; the blue tops of the towers kissing the blue open sky while inside the gray stone walls there was darkness; blacks and reds and deep steel grays threatening to swallow dwellers whole. And after what Ostrac had told her, it seemed that the same evil had silently creeped into the town like an invisible fog, coating every surface.

Was anyone else aware, but her?

19 – Mysarin

Mysarin sat on her bed the night before the first tournament, flipping through a book titled *"Fantastical Creatures and Terrifying Beasts; A Study on Pymith's Children"* that she had found in the library after giving up on reading the histories of Taurean Castle. They hadn't contained any answers to what she might be, and many of the texts had pages ripped out. The Loraenars must've not wanted anyone to know anything about the Danais unless it came from their own mouths. As she read through the small creatures and fierce warriors, she found herself staring at a single illustration.

A monster standing on its hind legs to tower over a human man was drawn. Its thick fur coated it from snout to elongated and barbed tail. A second pair of vicious hands and claws burst forth, counting four in total. Its red eyes matched the auburn colored fur and its elongated canines dripped in blood. Beneath the image was one of a regular wolf with the same coloring, only it was about the size of a horse.

Written in small letters above the illustrations read one single word: *lycanthrope.*

The full moon shone in the sky behind the bi-pedal monster, and Mysarin suddenly felt the urge to retch.

It can't be. I cannot be that. *It's simply a coincidence.* And yet it seemed to scratch at a memory deep within her that was too foggy to see. She began to read the passage written beneath as a sick chill crawled along her skin. Her hand rose over her mouth before she heard a knock on her door.

Her body tensed up, fingers gripping the leather cover of the book tightly. She wondered if it was Syndra, coming to ensure that her pet was prepared for the show tomorrow.

Soft linen grazed the back of her hand as she left her book beneath her pillow, next to Deime's letter. The balls of her feet touched down onto the cold wood with her heels never following suit. In the near silence accompanied by the crackling sound of the fireplace, she carefully put one foot in front of the other until she stood before the door. Her elven ears picked up breathing on the other side. Multiple inhales and exhales.

She shook out her hands and lifted her chin, preparing for the worst as she reached for the door handle.

"Supriseeee," the three men whispered in unison. Mysarin frowned as she took in Rionaes, Ostrac, and Delvuvius in tow with a bottle of wine and a basket of food.

"What are you guys doing here? I have to be at my best for tomorrow," she said, looking at the bottle of wine in Ostrac's hand. Looking at Del.

"Oh, this one's just for me," Ostrac said with all seriousness before cracking a smile.

Delvuvius smirked and placed a hand on Ostrac's shoulder as he said, "I decided to bring you some fun, before it all possibly goes to shit tomorrow." He leaned towards her as he continued. "You and I, we've been working hard on your magics and I thought we should celebrate how far you've come."

It was the first time anyone, other than herself, had ever thought to celebrate her victories. No matter how small. In the past, Mysarin had never wanted to draw much attention to any accomplishments of hers, because they had always been shrouded by her memories, her mistakes—her ongoing bloodthirst.

When she left Synsee and started working at the pleasure house, it was to run away from the trauma of losing her parents. This job that people living in Stonecrest would kill for, was only to get herself free. To buy herself more time to figure out what plagued her. Her quick run in the rain to Deime's bakery was the full extent of her celebration, and that was it.

Her goal was always to keep moving forward, never to stop and see all the progress she had made.

Now, she felt at a crossroads. Mysarin's mind was swarming with possibilities on who, or rather *what*, she might be and yet, here they were. Part of her wanted to tell them to leave, and the other wanted to thank them, to tell the three men what their offer of friendship, what her ability to *trust* them, meant to her. Terror clawed at her mind, and so did the desperate need to think of anything other than that image. To think of anything other than how the demon's claws had looked just like her hand before she passed out in the halls.

So against her better judgement, she opened the door. "Who do we think will feel the worst in the morning?"

They laughed as the three shuffled into the room.

Rionaes said, "Well if it is anything like last time, that would be you, Mysarin. And you did not even drink with us in the kitchens."

"Oh, Great Twelve. Don't remind me of how I ruined that lovely dress." Her fingers pressed against the curves of her face as they sat down at the table. Her skin felt cold and clammy.

"Do not worry, I had it cleaned for you," Rionaes replied.

Delvuvius' dark and straight brows furrowed in confusion. "You did?" Mysarin asked.

"What dress?" Del questioned at the same time.

Rionaes looked between the two, and timidly followed up with, "I had Telme sneak it out to Lila, they got it cleaned, and at the morning chirps, they brought it back. And,"—he looked to Del— "it was a dress I had brought from Oswes for her."

Mysarin tried to smile at Rionaes. "Thank you. Now I know what I'll wear tomorrow. I'm sure Syndra will approve." Her chest tightened further at the thought of the Princess.

"You had it made before you even knew her?" Del asked, utterly lost.

"He can see the future, you dolt," Ostrac nudged Del's arm.

Del continued, "But that still doesn't…"

"I try not to question it," Ostrac said as he wiggled around in his chair, trying to get comfortable.

"I do what the visions tell me." Rionaes shrugged.

Ostrac uncorked the bottle of wine with flourish, catching everyone's attention with the *pop* and poured four glasses into the goblets he had stowed away.

"To oracles, to trainers, and to Mysarin." He lifted his cup to the center. "And good luck to you two tomorrow. I'll be on standby when you become horribly injured." He looked at Mysarin and Delvuvius.

They laughed as they raised their glasses with him.

"And to our *encouraging* healer," Mysarin added.

Voices overlapped, salty snacks and sweet treats were devoured, and wine glasses filled and emptied as the night went on. Mysarin caught herself in small moments thinking back to the illustration. She traced over the word in the mind, trying it on. *Lycanthrope.* It echoed around before she realized she was looking directly at Del. His eyes slid in her direction after saying something she hadn't heard, as the other two burst into laughter.

"That reminds me, have I ever told you about that bird I found, Rionaes? The one with broken wings?" Ostrac said.

She came back into her body as Del turned his attention to her once more. He motioned for her to follow him by the fireplace, she felt a lump in her throat form.

Delvuvius leaned in and spoke quietly. "So, are we going to talk about it?"

It was hard to breathe.

"I hope not," Mysarin replied.

"Look, just let me say that I'm sorry. Normally, I'd ask before doing something like that." He looked embarrassed.

"Let's just forget it even happened, okay? I already have," she lied. Truth is, the moment when the guard offered to set them free if he could have his way with her had set her blood boiling. And since then, she had envisioned yet another corpse laying at her bare feet. Another slew of guts dangling between her fingers.

But that wasn't anything new. The hardest part of it all—the one she refused to dwell on—was that she wasn't mad about the kiss itself. Del had only done what he thought was right in the moment.

No, she was mad at *herself* for not being immediately and irrevocably disgusted afterwards. She should've found another man's lips like poison. He should've felt like another patron of the pleasure house, yet, even now she could still feel his muscular body pressed against her own. His smooth taste moving in perfect unison with hers. The softness of his hair brushing against her palms.

It didn't make her repulsed, and that enraged her.

"Okay… Deal." He continued to stare into her depths, eyes unreadable.

She wasn't paying much attention anyway.

"You're going to do great tomorrow, by the way."

Blood pounded in her ears as he spoke his kind words, and she felt the need to prove to herself that it was just a fluke. That she hadn't felt any aversion to him because she knew the kiss was not *real*. It was just like having another client in the pleasure house, and that was all.

"You have trained, and you have advanced forward at incredible speeds. I—to be honest, I'm in awe of you, Mysarin. You're so very strong, and whatever happens tomorrow, remember that."

She would prove it. Her fingertips found his callused hands.

"Thank you, Del. For everything." Her skin felt hot, and she felt naked in the forest once again.

He looked confused as she tried to open up to him.

"And I'm sorry, too," she finally admitted.

"For what?" His fingers intertwined with hers despite his hesitation.

"For charming Telme. I didn't know what she meant to you."

It was the truth, but it still felt wrong to wield it like a weapon. Many parts of her were beginning to all feel wrong. She wanted to crawl out of her skin, like she had when Telme had dressed her up like a Princess.

Lycanthrope.

Werewolf.

Monster.

"Another thing we can forget."

Her eyes flicked to his lips.

Her heart sped up like wild horses and she forgot all about the two men sitting inches away.

She looked back up into his eyes to find him wearing an intense gaze like it was the blood of her enemies. And she felt like a beast moving free from its cage.

The fox and the wolf trotting side by side.

She leaned in like she was starving.

"Mysarin… stop," he whispered, and yet he made no move to create more space between them. Their bodies were held stuck in time, inches from touching.

"Stop what?"

"Stop… looking at me like that." He turned away.

She stepped back, her mind once again becoming her own. She pulled back her hand as shame began to roil in her gut.

Great Twelve, what are you doing?!

Her inner monologue scorned her, for even thinking of testing her theory especially after their indiscretion.

She didn't need to know if she truly was a lycanthrope to know that she was a monster.

She reared back, feeling a sudden rush of air entering her head.

"Are you alright?" he asked, reaching out to place a hand upon her shoulder.

She moved before it could land and looked out of the window to find only a small sliver of the moon. It would disappear from the sky tomorrow, and she would feel hollow from its vacancy. The curse would fester on her skin, preparing to take her away once it rose again in full. But, she had only two weeks left here—all she needed to do was control herself.

"It's getting late." Her cheeks burned as she spoke loud enough for everyone to hear. "I need to make sure I rest well before tomorrow."

"Of course, we will get going," Rionaes said, smiling at the two. His lilac eyes seemed to sense the tension hanging between them.

"Oh! Before we head out," Ostrac fumbled for something in his pocket, oblivious to what Rionaes picked up on.

"I made this for you." He handed over a small vial of moonstone liquid, reflecting hues of blue and orange in the light as it sloshed around.

Mysarin opened her palms, accepting the gift from the healer.

"What is it?" she asked, holding the glass up to the firelight as she continually fought to keep her cool.

"It's a magics boost, though I doubt you'll need it." He smiled at her in earnest. "Think of it as an extra pool of magics, like you've trained yourself to use twice as much, just in case. Student healers learned to make them during The Pothalyan Battles. For the soldiers. The aftermath of using it will drain you of your energy twofold, though. So, use it carefully."

The Pothalyan Battles: a struggle for land between The Northern Reach and Pothalyr over the flatlands that lay between them. Ostrac must've been a student at the Open Palms School in Pothalyr while the small war raged just under a decade ago.

"That is so kind of you. Thank you." She returned the warm smile to Ostrac, trying to act as normal as she could.

"Thank you all again, for tonight, for your support. It means a great deal to me." She avoided looking at Del as she spoke.

The three said their goodbyes and turned to leave, after cleaning up their mess of drinks and food. As they left, Del hesitated in the doorway, turning back to Mysarin. He opened his mouth as if to say something, then closed it. He sighed softly, and shook his head.

"Goodnight, Mysarin. I'll meet with you after the tourney, to let you know if I find anything. Good luck." His face turned solemn as he then left her standing in her room, shoulders caving in on themselves.

20 – Mysarin, Estair, & Delvuvius

"Ah, I see you got your nice dress cleaned. I was afraid I'd have to let you wear one of mine." Syndra's voice was harsh as she encircled Mysarin.

They stood in the stable off to the side of the arena on the castle grounds, all ten guards present to ensure Mysarin followed through with her orders. She was a mess of nerves, exhausted from the new moon, and from the little sleep she got. She had been awake all night, haunted by the image in the book, and the way she had acted with Del.

And of course, thinking about what she had to do today.

They were right about Mysarin having to perform today in Syndra's stead; her single second of sleep was interrupted by guards grabbing her in her rooms, forcing her to bathe and prepare for the day, watching every move she made to ensure she wouldn't flee. Mysarin fought back tears as the men drank up her naked body, desperately trying not to think of the pleasure house. She had gotten out to come here, and yet it was starting to feel exactly the same. Telme had come by to get her ready again as well, putting her into that ridiculous costume of makeup and jewels. After last night, she hadn't even bothered to look at her reflection this time, either.

Syndra was already there petting the horses when the guards had shoved her in, whispering in her ear that she could easily be killed if she was to disobey their Princess.

"Shall I begin shifting into you, Your Highness?" Mysarin asked as she tried to steady her wobbling voice.

She felt like she could fall asleep right there. The new moon always had taken a strange toll on her; creating more vivid dreams, the need for more sleep than usual which was now exasperated by her lack of any at all, and a strange hollowness in her chest. Apparently now, it was also accompanied with erratic behavior. It was the only way she could explain to herself why she had tried to kiss Del last night.

Syndra huffed a laugh and that cold smile creeped onto her pale skin.

"You figured it out, didn't you? That you'll be doing my work today." Her silver eyes shone with a sick amusement. "Yes, you'll need to go out on the stage when the bell rings. It should be soon."

Syndra's hard exterior faltered only slightly, and only for a short moment; Mysarin saw the trembling in Princess' lithe fingers before she brought them to a fist at her sides. Syndra needed this to go well, or else her secrets could leave the Loraenars exposed. She stopped her pacing and turned to observe Mysarin, waiting for her shift.

Mysarin quickly gathered her strength, breathed in deeply, and summoned the glamor magics. Her heart raced as she prepared to once again impersonate the Princess.

"You will go out there," Syndra began to instruct as Mysarin shifted into her reflection, "and you will wave, and you will smile."

The words were all clipped and sharp. Mysarin could feel a chill in the air as Syndra walked closer.

"But do not look weak as you do it. Look strong, fearsome. You will then shoot Flame-Shot at ten floating barrels of hay, as fast as you can, and then you will put the fires out. Do not say a word the entire time."

Mysarin completed her shift and found Syndra inches from her face, her eyes wide.

"Once you are done, do not curtsy, just simply wave again and then leave. Come back here immediately. Do you understand?"

Mysarin swallowed back the feeling of rising bile. Her body began to shake from what she was about to do. Except, this time, when she felt the fear overtake her body, it wasn't just a withering, shrinking, fear, but the fear of a dog backed into the corner and ready to snap.

"I understand." Mysarin feigned the nonchalance of someone who was not simmering with rage as she spoke.

She had once thought Syndra the epitome of power, the saviour of Stonecrest, when she had first rescued her from the pleasure house. Now, she wanted to laugh at the pathetic liar before her. Syndra was no savior, she was no source of power. She was an impotent ruler, desperately clinging to her throne through a carelessly crafted plan to wield a monster.

A fleeting thought of watching her blue blood turn red atop the hay at their feet slithered through Mysarin's mind.

The large bell above the arena rang out, and her anger slowed back down into a quiet slew of nerves. Her palms were coated in a slick of wet, and she felt a bead of sweat tickle her back as it dropped low.

Mysarin barely managed to produce ten Flame-Shots while glamored as the Princess, and now she must put out the fires as well.

With shaking hands, she reached for the lambskin flask that the guards had allowed her to take from her room.

Mysarin turned her back to the Princess lingering by the horses and quickly downed her flask's contents. It tasted sickly sweet, with a strange tang to it, and it was thick as it made its way into her empty stomach. She fought the urge to hurl again, as she thanked herself from last night for putting Ostrac's potion into the flask. She then set her legs into motion.

The sweaty smell of the arena hit Mysarin first, as she took in the high walls covered in blood stains that encompassed a dirt battleground. Random pillars placed ambiguously around the arena bore deep gashes, and iron gates that lead into the underground pits were placed on either sides of the walls.

The crowd was bigger than she had expected. There were hundreds of people from all over the continent placed above and around the arena, all cheering for the Princess—for Mysarin. She could still taste the milky sugar of the potion as she realized she never noticed any of these people arriving at Taurean; how isolated she truly was in the castle. Banners of noble families and their cities flew near groups of people, showing who belonged to which house. The pale and sickly-looking people of New Grosham sat and applauded calmly next to their brown banner donning a two-headed fish emblem. She remembered Del telling her about their ritual of eating '*magical animal shit*' and held back a gag.

Next to them were the largely built brutes of Blackfall, all with big beards and mousy-brown hair. They spilled ale from their horn mugs onto their Crystal blue banner that had a slumbering dragon in the middle; its multicolored scales reminded Mysarin of the liquid she had just consumed. In the rows above them sat the varying shades of gray-skinned, lithe elves of the Northern Reach. Their black and white shades of hair blended them together almost seamlessly, and made the few red-haired ones only stand out even more. Their banner was a deep moss green with two golden lions in the center, fighting each other.

On the other side of the arena sat the people of Seawall, Pothalyr, and Synsee. The noble family of Perreway were more Loraenars, and sat with the King and Queen. Seawall was full of tan-skinned, blonde-haired people, their golden banner and sea-striker emblem waving in the wind. It seemed like the smallest group out of all the folks who had visited for the games. Pothalyr was made up of full-bodied people with varying shades of umber skin and dark hair, their orange banner displaying two snakes entwined to form a sort of "Y" shape. There were more humans among them than any other group.

Mysarin's heart sank when she took in the people of Synsee. The area was full of elves of every pigmentation with hair all styled in elaborate ways, their deep blue banner with a tome in the middle was showing off their Institute of Magics in front of one of their great Spiderbranch trees.

Finally, Mysarin looked to the Loraenars seated together directly behind the platform she was now about to climb up. She shoved aside her feelings of sorrow for the town she grew up in, replacing them with her newfound hatred of the royal family. They all had the same raven dark hair and sat below two banners. The one for Stonecrest which was gray with a bulls head, and the second one was white with a large raven soaring through it. Rionaes sat amongst them, standing out as a beacon of light amongst the vast night sky.

She began to wave as she was instructed, first to the Loraenars—to Rionaes—and then to the rest of the crowd. She held her chin high as though she were the most powerful woman there. Mysarin then rose onto the platform and faced the ten floating hay bales, held up with magics, in the air above the arena.

There were so many people here, and Mysarin felt that same feeling she had back when she was a courtesan, moments before receiving a new guest into her room. Like lightning floated over her veins, like a tavern performer was beating on a drum behind her ribs. She was there again, preparing to play the role of someone she would never be. She breathed in deep once, twice, three times.

Time slowed as she summoned the elemental magics to her palms, forcing the wild beast to obey her wishes. Heat scorned her hands, and power roiled through her blood. She breathed again, counting each beat of a palm hitting the leather drum.

She then skillfully threw each of her Flame-Shot fireballs at the bales in the air, hitting her mark every time. Her shoulders relaxed, realizing she indeed managed not to hurt anyone. Mysarin then looked around to the crowd, pretending to wait for more cheers as she tried to recall what Del had told her about the seed of magics, and the roots that burst forth. As she followed the branching paths back into the heart of her spell, she turned back to the hay bales, the crowd cheering at deafening volume, and reached out with her mind to the blaze before her. She recalled the element, watching each of the fires go out like the flame of a candle.

Power. Control.

It was something she felt for the first time in her life as she then turned and waved yet again, allowing a small smile to creep upon her face as Syndra often did. Coasting on that all consuming feeling, she floated towards the stairs.

She finally understood why people would undergo the Breaking—why they would sacrifice everything for the chance at more.

Yet, as one knee bent and the other extended, she felt the effects of Ostrac's potion wear off. The oncoming exhaustion slithered over her senses, that powerful confidence fleeting. The wooden railing felt stabilizing beneath her hand, and she went to take another step.

But the railing wasn't supporting enough because Mysarin stumbled just before she was out of view, almost falling to the ground. A few gasps in the crowd reached her ears.

A nearby guard quickly caught her other arm and allowed her to pass some of her growing weight onto him, preventing her from hitting the ground. The two continued their walk out of the arena as the extreme fatigue and dread filled Mysarin to her core. He felt sturdy, and his metal armor cool against her flush skin as she tried to count her heartbeats again. She struggled to take in the air. Once the two made their way back into the stable, the guard released her and watched Mysarin to fall to her face before Syndra's feet.

Today was the day that she could either get one step closer to freedom, or finally look her one fear in the eye. Win or die.

Estair was ready.

She chose heavy leather armor from the selection under the arena where all the fighters had gathered to prepare; the Loraenars had spoiled their fighters with selections of armor and weapons to ensure that the most skillful would win, rather than the wealthiest—and to ensure an entertaining performance from their grunts. Thick and pebbly dark brown leather clung to Estair's body like a second skin as she looked through the array of weapons for the best to use.

She made sure to take into account what the other fighters were picking and tried to decide which weapon would be the most strategic against them. One man, looking to be about fifty years old, picked up a large and heavy ax that paired well with his equally muscular and sturdy body. His tanned bronze skin and long golden-brown hair suggested he spent much of his time outside, possibly as another Stonecrest soldier or as a man working with the goods that arrived at the port in the south of the city. Estair watched as he tested the weight of the ax in his hands before striding off to practice his swing on hay bales. Even with all of his muscles and large stature, he moved with a noticeable slowness.

She wondered what he was fighting for. Was it the riches that were to be bestowed upon the winner that dragged him from his home? Or was the glory of being named the best warrior in all of Syrelle enough to risk his own life? She wondered if anyone would be cheering him on in the stands—if anyone would grieve upon seeing him laying lifeless in the arena.

Estair continued to observe the other two fighters, and set her sights on another man who was smaller than her and the man with the ax, yet still well built. He picked up a large shield and a long steel spear. The shield was made of metal and seemed to weigh down the red haired and dark-gray skinned elven man. As he held the spear in one hand, he began to twirl it mindlessly and skilfully. Estair thought it must be fairly lightweight if he could do so with such ease, perhaps hollow. His eyes were a searing blue and his blood red hair swept up into a pile atop his head. She wondered what lands he had traveled from as he clearly did not look like any of those who often dwelled in Stonecrest.

The third man in the strange cave under the arena that reeked of piss picked up a bow and arrows, with a small dagger tucked into a holster on his waist. He had sharp and cunning brown eyes, his skin was tanned to a light golden shade, and his closely cut blonde hair reminded Estair of The Golden Elf. She hoped this man would be whom she would fight today. He looked like a hunter dressed in lightweight leather clothing, and she imagined him tracking and slaying a minotaur out in the Heartwood forest.

Estair was told that there would be seven fights total over the course of three days, each a week apart, each granting their victor a step closer to winning the MoonDawn Games.

Each a step closer to Estair winning her freedom.

She walked over to the table of weapons and saw two longswords with engraved golden crossguards, carved to resemble sea-strikers. They were curved at the tips, and clearly made in the Twin Islands. So she picked them both, one for each hand, and made her way over to a hay bale. She did not swing her swords, did not practice any movements, did not give anything away to her competitors as she sat in the room and continued to observe.

The gasping of the crowd above the arena cut through their cheers as The Golden Elf walked into the rank pit.

"There will be four fights today," he said to no one in particular. "The girl and Dasra will be first." He had a slimy smile plastered on his face as he gestured to Estair and the man with the ax. "Next will be two from the other pit, then Zanira and Gionis are next," he turned to the gray-elf and the hunter, "and then the last two of the day. The winners will advance to next week's battles. Good luck." The Golden Elf smirked at Estair as he said the last words, probably betting coin on her death today. "Dasra and Zanira, please follow me to the other gate."

Her blood boiled as The Golden Elf and Zanira left the room, and she glimpsed Dasra sizing her up like he was about to eat her for lunch before he followed suit.

Delvuvius had no plan, not any that made sense, as he walked down the halls of Taurean Castle towards Syndra's rooms. He was an idiot for offering to snoop around for proof of the Princess's lack of magics—he didn't even know what he was looking for, if anything *could* be enough proof for the King.

If showing the King proof would even change anything at all.

He had decided this morning that no plan was to be the best plan, since there were too many unknown factors that could play into what he was about to do, and trying to scope the rooms out before today would only arouse suspicion with the guards.

Delvuvius sent a prayer to Talisi to guide him, to let his instincts lead him to what he needed. His heart thundered in his chest as he pressed his back into the lumpy stone wall at the edge of a corner just before the wing of Syndra's rooms. He controlled his breath as he heard two voices quietly murmuring to each other. *Only two guards, I can work with that. The rest of her personal army must be with her today, with Mysarin.* His stomach churned.

He quickly tried to think of a way to get the guards distracted for a moment while he still stood just twenty feet away. He silently glamored his hair into a shade of dull grayish blonde, and shifted his strong jawline into a weak and unassuming one. His stature shrank slightly, and he quietly thanked Mysarin for teaching him a few glamor magics spells during those days they trained.

Mysarin… the way she had looked at me last night—No. Now's not the time.

He had already spent all night replaying it over and over again. Had already allowed himself *one* single fantasy as he had stroked his own length—

He sucked in a deep breath. *Not the time for this*, he repeated to himself.

He set his now unrecognizable face into one of annoyance as he turned the corner and began to stride lazily towards the two guards as if he would rather be anywhere else.

He sighed loudly, gaining their attention before he spoke.

"Zendar said you guys can enjoy the battles today, and *I* have to be on guard duty."

They looked at him in confusion as they searched his face for familiarity.

Del continued on, "That's what I get for getting my ass kicked in training yesterday I guess. He says I'm 'too weak' to be fighting the 'real males,' and that I should probably stay inside with the women. Bastard."

His toes ached beneath his boot from kicking the wall as the two continued to stare at him.

The two guards faced each other for a moment, a silent conversation between their eyes.

One turned back and asked, "And who are you again?"

"Tyr Ventis," Del summoned persuasion magics to his throat before he continued on.

"Seriously, go enjoy the games while you can or go talk to Zendar about it for all I care, all I know is that dick got in my face telling me to come here instead of being at the tourney today."

He then rolled his eyes and leaned against the wall, making it clear he was not going anywhere.

The two looked at each other again, and one shrugged his shoulders. Delvuvius pretended to pick at his nails as the two sauntered off around the corner. *One, two, three...* He got to one-hundred before he relaxed, and tested the knob on the door to

Syndra's rooms. *Forgive me, Talisi,* he thought as he reached into his pocket and pulled out a long metal rod.

21 – Mysarin, Estair, & Delvuvius

Mysarin felt the frigid stone floor pressing into her cheek as she fought to rise. Strands of yellow hay stuck to her face. She struggled to get her arms beneath her. Panic riled beneath her skin and the hope of getting a deep breath evaded her when the world began to swirl into itself. Spinning, she managed to lift her head and look up at Syndra.

"You stumbled?" she asked her with an unnerving calmness in her voice. No, not calmness—icy, seething, rage.

"I'm sorry, it—it was more than I could handle." Mysarin barely spoke above a whisper, feeling every word scratch at her throat like claws.

"You made me look *weak*." Syndra's voice cracked on the last word, her anger tangible in the air around them. "I cannot afford to look weak like you. Great Twelve, you are worthless. I gave you every tool you needed and you still *failed*." Syndra bent down to get close to Mysarin's face as she continued. "You are not worth the air you breathe."

In the distance Mysarin heard the shouting of a confident man, introducing the first fight of the MoonDawn Games and going over as to what the tradition of it all was for.

"Better than what you could've done," she whispered as she looked into the harsh eyes before her, eyes she wished to scratch out.

The hand that Mysarin saw shaking raised into the air, and swiftly landed upon her cheek.

"You forget yourself. *Never* speak to me like that again." The fury coated every word out of Syndra's mouth, her will carried on flames.

She stood and turned to her guards as Mysarin's cheek stung red.

"Make her regret her failure, but leave her alive. I need her for next time." Syndra then left and made her way back out to watch the games as Mysarin heard a group of footsteps shuffle towards her body on the floor.

Then, Mysarin laughed as they began to slam their steel boots into her ribs, her face, and her legs. Over and over and over.

She never left the pleasure house after all.

Estair was ushered to the iron gate up two sets of stairs as The Golden Elf spoke to the waiting crowd, and spotted Dasra behind the gate on the other side of the arena. She drowned out the words the elf yelled to the crowd as she steadied her breathing, shifted her balance between her feet, and tested her grip on her dual swords.

Before she knew it, the gates opened, and the crowd cheered louder than a sea-striker could roar. Dasra slowly walked out into the middle of the arena and beckoned Estair to follow. She locked her sights onto his face as she ran full speed ahead. One foot placed carefully before the other, weight in her toes, breathing a rhythm. Battle was her favorite song. Dasra used the time to swing his ax around his head like a whirlpool, gaining momentum, and brought it crashing down to where Estair should've been.

But she was faster than him.

Dasra's ax landed in the dirt. When he yanked the weapon back up to his shoulder, puffs of earth filled the air. Estair used that second to advance on Dasra, slicing her swords against him as she lunged forward. He dodged, but not completely; the left blade sliced through the light leather of his armor, cutting into the bicep of his dominant arm. Blood dripped from the wound, the crowd growing wilder at the sight.

Dasra growled at Estair as they began to circle one another, eyes locked in a dance. Neither dared to break their path—straying may mean their death. Then she smiled at the large human man as if to say *you didn't expect this to be easy, did you?* It only enraged Dasra, causing him to swing again. Yet this time, Estair blocked his ax with the crossing of her swords just before her face, bending with the impact and using that momentum to shove the heavy blade away. Dasra's arms shoved up into the air creating a wide arch and he stumbled back. His face was shocked by her brute strength. Estair advanced forward with one, two, three steps and a twirl of her body. She thrust both swords using the momentum of her spin and again sliced through the chest of his armor, spilling more blood.

And still, he did not go down.

Dasra swung his ax held by his bleeding arm through the air as Estair retracted her weapons. Quickly, she jerked her midsection back just missing the attack by an inch. Her ankle twisted, shooting pain up her leg, and she lost her balance from the motion. She fell onto her backside and immediately rolled backwards over her shoulder as her body met the ground. She settled into a kneeling position, weak ankle down, watching as Dasra's ax embedded itself into the dirt inches from her body.

She snapped her head up, and before Dasra could retrieve the head of his ax from the earth, Estair sprung. She jumped forward from her kneeling position as her foot came down onto the dull extension of the back of the ax head, using it to propel her body further into the air and burying it deeper into the ground. Another shot of pain in her ankle almost made her falter as it crawled up her leg, but she was already airborne.

For a moment, Estair flew. Wind glided across her cheeks and blood from her swords spilled onto her hands.

And in the next, her dual blades crashed down into the sides of Dasra's neck, where it began to blend into his shoulders. Her feet were her upon his chest, crouching atop him, as she clutched her blades with all of her strength. She ignored the pain throbbing inside her body while she watched Dasra see the last thing he would ever look upon—her face—and fall onto his back. The crowd was silent as Estair removed her blades, still crouched upon his wide chest. She stood and immediately searched for The Golden Elf in the crowd. As they locked eyes, the arena burst into cheers.

The Golden Elf only raised an eyebrow to Estair before she dropped her blades on the ground and sauntered back to the gate.

Delvuvius, still glamored in case someone found him committing treason, fiddled with his metal rod inside the lock for longer than he expected. There were two locks installed on the door: one that locked from the inside, and one that locked from the outside. It was strange to see, yet Del didn't have the time to wonder much about it. Once he heard the *click* of the metal sliding out of place, he looked around once more and then proceeded into Syndra's rooms.

The first room was a personal dining space, covered in shades of cream and forest green. Massive paintings lined the walls that surrounded a large dining table. There were about 16 chairs lined up along its bright oak, and yet only silverware and fine plates set atop green linen were placed in front of one chair.

Del assumed there wouldn't be any secret evidence locked away within the first room of hers, and entered the door on the right wall. The next room was what must be the drawing room, if the chairs and small tables clustered around were any indication. It was engulfed in shades of teal and gold, with lush and flourishing plants every five feet. Delvuvius' eyes were drawn to the matching stained glass windows, intricate and reflecting the lovely state of the plants in the room. The trails of the stems led his eyeline up to the ceiling.

On it was a story painted, like most of the ornate ceilings in the grand castle wings, of previous family rulers. This one was the story of the original Stonecrest rulers. It wasn't obvious to the unknowing eye, but Delvuvius remembered the story from Telme who had whispered the castle's tales into his ear at night when he was a young boy. He looked up at the original King of Syrelle, Jurseca Danai, sitting upon his throne. His long black hair split into two plaits that trailed down to his knees, framing his tawny-brown skin.

A long and wavy red-haired figure stood pridefully behind the First King with a dark aura painted around him. It encompassed his mighty stature from his feet out to his red feathered wings, and brightened into a golden light around his head.

It looked like a depiction of a Deity, but not one that Del recognized. He paused for a moment, studying the man's sharp, bird-like features, as he recounted every one of the Great Twelve. He wasn't a scholar by any means, but he knew none of them had ever been described to look as this one was. A shiver ran down his spine as he stared up into the painting, into the eyes of a forgotten god. It felt as if his stare was searing its way into Del's soul.

Unable to look away, Delvuvius stood there, locked onto the painting as a voice in the back of his head was screaming to get away. He ignored the voice at first, completely entranced by the dark black eyes that bore their way deep beneath his flesh.

As if it was searching for something within him.

He wanted to reach out, to offer up whatever the painting craved, even as his skin crawled and his hairs stood on end. His neck ached and there was a dull humming that seemed to drink up his very being when finally, that voice in his head broke through.

"*MOVE AWAY, I COMMAND YOU,* MOVE!" A woman's voice, and one that tugged at his memories of a life before now. He ripped his eyes away from the ceiling and retreated back into the dining room, stumbling.

"T-Talisi?!" he exclaimed. "Was that you?!"

He caught himself on the back of a chair as he shook the hazy feeling from his head. His mind raced at the thought of his Deity speaking to him for the first time in so many years.

"Please, tell me that was you," he said. He could hardly believe it. Why she would choose now to reach out to him—despite every time he had needed her guidance, every time he had whispered his desperate pleas into her night sky—made no sense. *That painting...* It felt like a cloud was lingering over his mind, the room vibrating around him.

He blinked to try and restore his vision, taking deep breaths as he gathered himself. But the cloud lingered as he clumsily continued on in his search, entering the room connected to the left wall. He needed to hurry, and would think about whatever *that* was later.

In the room to the left of the dining room was a library, small and cozy. It was awash in warm shades of browns and oranges, with a fireplace alight. Del paused for a moment at the lit fire and began to scan the room for company. There was no one to be found, except, he noticed that something was *off* about the proportions of the space. Every room so far had been absurdly symmetrical from the viewpoint of the doorway, as plenty of rooms within Taurean Castle were. Yet this one extended further to the left than it did to the right, where the fireplace was lit on the wall.

Del smiled at what he likely discovered.

His hand waved before the fireplace, feeling the temperature of the air. Heat from the flames greeted him, but Del could feel that it wasn't real—it was magics. His smile grew as he unsheathed his sword and swung it at the wall. It went through as if nothing stood in its way, blurring the image of the wall as it soared across. Letting the heat swallow him, Del walked right through the illusion.

A new, darker, section of the library unveiled itself before him. There were still the same rows of books along the walls, and yet at the center, there was a table with an old, crumbling stone chunk surrounded by small items and half-melted candles.

Offerings.

An *altar*.

Slowly, Del made his way into the secret section and up to the altar. A red clay raven was displayed on the small table, with a circle of gold and black vines behind it. Its large wings were spread with its stomach facing outwards and neck stretching up and to the left. From within the beak, dangled a small silver chain. It looked hand-made, shoddy work at best with the paint bleeding over the lines, but it was clearly something someone—Syndra— had spent a lot of time on. He then examined the large stone in the middle. That same cold breeze made its way across the back of his neck. It looked like the same statues from the prayer room in the castle.

Yet the statue wasn't Gron, Deity of Disease. Even though it was removed from the room after the MoonDawn curse was blamed on him. It had to be that forgotten god in the painting. Del remembered the grip the ceiling had on him and quickly looked away to everything else on the table.

Below the raven were ancient tomes written in languages lost to time, but there was one thing they all had in common. As he looked through them, he noticed a blank space between words where a name might be. Del's hands trembled slightly as he opened the marked page of one of the texts, and stopped breathing once he beheld the drawing inside. There were two figures, one on their knees before the other, and one standing with arms spread.

Between them were strokes of all colors floating in the air, flowing from one person to the next. It looked like a transfer of some sort.

Like a transfer of magics.

Is that what Syndra is planning? To steal Mysarin's magics once she's strong enough?

Del ripped out the page, shut the book and continued to look around for more evidence. His mind raced as his eyes scanned the contents of the altar. Vials of strange liquid were organized neatly by color, next to written scrolls for single-use spells. On the shelf next to the table, Del saw a small locked wooden box wedged between books. He pulled out his metal rod and went to work on the thing, popping it open and seeing that inside there were many opened letters. He grabbed one and read the contents.

Dear S,

I have written some simple scrolls for you to use, should you need a quick fix. They will not and will never solve your lacking, but they will prove useful in a sticky situation. Use them sparingly.

Love, Z

He grabbed another.

Dear S,

These tomes, though difficult to read, may contain what you seek. Take notes, study, give offerings, and you may just find what you search for.

Love, Z

And two more.

Dear S,

Here are some recipes for small potions that will make you feel stronger. They will get those pesky flies off your back for now until we find a better solution.

Love, Z

Dear S,

I shall come by your rooms tonight so that we shall organize, I have some things I think you should like to see. There are ways to disguise the tracks of a raven's passing, so do not fret. I will do what you cannot.

Love, Z

Del placed the notes back into the box, and re-secured the lock. He pulled a deep breath into his lungs and tried to keep his panic about what he'd seen at bay. When he made to leave though, another spot on a shelf caught his eye. An array of shining jewelry and small talismans lined the wood. He didn't have much time to investigate but he knew that these were just another piece to the puzzle. He grabbed a small necklace, laying on the back of the shelf and one that surely wouldn't be missed, and tucked it into his pocket.

He felt the sudden thrum of magics swirl around him as soon as his fingers touched the amulet, and knew it was some sort of artifact made to strengthen one's power. His blood ran cold as the swell of magics beat through his limbs. Was this what it felt like to have received what was promised to him from the Breaking? He heard the crowd erupt with cheers down at the games as he turned and committed the contents of the secret room to memory.

Later that night, Del snuck his way to Mysarin's room, close to exploding with the information he had gathered today. He had spent every moment after his discoveries dissecting what everything had meant, how everything connected, and trying desperately to stave away the memories of last night. He burst through Mysarin's door with a smile on his face, too exhilarated to remember to knock. Yet, when he beheld the state that she was in, everything else vanished.

Mysarin was laying on her side atop a small deerskin rug in front of the fireplace, watching the flames dance. Her face was bruised, swollen, and crusted in her own blood along her lips and brow. Her beautiful gown was covered in dirt and her hands were wrapped around her legs, hugging them to her chest. Silent tears slid down her face and onto the rug as Del rushed to her side and dropped to his knees before her.

"Who did this to you?" he asked in a hushed voice, trying his best to conceal his fury.

Mysarin did not respond.

Del reached out to lay a gentle hand onto her shoulder, and she flinched at his touch. He remembered that this was not the first time she had reared back from him.

"Has this happened to you before?" His palms pricked in pain as his nails dug in deep.

Mysarin slowly nodded her head, keeping her eyes locked onto the bright orange of the flames.

He slowly inched his face closer to hers. "What can I do?"

He listened to her breathing, sporadic and hastened. She whispered a story to herself as tears continued to flow.

"Draw me a bath," was all she could muster after she finished, her voice small and hoarse.

Del was thinking more along the lines of murder, but he guessed a bath would do. For now. He rose without another word and began to prepare hot water for her with his own flames. His hands shook as he prepared the room for her, his jaw aching. He willed himself still before returning to Mysarin still unmoving on the floor. He lowered onto his knees again.

"It's ready for you," he said.

Mysarin put her arms beneath her and hissed as she tried to lift herself. Her hands immediately clutched at her ribs as she lay back down.

"May I carry you?" The words left his mouth before he realized what he was saying. But Mysarin just nodded her head again.

Slowly, Del reached out to place Mysarin's arm around his neck, and then gently lifted her from the floor. His heart was an orchestra within his chest as he held her close, avoiding looking into her beaten face. She was cold against him, hanging heavy in his arms. He steadily carried her to the bathing room just off to the side of where her bed was, careful not to jostle her sore body. When he finally stood before the tub of steaming water, he hesitated.

He cleared his throat. "Uhm. Your dress." His eyes still avoided her own.

"Take it off of me. I don't care." Del could hear the dread in her voice. She had already lost all of her dignity—there was nothing left that could make her feel lower than she did now. He understood the feeling well.

So, in a smooth and slow motion, Del set Mysarin down onto her feet, her hands bracing the rim of the tub and small sobs leaving her mouth. He got to work on the complex lacing and layering of her gown, making sure to avoid gazing at any bits of her bare skin. He would not continue her embarrassment any further.

Once she was disrobed from everything but her thin dressing shift, he picked her up once more. He dared to peer at her face again, and then fought the urge to tear this entire castle apart. She no longer looked like herself—her eyes and lips were swollen and turning to a sickly shade of green, cuts along her brow bore deep. It felt like his chest had hollowed out, a sharp pain ripping through his cavities. He blinked rapidly and placed her into the steaming water. A sigh of relief broke from her as she settled into the comfort of the heat.

Del turned to leave, to let her heal in private.

"Stay. Please," she rasped.

He thought about ignoring it. He thought about leaving to uphold the very precarious boundary between them. It would've been the right thing to do. But, when had he ever cared much about doing the right thing? So, he walked to the base of the tub and sat, back resting against the warm porcelain.

22 - Mysarin

She could still feel their eyes crawling over every inch of her skin. She still felt their metal boots bashing into her bones. The moment of her failure was etched into her very breath, each inhale and exhale a painful reminder. She sat in the warm bath, desperately trying to push her thoughts away, searching for a place within herself where she could hide. But everything she had been running from demanded to be seen.

She was a courtesan still—her body once more an object, used and battered. Bathing after a brutal beating.

It had become a ritual for her Lady Madame, Grenlide, to prepare her a steaming tub after each time a man used Mysarin for more than sex, for it was all she could do for the young girl before her. Though, that had stopped once it turned into Ixmon giving her the beatings for her misbehavior.

Tears slipped down Mysarin's swollen and hot cheeks, her body shaking even as the water warmed her skin. Images flashed through her mind, each mistake she had made displayed like paintings in a gallery, telling a tragic story. She should never have persuaded Telme to take that job, should never have become a courtesan, should never have left Synsee.

She should've never killed that man.

Mysarin's mind spiraled into a vicious loop, replaying the events of her life up until this moment. It paused on that one sliver of time during the riots when everything changed. That memory stood at the beginning and end of her descent.

It was of the man attacking her, because the Institute of Magics only allowed elves in, because the ruling families were only ever elves. The humans revolted. It wasn't uncommon for the two species to verbally attack one another, to stick to their own and shun any "other", but this time it was different. The humans of Synsee banned together, to protest outside of the school, and it spiraled out of control—two elves had come out of the school to bicker and to show why only they were allowed in. They displayed their magical abilities, and "accidentally" scorched a protesters arm.

And then chaos erupted. It escalated from there as the streets became a warzone and the humans broke into the school and began to destroy everything: tomes, artifacts, magical weapons, people. Mysarin was walking home from the library nearby when it all broke out into horror. She was the unlucky elf who was accosted by a man who looted one of the enchanted weapons rather than destroying it. He came at her, caught up in the storm of the riots, with a winter sword. He began to swing on her. He nicked her arm and she felt it go entirely numb from the cold.

Mysarin was untrained in magics, undisciplined, and she lashed at him with raw, unrefined, energy. She didn't think it through, no, she only knew to send a burst of the magics in the air around her. She acted before she thought, and as her mind caught up to her body, she watched his body ripple against the harsh current. He screamed at her back as she ran away, her body ravaged from using the pure power as she stumbled all the way home on a trail of fires to find her parents house alight in flames as well.

It was that night that she fled, and the first night she had forgotten. She awoke with no idea where she had ended up, with nothing other than her guilt at her side. It was the first time she wore those gloves made of blood.

Mysarin spent days lost in the Heartwood forest. Her arm regained feeling on the second night, when she had stayed awake the entire time listening to the sounds of the woods. She heard the minotaurs howl in the night, heard the owls and birds, and listened to the breathing of the trees. When the light broke, she picked a direction to go and promised herself not to stop until she made it out.

She got halfway through the Heartwood forest before she came across Grenlide for the first time. She was promised a cloak and a way out of the forest and all she had to do was pay her way through it with her body. From then on, at the age of fourteen,

Mysarin was trained to become a courtesan. Cursed to spend the next eight years in indentured servitude.

That night in Synsee, that man whose name she will never know the meaning of, was the start of it all. Had she not have killed him, had she escaped him and his beady blue eyes, she would've been able to stay. She wouldn't have turned into a monster. Or, had he killed her, perhaps she would be watching these events unfold through the Lands of Wind. Watching as Deime lived his life in peace, probably married by now to Yrana.

It felt like it had been so long since Mysarin had seen Yrana, and yet she was in the same place she had been when they became friends in the pleasure house, both physically and mentally. She was trapped here in the castle, surrounded by false luxuries meant to keep her complacent, and enemies seeking to break her. Except now she had the lingering image of that werewolf in the back of her mind as well.

Mysarin felt broken. She thought about what it would be like to submerge herself under the bathwater until her lungs filled.

But then she thought of Deime, of the wedding she still longed to have, of the simple life by his side. And she remembered Del, who was here, in the room with her as she spiraled.

"I was a courtesan," she said, breaking the silence that had felt hours long.

At first, Del did not reply, as if he was too stunned to say anything at all. Right as she was about to stop waiting for him to speak, he finally asked, "Why are you telling me this?"

"Because you once asked me if I was and I lied. Because I mourn the surname I used to bear. Because I feel as though I'm still a courtesan, selling my body for coin and sporting the bruises to prove it. Though this time they are not from human men seeking revenge against an elven girl or punishment bestowed by my Lady Madame, but something that's somehow worse." A sob rose in her throat.

It was so silly to hope. Mysarin had clung to the dreams that a child would conjure and allowed herself to think that it could be her reality. Was she going to be able to leave here? Or had she just traded one never ending nightmare for another?

She knew in that moment to never again get caught up in such fantasies. Never again would she let herself believe that it could be possible for her to live a normal life.

"Do you remember your family name?" His voice was bitter, as if he held in anger at the words she told him.

"Kileides. Mysarin Kileides." The name felt foreign on her tongue, wrong somehow, like a distant memory that no longer belonged to her. After years of servitude, stripped of her family name, it felt fake, like it had never truly been hers.

"My parents died in Synsee, and I was left alone with nowhere to go," she continued, omitting the full truth. "When my Lady Madame found me, she offered me a roof, a warm bed, food. But everything had a cost."

She paused to take a deep breath and sink further into the water. She wanted to hide from the shame of it all.

"I repaid it with my services, but I never really realized that I paid with my family name, too."

"Mysarin Kileides. A beautiful name. Though, your name could be Horse Shit and I believe I'd still find it beautiful." Mysarin smiled a bit at that, and wished she could see if he was smiling too. Her inner turmoil eased the slightest bit—talking with him about the things she never shared began to lift the dread from her chest. Began to drive away the monster within her. So she continued.

"I feel powerless, Del. I am afraid every day, and I feel like I never left there, like I'm back at the start, still sharing a roof with other girls all too young to be selling themselves." Her words were only whispers, as if speaking them at her regular volume would only strike more fear into her heart. "I am afraid. Afraid of who I might become by the time I leave here. If I leave here at all."

"Don't say that. You'll get to leave," he spoke the words clearly, believing them more than Mysarin did, "I won't let them keep you here."

"I can already feel myself changing, Del."

Mysarin's voice started to break, tears cooling the skin on her cheeks. She had gotten what she had wished for here—a lead on what she might be—and found herself drowning beneath everything that came with it.

"The person who I was before this, *she* will not leave here."

Delvuvius stood up then, his muscular back straining within his dark gray tunic. He turned around and finally faced her, locking those amber and emerald eyes onto her own platinum ones.

His eyes did not stray from hers to look unto her naked body beneath her now-sheer dressing shift as most men's eyes would. His fists constricted as he spoke to her with an even rhythm and tone.

"Then you will become who you are meant to be. I believe that everything that happens, happens for a reason. I know you might think it is silly and naive, but I believe that the Great Twelve are here watching over us, guiding us, and that whomever you become, will be even better than you are now. And I—I will be with you for every step of the way."

"Del…"

"No. You don't get to argue with me on this one. You and I? We're in this together, and dare I say we're…friends, now, and as embarrassing as it is, I don't make those easily. And I don't let go of them easily, either. So, you're stuck with me." He released a long breath, as if those words had been burning a hole in his lungs for a while. He seemed to remember that she was naked before him, and he dropped his eyes to the ground.

"I… I should tell you about what I saw in Syndra's rooms."

"No. Just… stay with me for now, and then you can tell me tomorrow."

23 - Estair

After winning the battle, Estair was immediately ushered out of the arena by guards, ensuring she wouldn't catch a glimpse of the other fighters or gain any further advantage over them. Still, the thrill of victory—the rush of besting another man—lingered in her veins, making her feel more confident than she had in years.

The fight lasted less than five minutes. Estair was accustomed to battling the Karnoch pirates—men whose blades sang through the air with lethal purpose—and knew how to fight to live. Dasra, despite his size, had clearly faced few battles where his life was truly at stake. Estair did not grieve for the life she took; she couldn't afford to, not after what they had done to Bea, not when winning meant her freedom.

As she was escorted back to the servants' quarters, Estair vowed never to mourn those who willingly signed up to die by her hand. Anyone who assumed victory upon seeing her was already dead. For each time someone underestimated her, she gained the upper hand. Though she hardly needed it. A smile tugged at her lips as the guards pulled her along the hallway.

She would win it all, for they did not know what she was capable of. She would annihilate each fighter and hold that wretched Golden Elf to his word. She would earn her freedom; something she hadn't truly thought of since being bought by the Karnoch. She had been so focused on surviving and making the best of her circumstances, that she had forgotten all about the possibilities of life if she were no longer bound by Boone Karnoch, or by the Loraenars.

And as she silently organized her plans, she saw her. A goddess before her own eyes, dressed in a flowing black gown with magenta and sunset orange orchids stitched into the fabric. Her head was held high, with elegant onyx jewels dripping down her slender pale neck. Her ashen uptilted eyes were narrowed in on Estair, on the plotting smile still plastered onto her face. Estair did not avert her gaze from the demanding presence of the woman. Instead, she let it linger—drifting from her night dark hair to her full lips, absorbing every inch of the regality that radiated from her.

"Ah, one of our victors. You seem to be pleased with the results of your battle today. I know I would be if I got to keep my head." Her voice was harsh, yet strangely comforting. Like a lullaby from the throat of a sea-striker. "Your fight was the quickest one today. I am shocked that a skill like that comes from a servant. Tell me, what brought you here? Why are you not a blade for hire?"

Estair remained standing between the two frozen guards who were stuck in a stupor in the presence of this woman. She let her smile grow as she replied, "I was bought by the Loraenars. Now I fight to be free." She let her bravado take the lead, showing no fear to the company that brought the usually barbaric guards to a standstill.

"If you were bought, why haven't you been placed within the ranks in the army?" Her arched brows lifted in questioning.

"The golden one, the elf, he said I wasn't to join because I'm a woman. He said I belonged among the servants." Estair spoke clearly, focusing on her pronunciation of each word. This woman clearly held rank within the castle and Estair hoped she could have that bastard punished for his stupidity. Each word that was spoken mattered.

But the woman just laughed. Her head tilted back and exposed more of the soft pale skin along her elegant neck. Estair wondered if this woman had ever seen the sun. "Sounds like him. He's an evil shit, but it *is* his army. So whatever he says, goes. I'll have a talk with him though, should you be the sole victor of the games. Talent like that should not go wasted." She then looked to the guards in a silent demand to move out of her way. The smell of incense and tiger lilies enveloped Estair as she stopped next to her to add on, "Should you win it all, perhaps you can be my personal guard. The heir to the throne should have the best after all."

The woman, no, *Syndra*, then smirked at the shock that lit up in Estair's eyes as she then walked back out to the arena.

Estair sat on Bea's old bed in the dark, damp servants' quarters, the room heavy with the scent of stale air. While everyone else slept, she remained awake, her thoughts drifting back to Qintra. In her mind's eye, she climbed a white tree, the scent of those small yellow flowers filling the air, her fingertips brushing against the velvet leaves. Estair was only 9 when she had tried to run away from her parents home. She told herself that she could simply live in the tallest white tree that she could find—she could sleep on the thickest branches, use the leaves for warmth and comfort, and she could fill her belly with all of the white berries the tree had to offer.

It seemed like the memory was no longer hers. It was so long ago when she tried to flee from it all; she always knew her parents had raised her to be sold, her name meant *expensive* after all. They fed her and looked after her, but there was never love behind their eyes. Like they were raising livestock. The only time Estair felt like she could escape it all was when she was alone, up in a tree where it took hours for someone to find her. It was the only time she felt loved. She knew now that it made no sense, that trees and plants and wind could not love. That they knew nothing of the concept.

Yet when she was still young and innocent, when she hadn't yet taken a life, she thought she felt it in those trees. It was what had chained her heart to Bea, why she grieved her so. The old woman reminded her of the single clean drop of water in the river full of poison that was her existence. And then they took her away. Silent tears made their presence known on Estair's face in the pitch black of the room.

Perhaps when she won it all, she would go back to Qintra and work as a blade for hire outside of the Karnoch pirates. She could make enough money to buy lumber and nails and build a home in the thickest and tallest white tree she could find, and live out the rest of her days in peace amongst the leaves. Isolated as she had always craved to be.

Or she could take up the Princess on her offer. Work for the people who bought her, slave away under the monarchs and serpents who had beheaded the one person to ever show Estair kindness. And then, when they least expected it, she would execute every last one of them. And then she would grab the fastest boat in the harbor and flee to another continent.

Estair finally settled down into her cot, letting the covers swaddle her into a sleep. She needed to rest well if she was to continue working in the kitchens and training in her spare time. Long days were ahead of her, days where she would spend every waking moment working towards that freedom, working towards the paths that laid before her. Only when she won her liberation would she decide what to do with it.

Pain shot from her ankle the next morning when she stood. Estair sat back down and inspected herself, seeing that her ankle had swollen to a larger size, and was forming a deep purple bruise. *Pretty*, she thought, and the image of Syndra flashed into her mind at the sight of it. She stood again on her good leg, and then slowly put weight onto the other. It was okay to walk on, but she decided to head to Ostrac right away. Her walk was uneven as she bounced higher on one side through the halls. She saw more of those strange-looking gray-skinned elves as she made her way, but this time they all had white or black hair flowing down their backs. She quickly looked away when one turned to her and flashed their sharp canines.

She was thinking of how she could get her own teeth to be so sharp when she reached Ostrac's door. The cries of a woman escaped through the crack beneath, stealing her away from her whetstone plans.

She bursted in to see what was going on without a second thought. Three pairs of eyes locked onto her in shock as she stood in the doorway:

Ostrac, who was only healing a patient, his hands glowing in a pure white light over the crying woman's ribs.

The crying woman, whose face was deformed and swollen much more than her own ankle with hair black as night and eyes like the Princess.

And a strong looking man dressed in simple merchant's clothing with a warning look spread across his face.

"Sorry, uh, I heard you crying. I wanted to see if you were alright," Estair admitted.

"Oh…" The woman wiped a tear from her face. "I'm fine. Thank you."

"Just wait a moment outside and I can be with you shortly, please," Ostrac said.

The broad-shouldered merchant relaxed his posture and immediately turned back to the woman, unamused by Estair. She gripped the door handle and slowly backed out of the room, closing it. The wall behind her offered to take some of the weight off of her bad foot.

"Who was that?" A male voice sounded through the door. The merchant.

"Her name is Estair, and she is a kitchen servant here. She's kind of my friend." The feeling of the hem of her sleeve between her fingers was rough, and distracting from her embarrassment. "She helped me make that potion for you, Mysarin."

"That's very kind of her." The woman spoke—Mysarin. A name meaning *blessed*. Estair lifted from the wall, deciding she would not eavesdrop on the three, and would simply come back later. She had chores to do anyway.

Watering the gardens was new. And tiresome on her throbbing ankle. She had to walk back and forth from the well and to the gardens, which were entirely too far away from each other, on opposite sides of the castle grounds. Someone dressed in fine clothing had asked her to do so, and no doubt they were told by that bastard who wanted to see her fail. But she grit her teeth through it anyway, happy to spend some time in the sun. It was her third trip back into the gardens when she spotted that velvet black and silken head of hair sitting beneath the grand fountain in the center. A white-haired, pale as death, lunar-elf sat beside her.

Stopping herself, and feeling cool water *slosh* over the edge of her watering can and onto her ankles, she nonchalantly allowed a rose bush to absorb her body just behind Syndra and the elf. Thorns pricked at her skin as she craned her neck to observe the two, wanting to know more about the Princess. That quiet curiosity bloomed deep within her chest as they sat next to each other and did not speak. The elf had his lithe body turning away from Syndra and he stared up into the clear sky. Syndra lazily moved her hand through the shallow water in the fountain.

Esatir's eyes clung to the ivory fingertips that searched for something in the blue waters, disturbing the white diamonds atop the surface and scattering them like syrk: the rat-like pests native to the Twin Islands that would intrude on the sweets Estair would stash in her beloved trees. Syndra hummed to herself until a red-haired and tanned skin Lady passed by wearing a scarlet red gown. Estair's sight trailed the extravagant powder blue embroideries in abstract swirls when Syndra finally spoke.

"What a wonderful dress you have on, Lady…" The Princess leaned forwards to study the pattern.

The woman curtsied. "Lady Amatrous, and thank you, Your Highness. It is an honor to wear something that the Princess deems suitable."

Syndra reached out and grazed her wet hand along the fabric, leaving a trail of where she had touched. The lunar-elf stayed locked in a trance, staring at the sky.

"Don't you think this is lovely, Rio?" Syndra nudged her elbow into his side.

He seemed startled, turning his head to the Princess. "Yes, it is very nice." His accent was thick and his voice was flat.

"Thank you, Prince." Lady Amatrous curtsied again to the lunar-elf, her gaze lingering on his handsome face.

"I would like to have it." Syndra said, commanding the Lady's attention back to her.

"I—I can have another made for you, Princess. It was done in Seawall, freshly made for the games, but I can send a raven." Lady Amatrous began to look around, for anyone near to come to her rescue.

"No. That will not do." Syndra stood, and tilted her head at the woman before her.

She moved with the smoothness of a cat as her hair glistened in the sun, cascading down her back like a waterfall of onyx.

"We look about the same size anyway. I think I shall take yours."

"Syndra…" The lunar-elf started in disapproval.

"I am the Princess to all of Syrelle, am I not? Soon to be Queen? The most important person in all of the realm?"

"Yes, yes, your Highness, whatever you desire. I shall go change and have it sent to your rooms at once." Lady Amatrous curtsied for the third time and then looked to Estair as she raised her body back up. She frowned and then opened her mouth to speak again.

The thorns scratched deeper into Estair's skin as she quickly turned and walked down the path leading deeper into the gardens, praying that she was not seen by Syndra herself. She dumped the rest of her water into a bush of golden Chrysanthemums, before leaving it there and heading straight back to the servants quarters of the castle. The plants had been watered enough. She limped straight to Ostrac's workroom and knocked, hoping he was not busy.

"Come in," he called.

She moved silently, still too embarrassed to make any noise at all, and sat down upon a cot. She breathed heavily and placed her hand upon her chest.

"Are you okay?" Ostrac said as he turned around, and began to reach for the scratches on her arm. His touch was a comfort she didn't know she needed.

She stared at him in silence as he grabbed a tin of that same salve Bea had given her, and began to apply it to her arms. While he was working, the sound of children's laughter flooded into Estair's mind. Suddenly, she was back in Qintra, training in the yard as she heard neighboring children the same age as her playing games of whimsy and imagination. *'She's kind of my friend.'* His words had embarrassed her out in the hall, as if they were said out of pity. Yet now as she heard the souvenir of her childhood spent in solitude, she felt a small smile spread onto her face.

"There is something wrong with my ankle, too."

"Quite the mess you're in, huh?" It was bright in the workroom, light shining in through a window above Ostrac's desk. It cast colorful shadows through the vials he had laying on the window sill. She decided that while Syndra's beauty is like her deepest bruises, his must be those rainbows.

"I hurt it in the tourney," she said. He stopped moving with a glop of salve on his finger.

"You're fighting in the MoonDawn Games?" A look of concern broke his usual mask of calm.

She brought her bravado back to the front, determined to show him that he was not to worry for her.

"I'm going to *win* the MoonDawn Games," she corrected.

He sighed. "Why does everyone I know insist on getting themselves killed?"

24 - Mysarin & Delvuvius

Over the next three days Mysarin had continued to heal her broken ribs with Ostrac. He had told her that while his healing magics could expedite the process, they would have to meet every day for the next week to complete it. Outside of that, her usual routine went on as normal; she awoke to a glamorous spread of nutrient dense foods, she healed with Ostrac, she read sometimes alone and sometimes with Rionaes, and she trained with Del. Today, though, had all been a blur for Mysarin.

The night before she had received another letter that Delvuvius brought from Deime. He stated he was to cater the ball that was to take place in four days—the same royal party that she had met him at all those years ago. It was the mid-point celebration where the castle opened the gates to most of the people in Stonecrest and now he would be working the ball again as Mysarin slipped back into living like a courtesan. The irony of it all had brought tears streaming down her face.

She knew it wasn't just a coincidence that the Loraenars had hired Sea Salt Bakery to cater the event. Somehow, Syndra must've known that they were engaged and likely hired him to unsettle her—a calculated threat. Mysarin knew too well the lengths Syndra would go to maintain control. The guards' steel boots slamming into her ribs were a painful testament to that. If Syndra could do this to her, what would she do to someone she didn't need? The thought of Deime suffering as a way to get to Mysarin tore holes in her gut.

Mysarin now sat in the dark, dreary room she had come to despise, waiting for Del. After he had shared what he found in Syndra's rooms—once Ostrac had healed her enough to where she could speak without pain—they agreed to keep it secret from him and Rionaes. The two had already risked too much.

It was like a tactical game unfolding before her eyes, and there were already too many players, who were all miles ahead of her.

She felt adrift, unsure of what to do, of what was right. Many roads lie ahead, and she had thought back to what Rionaes had said to her once, *"either way something is lost."* She finally understood what he had meant. She needed to get out, get away from Syndra before the Princess could destroy her any further and keep her here past the full moon. If she truly was a beast like the one she saw in her book, she could slaughter the entire castle. But if she were to flee now, what could it mean for Telme? For Del?

And now that Deime was to come here, was to work for Syndra as well—Mysarin couldn't do anything rash. Deime did not have magics, nothing that Syndra seemed to crave, but Mysarin could see him being used against her like a sword.

The right side of her head throbbed, the weight of everything threatened to crush her.

"Mysarin, you look miles better," Delvuvius said, relief sinking into his shoulders and chest. He closed her room door and inspected her face, now mostly returned to its normal state minus a few lightened bruises. "How are you feeling, though?"

"Starting to feel as normal as I can, under the circumstances."

Her headache eased as he pulled her out of a spiral. But the urge to see Deime, the need to protect him from her own fate nagged at her still. The wood on the table was smooth beneath her fingers as she prepared. *Deep breaths*.

"I need you to get me into the ball."

"The MoonDawn Ball? No," he chuckled bitterly as he sat down in front of her. "No, I will not do that."

"Why not?" She knew he was going to argue.

"Because it is the main reason why people from all over Syrelle come here, other than to watch the tournaments. Syndra will be at her most lethal and if she catches you, she will most likely make an example out of you. *All* of the ruling families will be in attendance and she will not do well to look weak or lenient in front of them." He grabbed her hand, stopping her from now scratching at the wood.

"It's not like they would know what's happening and Syndra wouldn't even have to know that I'm there. Please, Deime said he is catering and I need to see him. I need to tell him to leave," she countered.

"No, Mysarin." His eyes darted to the ash in the fireplace as he spoke. "Deime will be fine. What I want to know is why he would even take that job in the first place."

She sighed. "He doesn't get a say, his father still owns the bakery, handles the business. I assume it's because it would be very lucrative for them."

"He can't tell his own father no?"

"This isn't the point!" Mysarin pulled back her hand clenched her fists under the dreadful table she was sitting at.

The air felt thick and suffocating around her. She truly hated every inch of this room.

"I need to tell him goodbye. Tell him to leave so she cannot use him as a pawn in her sick game. I don't want to cause harm to anyone else because of this."

"You are aware you don't have to be the only one who suffers, right? I am here to help you, and Rionaes, and Ostrac, I believe they would help you too. You could run."

Tingles moved their way over her arms. "And endanger more people that I care about?"

Delvuvius pressed his fingers into his brow. "You're being stubborn."

Mysarin continued despite his words. "And if I run I'll still just worry about you and Telme, and now Deime, too. He cannot come with me. And… he cannot *be* with me. It'll never work."

Del paused in shock, his brows shooting up at her words. "Are you… calling off your engagement?"

"I—" Her eyes filled with tears as she realized it. It was her solution to this mess, in order to keep him safe. "I have to."

He was all she had wanted before coming to the castle, even as every part of her screamed that it would only end with his blood on her hands. Now, she was forced to finally make the right decision. The only one that could keep him safe if Syndra were to get any ideas. One day, hopefully, she would be free of Taurean, free of her curse, and she could earn Deime's forgiveness. But it was finally time to face the truth—he could no longer safely remain in her life.

Delvuvius was silent, he only stared at her.

"If I break off my relationship with him, perhaps Syndra will not think to use him against me. To force me to keep doing this for her. I, I don't know. Perhaps it will keep him safe."

"She will still force you to work for her, with or without Deime in play. If she wants to use someone against you, she will only find someone else."

"Not if I'm dead."

"Absolutely not. You are not going to *sacrifice* yourself because of that spoiled rotten bitch."

"What else am I to do?! She will drain me of my very being if I don't do anything, and then I will simply live as a husk for her to exploit until I'm no longer needed. Then what? I live the rest of my days rotting in the dungeons? I refuse to live a life like that, I would rather be dead. And she cannot stop me from doing it."

"And how do you think you'll do that? Huh? Will you take a dagger to your own throat? Bleed out in front of her? Or alone in this room until Telme or I come across your body?"

The harshness of his tone, his anger at her words, hit her like stones. Yet, she continued.

"I'll use her temper against her. I'll out her as a fraud in front of them all, and then she'll likely have me executed right there. Accuse me as an impersonator. Or she'll out me for being cursed. For being a MoonDawn beast. I'm sure that's her plan if I'm ever to disobey." The words left her mouth before she could stop them and she felt her heart jump into her throat.

Del stilled, staring at her with a deep ridge between his brows. She felt as if she couldn't move out from under his gaze.

He looked down at his hands and stood.

Then he walked behind Mysarin, spinning her chair around to face him.

She opened her mouth to take back what she had said, but he held up a finger. She felt his calluses cool her cheeks. They were breath to breath for a moment as he leaned down and stared into her soul.

"Don't ever say that again. Not here," he whispered. "Conjecture like that will get you killed."

Her breathing wavered, her heart close to bursting. It was the closest she had ever gotten to telling someone about what she does under the full moon. She couldn't tell if he took it seriously or not, his face unreadable.

"And as for your little plan," he continued, "it wouldn't work."

"How do you know that?" she asked.

"Because I won't let you."

"You don't get a say."

"I. Don't. Care. I will not let you. I will tell the King about her secrets first like we planned. Don't you remember?"

The aching in her shoulders eased at that—she hadn't even realized they were tensed up. She had forgotten it all, let her despair cloud her thoughts, let the threat of Deime and the entire castle laying dead at her feet seize her mind and send it into oblivion.

"We had a plan. Don't go trying to change it all on a whim because you have a death wish," he said.

Her eyes pricked with tears. She was letting herself be ruled by fear, terrified that those she loved would be taken away from her as they had before.

She almost spilled her one true secret before she even knew what it truly was.

Del softly wiped the tears away from her face as they fell.

"What if the King doesn't care?" she whispered. "What if he already knows and does nothing to stop her, what if he's as vile as she? What will we do then? We would have exposed what we know for nothing, our only advantage. It's such a risk."

"Just, let me handle it. Okay? You have enough to worry about." Del then got down onto one knee before her and she felt a cool breeze upon her cheeks in the absence of his hands, and then he took one of hers.

He sighed.

"I can help you get to Deime at the ball. Maybe I'll let you two even dance. I think you need some fun." He then reached into his pocket and pulled out a silver chain with a large amethyst dangling from it. It had what looked to be a family crest laying upon the stone—an owl head. Yet it was a family emblem she did not know.

"What is that?"

"I swiped it from Syndra's rooms. It works similarly to Ostrac's potion, without the side-effects, when you wear it." His voice had turned soft, gentle.

"Why are you…"

"So you can use it on the day of the ball. Whatever Syndra has you do before the games will likely wipe you out, but later you can wear this, and glamor yourself into someone unrecognizable. I'll escort you to the ball, you can see and speak with Deime, break his heart or whatever you wish to do. And then I will bring you back here as if nothing happened."

"And the King?" she questioned.

"Like I said, let me deal with it."

Del spent the next days training with Mysarin very carefully. She was treading a dangerous line with her mental state, with her injuries, and with her plans. He worried about her every second of the day, praying to Talisi, without any new reply, that she would help the elf through this. He tried to keep that moment when his Deity had finally broken her silence out of his head, because in an instant it had gone back to that painful stillness. He now sat in his room, trying to remember what it had been that sparked a response from Talisi in the first place. Perhaps he could replicate it in some way.

I was in Syndra's rooms and there was a drawing... no, a painting. Umakes help me, why can't I remember anything? It was only a few days ago.

And then like slipping into a slumber, the questioning in his mind had fallen away entirely. He resumed thinking of Mysarin and their current predicament, completely unaware.

In the moments when Del wasn't with her, he plotted ways to tell the King of their findings. And he also couldn't stop himself from thinking about her confession. He'd bite down onto his lip, a queasy feeling in his stomach, as he thought of the words she so carelessly threw out at him.

Was she a MoonDawn beast? Had Bea been killed because of Mysarin?

In sparse seconds, he'd glimpse at her during their training, trying to peer beneath her skin to find the truth. What was even worse, was that he wasn't sure if he could bring himself to turn her in if he found it.

He had to be very careful. He felt like those circus performers he'd seen once as a child, balancing on a tightrope in the same arena that the games were being held. Yet, if he were to fall, there would be no pile of hay to catch him.

All he could do was shove Mysarin's secret down deep inside of him, and focus solely on the one problem he could actually do something about—telling the King about Syndra. He considered bursting into court, revealing everything in front of the entire assembly. The King would have to act—or Fisrolf would throw him in jail for defamation.

Then, he thought perhaps he could spread the secret around the castle through servants until it eventually made its way to the King's ears. It would be a great way to avoid getting caught, but could end up with more servants losing their heads. It was an idea that would hurt too many innocents.

He then thought about the notes exchanged between Syndra and "Z". Perhaps he could go back into her rooms and collect them all, then slide them into a place where the King could find them. Surely he would be upset at the thought of his daughter sharing secret notes and meetings with a man who was not Rionaes, her promised betrothed. But it would be easy to claim that they were doctored, or that it was not Syndra receiving the letters. They were coded enough that it was hard to pin-point who wrote them and what information, exactly, they contained.

But it did spark an even better idea. The simplicity of a note. Del, perched on the edge of his narrow cot, grabbed a quill and parchment, and began to write.

Your sole heir, your only child, is believed to have no magics running through her veins.

The one who has made the grand display is an imposter. It is done only by the will of the Princess.

I implore you to intervene.

Explore her rooms. Go through the flames.

Delvuvius folded the paper and sealed it with wax from a nearby candle. He then tucked the note into the pocket of his trousers, glamored his hair to be red and short to make himself less recognizable, and left his broom closet room. He walked through the castle, all the way to the soldiers' training grounds, while making sure to keep an eye out for Zendar. He needed to make sure no one would notice him.

It was a great, open field on the eastern side of the Taurean Castle grounds, spanning out to the towering walls. Filled with men practicing battle magics and swinging wooden swords at dummies made of burlap and hay, the air hung with the smell of sweat and blood. He kept his head down, posture unsure, to avoid drawing any attention to himself. Seeing his old friends and rivals training stirred a familiar bitterness in Del. His mind swirled with the echoed thought: *I should still be here.*

He shook his head as if to shake the thoughts away. It didn't matter anymore. He looked around until he saw what he was looking for: an ambitious looking young fighter, looking to get ahead and make an impression. He was secluded from the other men, training on his own with a dull sword and a dummy by the wall. So Del walked right up to him with urgency in his movements. He summoned the warmth of persuasion to his throat before he spoke.

"Soldier, I've been told you can be trusted with a pressing task. Is this true?" He lifted his chin and displayed an air of dominance to his presence. As if he was some high ranking commander looking for a grunt to do a job for him.

"Uh. Yes, Sir." The man was tall, a little shorter than Delvuvius, and muscular.

He looked young, his light brown hair cut short to his brow only made him look younger. His blue eyes scanned over Del for any familiarity.

"Forgive me, Sir, but who are you?"

Delvuvius let out a short, sharp laugh. "Someone who outranks you, worm." He leaned in, his voice low and edged with menace. "I suggest you keep track of all those who are above you if you want to succeed."

"Yes, Sir. Sorry, Sir," he replied, without losing any confidence in his stance, though his blotchy skin turned wholly pink in embarrassment. He wondered if this one would make it past the Breaking, make it further than Del had.

"Perhaps I'll find another runt to do this task for me. Someone who deserves it more." Del turned his head towards the rest of the field, as if searching for another inferior to do his work.

"N-no. Please, allow me, Sir. What must be done?"

Del fought the urge to smile at his words. The poor soldier fell right into his trap.

He turned his head back to the human man before him and let out a heavy breath as if to say *'fine, I guess you'll do.'* He reached into his pocket and retrieved the paper from within.

"Take this letter, *do not* open it. Deliver it to the King during court, *discreetly.* Ensure he understands that time is of the essence with this information as well. Do you understand?" He extended the letter and willed his hands to keep still as he waited.

"Yes, Sir, thank you. I will not let you down." The man quickly grabbed the letter and pocketed it. He took a moment though, to stare into Del's glamor as if trying to search past it. Perhaps he could see who lay beneath.

"Well, what are you standing around for? Go, now." Del pointed towards the castle in command as he felt a cool breeze highlight the sweat in his underarms. He finally relaxed when the soldier simply nodded and began to make his way, letting the persuasion magics ease away from his throat.

Step one of Del's plan was complete, but unease gnawed at him. The soldier seemed eager enough, but that alone wouldn't suffice. The king had to take this seriously—or everything would fall apart. Without hesitation, Del moved on to step two.

In the middle of the shopping district, Del set up at his same old spot, smelling the salt of the Fallen Waters on the breeze and enjoying the distant chatter from merchants and peoples amongst him. The orange blooms of Ikaamte hung from the edge, their vibrant color drawing the eye as he began his usual routine—peddling false hope to the desperate. He sold a few elixirs to a woman addicted to Prunn, one to a servant of one of the rich families who lived in the upper parts of the city, five to a fisherman. It wasn't just a usual day for Delvuvius selling his "cure all" though—he wasn't as eager to swindle.

His attention instead had caught itself onto a beggar on the sideline of the large oval shaped area. The beggar was old, haggard, oily, and in a tattered cloak. Her hair was a mess, strands of gray and black intertwined and matted. She used her bony fingers to rattle an old mug at people passing by, and yet she never called out to them as usual beggars do.

In between his persuasions and lies, he studied her. He watched the way her eyes flitted about, accounting for every detail of the people who roamed around. He saw the way she stretched her frail body towards commoners so that they could see her mug, and so she could listen in to what they said.

She was a Voiceless. Another leg of the group of spies who worked for the Loraenars. While the Faceless were the Queen's, the Voiceless were the King's.

Del recalled the whispered tales from his training days—of hidden Voiceless with tongues cut out, ensuring they could never betray the secrets they gathered. And he knew that the

Voiceless on the street posing as a beggar only accepted information in writing.

He continued to watch until the day was close to coming to an end. He saw a guard pass by and open his mouth to the beggar in silent questioning. The woman only opened her mouth in reply, revealing the gruesome state of her black and purple tongue. He passed her a sack of coin, and then moved on with his route.

When the sun began to set and the shadows grew long, Del gathered up half of what he made with his elixirs into a small burlap sack, and added in a copy of the note he had given to the soldier earlier today. He then packed up his displays into his small trunk, and wandered over to the beggar. She was still shaking her mug at the few people leaving the shopping district, and Del made sure he was one of the last to pass her by.

Her fingers were crushed and bent in unnatural ways as they tried to hold onto her mug handle.

He stopped just before her and looked into her fierce glacier blue eyes, and opened his mouth. She did so in response. *I guess she takes information from anyone*, he thought to himself. So, he tossed her his sack of coin concealing his letter and strode his way back up to the lion's den.

25 - Mysarin

"Raise your right arm above your head." Ostrac said while examining Mysarin the day before the next round of the tournaments and the ball.

She raised it without strain, but still felt that sharp sensation pressing in under her right breast.

"And now both arms."

She hissed in pain with them both raised, and flinched back as Ostrac prodded her ribs with his fingers.

"Yep. Still hurts."

He looked up at her over his enchanted lenses that allowed him to see the bone and flesh beneath her skin.

"Sorry, just making sure." He relaxed back into his seat placed before her bed as he crossed his arms over his chest. "You should be fine for tomorrow, just try and take it as easy as you can. Or as easy as Syndra will let you." He then reached down into his leather satchel to retrieve a vial filled with dark brown liquid, and then handed it to her.

"It's not another power boost is it? I don't want to risk stumbling in front of everyone again," she said.

"No, it's just a strong pain alleviator. Take it only after you're done with everything tomorrow. It'll cause you some drowsiness." He handed the vial over before continuing. "And, I'm sorry, about what happened." His eyes dropped away from hers as he spoke, and his body tensed up more than usual.

"It wasn't your fault, you told me the risks and I took the boost knowing them. I needed it anyway."

He absently nodded his head at that, then forced his glance to meet hers again. Those deep mahogany eyes seared into her own. "Are you… are you doing well? Mentally, I mean."

"Do I not seem like my chipper old self?" She tossed a playful wink his way.

"I just… I can't get the way you looked that night out of my head. And Del… I haven't seen him so panicked before." His arms returned to his chest.

She sighed. "I'm okay. I'm better than I was that night, at least."

"Good." He cleared his throat as he stood and took off his magical lenses. "If you need me again though, don't hesitate to call."

He began to pack up his kit into a small trunk like the one Del had used for taking his elixirs and decor to and from the shopping district.

"Ostrac?" she asked.

"Yes?" he replied.

"How do you have time for us all? How do you risk punishment each time you come to our rescue, to heal a non-noble?" Her palms felt slick as she rubbed them against each other.

"I—uh," he took a moment to think, "I may be a Royal Healer, but I believe everyone deserves good health and good care. No matter their standing. I simply make the time, find the way. Try not to stress myself out about it." He stood, trunk fully packed.

"That is very honorable of you. Thank you."

Rionaes came by to share silence as the two read by the fireplace later that night. It had become a ritual of sorts; one of them would end up walking down the dark hallway, burning candle wax in one hand, a book in the other, laying a gentle rap on the other's door.

The fire crackled softly, its warm balm keeping out the chill that had begun to take over the air. Fall was coming. She stared at the image of the werewolf in her book across from Rionaes, hoping he would be too lost in his own world to wonder why she had been reading the same thing every night.

She dropped her eyes back down over the text she must've read hundreds of times by now: *It is speculated that these shapeshifters originated from Pymith, The Huntress, Deity of the Wild, Nature, and Creatures Big and Small. Others believe they were here long before humans and elves, as they were birthed from the misguided magics of the Fey. The cursed elven-like beasts were the first creations of the gods, and were soon left behind for their wild magics and...*

Mysarin's silver eyes slipped off the pages of her book and into the night sky, her focus landing on the white half moon encompassed by gossamer clouds. They looked grayish blue from the cast of her personal clock. The world spilled into a blur around her as she was caught in a trance, as the eternal white light stared back at her.

Rionaes noticed the subtle shift, and began to silently observe Mysarin. She felt his words just behind his lips and yet he didn't dare to break the quiet between them. She almost left it that way, not wanting to threaten the peace between them. Almost.

"What is she like, when she's with you?" Mysarin's words came out softly as she shook off the allure of the moon's presence. She turned to Rionaes to see him wiggle around in his seat.

"It is... not what you would expect," he replied, playing with his white curls. "She seems sometimes torn. Between a Princess, who she is expected to be and... someone else."

"How?" Mysarin scrunched her brows together. Not at all what she was expecting.

"She is demanding. She is obsessed with playing games with others, but sometimes... Sometimes I see her eyes change. After she has won. Perhaps she feels guilty." Rionaes' neck bobbed up and down.

Copper swept over her tongue from her lower lip squished between her teeth. It was hard to hear that perhaps her enemy was more human than she thought. She dared to ask more, needing to know the full truth. "Have you seen her in any of your dreams?"

"Yes," he said quietly.

"And what does she do?" Her hands gripped her book a little harder, turning her fingertips white.

He studied Mysarin's face before answering, eyes darting back and forth between her own.

"She waters her plants, she stares out into the gardens, she screams in fear from ghosts, she lays awake at night. Alone. All of it alone."

Mysarin snickered at that.

"But she also tortures those she deems less worthy. She sets fires to small villages. She kills the silver wolf, over and over."

Her mocking smile vanished as quick as it appeared. "Have your dreams ever been wrong?"

"I have deciphered their meaning incorrectly, but… there is always a truth to be found."

A tremor passed through her as she recalled the reason for Rionaes's visit to Syrelle.

"Do you still plan on marrying her?"

"I believe I must."

"I'm sorry," she whispered.

Rionaes shrugged his shoulders in resignation rather than acceptance. "It is duty. I am Prince of Oswes. There is no marriage for love." His eyes grew softer as he spoke the last few words, his head turning to the blazing fire.

"If you could choose another destiny—if you weren't born as royalty—what would you be?" She thought of the painted ceiling in his room as she studied his delicate fingers. *Perhaps he would be an artist.*

"I—" He jumped in his seat and looked over his shoulder at nothing before he could say more. His cheeks turned pink as he bashfully laughed to himself about his behavior. "I would be anything if it did not involve that."

26 - Delvuvius, Mysarin, & Estair

Delvuvius had heard nothing about whether the King had received his letters or not. Yet, he didn't quite expect to. He knew that whether or not the King took the information seriously, he would be sure to keep the entire thing quiet. If the information got leaked to the other powerful families, especially while they were here in Stonecrest, it could result in a full on war.

Which is what brought Del to the games today.

He paid his five gold to the guards at the door and found a perfect seat up in the bleachers, right behind the Chaehora family. It was a terrible seat from a spectators standpoint, offering a limited view of the arena thanks to the Seawall banner placed directly in front of him. But he wasn't here to watch the fighting— his eyes were on the real battle unfolding among the Stonecrest court.

In his pocket he had two more handwritten notes, both containing the same words that were passed to the King. If Del

needed Fisrolf to take the information seriously, then he needed to
turn up the heat. Raise the stakes. And what better way to do that
than to give that very sensitive information to the hands of the only
family who could take down the Loraenars.

But he had to be discreet. And so for now, he sat, and
waited for the games to begin.

Mysarin's morning was the same today as it was a week ago.
Guards bombarded her, forcing her to bathe in front of them.
Except today, they threw a new dress at her. Telme came in again
to help her get into it and paint her face. Mysarin wondered if
Syndra was different around Telme—if the auburn-haired woman's
motherly instincts extended to the Princess, turning her more
gentle in the handmaiden's presence.

The dress was a deep shade of phoenix red, and a little too
small on Mysarin's curvy body. There were delicate embroideries
of abstract swirls and mazes on the skirts in an airy shade of
powder blue that reminded Mysarin of the sky on a clear day. The
neck was low, showing off any cleavage and leaving Mysarin
feeling exposed. A scream trapped itself in her throat as she
noticed a guard's eyes inspecting her chest when she was finished
putting it on. At least there were long sleeves.

She was rushed from her rooms, and in the chaos of
ushering Mysarin out, she was able to quickly swipe the amulet
Del had given her from under her pillow. She felt the sudden
expansion of magics deep within her as the lumpy silver poked at

her breasts inside of her corset. Either not one of the six guards seemed to notice, or they simply didn't care that she grabbed a necklace to take with her.

The walk from the empty castle to the arena was unchanged, with guards encircling her to shield her from prying eyes. Mysarin focused on her breathing the entire way. She begged herself not to puke again, to just do what she had to do today and get through it. And then later she would make her way to the ball. She would see Deime again, possibly for the last time.

Mysarin knew what she would do. She would let go of her dreams of a simple life, and thus, let go of Deime. She wasn't good for him and she never would be, no matter how much that realization had broken her heart.

"Hm, that dress looks a little small on you." Syndra's eyes surveyed Mysarin's body as she spoke in the stable off to the side of the arena.

Mysarin resisted the urge to roll her eyes.

"You can change into me now," Syndra said.

"Yes, your Highness." Mysarin began the change; pins and needles tingled along her skin, the smell of roses filling the air as the glamor magics wrapped its way around her body, squeezing and reshaping.

Once it was completed, she still felt plenty of magics left in her veins. It was strange. Not only did the hidden amulet offer her more power, but she had been training relentlessly with Del— she had also gotten stronger. Her mind jumped to the first time she had transformed into Syndra, how drained she felt immediately afterwards. Now, she felt she could do it ten more times.

The power of that knowledge—of all that she could do simply if she wished it—felt *good*.

"Today is more basic elemental stuff. Should be easy, if you practiced everything I underlined in that book," Syndra explained. "You'll go out and set a wall of hay ablaze, and then summon a wave to extinguish it."

Syndra snapped in front of the face that was the reflection of her own.

"Pay attention."

"I am," Mysarin said before checking her tone. Her eyes flicked over to the guards, seeing if they had bristled.

Syndra snickered. "You're getting good at pretending you're me," she walked towards Mysarin and lowered her voice, "but I still know that you're just a whore."

Mysarin kept her mouth shut as she heard the blood rush into her ears. She held Syndra's stare. Her teeth ached, a flicker of anger flashing in her eyes. She imagined flames licking up Syndra's self-satisfied smirk.

"Just don't fall this time, or you'll end up worse than before." Syndra reached out to Mysarin's chin and turned her face over, examining it.

More power plays. Any way the Princess could find to display the command she held over others, she would use. She was insecure, an heir to a throne she did not deserve, could not protect. Mysarin saw every hidden wound Syndra had disguised.

She lifted her own hand and gently removed Syndra's from her face as she held her stare.

"I won't." Last week she had gotten too arrogant, but now, with the necklace, she knew she had the real power here.

Syndra's eyes lit up in shock, so quick that Mysarin thought that she imagined it, and then settled back into her usual glare. She then smiled her usual goading grin.

"Good."

Mysarin turned and led herself to the door where she would wait. The bells would ring any second.

She was desperately trying to play it cool, but the move she just made—*touching* the Princess—made her feel the gag rising in her throat. She felt all the eyes on her back as she stood there, counting down the seconds. She was sure Syndra was fuming. She wanted to look, to see the crack in her fine porcelain skin.

The bells sang their foreboding song as Mysarin was about to break and turn around.

She sucked down a deep breath of air and made her way to the platform above the arena. Her eyes scanned the same few faces in the crowd as last time, marking all of the noble families. She smiled Syndra's signature evil smirk at them as she waved. Turning around she saw the King, the Queen, and Rionaes sitting next to an empty seat nearby. His lips turned upwards when they locked eyes.

The crowd was screaming for her at that same incredible volume, and instead of feeling all of the pressure of this performance weighing her down, all Mysarin felt was the immense power roiling inside of her. Instead of a glass of water, her magics was a lake. She faced the twenty foot hay wall and began to gather up her strength.

The elemental magics burned at her fingertips, searing its way up her arms and into her core, until she was living flame. The heat clung to her, fueled her, before she thrust the magics forward, sending a stream of fire into the wall, engulfing it entirely. The smell of burning hay filled her nose. The crowd gasped, some jumped in their seats, a few screams rang out.

Mysarin smiled—a genuine smile—at what she had done. At what she was still *doing*. The flame that erupted from her had climbed to the height of the wall, and then it kept going higher and higher.

Mysarin saw the oranges and reds swirling together, reaching above the height of the hay as she tried to pull back. She tugged on her connection to the roots, struggling to reign it in. But there was no use; it had become its own being, with its own will. Droplets of sweat upon her forehead broke the heat from the wall, and she felt the metal of the amulet between her breasts start to burn.

The fire raged. Higher. Hotter. Uncontrollable. And then— a breath. A thought of cool waters, and the magics shifted.

She tried to remind herself of the scent of the sea, of the salt in the air in the shopping district. Of the sound of the waves that splashed against the cliffs when Del had taken her to see Deime. The grotesque taste of raw element. She felt her temperature drop drastically. Felt the silken water magics take over her body, letting it glide its way along her skin. Her arms dropped to her sides before she slowly raised them up, a wave of water forming before her.

It climbed up, up, up, and then Mysarin sent it crashing down onto the wall of fire, splashing herself and everyone in the first few rows of the arena. Cool steam brushed her cheeks as droplets of water fell onto the face that was not her own.

Everyone stood to clap, to cheer, to scream Syndra's name. And Mysarin remembered herself. Her eyes frantically searched the crowd, scanning the faces that cheered not for her. She waved to them all, trying her best to continue playing her role. Her heartbeat began to pump loudly in her ears, and she felt hot with rage. Her nostrils flared thinking about how she was able to do all of that, and yet the glory of it was not hers.

She turned to leave when her eyes snagged on Del.

She could only see part of him—most of his body was covered by the golden banner of Seawall. But she could see him clapping wildly and his face full of pride. She relaxed a bit, smiled at him and at him only, before she lifted her chin high and escorted herself back into the small building where Syndra resided. At least he would know.

If Del hadn't needed to be covert for his secret mission, he would've been cheering louder than everyone here combined. Mysarin had glowed during her performance. She had turned that entire wall to ash upon the ground and soaked about half of the people here. It was incredible to see. Incredulous to think that she could do such a thing without undergoing the Breaking, even with the amulet.

He was struck with awe while he watched her make her way out of the arena. He realized that all of the worrying he had been doing about her was for naught, that she was growing into someone who could hold their own. She was truly transforming, and he wished he could run down there to be with her, to witness her blossom—

He paused, frowning.

If she was so powerful, and also monstrous, he should feel much more concerned. But something about his fear of her had shifted into something else entirely. It felt like his admiration of the gods. It felt like loyalty.

The crowd was still standing and chanting for Syndra, and his fingers shook slightly as he reached into his pocket. Fumbling around for the slip of paper, eyes remaining on the wet ash in the middle of the arena, he grabbed one and brought it up into his clapping hands. Casually, he let go of it when he drew his hands apart, letting it fly away towards the middle of the Seawall crowd. He kept his face straight ahead as it soared, as if he was unaware.

Out of the corner of his eye he watched his folded up parchment land in the hood of a blonde elf's cloak.

Estair descended into the familiar, damp, cave-like room beneath the arena, awaiting her fight. She grabbed the same armor and twin swords that she wore in the previous battle and sat to watch the only other person in the room with her—the gray-skinned red-haired elf. He must've killed the man that reminded Estair of The Golden Elf. She wondered if they would be fighting today, or if she would finally get to see who else waited for her in the other room under the arena.

"Your fight was the quickest one of the day, last week," said the strange looking elf. "I wonder if you'll be so lucky again." Airy pitch and distinct pronunciation made his words sound like honeyed-venom.

Estair stared into his cerulean eyes, saying nothing.

"Oh, where are my manners?" He displayed those same elongated canines as the other gray-elves had, feinting a smile. Estair knew, though, that he was simply baring his teeth. "I'm Zanira Fethe, a soldier from the Northern Reach."

He then bowed his head to Estair as she crossed her arms, the same hay bale feeling lumpy under her behind. When she still did not deign to respond, Zanira continued:

"I wasn't able to watch your fight, unfortunately. Though I wish I had. I'd love to know how you took down Dasra. I'd heard stories about him even all the way in the Reach. He was a skilled warrior, known to take down a few minotaurs in his day. They even said he helped to kill the Danai family all those years ago."

He turned to pick out his same spear and shield as he spoke.

"I guess retirement dulled his edge. I heard he traded his sword for a fishing rod after meeting his wife. They mated, you know, under the eyes of Talle. So sad, she has to spend the rest of her life without her one and only. It's so rare to find those nowadays, too."

A pang of guilt pierced her like an arrow as she thought of Dasra's wife, but she quickly buried it, her expression unyielding.

"Still nothing, huh?" Zanira turned back to look at her. He twirled his spear in his hand again as he stared her down. A thought visibly crossed his mind just before he threw it at a target near her head. Estair felt the air move through her hair, heard a whistle above her, and knew without looking that it struck true in the center of the red bullseye.

She tensed. "I'll rip those dog teeth out of your skull."

Zanira smiled in satisfaction when he walked over to retrieve the spear. He leaned down to whisper in her ear as he did, "I hope I get to fight you today. What a pleasure it would be to see you bleed."

Estair debated on killing Zanira right there. It would be easy to break apart his spear and use the pointy end to stick into his sky blue eyes.

Instead she remained where she was and began to sharpen her swords with a whetstone. He went on smiling to himself as he sat and ate an apple, still staring at her from across the room. She continued on ignoring his obnoxious chewing when The Golden Elf walked in.

"The girl will go first again today," he claimed from just beyond the threshold.

"And will we be fighting one another? I want to know what her screams sound like." Zanira never broke his stare as he spoke.

The Golden Elf laughed. "Don't we all." Estair looked up at him with rage on her face at that. "Come, girl, it's almost your time."

Estair silently got to her feet, throwing the whetstone at Zanira. She heard a growl rip from him as she followed The Golden Elf. The sound made a smile spread across her lips. The two walked the stone stairs up to the gate of the arena, and The Golden Elf left her standing behind it as he went through a small wooden door to the other side.

This time, she listened in on whatever the elf was shouting at the crowds from the platform.

"Today is the midpoint tournament of the annual games. Twenty years ago, King Fisrolf was one week into battle with the Danai family." He paused to let the crowd cheer. His face was smug as he looked around at the people in the arena, and then he held up a hand to shush them before he continued. "Many men had been lost on both sides, but today was the day that Marista Danai, the MoonDawn Queen, gave her life for her family. She appeared in front of the Loraenar ranks in her beastly form to fight amongst the first line.

"But she was no match for our army. Men came together to take her down with their battle magics, and I was one of them." The crowd cheered yet again. He waited for them to quiet down on their own this time, letting them scream on. "I was the one who dealt that killing blow with one of my golden arrows. I shot it directly into her heart, ending her terrifying reign. The battle was won after that, and though we still had a war ahead of us, we celebrated that night. And that is what we will do again, here, tonight! We will continue to celebrate our victory over Stonecrest, and continue to celebrate the end of the MoonDawn curse! And we will do so for years to come!" He was yelling now while the crowd roared. "And with that, let the second round of tournaments begin!"

27 – Estair, Mysarin, & Delvuvius

Estair finally learned her enemy's name as the gates opened and she walked out onto the arena ground. The crowd chanted "*Zendar*" over and over. She didn't even pay attention to whoever was entering the arena on the other end as she stared up at him, still on the platform. He stared right back at her with that slimy smile still on his lips.

She smelled ash, and the ground was like mud when she looked down at her feet. A burst of air knocked her back, and she landed on her arse. The mud was sticky—a thick paste that slowed her down and grabbed at her feet like a thousand hands. But that meant it would slow down her opponent as well. She looked up and got her first glance at the man.

He was tall and slender, with long auburn hair flowing down his heavily armored back. He wore a matching silver helmet with two great horns, and through it, Estair could see his glowing yellow eyes. He had no weapons with him and as Estair was trying to search for one, he lifted his hand up to the sky and brought it down fast in a fist to his chest. The crowd was silent, and all that could be heard was a shrill tone ringing out through the air.

Estair scanned the crowds; they were all looking up at the clouds, and before she could follow their line of sight, a glowing yellow sword fit for a giant slammed into the ground before her. She screamed as the impact reverberated in her teeth, and all around the arena, causing the crowd to go insane. Soft earth wedged its way under her nails and between her fingers. She shook off the vibrations in her bones and scrambled to her feet. The man's eyes grew brighter as he retrieved his sword, as it flew in the air until it landed in his outstretched hand. It was twice the size of him, and yet he held it like it weighed nothing.

Because it was only magics.

Estair, wet with mud, made to advance when the battle mage flung out his magics at her again. The sword made a high pitched shriek as it came through the air and swiped at her midsection. She bent her knees to jump, but the thousand hands grabbed onto her feet, keeping her grounded, and she fell onto her backside again. The crowd erupted into laughter as the sword made its way back to the mage's hands.

Then Estair felt it.

Burning, searing pain ripped across her flesh. The side of her armor on her stomach was sliced open, shredded. Her skin beneath bubbled with black pus, boils spreading where the sword had touched her. She held her second scream in as she rose again, using her swords as leverage. The man raised the sword up above his head as he faced the crowd, egging them on. She tried to run while he was distracted, slowly dashing behind him. But it was like he knew where she would be.

In the blink of an eye, he whipped around and thrust his magics towards her, letting the sword leave his hands again. She intersected her own two swords and caught the attack in the cross. Her side shot daggers of pain up her ribcage as she tossed his sword away. It soared through the air, singing its dreadful song, until it hit the arena's stone walls, creating a deep crack. The entire place rumbled again as the crowd screeched. *Not* made *of magics, just surrounded by magics*, she thought, *that's good. I can work with that.*

While the mage was unarmed, Estair advanced toward him. He reached out his hand to summon the blade back to him as she sent herself into his direction. He stood with full confidence, hand waiting patiently for the return, shining hair caressing his silver armor, when Estair reached him. She swung her left sword at his head and he moved like silk to avoid it. Then while he danced, she swung her right with full force, stinging her midsection again. His helmet rang out like a bell upon impact, causing him to stumble. Estair made to advance when she heard the sharp whistle again coming from behind her. She careened to the side before her knees hit the mud.

The yellow sword returned to his hand for only a second before he hurled it back into the sky. Estair staggered to her feet, eyes following the blade's ascent. A sudden gust of wind hit her wounded side, tearing through her concentration. It pressed against her boils, forcing a scream from her throat as they burst, releasing a stream of black pus that seared her skin further. Despite the agony, she managed to stay upright, gripping her swords—planted firmly in the mud—for support as the force of the wind threatened to knock her down.

The violent song drew close, and Estair quickly used her magics to create a shield of water to surround and encompass her.

The mage's magics sliced through it, against all odds.

It brushed past her arm, creating more boils against her skin. She winced at the pain as she held up her shield and then drew in an unsteady breath. With the mud and against this strange form of magics, she knew she wouldn't win this on strength and speed alone. She needed an advantage.

That's when she noticed that the yellow sword's light began to fade behind her water barrier. She heard pounding against the shield echoing around her, from his fists or spells, she was unsure. The opaque water raging around her blocked her sight. She couldn't see what he was doing.

And he could not see her, or his sword.

The light began to dim more and more the longer she held her shield up, but she hadn't undergone the Breaking. Her magics was about to run out. She had to think fast.

His eyes glowed with the same shade of yellow. She smiled to herself as she let her shield down, letting the mage finally summon his sword once again. The color of his eyes and sword glowed bright as they were reunited.

Mysarin shifted back into her own skin once she returned to the stables where Syndra waited. She continued to stand tall, only feeling a slight fatigue from her performance when she would otherwise feel completely drained. She locked eyes with the Princess, and then bowed.

"You've improved," Syndra said, her words clipped. "I'm impressed you did all of that without any Breaking."

"I've been training everyday." Mysarin lifted her head to meet Syndra's cold, hard, stare. Her jaw and fists were clenched, her eyes glowing with the same sort of rage Mysarin had felt earlier, when the magics was still rising within her blood. She bit her lip as she wondered if Syndra knew about the amulet, if she noticed it was missing.

"It would seem so." Syndra's lips were tight as she continued on. "Well that's all I need you for. Someone will retrieve the dress from you later, I can't wear it now that it's soaked." The guards moved to grab Mysarin, to bring her back to her room the same way she was brought here.

Their cold metal hands gripped onto her arms and they surrounded her. Mysarin turned back to see Syndra staring at herself in the reflection of a mirror nearby. She released a breath, thankful there were no more questions regarding her strength today.

Del was entranced as he watched the first round of the games. He was still thinking about Mysarin's performance and now desperately trying to get a look at who was fighting in the arena.

He had heard of the man before—Garlin Zraxoy, a member of the noble family that oversaw Synsee—but the woman… She seemed familiar. He racked his brain on where he'd seen her before while she continued the outstanding battle against the mage. Garlin—who trained among the best magics wielders in Synsee at the Institute of Magics and possessed a bloodline that harnessed and enhanced the sea-striker's acidic magics—was a fierce warrior. Del was stunned by how the woman had gotten this far.

Caught up in the fight, Del nearly forgot his mission. He reached into his pocket for the letter as the Chaehoras were also engrossed in the battle. Discreetly, he dropped it on the floor near the seats occupied by the noble family and used his foot to nudge it forward. All while he kept his eyes fixed on the water shield the woman had summoned.

The letter landed a few rows down by the feet of another Chaehora. They looked down in confusion and picked it up to read it. Garlin threw spell after spell against the shield with no gain. Whispers spread among the crowd, with the name *"Syndra"* echoing repeatedly.

Estair was biding her time, trying to reserve her energy for the right moment. The mage lashed out with his glowing blade again, standing still in the mud as he maneuvered with his magics. Estair tried to dodge out of the way, and that vile magics chased the skin of her ankles. Another slice, more boils and pus, more daggers as she moved. A bark of pain erupted from her throat. She started to feel lightheaded, the world beginning to spin.

She slipped on the mud again, barely catching herself as the mage's laughter wormed into her ears. *It needs to be soon.* But he was taking his time with her, taunting her. The next time he whipped his sword at her, she moved just a little too late, allowing the yellow sword to slash her again. Blood and pus oozed down her chest just below her neck. The air grew thicker, her lungs drew breath slower, and Estair dropped to her knees before the mage. He slowly walked toward her with his glowing eyes only growing in intensity.

He looked to the crowd with his arms spread wide once he was a few feet before her. The crowd cheered yet again, louder than it had been before—they were thirsty for blood.

But so was she.

He sent his sword high up into the air, and Estair watched as it soared, gasping for air on her knees. Once it was out of sight, she looked at him and let her smile show. He hadn't noticed her hands submerged in the sticky and thick mud, and was too slow to move when she threw it into his eyes.

He staggered back, and before he could simply wipe it away, Estair summoned her flame—the last bit of her magics—to surround it. To cement and meld it with his helmet, creating a clay shield that blocked his vision. Then she got up from her knees and dragged her feet behind the mage as he scratched at the clay visor. She heard the singing of the blade again as it flew down towards the earth, headed for where she was kneeling.

Estair raised her leg and kicked him face first into the spot where her knees were planted, right as the mages own sword came down and crashed into the back of his armor, piercing through it. He was still alive, impaled by his own weapon, as the glow began to fade for good. Yet, it wasn't before the acid of the blade melted the armor surrounding it and exposed the skin of his back. The smell of melting flesh, toasty and ripe, filled the air. Estair walked over and struck her own sword right into where his heart would be, before she collapsed to her knees from the exhaustion.

The crowd exploded again, and Estair knew that they would start chanting *her* name this time if only they had known it. She looked up to Zendar still watching from above, and by the look on his face, he knew it too.

Del cheered along with everyone else, besides the Chaehora's, who were caught up in the information he had dropped into their hands. He looked over to the woman whose hood his first letter landed into, and noticed it now missing. His mission was complete, and he didn't care to watch the rest of the battles now that the woman was done fighting for the day, so he easily slipped out of the arena among the chaos.

He made his way back to his room in order to get prepared for the ball, and to prepare himself to escort Mysarin to see Deime.

Mysarin was having her own celebration back in her room. She opened a bottle of wine that she had a servant grab for her, as she changed into one of her own dresses. She chose her nicest gown, besides the one Rionaes had made for her. It was a hunter green shade with minor black embroideries along the edges. Nothing extravagant, but it was well fitted with long flowing sleeves.

She kept the amulet on, showing it off like a Lady with her fine jewels. She knew taking it off would result in her feeling drained rather than slightly fatigued, and she needed to make it to see Deime. She swept up her hair into a pile atop her head before glamoring it into a sandy blonde shade. She changed her olive skin into a golden tan, and shifted her eyes to a chocolate brown. Her nose was adjusted into a slightly longer shape, with a bend in the middle and she shrank her mouth down to a smaller pout.

In the mirror, her eyes drifted to the amulet, and she knew she would have to hide it in case Syndra noticed her at the ball. So she experimented. Mysarin had never tried to glamor an object, let alone one that contained its own magics, but she thought to herself *how different could it be?*

She started with the silver owl's head emblem on the front of the amethyst, trying to shift it into a more simple shape—a heart. She struggled for a moment, letting her glamor magics poke and prod around the intrinsic magics of its own. She searched around for holes that allowed her to get past its barricade of protection as she sipped at her wine.

Finally, she found a space to slip past and was able to alter the owl into a heart, and the stone into a black one to go with her dress. She looked into the mirror and smiled at her own reflection, ready to have a little bit of fun for the first time in what felt like years.

Perhaps with this amulet, she wouldn't need to break off her engagement with Deime—she felt as if she could level this entire castle if Syndra so much as dared to threaten her beloved. And perhaps, more magics meant she would be able to prevent herself from shifting into a beast.

28 - Mysarin & Estair

Del arrived around sunset, and Mysarin opened her door with a smile spread wide across her face. Their eyes both lit up with shock at the appearance of the other. Del took in Mysarin's glamor while she enjoyed the view of him in his tailored all black outfit.

"What is this?" she asked, soft cotton gliding smoothly beneath her hand.

The tunic and matching pants were similar to what he usually wore, except they fit his body exceptionally well, showing off the curves and contours that prove he would do well in battle. She inched her face closer, noticing the dark hunter green embroideries of what looked to be lightning bolts and storm clouds along the sides.

"Del... We are matching."

"Well, would you look at that!" He laughed as he ran his fingers through his long, dark chestnut hair that he wore undone for the first time Mysarin had seen.

The soft waves framed his chiseled jawline and contrasted against his light golden tanned skin.

"And you look… well you look nice but it's not the same when it's not *you*," he said.

She barely registered his words as she stared. With his hair down the amber in his eyes seemed to pop even more, taking over the spots of dark green. She thought he looked rather… Princely.

"I guess us matching works in our favor, I can pose as your date for the night." She winked at him.

"Excellent idea." His cheeks turned slightly pink as he extended his elbow to her. "Shall we go then? It starts soon."

She nodded her head as she linked her arm into his and made way to the ballroom in the center of the castle grounds.

The ballroom was similar to the rest of the castle with its dark and extravagant decor; the walls were black and gray with gaudy gold trim; the floor was a deep red marble with busy light gray rugs lain beneath long mahogany tables; and the paintings hung on the walls were larger than three of Mysarin's length all stacked on top of one another. When she had first arrived at the castle, she had felt inspired from all of the colors and ornate details thrown about, but now, after living here for a few weeks, she despised it all.

The one thing about the space that Mysarin could stand to look at was the open ceiling, allowing full view of the stars beginning to sparkle in the purple and orange sky. Inside of these walls, it was a dark dungeon, but out there, it looked like freedom.

"I don't see Deime yet," Del whispered to her side, bringing her back to reality.

"I guess we can enjoy ourselves until he comes around. Shall we get something to drink?" She eyed a table filled with golden goblets containing more wine.

Del followed her eye line and that mischievous half-smirk spread across his face. "Lead the way."

The two walked arm in arm to the table to help themselves to small confectionaries and the delicious cherry wine. Mysarin softly moaned with pleasure at the taste of it, savoring the warmth it brought to her stomach and the calming of her nerves. She looked around at all the people now entering the ballroom, examining their fanciful dresses and sparkling jewels, her eyes scanning the crowd for any signs of Deime.

Her gaze halted upon seeing Rionaes and Syndra enter the room. The wine in her belly began to whirl. *No,* she thought to herself, *stay focused.* Whispers took over the room at the sight of the Princess, and Mysarin strained her ears trying to make out what the people were saying.

"Looks like the party has finally started," said Del from behind her. "I may have set a few things in motion earlier today."

She whipped her head around to look at that fox-like twinkle in his eyes.

"What did you do?"

"I made sure the King will hear us." His eyes scanned the room. "I need to—"

Wonderful, swelling, music started to play, cutting off what Del was saying. People around joined hands and began to dance as if it were a routine, and he turned back to look at her. That same look filled his face as he offered her a hand.

"What would you say to a dance while we wait?"

She looked him up and down, feeling the suspicion fix onto her face. "I'm not too sure…"

"Oh c'mon. It's considered impolite at these things to skip the first dance of the night."

It was true. As a courtesan she had danced with a stranger that night wishing the whole time she'd had the nerve to ask Deime. She scanned the room once again for her favorite elf, and when he was nowhere to be seen, she silently placed her hand into Del's.

"You better not step on my toes," she said.

"I'm actually quite good at dancing, but thank you for your faith," he teased.

He led her out into the center of the floor as her heart beat in time with the music. Violins inflated and horns hummed. Del placed one hand gently on the small of her back. He lifted hers to the sides of their faces and began to guide her in a sway. They went forwards, and backwards, then twirled around as they stepped to the side. She couldn't stop the giggle that left her mouth as he lifted her for the spin.

"Wow, you weren't lying. For once." Up this close, he smelled faintly of a warm spice—clove.

He squinted at her. "Ouch. Don't you remember that I have feelings, too?"

He released his arm around her as he took a step back, and lifted their hands above her head, spinning her. Her feet slid with ease across the marble flooring, reading what he planned to do. She thought of their bickering like a dance of its own—there were two parts to play, and they seemed to read every intention of the other as a new move was made.

"How could I forget?" She stepped back into his large chest, feeling his sturdy body against her own. "You never fail to remind me. Matter of fact, you never forget to say *everything* that's on your mind at the moment."

"I'll have you know that there is *plenty* that I do not share with you." He brushed away a bit of hair that fell into her eyes during the spin with the warm pad of his thumb.

Her breath left her from his much-too-intimate gesture, and at how easily it came. "Oh please, like what?"

His eyes turned serious. He looked like he was internally debating himself as they went around in another circle. Yet, when he opened his mouth to speak, she felt her back bump into someone else's. She turned around to apologize, and immediately pushed herself away from Delvuvius. It was Deime she had run into. And he was dancing with Yrana.

Estair desperately needed a healer when she was done with her fight to cure the gashes and boils, and the burn marks they left behind. Hobbling her way through the now quiet hallways, she made her way to Ostrac's workroom. He greeted her with few words, and went silent as he got to work. Which she was thankful for—she was much too tired for chatting. He tended her wounds quickly with ointments and a white glowing from his hands, but she had quite a few to be healed. She was told that as a fighter, it was mandatory to attend the party that was to take place tonight, yet the healing was taking so long she thought she might miss it all together.

"Almost finished." The first words he had spoken in the few hours he had worked. Estair frowned at him. "What, you want to be here all night?"

"I'd rather be here than the party. What am I supposed to do there? I don't know anybody." She fiddled with the white linen on the cot beneath her. Large crowds, dancing, small talk—it made her feel strange. She wasn't afraid, she was just better when there was no talk to be made, with a sword in her hand. Perhaps, that's why she never had many friends.

"You let the noble families leer at you. Some may ask about your previous battles. Some may want to bed you," he said as he pressed his hands over the boils on her leg. She winced at the pressure for a moment, and then felt instantly relieved when the white light of his magics mingled with the herbal paste he had spread over the area.

"Now I *really* don't want to go." She watched him remove his hands to reveal clean, supple skin.

"Don't you have anyone there you'd like to see?" he asked.

"No." His mahogany eyes dropped to her hand still fiddling with the blanket. She went still.

He looked up to her with an odd look in his eyes, something like pity resided there. Her shoulders slumped.

"Well, I'll be there, and I can help you fend off the unwanted attention from the noble families. I need a date anyway." He offered his hand to her. It was still covered in the medicinal paste, yet she shook it anyway. She didn't want his pity, but she thought it would be nice to know *someone* if her attendance was required. Plus, he himself had said they were friends now.

"Not a date," was all she said back. At least she knew he would be comfortable sharing a silence with her. Perhaps she would get to see that lovely woman, no, the *Princess*, again. And get a look at whomever stood in her way from winning the entire tournament. After today, it would be her and one other opponent. She wondered if it would be Zanira, or if his arrogance had gotten him killed.

The door to Ostrac's workroom opened, and standing there was another Royal Healer by the look of his uniform clothing, matching with Ostrac's. The Stonecrest bullhead seal seared its beady eyes into Estair's as the older man with graying hair stood in the doorway.

"I, uh, I came to speak with you about the King. He has need for us on the morrow." His green eyes darted back and forth between Ostrac and Estair. Ostrac's body had gone completely still, his face remaining stone. "It seems you are busy, though. I shall meet with you later."

"Thank you, Inamon." Ostrac's voice sounded strained. Monotone and similar to when he spoke of the girl he had watched die before his own eyes. Inamon then took one last look at Estair, at the fighting leathers she had still worn from her battle, and then at the medicinal herbs and paste on the table close to them. He left and closed the door quietly behind him.

"Inamon won't say anything. He understands," Ostrac said, mostly to himself.

29 – Delvuvius & Estair

Delvuvius felt his face burn. He'd gotten too carried away, dancing with Mysarin like she wasn't here to see Deime. And now there the man was, oblivious of this indiscretion *and* the one from the tunnels.

"Oh, my apologies," he said as Mysarin just stood and stared, mouth agape. Either she forgot that she did not look like herself, or she was shocked to see Deime with what looked to be a courtesan by the way her dress cut incredibly low on her chest. Del wasn't sure what to make of the two himself. Yes, it *was* impolite to sit out the first dance of the evening, and he didn't take Deime for an impolite man, but he could only imagine what was going through Mysarin's head at the moment. Yet, she had just been doing the same with him.

"Yrana?" she asked.

"I'm sorry, do I know you?" The courtesan with deep golden skin and tightly wound curls replied, her hand moving dangerously low on Deime's back.

"I-I know his betrothed. Mysarin. She's told me about you." Del held his breath as Mysarin shot daggers from her eyes when she turned back to Deime.

"Is she here? I was hoping I could see her," Deime said, finally releasing Yrana from his grip.

"No. She wasn't allowed to come." Mysarin's words were laced with resentment as she spoke. She turned around to grab Del's hand and dragged him off the dance floor. He made a wave to Deime as they headed back to the drink table, watching him wave back in confusion.

She reached for another goblet of wine and drank the entire thing in one go. Then began pacing. Del wasn't sure if he should say anything to her, if he should point out that they were just doing the same thing she caught Deime doing. That it wasn't a big deal.

He opened his mouth to say as much when she put up a hand to silence him.

"I know."

"Then why are you so upset?" He reached for her hand, grazing the smooth gold of the new goblet she was bringing up to her lips. She turned that angry look on him.

"I don't know! I just… Leave me be for a moment. Let me sort myself out." She downed the wine.

"Are you sure now is the best time for that?"

She laughed bitterly as the dancing came to an end around them. "I'll be fine. Go do whatever it is that you need to. I'll be here."

He simply nodded his head and slithered his way through the crowd of noble families and commoners alike, hanging onto every softly spoken word. Trying to ignore the drum in his chest. The news of his letter was spreading. Soon, the King would be forced into action, Mysarin would be set free, and the weight that had been pressing in on his chest would be lifted. Del brought with him more copies of the incriminating note, in case it was not enough that the Chaehora's knew, but it would seem that the people of Seawall liked to talk. He fought the urge to smile as he continued to listen in on the quiet conversations that were spreading like wildfire.

"Did you hear about Syndra Loraenar?" was commonly spoken amongst the group. "How is she to protect the Kingdom?" was another. His personal favorite though, was, "The Chaehora's aren't going to let this slide."

Delvuvius wouldn't mind if a war broke out over this, if Syndra's secret was the beginning of the end for the Loraenar's rule, if it meant he could prevent Mysarin from suffering any more. He knew it would feel good for himself too—to see the people who Broke him and rejected him from his destiny fall. He had an image of Zendar's smug head removed from his body appear in his mind, and he smiled at the thought.

If the entire castle broke out into a battle tonight he'd only need to get the servants out, get Mysarin, Deime and Ostrac out. Possibly Rionaes, but he assumed the Oracle would know what was coming and flee the first chance he had. Everything was falling into place…as others seemed to fall apart.

He figured it had been enough time and turned around to make his way back to Mysarin when he saw Fisrolf enter the room. The crowd cheered at the sight of the King, whose face was set into a hard mask of anger, and Del made sure to clap harder than everyone else just to be annoying. The Stonecrest crown laid upon his short dark hair, the silver of the stars and horns glinting in the light and mimicking the color of his eyes. His face was round like Syndra's with almond shaped eyes and light olive-toned skin. The genetics in this family ran true.

Fisrolf's obvious displeasure was too much of a distraction for Del to look for Mysarin anymore. He watched as the King made his way over to Syndra, pulling her aside from Rionaes. They spoke for a moment, too far away for Del to hear anything they said, but he could probably guess what it was about. The two then left the ballroom as the Queen made her entrance.

Yegaran Loraenar received cheers as she waved to the people. Guards escorted her through the crowd and up to the dais on the opposite side of the large doors from which she entered. She held the same regality and demanding presence that Syndra often carried with her; her nose upturned, her eyes expressionless, her manner reeking of boredom. Her smile seemed tight, forced, as she sat upon one of the black thrones of the dais. Her brownish-red hair was long and curly, holding a crown identical to Fisrolf's atop her head. She looked into the crowd, waiting for them to quiet before she spoke.

"I would like to thank you all for joining us here tonight, and during these three very special weeks." Her voice was solid, confident, and melodic. "I know some of your travels may have been difficult, but after the battles you have witnessed today I assume it was worth it." The crowd cheered again for her words. Her smile grew, straining her face further. She lifted a hand to silence the sea of people. "Tonight we celebrate as we did twenty years ago, except this time we are not in a war camp."

Laughter rippled around Delvuvius at that.

"We celebrate with our victors of the day who will have to battle yet again in a week, where we will see who shall take home the title of the MoonDawn Warrior. The two should be arriving here soon to feast and dance amongst you all. And speaking of feast, I have a very special surprise for tonight." Her hand motioned towards the door from which she came, and in walked Deime and his father, carrying a cake at least ten tiers high. "And with that, I implore you all to have a *fantastic* time."

Del searched for Mysarin as the two walked the cake up to a table in the center of the room. He couldn't see her anywhere, and so he tried to get Deime's attention by *wooing* loudly. They locked eyes for a moment, and Del tried to suggest with his eyes that they would need to speak. Deime simply nodded back to him.

Yes, later, he seemed to say. So Del continued to blend into the crowd as the music began for the second time.

Estair arrived with Ostrac just after they brought the cake in and was immediately surrounded by people of all sorts. She felt her blood boil as they drank her in. She felt her ears ring at the *volume* of the room. She spotted a few Chaehora folks and thought back to the night they had attacked the Karnoch. The Silent Crossing, they had named it. She was lucky enough to have been stationed at the docks in Quantis when the people of Seawall crept up to the Karnoch battleships on small dinghies. And even luckier that she only had to fight off a few that slipped past, while the real battle took place out in the Fallen Waters and attracted a sea-striker.

"It's not common for women to fight here," Ostrac leaned in to say quietly, breaking through her memories.

They moved side by side through the packed room.

"They just want to see what kind of a girl could do what you did today."

Estair looked at him with furrowed brows.

He laughed softly before clarifying, "I don't agree with them." He hesitated for a moment. "You did do amazing today, though. Where did you learn how to fight like that?"

"I used to be a part of the Karnoch," she said.

She felt strange receiving compliments on her fighting. She never really had before now. Never had anyone, let alone an entire *crowd* of people, celebrate her. Her confidence—her trust within her own skills—came from only *her* believing in herself. Even when she trained with the pirates, they always pushed for more, for better. Yet, the night of The Silent Crossing had truly taught her how talented she could be with a weapon in hand. She smiled remembering the four bodies that had lain at her feet.

"That's right. You'd told me when I was focused on not puking my guts out… How did you end up with them?"

"My parents sold me to them."

She looked around at all of the eyes still lingering on her, she took in their faces. She studied the blonde Chaehora's heads of hair, and thought of those same blonde strands coated in blood.

"Oh. I'm sorry." Ostrac tensed up beside her.

She looked back to him, confused. "Why? You did not raise me to be sold."

"No, I mean, I am sorry that they did that to you," he replied.

"Do not be. Only they need to feel sorry for it."

"Agreed." Ostrac noticed her hands at her sides, then looked back up into her still frowning face. "Let's go get some wine. It's always really good at these types of things."

As they continued to make their way through, it seemed that Estair's novelty was beginning to wear off. People were staring less at her and more so at the giant cake in the center of the room, or they were too busy dancing to the lousy tune that filled up the space. She felt relieved. A blue-eyed and black-haired woman came up to Ostrac just before they reached the table filled with golden goblets and asked him for a dance.

He looked back to Estair. "You wouldn't mind, would you?"

She shook her head. "Go have your fun. I'll wander around here." At least she didn't have to worry about people staring at her any longer.

He smiled at her and grabbed the woman's hand before they headed to the area where many couples joined together in a strange dance. Estair watched as she grabbed a goblet and tasted the wine.

She wanted to spit it out as soon as she tasted it.

It was way too sweet compared to what she was used to. So she raised the glass back to her lips and tried to let it subtly pour back into the cup.

"Leave me alone." Estair heard a woman's voice say near the drink table.

She looked around for the source and saw an elven woman with sandy blonde hair standing a few feet away. A human man much older than her with graying hair stood before her. He was obviously drunk already on that horrendous wine.

"Oh, you don't want to be rude, do you?" She watched as the man leaned in to grab the tips of the woman's ears. She smacked his hand away.

"I said to leave me alone." The woman's voice was shaking as she spoke.

Estair moved closer as the woman frantically looked around for someone she knew.

"Spoiled *poivachikk*. What, you don't want to dirty yourself with a human man? Is that it?" He stepped closer, his already pink skin growing red in his frustration.

The woman moved to step back when the man grabbed her arm. Estair's veins pulsed at the sight. The woman tried to shake off his hard grip to no avail.

"Go away!"

She splashed her drink in his face, and in a split second the man raised his fist in his fit. But Estair was there in an instant.

Instead of the man slamming his knuckles into the face of the blonde woman, Estair slammed hers into *his* face.

He fell back onto the ugly rug below them, dripping that dark blood-red wine from his face onto it. Estair took her own goblet of wine and dumped it on top of him.

"The lady said to leave her alone. I suggest you do that."

He blinked the wine out of his eyes before seeing all of the nearby elves who heard what he had called the woman next to Estair. '*Poivachikk*.' A hateful Diarmar word used against elves. He scrambled to his feet and made his leave without another word.

"You know what, I think the rug looks better like that," said the woman.

Estair laughed. "I think so, too."

Then she looked at the once pretty dark green dress now stained with spots of wine. The two colors mixed together to make an awful shade of brown.

"Your dress does not, though."

"Shit, I really liked this one." The woman's hands were shaking as they reached up to touch the drenched cotton. Estair could hear her uneven breathing.

"Are you okay?" she asked.

The woman tried to steady herself, to take a deep breath. She then finally looked to Estair and her eyes flashed between brown and silver. Estair took a step back and the woman's face scrunched in confusion. Her hair then changed from the light blonde color into a full head of raven black hair.

"Your… your hair." Estair took back another step.

"What? Wait, don't I know you?"

The woman then sloppily grabbed a stray piece that was not atop her head and examined it. Her brown eyes turned silver again as they went wide.

"I have to leave," she slurred.

Estair's face mimicked the woman's look of confusion.

"I-I'm sorry. Thank you for your kindness," the woman said on fluttering breath before she ran out of the room, covering her face.

30 - Syndra

"You need to fix this."

Fisrolf Loraenar was pacing back and forth in a small study down the hall from the ballroom. Syndra sat before him on a tall and mighty wooden chair, picking nervously at her nails.

"How could you have let this happen? You foolish girl."

"I don't know. I did everything you told me to do, father." She needed some water. Her mouth felt like sand.

"Well it was not enough!" Fisrolf slammed his fist into the desk before him, creating a crack in the wood.

Syndra jumped in her chair from the sound, and her mind began to race.

Fisrolf knew from the time that Syndra was a girl that she had no magics, and he had slaved away to hide it from the world. He, and his right hand Zendar, had tried endlessly to find a way around it. Yet nothing had ever worked. Yegaran had even tried to produce another heir, one Syndra's parents had prayed to the Great Twelve would be a boy, but to no avail. Elven males had always had a difficult time successfully impregnating their female counterparts. And now the two were burgeoning on the age of never having any again. They had an abomination of a child, and now Syndra was doomed to live a life feeling empty, weak, less-than. She knew she was about to lose her claim to the throne, that her own father was moments away from throwing her out into the cold as a reject. She was panicking.

"I can do more. I can do better," she pleaded.

"No. We now have a war on our hands girl. Seawall *knows*." He walked over to her, getting inches away from her face as he worked through his rage. "Someone out there is leaking our secrets. It has to be the girl. I should've known you were too weak to control her."

"I still can," she said quietly.

"How?" Fisrolf's face had turned beet-red, his mustache twitched above his lip.

"I-I can Break her. She can go out as me again at the tourney, and do anything I tell her to. Then I can use the spell and take it all from her. He said she'll be strong enough after Breaking. Once I have her magics, I'll make them second-guess their information."

She picked at her nails again, fingers stinging as she ripped delicate skin. She felt her lip begin to quiver, so she bit down onto it.

"How would that change anything?" Her father backed away, returning to his pacing across the room.

"She's strong. Didn't you see what she did today? It was before any sort of Break. Imagine what she could do after that. Imagine what I could do once I take it."

"I am not worried about her might. I am worried about *your* credibility."

His words were like an arrow through her chest.

"How will you control her? How will you prevent this from spiraling any further?"

Zendar cleared his throat from the other side of the room, behind Syndra. "If I may, your Majesty."

Fisrolf turned those molten eyes over to the Commander. The shadows of the candles highlighting his gaunt features.

"What?"

"If we were to Break this girl, perhaps it would break her will, too. I've seen it happen plenty of times, among soldiers, it's why we always insist. The more brutal the Breaking, the easier they become to control. Then, it will be easier for me to do the transfer." His voice was steady, speaking from experience. "We will do it after, as soon as we can."

Fisrolf stopped his death-walk. He turned back to his daughter, and the rage dissipated. Syndra knew he loved her, knew that his rage was all for her, to protect her.

He sighed.

"Your last chance, Syndra. Because you are my sole heir."

"I will not disappoint you," was all she could say.

"You will not because if this does not work, then you are no longer a Loraenar. You will lose your titles, your standings. I will send you on your way to live out your days on another continent, or I will have you killed. Otherwise I risk losing this kingdom. Do you understand?"

"Yes, father." Syndra stood from her chair, knowing now what she had to do. She left as Zendar and her father continued to discuss how to work around the scandal, meeting her usual ten guards outside of the room.

She released a breath she didn't realize she was holding when the door shut and she began to make her way back to the ballroom. The guard's melodic footsteps echoed her own as she pushed back against the tears in her eyes. She would not let them see her cry.

Then a woman with wine spilled down the front of her dress burst through the ballroom doors, hands covering her face.

Syndra paused, right when the woman did, noticing who was in front of her. The woman's eyes went wide with fear and despair. Syndra was about to ask if she was alright, if she needed help, right when the glamor faded away.

It was Mysarin.

"Seize her."

"No. No!" Mysarin frantically looked around as the guards rushed in, grabbing her arms.

She flailed around like a fish caught in a net as she struggled against them.

"No!" she screamed. "I did everything you asked!"

The ground started to shake beneath Syndra's feet. She stepped back in fear of her power when she spotted the amulet around Mysarin's neck. The emblem on it flashed between a heart and an owl's head. *So that's where it went, that little thief,* Syndra thought. *No wonder she had so much power today.*

Syndra stormed up to Mysarin as she struggled to fight against the guards with her magics. Her hand lashed out at Syndra as she reached out and ripped the amulet from Mysarin's neck. Her hand burned as she threw the amulet to the floor and brought her foot down atop it, shattering it.

"De—" Mysarin tried to shout before a guard used the pommel of his sword to smack her on the back of her head, knocking her unconscious.

"Quickly, bring her to the dungeons before anyone notices," Syndra said as she watched Mysarin slump between the guards' hands. She looked down to where Mysarin had scratched her, at the deep gashes in her skin.

As they dragged her away, Syndra felt a knot in her gut grow. She never wanted it to go this far.

<h1 style="text-align:center">31 - Delvuvius</h1>

Delvuvius could not find Mysarin anywhere. He felt the magics in the air when the castle rumbled moments ago, and immediately began his search. *I shouldn't have left her alone, Great Twelve, what was I thinking? Idiot idiot idiot.* He scanned every panicked and confused face in the crowd, searching for Mysarin in her glamor. When he had checked every corner of the room twice, he decided to alert Deime. He was standing in the center of the room by the ridiculous cake, cutting and handing out pieces.

He sauntered over, cutting the line that was forming to take the next slice.

Del leaned in close to Deime as the people behind him grunted in frustration, "I need your help. It's Mysarin."

Deime's eyes went wide before he nodded his head and turned to his father. "I'll be back later."

The two then began to weave their way through the crowd, scanning each and every face.

"Why was she here? I thought she wasn't allowed."

"She glamored herself to come here and see *you*, dummy. That was *her* you bumped into. She came to warn you." Del didn't want to be the one to break the news of their engagement to Deime, so he tried to keep it vague.

"Warn me of what?" Deime set his sights on the back of an elven woman with long black hair and reached his hand out to grab her shoulder.

Del lowered it for him, "She *glamored* herself. The blonde woman I was dancing with."

He avoided eye contact as he spoke the last bit.

Deime furrowed his brows in confusion.

"She can't change herself completely," he said before adding, "can she?"

"She's gotten a lot stronger since the last time you saw her."

Deime said nothing in response and continued to walk through the ballroom, scanning faces all around for any sort of familiarity. A few feet from the door, Del's gaze landed upon the fighter he had seen in the tournament earlier that day, rushing towards the exit in the same manner as them. She locked eyes with him, taking in the tightness of their shoulders and the look of uncertainty on Deime's face.

"Did you see what happened to that woman? Her eyes and hair were changing colors," the fighter said. "I think that tremor was from her, too."

"Where did she go?" Deime asked, eyes panicked.

The fighter pointed to the door that separated the ballroom from the rest of the castle. Deime nodded to the fighter as Del stormed forwards.

The two burst through the doors just in time to witness a woman with long raven hair at the other end, about to disappear into another corridor.

"Mysa!" Deime shouted.

"*Shit.*"

Del looked to Deime, who looked like he was about to throw up as Syndra stopped and slowly turned around.

She was standing there alone, and yet Del could hear the echoes of her guards' metal footsteps marching just out of sight. The *clink clank* of the sound was accompanied by a subtle dragging noise. Del's stomach sank.

"Halt." Syndra turned to the guards just around the corner as she spoke, and the dragging noise stopped with them.

She looked back to Deime and Del, and tilted her head to the side in a predatory move. She smiled.

"Sorry, wrong person. Heh, he's had a lot to drink." Del made a grab for Deime, who was frozen in place, and redirected him back to the ball. They needed a plan, *now.*

"Stop," she commanded, and Del heard the sound of her footsteps walking towards them as the two paused in place. "I know you."

Delvuvius felt sweat start to coat his skin as he leaned in and whispered to Dieme, "Let me lead. Act drunk."

The two spun back around as Del raised an eyebrow to the Princess.

"Well, I certainly know you, Your Highness. Don't you remember our little chat with the Queen?" Deime's breath caught in his throat as Del made to bow to Syndra.

Her smile dropped. "No, not you," she pointed to Deime, "*you.*"

"M-me?" Deime stepped back as Syndra prowled closer.

"My handmaiden told me about you," she said, a light in her eyes growing as she moved in on her prey—as she crafted her plan. "You're Mysarin's husband."

Deime was stunned into silence. Syndra moved closer.

"Sorry about him, he's a bumbling idiot currently. But I believe you are mistaken Princess, no one is married to this scoundrel." Del nudged his elbow into Deime's side as if they were long time friends.

Deime nodded in agreement. Del could see the glint of sweat on the bridge of his nose.

"No, I checked if the information was correct when my mother hired you and your father for today, for the cake. Tell me, what was your name again?" She was now standing directly in front of the two, arms loose at her sides as she prepared to strike.

"Deime Thunshire," he said, voice shaking.

Del wanted to smack him for dropping the act.

"Come with me, Deime. Mysarin is hurt. She needs you." Syndra's smile did not reach her eyes as she reached out and grabbed Deime's hand.

"Where is she?" Del demanded as he grabbed onto Deime's shoulder, preventing him from leaving.

"Do not stand in my way," Syndra's cold stare froze Del to his core, "or you will meet an early grave."

Six guards now walked back down the hall, hands upon their swords.

Del knew they would kill him. He had no weapons, no armor—only the flimsy clothing he had worn to hopefully impress Mysarin. He had no magics that could contend with theirs. Even if he had tried, there were more guards in the ballroom behind him. He looked at Deime, who nodded his head at Del, lips pressed into a tight line.

Del swore under his breath as he stepped back.

He watched helplessly as Syndra led Deime away, the guards now forming a wall between them and him. He saw the fear that had resided in Deime's eyes, the subtle tightening of his jaw despite his attempts at looking calm. He needed to figure out a way around this. He needed to save them.

Think, you idiot, think! He smiled at the guards like he was complacent before he turned back into the ballroom. The sounds of music and the murmurs of the crowd filled the space. Perhaps he could persuade that fighter woman to help him. The two of them surely could take a few guards. His mind raced, his heart was hammering in his chest, *fuck fuck fuck* was all he could think. He didn't care if talking to the fighter was a shit plan, it was all he had. He searched around for her as the sounds of the room pressed in on him. They grew louder and louder as he stormed past them all, bumping into Lords and Ladies with no regard, on a hunt for the tall woman with short hair.

Rionaes appeared before him as the walls began to close in. He reached out to grab Del's arms, and his mouth moved without any sound coming out. Del went to shove him off. He had to focus. Rionaes just held on tighter and began to shake him.

Finally, Rionaes' voice broke through the panic.

"We have to go."

"What?"

"We need to *leave*."

Rionaes dragged Del away.

It had been two days since Syndra stole Deime and dragged him off to who knows where. Mysarin still hadn't shown up either and Del knew it was no coincidence. They had to be locked up somewhere, suffering. He'd been a mess since Rionaes dragged him out of the ball; he hadn't slept, hadn't been eating, hadn't done much of anything.

It was his fault.

His plan to tell Fisrolf about Syndra and her plans had erupted in his face—there was apparently a very unflattering conversation held between Pryse Chaehora and Fisrolf Loraenar at the ball, unnerving guests. He hadn't dared to ask Ostrac for any other details about it, he was too busy holding in the contents of his stomach at the time.

Clearly the Loraenars had taken a different approach to the threat of war than Del had thought. His misstep was going to cost him something that he wasn't sure he could handle losing.

Now, he sat in Rionaes' room, as they built a plan. Rionaes was tipped off about what was likely happening to Mysarin, to Deime, by whatever it was that told him all the secrets of the castle. He whispered it to Del, saying he was the only one he trusted to put a stop to it all, as they left the ball early. Del was in denial at the time, refusing to believe that he had screwed up so catastrophically. Yet there he was, two days later with no signs of either elf.

"We have less than a week," Rionaes said after sending his handmaiden on a fruitless quest to find an *Infen*, a native crop to Oswes, at the port. The darkness beneath his eyes had grown, bruising deeply.

"Less than a week? We need to help them *now*," Del argued.

"We can not." Rionaes shook his head as he sat down onto his oversized bed.

"And why not? I can't sit here and let Syndra do whatever she wants with them." He clenched his fists, feeling his nails dig into his palms.

"Because my plan involves waiting until the third game."

"Well make a new plan!" Del's whispers raised into hushed shouts.

"I do not have another." Rionaes looked too calm for Del's liking.

"Neither do I. *Shit*. What if we ask Ostrac? See if he can think of anything."

"I know you do not see things as I do, but you must listen to me. There are only few ways that this can be done, and involving Ostrac will only endanger him…" Rionaes swallowed, his eyes drifting to the floor. "Much is concealed, but I have seen the inevitable."

Del said nothing. He was in an impossible position. He knew he should listen to Rionaes—he was helping him for nothing more than because it was the right thing to do, because only he could see the right path.

He sighed. "Okay. What's your great plan, then?"

Rionaes stood, and began to pace over the piles of clothing and books along his bedroom floor. "Syndra has said that Zendar brought in minotaurs. For her to kill. For the display."

Del watched as he waited for him to finish.

"We release them early, while people flood into their seats. Syndra and I are always the first in the crowd, before she leaves to the stables to get to Mysarin, to switch. We set the minotaurs into the arena, and everyone will see as she does nothing. Then we grab Mysarin from the chaos, and we leave."

"We? You're coming with?" he asked.

Rionaes solemnly nodded. Del noticed that the Prince looked thinner than he had when he first arrived here. He had a feeling that there was more that Rionaes didn't share with him. That something had happened to him while he had been staying here. He did wonder though why he would not just leave and go back to Oswes, but now was not the time to ask.

"What about Syndra's guards? She has an entire personal army," Del said.

"They will be too concerned with the Princess' safety. That is their first priority."

"Alright. And then we have Mysarin disguise herself. Smart. What about Deime?"

Rionaes stopped, and looked at the ground. He said nothing.

"What about Deime, Rionaes?"

His strange eyes drifted their way back to Del. "He will not survive that long."

He refused to believe what Rionaes had said. That Deime would not make it out of here. There would be a way to get to him—they would break him out or cause an even bigger distraction, *something*. Del had always worked better without a set plan anyway. There would be a moment, an opportunity he would seize, he swore it. He paced around the castle grounds as he searched for ideas. Perhaps he would overhear some information or—

"You!" A blonde elf stormed up to him. "I know you! Tell me, do you know where my son is?"

Then Del recognized him; it was Deime's father.

He sucked in a breath as he faced the consequences of his decisions. His eyes scanned about the hall they were standing in as he debated telling Deime's father what had happened. Perhaps he held the idea that Del had been looking for.

But then his eyes landed on a dark mirage against a far wall, behind Deime's father's head. He squinted at it. The shadows moved like smoke in the air, and something slowly emerged.

A Faceless, just barely visible within the black fog, listening to what Del would say. It was a threat. He flicked his sight back onto the worried father before him.

"I..."

He was trapped. He couldn't say a thing to Deime's father, could not say where his son had gone. He tried, but the words refused to leave his mouth. He looked back over to the Faceless, and they tilted their head in waiting.

"I don't know."

Deime's father turned around just as the Faceless slipped back into the shadows. Frustration spread across his tired face as he whipped his head back.

"Last I saw him, *you* pulled him away. He hasn't been home in days and… it's very unlike him. Please, tell me." His blue eyes welled up with tears.

He knew something had gone horribly wrong.

Del wanted to scream. If he talked, it would mean his head, Mysarin's head, and definitely Deime's. It would seal the poor elf's coffin before Del could come up with another plan.

"I'm sorry, but I don't know. After we spoke, he went back into the crowd at the ball and I just assumed he went back to work with you." His gut twisted.

"You're lying!" he yelled into his face. "You ungrateful human, I know you know where he is!"

He grabbed onto Del's shirt in a fist and pulled him in close.

"Unhand me!" Del said as he yanked the elven man's hand out of its grip, throwing him off balance and onto the floor. "I told you, I don't know…"

He had never felt more like a selfish arse than in this moment, as he stood over a desperate father, begging for clues. His muscles shook with fatigue. The hall began to shrink.

"There are twelve gods and yet not a single one shall show you love. I pray for it. I'll relish in the thought of you calling out for an answer to only be met with cold silence." Deime's father stood, and spat at Del's feet.

Del said nothing in reply, as he watched Deime's father walk away, as the walls grew closer—inch by inch, second by second—as air evaded his burning lungs.

32 - Mysarin

When she awoke she was in a strange room. The walls were dark like the rest of the castle but in the dim light of a few torches on the wall, Mysarin could see that they were made of stone. *Am I outside?* Mysarin went to look at the floor, to see if there was dirt or cobblestone beneath her feet, and yet she could not move her head. She blinked a few times, trying to peer into the darkness at the space before her as she struggled to fight against whatever held her head in place.

At that moment she realized that her hands were also bound. She thrashed about, trying to break free from the cold metal around her wrists, her heartbeat quickening. She blinked furiously until her eyes adjusted to the dim light, and saw that embedded in the stone before her were five iron cuffs. One for the neck and jaw, two for the ankles and two for the hands. She tried to lift her left leg, her skin scraping against the iron. She could hear the sounds of flies buzzing around her head, waiting for rot. The smell of piss and sweat and iron hit her senses and she began to hyperventilate.

Mysarin was in a dungeon.

A *creak* broke through the air as Syndra opened a metal gate and stepped into Mysarin's view. The torches behind her cast Syndra in the shadow, reminiscent of the figure Mysarin had seen in her dreams too many times.

"Bring him in." Syndra's voice was hard, devoid of any emotion as she spoke.

Mysarin squinted to see past the cloudiness in her vision and at the look on her face. She felt dizzy, and her head throbbed where it was hit.

"You've taken quite the beating in your day, or so I've heard from your little boyfriend." Syndra continued to speak as Mysarin heard steps creeping towards the cell. "Zendar tells me that your history could make this quite time-consuming. And well, I can't afford that. And I can't have you looking all banged up and injured like last time, either. So we will have to take the easier route."

"W-what's happening? Why are you doing this?" Mysarin's voice was sore from her screaming earlier. She spoke through her teeth, the metal collar around her neck stopping any movement.

Had no one heard her? Had no one come for her?

Syndra's sigh cut through Mysarin's thoughts. "I could explain it all to you, but again, I really don't have the time." She turned her head to where she came. "Zendar, chain him to the wall."

Into the room walked the Golden Elf, his matching glowing magics wrapped around Deime's hands. The elf shoved her love forwards and into the wall. His hair was disheveled, his nose bleeding onto a rag in his mouth. He walked with a limp.

"Deime? What are you doing to him? Stop!"

Her restraints cut into her skin again, yet she barely felt it. She tried to summon her flame magics, tried to burn them off, but she was so drained. There was nothing left. Syndra had taken the amulet, smashed it, and now Mysarin was back to having only a speck of magics in comparison. She sagged in defeat. She knew this would happen, but she wasn't fast enough in warning him—she let her own jealousy get in the way.

"Deime… Deime, are you alright?"

"Oh, he's fine. For now." Syndra moved out of view as she spoke, and Mysarin saw Deime clearly in the light of the torches on the wall beside his head. Fear was a rabid beast in his round eyes.

There he was. Her doe.

Mysarin heard a cry leave her mouth. Zendar then pulled out a small dagger, and cut Deime's yellow tunic down the center, revealing his bare torso. Deime flinched as he did.

"Please, please do not hurt him. He didn't do anything! Please!" Mysarin used her dwindling energy to fight against her shackles again, but to no avail.

She was trapped, and so was Deime.

"I did everything you asked!" she yelled.

Syndra and Zendar said nothing. Syndra walked back into view, striding to Deime. She handed what looked to be a long rope to Zendar, and then placed her hand upon Deime's skin. Mysarin felt her blood heat as Syndra stroked lazily up and down Deime's torso. Mysarin could hear his breathing from across the room, coming out heavily through his nose.

"You can begin," Syndra said quietly to Zendar as she moved back a few paces.

That's when Mysarin saw what she had handed to Zendar. It was a whip. He lifted his hand as Mysarin watched frozen in horror.

The *crack* of the sound rang through the stone cell, and Deime's muffled scream followed. His perfect, soft, skin had turned into a red, angry, line going diagonally down his torso, and Mysarin realized that she, too, was screaming. The tip of the whip was metal, slicing open his skin. Blood dripped from his shoulder down to his navel, as Mysarin felt tears sliding down her face. *Crack!* Zendar sliced the whip through the air again. She felt nauseous, her heart pounding in her throat.

She tried to talk around the beats. "What do you want from me? I'll do anything, please, just stop." Mysarin's voice shook as she begged.

Syndra turned back to Mysarin. "I want you to *Break*. I want you to prove to the world that Syndra Loraenar is not to be trifled with. That Stonecrest is not as *weak* as people may think."

"Then break *my* body, *my* bones, but leave him out of this!" Mysarin was still looking at Deime, at the angry gashes on his chest.

Syndra laughed. "It's like you don't even listen."

Crack! Another slice across Deime's skin, making a bullseye.

"It would take too long to Break you through more traditional means. But taking an alternative direction, breaking your *soul* rather than just your body, will prove to be much faster. Right, Zendar?"

Crack! Crack! Crack! Deime's body was covered in blood, the trill of his screams reaching new levels. He squeezed his eyes shut.

"Correct, Princess," Zendar said.

Mysarin began to sob as she watched the torture of Deime continue. She felt so helpless compared to the potential that had roiled through her at the games.

How long ago was that? How long was she unconscious for?

She began to pray in her mind, to any and all of the useless Deities, begging for their help. For an intervention. *Please, save Deime. Take me instead, but please spare him,* she repeated over and over to anyone who might be listening, begging for a miracle.

She believed that someone had listened when Zendar set down the whip and said to Syndra, "This could take all night, a few days, perhaps. We should get back, let them suffer a while."

It felt like days had passed. Time was difficult to keep track of in the dungeon, in the darkness. They snuffed out the torches when they had left, leaving the two in pitch black. Mysarin thought she had a concussion, her head continued to pound and swim around in circles. She spoke to Deime all throughout the night. She talked about anything, everything. She told him of her new friends; Rionaes, Ostrac, Del. She told him of the gardens and what they had looked like, how her performances at the games were like. Whatever she could think of to hopefully distract him.

She almost thought about telling him the truth about her that she had kept hidden away all this time. Yet, her stubborn hope of still somehow finding a way to be with him stood in her way. He made muffled noises through the rag around his mouth to let her know he was still there.

"We're going to get out of here. I promise," she said. "Someone's going to come for us."

He didn't reply.

She must've fallen asleep eventually. She only knew she awoke in another daze, to pitch black, to a starving stomach and sore skin.

"Deime?" she called out.

No reply. She listened closely before letting panic sink in. He was breathing still. She closed her eyes again, letting the haze take her mind back into sleep.

Cold water hit her face, waking her. The torches had been lit again, except they were almost blinding now. She blinked, trying to get her bearings. Once her vision cleared, she saw the dried blood and long open wounds across Deime's chest. His hair was wet, too. Zendar was there again, whip in hand.

"Good afternoon," he said with a sick smile on his face.

She felt bruises forming against where she was cuffed as she struggled again.

He clicked his tongue. "You know you're not going anywhere, don't you?"

He then raised the whip and the dreaded sound rang out again. *Crack! Crack!*

"Please, stop," she begged.

"Then *Break*."

"How?" *Crack!* "Tell me how!"

"This. is how. you Break! You watch the man you love be tortured at your expense and it *breaks* you." *Crack!* "Know that this is all your fault." Zendar turned around, and threw the whip to the ground. "This wouldn't happen if it weren't for you. Doesn't that make you feel ill?"

She swallowed.

"Doesn't that cause pain in your chest? Doesn't it make you want to kill me? Go ahead. Try."

She did want to kill him. She struggled again, trying to reach him, even though she knew it was pointless.

Zendar laughed. "Pathetic."

Her magics still felt small inside of her, not fully regenerating through her strange sleep. She tried to summon fire, bringing the heat to her palms, but as she pushed it towards him, it fizzled out.

He turned away from her, eyes back on Deime. "Perhaps I need to kick it up a notch."

Deime was covered in his own blood. His lids drooped, his breathing turned labored. The rag covering his mouth was soaked with cold water, sweat, tears, and blood. Mysarin watched as his teeth grinded down onto it, as he screamed, as she did, as Zendar cut off a toe.

More time had passed. It had both felt like hours and weeks in between Zendar's macabre sessions. He came at seemingly random intervals, and she never knew how much time she had in between. The waiting was almost worse. She tried everything she could, constantly pulling at the cuffs, trying to break free. She tested her magics. They never made a difference.

She tried to not let her mind focus on what was coming next, and when, but it haunted her regardless. She kept trying to talk to Deime, but he became less and less responsive.

Mysarin tried to Break. She had tried with everything that she had, let every terrible memory haunt her mind in the darkness as Deime got a few hours of sleep. Tried to will her way into it and yet, nothing. She felt like she was slowly losing herself in the dark, the buzzing of flies getting louder as each conscious second passed.

Zendar had cut off all of his toes.

He mutilated Deime's ears. He cut off his manhood… And Mysarin watched through it all. She wanted to close her eyes, to try and drown it out, but she forced herself to spectate. It was the only way she could try and speed up her Break, because at this point, she wanted it just as much as they did. Deime stared back at her while it happened, if he could. The only time he looked away was when that evil bastard pushed a red-hot knife through his left eye. She could still smell the burning flesh.

She wondered how he hadn't run out of blood to spill.

There was so much.

"Great Twelve, Zendar…" Syndra said as they lit the torches. She hadn't witnessed any of it, she was only here for the whip. In a sick way, Mysarin missed the whip. "I—I'm going to retch." Syndra ran out of Mysarin's eyeline.

She heard gagging and the *splash* bounce around the room on the other side of the iron bars. Deime's left eye was swollen shut around a thick layer of yellow pus, blood, and crispened flesh. His pants were soiled, a few times over, as well as her own dress.

"Get used to it, Princess. There is a war brewing and this will not be the hardest part." He smacked Deime's face, waking him, causing a clump of pus to drip down his cheek.

Deime groaned through the same cloth still tied in his mouth. Two flies flew from his wounds. Zendar turned around to look at Mysarin. He picked up a bucket of water and brought it up to her mouth.

"Drink."

She gulped it down, trying to fill up her stomach enough that she would forget about food.

"Mm mmmm," Deime said through the cloth.

"What was that, worm?" Zendar lowered the bucket from Mysarin's lips, walking over to Deime. He leaned close to him, putting his pointed ear next to his mouth. "I couldn't quite hear you."

"Mmm mmmmm."

"Quit playing with him." Syndra walked back into the room. "Ugh, they stink." She drew a handcloth from her bosom and placed it over her nose.

Zendar pulled the rag out of Deime's mouth.

"Kill me," he said, voice like shards of glass.

A silent river carved its way down Mysarin's face. Her heart shattered.

"You see that? You see what you're doing to the man you love?" Zendar said, putting the cloth back into Deime's mouth. "Why. won't. you. Break? Do you not love him? Did we get it wrong?" Mysarin continued to sob as Zendar's voice strained.

Syndra stood in the corner, avoiding looking at either of them.

"You don't, do you?" He let a cruel, mocking laugh loose. "Your heart belongs to another. It's that *rat* that lurks about the castle, isn't it?" He laughed to himself again.

"No! I love Deime, I do," she sobbed. Deime scrunched his brows, groaning louder this time.

"Mmmmm. Mmmmmmmmmm."

Deime was owed more than this. He hadn't ever hurt another person. Mysarin once watched him struggle to kill a spider because it hadn't deserved to be crushed by something so much bigger than it just for existing.

She had ended up shoving him out of the way to do it herself.

"This is taking too long, Zendar," Syndra's voice cut through, "You said this would work. The tourney is starting soon."

"Perhaps it is not enough. Perhaps we can go further," he said as Mysarin cried harder, realizing how long it had truly been.

A week of torture, of starvation, of vibrating silence and absence of light. Zendar looked into Deime's face, saw how Deime refused to acknowledge neither him nor Syndra. Zendar then turned and followed his victim's line of sight, to see Mysarin staring back at him.

"She still has hope," he snickered. "I know what to do."

Zendar then raised the fire on the torches in the room with his magics, the flame glowing brighter. Another scream ripped through Mysarin at the full sight of Deime in the blaze.

"Please," she howled, "please stop! Stop! I'll do anything, I'll be *anything* you want!"

Zendar smiled at the sound of her anguish as he grabbed a dagger from his belt, and Mysarin could only watch as he plunged it into Deime's heart.

Mysarin was still wailing when his eye finally closed and she split in two.

Then, Mysarin felt it.

For it was not just her heart that had broken into pieces but some internal, *integral*, part deep within her, had snapped. She felt the magics expanding like a constellation unfolding across the pitch black night sky. Every second it was as if a new star blinked into existence, each one a new level to the depths of her magics. In that same instant, Mysarin felt the spell that was placed upon her when she was twelve begin to lift.

The fog cleared and as the stars continually lit up that dark sky, a full moon arose.

Mysarin remembered who she was.

Memories from a lifetime ago came flooding into her mind. The bog in the summer, golden light shining through skinny and ancient trees and reflecting upon the pools of water that slumbered between the tall grass. Small, simple houses built from the land around them creating a miniature village—Crelde. Hers was closest to the edge of the forest, in case she ever had to run.

She remembered the day that she did. She remembered the last embrace from a woman with golden wavy hair and beautiful honey-brown eyes. Her mother.

Marista Danai.

Mysarin could still smell the herbs that burned alongside the entire village as they sat in a large circle, Mysarin in the middle. They had all worked together casting the spell upon Mysarin before she was sent to live in Synsee, with people whose blood was not her own.

"*It's to keep you safe, my yshk*," Marista's soft and low voice whispered into Mysarin's dark hair.

More fragments of memory, of a the life she had lived, slammed into her mind: large wolves racing through the woods, small animals dropped from their maw before the young children in the village, the fog that floated through the wood in the early gray mornings, the strange green women with rows of teeth lingering at the edge.

Her mother was the clearest image out of everything. The Loraenars, Zendar, had thought her dead all this time, and yet Mysarin had such a clear picture of living with Marista in Crelde all those years ago. *After* the siege. The smell of plums that had engulfed her each time Marista had held her in her arms. The lull and sway of her voice as she told stories to Mysarin.

The Loraenars had it wrong.

Marista had escaped somehow, Mysarin knew it. The memories, the feelings, they were too real.

Which meant that Mysarin was not just an ex-courtesan that happened to be a talented mage.

She was Mysarin Danai, the rightful heir to the throne. The next MoonDawn Queen.

That is what had caused her lost nights. Some side-effect to the spell, some protection placed over her mind to keep her from knowing who she truly was. She had spent ten years living a lie, and ten years without turning into her wolven form. The image of the werewolves from her book had finally slotted into place; the monster was an evolution of the wolf. It was called a sentinel. It was a curse, and it was a gift. The MoonDawn wolves were made for peace, and when she had spilled the blood of that man in Synsee, she had broken that peace.

She had unknowingly paid the price, and it caused her to take the monstrous form every full moon.

Her skin burned, a sticky sweat coating it. She looked to Zendar and Syndra who had their backs turned as they examined Deime's corpse. Zendar pulled out his dagger from Deime's heart, and Mysarin felt as if she were about to explode. The full moon was that night, and with the trauma of everything before her, inside of her, the beast wanted to come out that instant.

She fought with all of her strength to fend off her second skin, to keep the wretched thing at bay. But she desperately needed a release.

She needed to escape. She couldn't let them know who she really was, or she would end up with her body hanging from the castle gates. She'd be made into a spectacle, with her mother hunted down. Mysarin began to reach for the magics now roiling inside of her, the stars that had surrounded her full moon.

Flame suddenly burst from her, directed at where Zendar, Syndra, and Deime's body stood.

But a wall of magics stood in her way, and she heard Zendar laugh as her flames dissipated into nothing before them.

"Well, I told you it would work." He turned to Syndra— Mysarin's second cousin.

Syndra smiled, unaware of what she had truly done, of who she unleashed. "Outstanding. She couldn't do a thing before, and now look at her."

Syndra moved closer just before the invisible barrier between them. Mysarin squirmed. She *needed* to shift. It took everything inside of her to hold it back, but it was only a matter of time before she grew tired.

"I guess our work here is done, and we have the game to get to," Syndra said.

At least the burst of flame had taken a bit of the edge off.

Zendar came over to her and unlocked her cuffs, grabbing her.

"If you do *anything*, if you even look the wrong way, you'll end up like him. And I'll really take my time with you."

The three left the dark cell with another *creak* of the door closing, and then locking behind her. Deime's body still clung to the wall there. She felt her eyes swell as tears rolled down her cheeks. Her blood pounded harder with every moment she spent walking out of the dungeon, fighting against her second skin.

Her chest felt heavier than it had ever been.

She fiddled with the engagement ring on her finger as the beast thrashed and raged deep inside of her, howling. She grit her teeth, closed her eyes, holding it all in. She did not have the time to mourn. When she opened her eyes again, she blew out a deep breath and prepared to display her magics.

33 – Delvuvius, Estair, & Mysarin

Del put on his old suit of armor. He grabbed his blunt sword and attached its sheath to his waist, his hands shaking through it. He quickly threw any extra clothing, dried meats and cheese, Rionaes' velvet pouch and a lambskin flask into his elixir trunk and was almost ready to leave until he thought about Telme. He couldn't disappear without saying goodbye to her, or saying goodbye to Ostrac, and yet he could not tell them where he was going.

Quickly he grabbed a quill and paper, and wrote a quick note.

Telme, Ostrac,

My time has come, I must move on. There is nothing left for me here and so I search for a new horizon. Telme, thank you for everything. Ostrac, thank you for being a friend.

See you someday,

Del

He then set the letter atop his cot, and left the room for the last time. He made his way out of the castle grounds early in the morning, bringing his trunk to the edge of the forest. He found an old Heartwood with a gaping hole grown into its side, and shoved it in. He grabbed a few leaves and a handful of soil to throw on top of it. He stood back and examined it, thinking that no one would notice unless they knew to look.

Estair was still thinking about that woman from the ball. How her features had changed before her eyes, how the woman had claimed she knew Estair. She tried to convince herself that the elf must've recognized her from the games, but down in her gut, she knew it wasn't true. She saw the fear in the woman's eyes as she waited for her last chance at freedom in the cave below the arena. Alone.

Only now that no competitor was around, would she practice. The weight of her swords in her hands pulled at her skin as she maneuvered around a dummy. Her feet pressed into the ground with confidence, each step a calculated pattern. She stopped to stretch her muscles, letting the soothing tension build and release. The woman's dark hair and silver eyes flashed into her mind again. She looked like the Princess.

But it was not Syndra Loraenar, it couldn't have been. What would the Heir to Stonecrest be doing disguised as another woman?

"Zendar has not yet shown." A man's voice rang out at the bottom of the stairs. "We're going to go ahead and start the games, and Syndra will finish the event today." Estair stood and turned to see a tall, tanned man with dark curls standing before her.

"Who are you?" she questioned, twirling her swords.

"Eldred Henz, Second in Command under Zendar Paelos." His chest was wide, sporting that same Stonecrest uniform Zendar had always worn. "Let's go."

Nerves bubbled below in her stomach, fluttering along with her heartbeat. It felt like she had fresh land-legs as she nodded and followed him up the stairs to the gate. He locked the gate behind her, and she stared into the arena through the bars. No mud this time. She tried to even her breathing as she scanned the crowd, seeing the same faces that had been cheering for her death. They all had strange crowns on their heads with two metal pieces shaped like wolf ears, and their faces were painted brown and yellow.

It was unsettling. Like she was about to be sacrificed as a part of some strange ritual. She looked away from the people taking part in a culture she did not understand.

Eldred began to speak to the crowd, finally introducing her to the people who wished to see her bleed. They cheered as he said her name. Then, they cheered louder as he introduced Zanira Fethe. *So he survived the last round. Where was he at the party?* She squeezed the soft leather of her swords tight, then eased her grip. *Perhaps he was injured as well.* There was a ticking clock in her mind. A countdown to her death.

The gates opened.

Del panicked when he heard the cheers of the crowd from the outer walls of Taurean. They had started the games early. *No no no no,* was all that rushed through his head as he broke out into a sprint towards the arena. *I missed our chance? How could I miss it?* He looked up into the sky at the angle of the sun—it wasn't yet midday. Everyone should only just be arriving now.

"Why?!" he screamed.

A few Dwentil nobles from Pothalyr were flooding into the gates as he ran up behind them. They turned around with painted faces and wolf ears atop their heads and looked at him with a questioning look. He hardly noticed. His chest was about to burst as he quickly dropped the coin into the doorman's hand and ran up to where he could see Rionaes sitting next to an empty seat. Shoulders brushed past his own as people shuffled around him for a seat.

They locked eyes, the Prince looking as panicked as he felt. Del shook his head. Rionaes looked like he was about to be sick in response. The pale elf then stood, murmuring something to his handmaiden and the Oswesian Knight behind him. He gestured to Del to meet with him outside the arena.

A new plan had to be made.

Estair was already out of breath. Zanira was fast, faster than her. He blocked every attack with his shield bringing parry after parry. They circled around each other now, waiting for the other to make a move. He twirled his spear around in his hand as his deep blue eyes trailed her every step. She feigned forward, testing his reflexes. He jumped back faster than a serpent could strike.

He took it as an opening, rushing towards her. The hot air, the last day of summer, beat down onto the back of her neck as he plunged his spear near her side. She dodged, and used the moment to swing her swords towards his head in a duel attack. His steel shield blocked the first hit, absorbing the impact, and then she felt the weight of her attack press back towards her on the second. She stumbled back onto her feet. He leapt backwards. They were at a stalemate—neither one was able to touch the other. Perfect foes.

Their circling resumed, both trying to find a way, a weakness. Then the lighting changed. A storm cloud rolled over the sun, casting the arena in shadow. Warm air mixed with the cold swooping in, wind blowing stray pieces of Zanira's crimson hair around his face. It looked like fire. She then noticed how he was putting less weight onto one of his feet.

He was *injured*.

She dashed in an erratic pattern towards him, trying to prevent him from predicting what she would do. She swung with her left, a hefty smack, as he parried her again. She used her right arm to seize the moment, swiping at his feet. He jumped and she interrupted her swing, reversing it back below his feet in a jagged motion.

The weight of his body landing down on her longsword brought her chest down, bending the metal and her legs. Then she threw the sword in her left hand to clasp onto the handle of the right beneath his foot, and used her might to bring it up above her head. His ankle rolled and he fell onto his back. Her sword was now unbalanced, rendering it harder to wield. So she jumped forward and slammed her foot down onto the wrist of the hand that held his spear. Her knee pressed into his chest.

He was pinned. She watched as droplets of rain began to pour down onto his gray skin. Then he bashed his shield into her side, over and over. She resisted it. Bringing her bent sword down into his bicep, she summoned her fire magics, and began to blast at his metal spear with everything she had, attempting to melt it. He growled as his hand burned beneath her foot, as the metal warmed in his palms. But the rain and the wind thrashed about, keeping her fire too cool to melt it completely. Then Zanira used his elongated canines to bite right into her thigh, as he slammed the shield into her head.

She screamed and toppled over. Zanira pulled the sword from his arm and threw it before he followed and straddled her.

The crowd grew silent as Zanira wailed his fists down upon her forearms hovering above her face.

"This is boring now isn't it?" A voice rang out over the silent arena.

Zendar had arrived.

"Let's raise the stakes, shall we?"

Thunder boomed in the skies as the people raged for death. Foot stomps rattled her bones. She heard the crowd start to actually *howl* in anticipation.

Zanira was distracted, and so Estair grabbed onto his wrists as she lifted her legs to his back, and twisted. She used a boost of wind magics to propel him off her, and he rolled against the dirt. Then the gate from whence he came opened again. They both scrambled to their feet, heads turning to see their new surprise opponent.

But it was not another human or elf walking through the gate. It was a minotaur.

Its eyes glowed like Zanira's hair, a crown of that same red misted around the horns the size of Estair's arms. Rain continued to pour, as steam shot out from the beast's ox nose. It was twice the size of her and Zanira, covered in fur and muscle. Its torso was man-like with hairy legs and hooves the size of Estair's head. It roared through the arena. Estair looked to Zanira, standing a few feet before her now. Then she searched for the unbent longsword she had tossed, and made a dash for it beside a column.

The ground rumbled, mimicking the sky above them as the beast charged at Zanira.

Mysarin watched from the stands, squished between two of Syndra's guards. They had stripped her naked and doused her with soapy water before shoving her into a spare beige servants gown. Now she watched as they shoved that innocent beast into a cage to be butchered.

They had arrived late, in the middle of the fight, as Syndra had told her to '*just sit still until it is over.*'

So she sat there, empty. Her eyes were strained against the outside light, her body gone numb except for the wolf inside of her continuing to rage, to grow in anger against her skin as her grief threatened to end her. She watched the minotaur, and she felt pity for it—related to it. The rain began as she sat down, reminding her of that day when she had thought she was free, when she had run through the streets of Stonecrest to find Deime.

When she had still clung to that silly dream.

Now, it was transformative, the storm. The clouds rumbled above them all as they cried for her. The sky wailed in pain at the atrocities she witnessed. She longed to shift and run through the droplets, letting them soak her thick coat. Her head pounded. She needed another release of her magics if she were to contain her other form.

The crowd howled again in mockery. They all mocked her, her family, with their repulsive wolven crowns and face paint. With the way they growled for blood and barked in excitement. It was a tradition to dress up like the MoonDawn rulers at the third game, to further rub in the horror of her entire family being slaughtered in their ancestral home. Rage simmered further beneath her skin.

She watched as the two danced around the arena, soaked and terrified for their lives. The beast charged towards the gray-elf, just barely missing. The gray-elf then thrust his weapon into the side of the minotaur. It only poked at it, though, as the woman had melted the sharp edge into a dull curve with her magics. Mysarin's eyes slowly slid towards the woman, unengaged. She examined the way the woman rushed to a far away column, most likely seeking solace from the beast as it attacked her foe.

Mysarin then squinted down at the woman as she breathed heavily against the column.

It was the girl from the ball.

The one who had saved her from that perverted and entitled man. The one who had burst into Ostrac's workroom because she had heard a woman sobbing. The one who had helped him make a potion for a woman she would likely never meet.

Suddenly, the game had become more interesting. Mysarin had found someone to root for.

She looked back over at the gray-elf to see the minotaur grab him with both hands, and thrash him against the walls of the arena. *Thud thud thud.* A web grew in the stone wall. The sky bellowed in opposition as the crowd feasted upon the senseless violence. The elf was likely dead, laying limp between the minotaurs hands. It roared to the crowd around them as it hurled the corpse like a doll. A loud *crack* filled the arena as the gray-elf slammed against a column, snapping it in two.

It sounded eerily close to the whip hitting Deime's body.

Mysarin flinched.

The red crown surrounding the horns of the creature flashed in and out of existence. It was being controlled by someone else. Mysarin looked over to Zendar through blurry eyes to see that same shade of red swirling around his body. It screamed again as the red glowed steadily, regaining full control over its mind.

That's when it saw the woman, who had been watching from around another pillar. Mysarin's skin flushed, zaps of untapped magics rising along her bones. The wolf rammed into some internal door, breaking it down. Her hand spurted claws, and she quickly tucked it beneath her. She watched out of the corners of her eyes to see if either guard had noticed. But they were too focused on the game. The minotaur then ran full speed ahead at the pillar the woman hid behind. She fled as its horns crumbled the stone.

Mysarin felt like throwing up. Her mind began to crack like the pillars. Like the whip. Images of Deime's battered body flashed into her mind. The wolf rammed again, shattering the door. Lightning struck the sky. Mysarin ached for a release. The minotaur wailed in desperation, begging to be put out of its misery. Deime was dead. The crowd howled in unison. The woman who had been so kind stood no chance in the arena. *Deime* was dead. Mysarin's eyes slid to Syndra sitting in front of her, she wanted Syndra dead.

Tears rolled from her eyes. A tiring feeling.

She was now a slave to the people who had murdered her father. The people who spent three weeks and thousands of coin to celebrate it every year. The crowd was full of those who celebrated it, looked forward to the event and planned their year around it. It was all a cruel, contemptuous ridicule of her.

Deime was dead.

Crushed like the spider beneath her hands.

Like a doe ripped to shreds to feed a pack of wolves.

And now the woman's life was going to be stomped out beneath the Loraenar's giant foot.

Mysarin had thought she was cruel. That she was the monster. Both things were true, but in the face of everything before her, she seemed more like the lamb instead of the beast.

It was all too much. Everything poured down onto her like the rain from above and she couldn't hold it in any longer.

She steadily rose from her seat, and gathered up all of her new magics. A roaring tide climbing tall enough to swallow this city whole. It was so heavy within her, that it felt as if it could pulverize her own bones into dust.

As the minotaur howled back to the crowd and began its stride towards the woman, Mysarin channeled that raw tide into her hand and pushed out, releasing a burst of pure magics at the creature in the arena.

It shook the stone, screaming replaced the jeering barks, and the beast fell lifeless to the ground.

The release flung her body backwards, her spine ramming into the edge of the tiered seats. She felt the guards hands around her wrists, now back to normal, before they shoved her face into the stone at their feet.

"What did you do?" Syndra hollered, her voice drowned out by the panic filling the air.

The noble families fled, trampling over one another, shoving others out of the way.

"Mysarin what did you just do?" The princess dropped on top of her, flipping her around to face her, shaking her.

"Now it was all for *nothing*! Deime *died for nothing*!"

She had never seen the Princess completely lose her carefully crafted composure before. Had never heard this side to her voice; the terror, the cracking tone as she spoke. Mysarin laughed maniacally as blood dripped from her nose down into her teeth.

Syndra stood, her face unrecognizable. A tear dropped from her cheek.

"Take her back to the dungeon. Lock her up, and leave her to me." A deep, rattling breath. "I'll be there soon."

The crowd was chaotic as the guards ushered her out of the arena. She laughed still, emptied of her magics, as they led her to her death.

"Mysarin!" Del's voice called out. She dared to look over. He was standing there next to Rionaes, outside of the arena. She mouthed *I'm sorry* in their direction. The guard turned her head back to the front, back to her fate.

They locked her back in that same, raw and putrid smelling room. Deime's body was still there. They hadn't even bothered to move his remains. To bury him.

They left her there, to let her think about what she had done as Syndra scrambled to clean up her mess. Mysarin smiled to herself. She imagined what the King and Queen must be thinking about their prisoner. How they would punish Syndra for not keeping her under control.

"They're going to behead me soon," she said to Deime's corpse. "Or torture me, like they had you."

His limbs dangled against his cuffs.

"You should've seen the look on her face," she laughed to herself again. "Stupid bitch. I should've killed her instead."

She tossed her body within the cuffs again, testing, as her wolf reawoke within her.

"I want to kill her. I want to see her bleed. I need to make her pay," she growled, pulling her body against the restraints.

"I need to make her pay! No one else will do it right, but me!"

"Hey! Quiet in there," a man's voice said lazily, a single guard. She decided she could kill him; she couldn't let them kill her, she needed to find a way out. If no one would come, she would save herself. All so she could watch as life drained from Syndra's eyes.

Del and Rionaes arrived at the entrance to the west wing of the castle. From there they made their way out into the gardens, checking behind their backs at every turn. Castle-goers had fled the grounds from the arena, which left it all solemn and empty, besides the two of them.

"Are you sure you want to do this? You're supposed to be the Prince of Oswes, supposed to marry Syndra. It's not too late to back out," Del whispered as they crept through the rain soaked labyrinth.

Rionaes looked at Del as they made their way to the large fountain that loomed over them. The sound of heavy droplets splashed into the water. No longer was the look of a regal Prince, but the hollow ghost of him. A man ready to abandon what he was raised for.

"I have always prepared for the day I might run. I just did not know when it would be." He shrugged his shoulders as he said, "Now seems like a good time. For a good cause."

Del nodded.

"Is this how we can get in?" His hand gestured towards the sparkling waters that streamed into a pool. At the bottom of the stone fountain, he saw two large grates.

He nodded back.

"Let us hope the armor will not weigh you down too much," Rionaes said with a nervous grin on his face.

He climbed into the pool and began an attempt at lifting the grate out of the way, soaking his fancy deep purple tunic and pants. Del looked around for guards one last time before hopping in to help him.

"How'd you know about this anyway?" Del grunted as the two men wrapped their fingers around the grate and yanked.

The water flowing through worked against them, making it harder to lift.

"Like I said, I always knew I would run." The two yanked and pulled again, their fingers straining to hold onto the slippery iron. "I snooped around not long ago and marked this as a potential exit. Then the library had an old map that told me this was connected to the sewers."

They yanked again, and finally they pulled the grate to the side, revealing a narrow slide just big enough for a person to squeeze into. Del grabbed a piece of crumbling stone from the fountain lip and tossed it down into the darkness.

They waited a couple of seconds before they heard a *plop* of the stone landing in the water below.

"And I'm guessing 'the wind' is saying the sewers also connect to the dungeon?"

"You would be correct." Rionaes squatted down in the crystal water, ready to plunge into the deep, murky, sludge.

Del frowned.

"Are they ever wrong?"

"Sometimes."

And with that, Rionaes slid down into the chamber beneath them.

"Please don't be wrong," Del murmured to himself as he sat down on the fountain floor, and shimmied himself into the grate hole.

He looked up at the fountain statue made into the image of Talisi as rain poured into his eyes. "Now would be a good time to say something. Anything."

He did not wait long for a reply.

Darkness took over as the water rushed him along and before he knew it, Del was falling into the pitch blackness. He splashed as he landed, the water rising just a few feet above his head, and he held his breath as he tried to rise. But his armor *was* heavy, and he fought beneath the stream. He saw a light appear above the surface, shining bright lavender, just before a hand plunged down to grab onto his. Rionaes pulled him up and onto the slim stone sides.

Once standing and safe, Del turned around to look at the water that he'd just emerged from. The smell of it hit him at the same moment.

"Remind me to puke later," he said while looking down into the muddy waters. His stomach churned as the stench of himself and Rionaes clung to his nose.

"Yeah, not pretty," Rionaes replied.

"Let's keep going." Del swallowed, a look of disgust on his face. "Where to?"

Rionaes stood silent for a moment, listening to directions that Del could not hear. He moved the glowing light, like an orb above them, to a crossing, and then to the right.

"That way."

For what felt like an eternity, they trudged in silence through the stinking sewers, the only sound the squelch of their footsteps. Then, it broke through—the screams. One voice, raw and broken, echoed down the narrow tunnel, tightening Del's chest.

"We need to hurry," Del said.

He surged forwards, towards the screaming.

"Is… Is Deime…?" he questioned.

Rionaes had said he wouldn't survive, yet Del never wanted to believe it. He had hoped they would be able to save them both, that Rionaes' information was wrong.

Rionaes shook his head.

"Deime has passed," he said softly.

Del felt his body light up with chills, his stomach twisted. *It's my fault. I dragged him into this. I didn't stop her. I didn't save him.* He pulled his sword out of its sheath. He set the tip of it against the ground as he lowered onto one knee, his trembling hands clasping around the hilt. He bowed his head.

"Talisi, Harbinger of Light, guide this soul into safer lands. I did not know Deime well," his breath hitched, he owed the man more than this.

He owed him a proper burial, a real goodbye, *something*, yet all he had to give was a meager prayer to an absent deity.

"For fucks sake I didn't even like the man, but I ask you to give him safe passage, and to help Mysarin through this time. Be gentle, be kind, in the name of Justice and Sacred Fire."

He rose to find Rionaes kneeling as well, sending out a prayer of his own to Siefris, Saintess of Stars.

The two continued to creep onwards in a respectful silence until they arrived below another gate. The feral screams had softened into quiet whimpers. It was Mysarin, crying in the dungeon. Del felt an ache rip across his chest from her agony. He should've done something more.

"Lift me," Rionaes whispered.

Del swallowed, trying to bury his guilt and focus on their mission. He bent down, feeling Rionaes' wet shoe press into his hands.

34 - Mysarin

Mysarin had found nothing in her cell, nothing to help her escape. She was about to let her wolf take over, let herself shift and end her suffering. Just so she could feel that part of herself one last time. But then she heard a scraping against the floor. Her heart pounded in her ears and her skin heated at the sound, her second skin preparing to take hold.

The guard who had been listening to her spiral stood, and she heard his sword unsheath.

"Uh, Prince Rionaes? What are you doing?" he slurred.

This had to be the dumbest guard in all the lands. A desperate, numb laugh almost burst from her lips. Someone had come for her.

"Who is that?"

"Oh hey, Vixcor." It was Del.

She did laugh now. A burst of nervous, demented laughter. She heard steps advance, steel ringing against steel, and in a matter of seconds, the sound of a body hitting the floor.

"Mysarin?" Rionaes called out to her.

She began to cry through her laughter at the recognition of his voice, but her wolf pushed harder against her skin.

"I'm here," she cried, "I'm here." Her voice felt raw.

She heard two pairs of footsteps rush towards her, to the gate that separated them from her.

"Fuck," Del whispered.

Then the shrill sound of metal scraping against metal as he tried to pick the lock. It snapped open and Mysarin cringed at the harrowing *creak* of the cell gate.

"Get me out, get me out," she whimpered, eyes still locked onto Deime's broken corpse.

"Please, I can't look at him any more and my skin is on fire. Get. Me. Out!"

She wept as Del and Rionaes rushed into view, avoiding Deime's body. Del, his face splattered with blood, picked at the cuffs around her wrists, and flinched when he touched her skin. He looked up at her for a moment, opening his mouth to speak, and then stopped.

He resumed lockpicking without a word, which Mysarin was thankful for. She couldn't explain it right now, maybe not ever. Rionaes walked in front of Deime's body and made a strange gesture towards it, and then turned to face Mysarin, blocking the deceased from view.

Del freed her hands and feet in silence and then stood to start working on the metal around her throat.

His eyes flicked up to hers, "You're going to be okay. We're getting you out." His voice was soft against her ears.

It settled her wolf for a moment. Until she realized what he had said: "*you*," as in singular, as in *not Deime*.

"We can't leave him here to rot," she said.

Del's hands shook as he fiddled with the lock, and his eyes looked back up into hers. His face went tight as he spoke.

"We can't take him. I'm sorry, Mysarin."

"We can't leave him," she repeated.

"He is right, we do not know how much time we have and dragging him through the sewers... will slow us down," Rionaes said, eyes gazing at the ground.

The collar around Mysarin's neck released, and she fell forwards. Del caught her in his armored arms, and the metal felt cool against her skin. The string inside of her that held her second form inside tightened at the release, and frayed.

It was close to snapping. Another ram into the door.

She knew they were right, that she needed to leave as soon as she could or risk showing everyone who she truly was. But what she had to do and what she wanted to do were two very different things. She grabbed the lockpick from Del's hand and stood, legs wobbling, and walked over to Deime. She began fiddling with the rod in the locks as she had seen Del do, the scraping of metal on metal scratching her ears.

"Mysarin—"

"We can't leave him," she repeated, growing frustrated with the evidently immovable lock. She grunted. "It's not working."

There was silence from the two men behind her, the only thing she could hear was the sound of her breathing and the scraping iron. Her hands were shaking and her forehead beading with sweat, while the wolf within her still demanded its freedom.

"It's not working! Why isn't it working?" she said. She began jamming and forcing, her breathing becoming more erratic as she felt the passing seconds of time she was wasting. "Help me with it! It's not working!"

She heard steps draw nearer, slow and hesitant, and then she felt the panic in her rise when the *snap* of the steel rod broke inside of the lock around Deime's neck.

"Give me another one. I know you have more," she said, still staring at the lock in her way.

"You jammed it. It-it won't work."

"No, no, there has to be a way to break it open then, right?" She slipped her fingers between his skin and the collar, trying her best not to notice how cold he already was. Then she began to pull.

Del set his hand on top of hers, stopping her, and forced her chin to look at him. "We *have to go*. You have to *leave him*."

Even though it was impossible for her to break any further, it felt like she did. Like there was a gaping wound in her chest to match the one Deime had. She let go of the metal, her face going numb.

"I'm so sorry, Mysarin," he whispered.

His hand delicately rested upon her shoulder as she took one last look at Deime's lifeless body.

"I hear footsteps coming," Rionaes interrupted. "They are not far, we need to go now."

She heard them too with her elven hearing, and the string beneath her skin only grew thinner. So, she closed her eyes, and turned away from Deime for the last time.

The three of them rushed to the grate, stained with a trail of Vixcor and Deime's blood on the floor, Del and Rionaes jumping in first. She looked to the body of the drunken guard that Del had just killed to save her. She would have to remember to thank him later. They then both reached up to help Mysarin down, helping her to softly land on her feet into the sewers.

"Which way is out?" she asked, her skin turning molten.

Rionaes summoned a lavender orb of light that began to lead the way, and she burst into a sprint after it, the two following behind.

The ringing of their footsteps bouncing off of the walls and water mimicked Mysarin's labored breaths. Her pulse had become a steady spiral. Her legs grew more fatigued with each step, and her throat felt like she was swallowing glass with each breath. She continued to run anyway.

After what felt like hours of running through the fetid sewers, Mysarin began to hear the sounds of waves. The glowing orb of light that led their way started to fade—it was closer to reaching its destination. The pungent smell started to disperse as Mysarin followed the guiding light around a corner, and she stopped.

The salt of the sea smacked into her, the wind flowed through her hair and cooled the sticky coat of sweat covering her skin. The wolf within her howled, begging her to let itself be known. She closed her eyes and shoved the wolf further down. Her skin burned and ached further at the resistance and not even the sea's cool breeze was able to bring her comfort.

She looked down at her hands and saw the blood stain coating them. She tried to wipe them onto her dress, scrubbing her skin against the grainy linen. White noise drowned out everything around her and she tried to count her breathing. But the stain of her guilt was still there.

As the silence grew louder in her ears, Mysarin resumed her sprint all the way to the edge of the sewer line and jumped into the sea.

The icy waters caressed her skin as she sank down beneath the black waves, finally offering a bit of relief to her fever. The ripples glided between her arms as she slipped further down, unmoving. She allowed herself to sink and touch the shallow sand settled beneath, letting its silky texture slide between her red stained fingertips. Her lungs pulsed, her hair spread out like tendrils of ink.

It was so still down there, so peaceful.

Until the image of Deime's body, ravaged and chained to the dungeon wall, pushed its way to the forefront of her mind.

She opened her eyes under the water, searching for something to distract her. Deime was still there, now lifeless and floating before her. She reached out to him, swiping at his image, distorting his body. She felt nothing but the frozen water flowing between her fingers. A sob broke through her, forcing the sea inside of her lungs, and she began to struggle. Her pulse pumped at erratic speeds, her mind fraying between what was lost—Deime, her life before this nightmare—and who she was to become.

Mysarin flailed around her arms. She pushed her feet against the sand and shot towards the surface.

A hand plunged down to her and gripped her arm, pulling her all the way up and out of the filthy waters

"What are you doing?" Del whisper-shouted to her as she coughed up water and climbed onto the shore.

She looked around at the world outside of the sewers and realized they were just outside of the city. She shook her head to clear the images of Deime. The sun glistened upon Del's face, A beacon of light, and she watched the rain recede.

Del reached under her arms to help her to her feet as gently as he could.

"I needed to cool off," she struggled to say between coughing. She inspected her hands, afraid of him seeing her guilt plastered onto her like a scar.

They were clean.

"In the Fallen Waters? You're lucky nothing pulled you in further." His brow crinkled into a hard look of anger. "We need to get into the woods, make camp. We got you out but we aren't far enough."

He turned to look at Rionaes for answers, directions.

The purple beneath his eyes had grown deep, and he seemed more distant than usual. The running and all of the magics must've taken a toll on him. He shrugged his shoulders at the two. "They have not spoken in a while."

"Alright then, follow me." Del marched onwards without another thought up the grassy hill, towards the Heartwood forest.

Mysarin's skin was already drying, already heating back up. She wanted to ask Rionaes what changed his mind, why he decided to run with them, but it took every bit of her focus to continue to keep her wolf inside. *When they go to sleep*, she promised herself.

The three traveled quickly and quietly until they were far enough away from the castle and the city that they were able to walk normally towards the forest, yet they continued on in silence. Perhaps it was to ensure no one would catch them out in the open fields, but Mysarin had a feeling it was more.

She had no words for them, she was too preoccupied with containing herself, with the heavy fog of loss clouding her mind. The sun began to set over the horizon, and Rionaes was exhausted, stumbling about every few minutes as if he would collapse right there.

Del, though... Del always had something to say. Mysarin felt the back of her mind wondering what kept him silent as they moved through the tall grass. His face revealed nothing.

Movement in the treeline caught her eye, they were only a few feet away from the Heartwoods. The primordial, omniscient trees loomed overhead, hiding what lay beyond. The sun sent golden rays through the sky, illuminating paths through the thickets, and casting where Mysarin looked in deep shadow.

She squinted her eyes to focus on what lurked in the dark. She saw slight movement, like the shadows were alive.

Perhaps it would be prey—a deer, or rabbit—something she could sink her teeth into as soon as her true form took shape. Her mouth salivated at the thought. Her wolf stroked claws down her insides.

"I need to rest. Soon." Her jaw clenched down as the words broke their way out.

"Just a little further," Del replied. "The Heartwoods will provide us with cover while you two sleep." He walked up to a tree with a large hole in its side, reaching in and pulling out a trunk.

"Are you not exhausted?" Rionaes cut in.

"Someone needs to keep watch," Del grumbled as the three passed the beginning of the treeline.

The deep golden lighting fled and the encroaching gloom of night engulfed them. The smell of wood and pine swirled around in the air mixed with something sweet. The sweet smell reminded Mysarin of the potion Ostrac had given her for the first game. Del brought a string of golden light into the world beyond them. Shadows and branches, bushes and insects filled in the gaps all around. It sounded like there was breathing, humming, coming from the trees.

"I'll keep watch. You two have done enough for me today." Mysarin's voice was still hoarse as she refused to let Del watch her turn into a beast.

"You just said you needed to rest." That frown appeared again on Del's face.

"I… I need to stop moving and… process. I doubt I'll actually get much sleep anyway." A lie. She *was* exhausted, her eyelids felt heavy, her muscles weak, but she couldn't let her guard down. If she slept before shifting, she might kill them both.

"Mysarin—"

"No," she cut him off, "I need some time alone tonight. I'll be fine. Please."

Rionaes stayed silent as Del nodded his head in defeat.

Mysarin sat with her back against a Heartwood tree as she watched the flames dance before her. Rionaes fell asleep the quickest, jerking and jumping from whatever haunted his mind every so often. Del laid still on his side, with his back facing the fire. Mysarin waited, straining her ears to hear the deep even breaths of sleep. Her blood thrummed in her body, her skin still burning as hot as the embers before her. It threatened to break through her concentration on Delvuvius.

But this was what she trained for. Some of her memory was still hazy, still making its way back to her, but this, she saw clearly.

She remembered training with her mother, with others like her. They were all there in Crelde, shunned from the cities and left to pass down the wolven bloodline until they'd been forgotten about. They had discovered ways of controlling it, of taming the monsters that dwelled within them. Mysarin began her training from a young age; the first time she turned she was five, and from then on her mother made sure Mysarin would never again turn unless she herself willed it.

Painful as it may be, it was possible. It was possible all along, and yet her cousins, the Loraenars, killed her father for it. Slaughtered him like the monster they thought he was. They thought they had killed her mother, too. And they *celebrated* it. Fisrolf, her fathers own cousin, killed his own blood. And for what? To protect people from a beast. A beast who was tamed, caged, under control. And Fisrolf betrayed his own kin for glory.

Her skin heated further, her eyes settled onto Del, on the slow rise and fall of his chest. He wanted to serve them. He was going to fight in their wars. Slaughter more families. He was inches away from being the one who drove that dagger into Deime's heart. Her mind was racing with all of the information that was taken from her—with the family that was taken from her. Her wolf slammed into the door again, claws slicing into the palms of her hand. She glanced over to Rionaes, the foreign Prince who was promised to her second cousin. Would he kill her too? For the so-called monster that she was? Would his deity order him to forsake her?

Mysarin quietly moved to her feet, her body poised to strike, her heart beating like a war drum. Then she heard the sound she had been waiting for coming from Del—the rhythmic breathing of deep sleep—and she smiled. The growing energy in her body gathered to the balls of her feet, and before the two knew what happened, she ran off into the forest.

35 - Estair

Estair was called into the throne room the next morning shortly after she awoke. All of the people who had been at the game the day before, the same people who witnessed her fighting, were gathered in the throne room with her. As was Zendar. Estair rolled her eyes at the sight of him, and took up a spot near the back of the room, by the large wooden doors. The crowd was still filled with anxieties, murmuring about the woman who dared to interfere with the annual games. Estair's savior. She just wanted this to be over, wanted them to announce her freedom so she could decide what to do next with her life. Perhaps, she would find her savior, and thank her.

She knew she would've stood no chance against that minotaur after the way it had killed Zanira within seconds.

She was picking at her nails when the doors opened and the crowd went silent. She glanced up to see who must be the King striding down the long hallway up to the dais, with Syndra and her mother in tow. Syndra's face was swollen around the eyes, as if she had been crying all night. Estair felt confused. Why would the Princess be so upset?

The three took their places on the dais, Syndra and her mother sitting on small thrones that flanked a larger one in the middle. They were all made from pure black stone, and they glinted slightly in the light that came in through the floor to ceiling windows behind them. A man in platinum armor and a scythe at his side stood near, with a small lunar-elf woman beside him. She looked afraid. Estair stared at Syndra in her chair, and felt her throat run dry. Something was very wrong.

"I've called on you all today because the Crown Prince of Oswes has gone missing."

The crowd gasped at the words Fisrolf spoke.

"Rionaes Theinguard has been taken away in the night while under the protection of the Loraenar family. I do not take this lightly."

The king looked around with his dark steel eyes at the crowd before him, as if he might find the person responsible within this room.

"Therefore, our celebrations have been canceled for the time being, and there will be no ceremony to announce the winner of the Moondawn Games."

Estair felt her body grow tense and her heart drop into her stomach. Was it all for nothing?

"To add on to that," Fisrolf continued, "due to the unlawful meddling of the very disturbed woman who had interfered with the games, we can't in good conscience name our last fighter as a victor."

He rose to his feet. "I call on that last fighter to make her way to the dais. As well as The Golden Elf."

Estair, feeling as if her soul had left her body, began to push her way through the crowd. More of those faces drank her in; her height, her stature, her figure, all consumed relentlessly by the peoples of Syrelle. Zendar stepped up with her. He stopped before the platform and got down onto one knee. Estair wanted to kick him over, see him topple. But she did not want to lose her head, so she bowed with him.

"What is your name?" Fisrolf's voice boomed in Estair's ears, reverberating around her skull.

"I am Estair." She bowed her head, and heard the crowd giggle at her lack of title and surname. When she gazed back up into the face of the King, he only raised an eyebrow to her before he continued on.

"I wanted to offer you another chance to earn the title as victor, yet now is no longer the time for celebration and cheers, but a solemn one meant for prayer to the Great Twelve," he said. "But Zendar Paelos, our Commander here, said there may still be a way to earn the title while also continuing our duty of finding the Prince of Oswes."

He smiled now as he looked down to Estair.

"You shall go out and search for Rionaes Theinguard and his assailants. You have proven capable of doing so in your battles, you have shown strength in both body and mind, and shall you bring back the Prince, you will be named the winner."

Estair waited in silence, brewing with anger, as Zendar stood and began to speak to the crowd next.

"I will be searching for the Crown Prince as well, and if I am to find him first, then our competitor here will be named the loser. Instead of crowning her, I'll take her head."

She turned to see the Golden Elf standing there, a look of bloodlust in his eyes.

"Either way, Rionaes Theinguard will be brought back to safety, his captors will be punished, and you all will still remain thoroughly entertained." Fisrolf sat back down onto his throne. "You may rise."

Estair got to her feet as she looked over again to Zendar. For the first time since she met the Golden Elf, she noticed he looked concerned. She swallowed. This was not going to be an easy task. The crowd cheered happily behind her as she felt guards come to her side. They began to lead her out of the throne room, following Zendar's lead.

36 - Delvuvius

Del awoke early in the morning to find himself alone in the makeshift camp with the fire turned to a pile of ash.

Mysarin and Rionaes were nowhere to be found, and he immediately sprung up into action.

Did Rionaes betray us? He grabbed his sword. *Were they both captured?* He began to look around for any clues, any footsteps leading off from the small clearing. *How could I have slept through this?*

"How?" he yelled.

Del whipped his head around toward the sound behind him: a soft, heart-wrenching sob that cut through the air. It was Mysarin. He bolted into that direction, running through bushes and thorns, scratching his face as he followed her cries. He'd already led Deime to his death because of his mistakes, he wouldn't let it happen again.

Not to her.

Not Mysarin.

He wondered if he'd only led the three of them into a death march as he ran into another small clearing. He jolted to a halt at the sight.

Mysarin was covered in blood crying as Rionaes sat behind her on the forest floor, his arms wrapped around her as she struggled to break away. He felt his stomach drop.

"Let her go!" Del yelled as he drew his dull sword and charged forwards. Rionaes looked at him with something in his eyes that Del could not place.

"Stop. You cannot win this fight," Rionaes said into Mysarin's ear as she thrashed against him. "Tell him."

Del raised his sword, heart pounding in his throat, ready to sever the Prince's head—but, Mysarin. If he struck, he'd harm her. He froze, torn between his need to protect and his fear for her safety.

"Let her go before I kill you." He stood just before them, and he forced his eyes to remain locked onto Rionaes, instead of all the blood on Mysarin.

"Tell him," Rionaes urged her again.

"No!" she cried.

"Tell me what?" His eyes drifted down to Mysarin's body, to the blood. *So much blood.*

"Look." Rionaes tightened his grip on Mysarin as he nodded his head to the left side of the clearing.

Del kept his sword raised, poised to strike Rionaes should he dare to make any sudden moves, as he flicked his eyes into the direction. It was a body.

A man sprawled face down in the dirt, blood pooling beneath him. His guts spilled out of his back—a grotesque tangle of innards that stained the grass—and his head was almost torn clean off. A bow was slightly tucked beneath him, a quiver of arrows on the ground spilled beside him with the strap torn. Del looked back to them as he lowered to his knees before Mysarin.

"What happened?"

The two said nothing. Rionaes seemed like he was waiting for Mysarin to say something. But she was so upset. Del looked at her cheeks, they were covered in the same blood, her eyes never leaving the man's corpse. Her hair was matted and stuck to her wet face.

"Mysarin," Del said softly.

She turned her attention to him with wild eyes, the silver glowing more fiercely than they had before.

"Tell me what happened."

Tears rolled down her face as her gaze slipped back over to the corpse. Her chest rose and fell violently.

"I... found her trying to save him," Rionaes said at last.

He kept his eyes down as he spoke, down at his hands also covered in the still wet blood. His white brows pinched close together. "A minotaur must have killed him."

"No," Mysarin whined.

Del saw what looked to be a chunk of flesh tangled into her curls and he gently pulled it out. He felt his heart break for her. For the storm raging within her. It clearly was not about the man they did not know, but about what she had just gone through. Deime, her betrothed, was dead. They had Broke her, which Del remembered was traumatic enough, but to do it in such a way… She may never be the same again.

"Let's find a river, clean you up, and then we need to move out."

"Where do we go?" Rionaes looked at Del, that strange emotion on his face that Del couldn't place. Mysarin stopped thrashing, and Rionaes slowly loosened his grip around her.

"I don't know, I was hoping you could tell us that," he replied, watching the Prince's arms release Mysarin from their hold, and begin to stroke her arms in an attempt at comfort. He felt his pulse quicken at the sight of the Prince's hands around her body.

Mysarin whispered something to Del in between her sobs, silent tears creating a river of their own down the blood splattered across her cheeks.

"What?" He grabbed her hand gently and noticed her fever had broken.

She was so warm the last time he had felt her skin, as if she could've given him burns. He felt a feather lift from his shoulders, one less thing he had to worry about. Her eyes seemed to see clearer than they had too, even with what lay just a few feet away from them.

She looked at him with a hardened expression. Her eyes were swollen, with deepened purple beneath them. She must not have slept at all.

"She's dead."

"Who?" he asked in a soft voice. He rubbed his thumb lightly against her own, swiping back and forth.

"She's dead," she said again.

But the body in the meadow was a man. No, she wasn't talking about him. She wasn't talking about Deime. Del furrowed his brows in confusion.

"Who's dead, Mysarin?" But as he said it, he realized what she had meant.

Mysarin was going to kill Syndra Loraenar.

Acknowledgements

Wow, I wrote a book! It feels good to say, and I want to do so over and over for the rest of my life. So first and foremost, if you're here reading this, I want to thank you for being here and supporting me.

To Marley, my sister, you're an icon. Thank you for getting me back into reading with your suggestions and for listening to me rant about how I was going to write a book for the first time. You were my target audience, and kept me going with your encouragement. Also, I want to say thank you for all of your help in terms of publishing this. I wouldn't have done it without you.

To Christian, my love, who sat beside me listening to the same excerpts hundreds of times because I changed one little thing, you are my best friend, and my biggest supporter. You helped me with the logistics of things and characters (especially Delvuvius), and with refining my big ideas into things that I can actually incorporate into this world. Also, thanks for letting me borrow your cool last name.

To Cassandra, who has always been such a supporter to all of my artistic endeavors, thank you for taking the time to read my stuff. Love you forever.

And to my family; my mom and dad, my grandma Kathy, and everyone else, I love you guys.

Stay tuned for a chapter of *Heir of Monsters: MoonDawn Series, Book Two!*

1 - Estair

"You mustn't tamper with it, or its magical properties could react in unpredictable ways," Estof, the court artificer, said as he secured a metal cuff around Estair's ankle.

She sat upon a table in a large room dedicated to planning war strategy. She stared down at his creamy-white balding head. The cuff felt sharp against her and she hissed at the quick prick of a needle sliding into her achilles. Once blood was drawn, she watched a faint red line fill in the swirled engravings around the hinges.

"Unpredictable? Like how?" Estair's mind thought to Boonefaentelle Karnoch, The Pirate Prince of the Twin Islands, and the time he had once tried to train and domesticate a pack of syrk. The little rat-like climbers had then chewed all of the *Jiofornia* and subsequently died from an overdose of the sweet flower used to create prunn, leaving the Karnoch with no supplies to sell at the ports.

"Let's just say you aren't to tamper with it unless you'd like to lose a foot," Estof said.

Estair nodded.

"It is also bloodlinked to a raven that will be able to travel between you and Princess Syndra. Should you go astray from your objective, then it will also be able to track you down and lead an army directly to your location as well. So unless you'd like to lose your head…"

"Right. I will behave."

The door swung open with a loud thud.

"Speaking of her Highness, hello, I was just informing your warrior on how the cuffs are to work."

Syndra stood regal before the two, and Estair felt the breath escape from her. Those silver eyes roamed over her, reminding her of the gray that was the Fallen Waters in a storm. "Thank you, Estof. Is she ready to leave?"

"Yes, Your Highness."

"Then you are excused. I'd like a word with our warrior here." Her silken hair poured from her head like fine wine.

Estof stood and bowed before the Princess as he made his leave. Estair could find no words, still lost in the ethereal aura of Syndra's night. She seemed to fly over to where Estair sat—her wide skirt hiding the movement of her legs and feet. She sat beside her on the bench and placed a pale hand atop Estair's deep brown one.

"We will be in direct contact the entire time. I want to know everything about your journey," her voice was strangely soft.

"I can do that."

Her grip tightened and she leaned in closer. "I mean it. I want every detail. I want to know where you go, what you see, what you eat for breakfast, what you think. Retrieving the Prince is our utmost priority, and I know him best. Perhaps there will be a clue or some detail you miss. And I shall be the one to tell you."

Was this supposed to be threatening? Estair let a small uptilt of her lips come forth. "As you command."

Syndra relaxed. Her hand floated back to the other one sitting atop the velvet fabric covering her lap. "I am aware that you are somewhat new here, but you should know by now that I am the heir to the throne. You should be curtseying and speaking to me with proper titles. 'Your Highness' is standard."

"I apologize, *Your Highness*. But I serve no King. I am here only to gain my freedom," Estair replied.

Syndra conjured a smirk of her own at that. "It seems we have a dissident on our hands. Very well then, you may serve whomever you like as long as I get Prince Theinguard back and his captors in chains." Syndra stood, letting the dark maroon velvet flow back around her feet. "I shall expect a new letter of your journey each day."

Estair reached out to grab Syndra's arm as she moved towards the door. Syndra stopped in place, and slowly turned her head towards Estair in amused opposition. "Will there be supplies for me to take? Or coin to buy some along the way? This journey could be many days. Months."

"Zendar will be here in a moment to set you up with that." She looked down at Estair's rough hand still wrapped around her arm. "And another thing on court etiquette—never touch the royal persons unless invited to."

Estair dropped her hand. "When is anyone ever invited to touch another? Doesn't that spoil… intimate moments?"

A slight pink rushed to Syndra's cheeks. "Pirate brute," made its way from her equally pink lips.

Another thud of the door hitting the wall sounded out as The Golden Elf made his entrance. Behind him trailed a smaller man carrying armor, the two swords Estair had used in the MoonDawn tourney, and a pack of what was hopefully supplies.

Zendar walked to the table before them and spread out a map of Syrelle. He said nothing as he then walked over to a cabinet and pulled out figurines that vaguely resembled chess pieces. Estair turned her sights back onto the Princess, who immediately looked elsewhere after their eyes had grazed. Syndra crossed her arms and huffed. Zendar placed the bull piece with a back flag onto the map atop Stonecrest. He then placed a soldier piece west of the king, and a knight to the north. Two wolves were then set on top of New Grosham and Synsee.

He looked up at the two women, and snickered. "Arguing already? Is it that time of the month?"

"Is it courtly to ask the royal Princess about her moon?" Estair kept her eyes on Syndra.

She rolled her eyes. "Leave it alone, Zendar. What is the plan?"

Zendar shook his head with that toothy smile. Estair thought of the syrk again, and decided if Zendar were to morph into an animal, it would be that one. "We are here," he pointed to the bull, "and our targets have likely gone here." His fingers roamed over the Heartwood forest to land upon the two wolves. "I will begin the search between us and New Grosham. The girl will begin looking in between here and Synsee."

Estair stood and looked over the map before them. There was a path through the forest towards the northwest leading to another town called Perreway. "What about there? Shouldn't someone look that way too?"

"Perreway is Loraenar territory, girl. Only a fool would head there."

"Perhaps that would be the best place to go, then. If I were to run away, I would go to where the enemy is least likely to look."

Zendar raised his golden eyebrows at her, deepening the creases along his forehead.

"I guess our warrior isn't just a brute afterall," Syndra said. "We have sent a raven to our cousins in Perreway. They know to keep the perimeter secure."

"And we aren't about to waste Stonecrest resources on something so unlikely," Zendar added.

"Waste resources? I thought this task was of utmost priority. Are coffers running dry?" Estair challenged.

He looked at the Princess with an expression of disdain. They had a silent conversation. "This topic doesn't concern you or your objective," he finally said.

"Fine." She glanced over the map again, studying the woods between the sea and a small lake. "I'll head there and begin my search today."

"Good. Vixcor—I-I mean *Hans* here, brought your supplies." For a moment, Zendar looked anything other than arrogant and vicious. His slimy trout lips dipped into a frown at his mistake in name. He looked at the man standing in the corner and motioned for him to hand over what he had to Estair. "I will be heading out now as well, and remember, if I find them first, I'll finally get to see you bleed."

Estair held out her arms as Hans dropped the heavy load into them. She looked it all over as she thought of anything else she may need. "One more thing."

"What else is there? We can't hold your hand through this more than we already are," Syndra said.

"I'll need a Healer."

"For what?" she asked.

"If I get hurt in battle, or injured from traveling. What if a minotaur takes me for lunch?"

The two looked at each other, another silent conversation taking place. Estair decided she wanted to be a part of it. "When I was with the Karnoch, we always had a healer of sorts with us on the warships. Even when we docked at the Venom Isles for *Jiofornia*. Everyone gets hurt. Even pirate brutes."

"Fine," Syndra broke first. "Go find a man named Ostrac. He lives by the ports, and he recently lost our patronage. I'm sure he has nothing better to do."

"He was?" Estair thought back to that moment in his workroom when another Royal Healer had walked in on the two. When the other healer witnessed Ostrac healing someone who was not of nobility.

"Enough questions. The more time we waste, the further our captors get. Retrieve the healer if you wish, but it will put you behind me. And if you plan on winning you'll need every advantage you can get," Zendar said as he rolled up the map and handed it to Estair. He then looked down at the cuff around her ankle. "Be sure not to get lost, or we'll take that as abandonment."

The air had begun to calm down around her as late summer settled into fall. Estair scanned through alleyways, and peaked into booths selling goods for the fisherman down at the port. Her magical cuff thrummed against her ankle and a small shadow above her head appeared. She reached down to scratch at the skin beneath her new weight. Little talons lightly gripped onto her as she stood.

She stopped moving and looked to what had landed upon her shoulder.

It was a raven, and attached to its stomach was a sort of bird-sized pack. The bird ruffled its feathers at her before tilting its head. Then it cawed in her face when she continued to stare.

"Bad bird." She wove her calloused fingers over the closing on the tiny sack, and pulled out a note.

Do hurry on your departure. Zendar has already left, and I do not want to see you fail due to a headstart.

And do not forget to write back before sundown.

Also the raven's name is Gustefhan. If you were wondering. He likes raspberries. If he acts ornery, then give him some to settle him.

Syndra

Estair balled up the note and threw it over the shoulder that Gustefhan was not occupying. She continued to walk down the path along the rows of large ships, and Gustefhan remained stationed upon her. She sent a finger to graze the top of his head, and he nipped her.

"Ow, Gustefhan. Be nice," she said as she tried to shake him off her shoulder. He gripped deeper into her skin in defiance. She groaned in annoyance.

Where the path began to meet the stoney beach, Estair spotted a group of men all gathered around. She made her way towards them, prepared to give Ostrac's description.

"Ahhhh! Fuck!" A man's scratchy voice called out, and Estair sped towards the group. She found the men standing in a circle around a large sunkissed and burnt man on the sandy ground with a fishhook tearing through his cheek. And Ostrac kneeling beside him.

"Stop talking or you're going to make this worse." Ostrac's hands illuminated the space where the hook intersected with tender and squishy flesh. A larger incision was made, and Ostrac steadily pulled the metal out the way it came.

"Great Twelve, that's nauseating," a man with blonde hair and the same shade of sunkissed skin standing next to them said. His lips were incredibly chapped, and made Estair think of her crew mates back in the Twin Islands.

"Don't you dare look away, buzzard! You did this to me, you should have to watch," the man with brown hair on the ground replied.

"Shut up. I'm almost done and *then* you can berate him," Ostarc's voice was steady as blood covered his fingertips. He wove a white glowing needle through the man's face, with a matching thread trailing behind it, helping to suture the skin back together. Estair continued to watch without saying a word, looking over the shoulders of the other fisherman gathered around.

She desperately wanted to say something, wanted to hurry up and get Ostrac to come along with her already. But she knew to keep quiet and let him finish. A part of her was also entranced with his perilous focus. He finished stitching the skin with his magics, and then he placed his palms down onto the wound. Another glow of white, and a swipe of Ostrac's arm over his forehead to remove the sweat, and the wound was gone.

The blood and what looked to be a dark pink scar lingered on the man's face, but other than that, it was like it never happened.

"Okay, you're done," Ostrac said as he stood, still unaware of Estair's presence.

"You son of a bitch!" The man stood and immediately jumped onto the blonde man, tackling him to the ground.

Estair slid past them and walked over to Ostrac, who was rinsing his hands in the ocean. "Wow. You've gotten a lot more heroic since the last time I saw you."

He finally looked over to her and smiled, showing off a single dimple. "And you've got a new friend I see." He gestured to the raven still clinging to her body.

"His name is Gustefhan. And 'friend' might be too generous." She gave her torso another shake, and the raven cawed into her ear. "What are you doing here?"

"Helping poor souls, of course," he looked over her shoulder to the men figuring out their differences, "I might still be needed."

"Well, I'm sure you heard about Prince Theinguard. I'm off to look for him."

Ostrac sighed. "Finding new ways to endanger yourself. I heard about his 'captors'. I'd wager he simply no longer wanted his crown."

"Either way, I need to find them. I was hoping you'd join me."

"Join you?" He laughed. "What could I do other than get in the way?"

"You could do plenty. You know about herbs—what's safe to eat in the forest. If I get hurt, you could help me. You can keep me company. Plenty for you."

"I don't know."

"Syndra said you lost their patronage. What else do you have to do?"

"Yeah, after they saw me healing *you*."

Her body stiffened at that. She felt her chances at finding the three, at finally being free, begin to shrink. She needed Ostrac to help her. "I apologize."

"No need. It was my own doing. I knew it was a risk, and I took it anyway." He looked out into the ocean. A cool breeze rolled over the two.

"This would be risky, too. There are, most likely, more minotaurs out in the forest. I don't wish be face to face with one again." She thought of the way the minotaur in the arena had grabbed onto Zanira and slammed his body against the concrete walls like he was nothing but air. She shivered.

He contemplated for a beat, his eyes scanning the horizon. "My friend Delvuvius left a letter saying his goodbyes the day the Prince went missing. And another woman, named Mysarin, I have not seen her in some time either… Do you think it could be them?"

Estair shrugged. "I find it hard to believe it was a coincidence for other people to disappear on the same day. And the

Loraenars think so. They said the people I was looking for went by the same names.”

“Did they tell you to kill them when you find them?” His jaw flexed.

“No. Just to tell this raven when I do. And then they will come get us all, and bring us back to Stonecrest.”

He looked at her then, his angular face held firm in his calm disposition. “And what if they left for a good reason?”

“Either way, I’m turning them in. It’s what I have to do.”

“Could I change your mind?”

“Probably not.”

He smiled a bit. “Let me pack a bag and we can go.”

“Really? You’ll turn in your friends?”

“I never said that.” He took one last look at the two men, now standing back up and shaking hands, and then began to stroll back towards the city.